MEMORY OF THE BLOOD MOON

SANGUIS AMANTIUM
BOOK 2

REBECCA BYRON

*For those who feel a pull they don't understand,
a voice they can no longer ignore.
When something refuses to let you go,
perhaps it's time to stop fighting—
and discover the curious magic
you were meant to wield all along.*

CONTENTS

FOREWORD
A NOTE TO READERS

If you've read *A Memory Not Mine*, Book 1 in the *Sanguis Amantium* series, you know my stories are intended for mature audiences. But in *Memory of the Blood Moon*, we enter darker territory. 14th-century Romania was a brutal place, and within these pages you will encounter the tragic origin story of one of the characters.

Because your mental well-being matters to me, I want to make you aware of elements that may be difficult to read:

- Graphic violence
- Sexual assault (told from the survivor's perspective)
- References to the death of a child & spouse (non-graphic)
- References to the death of an animal (non-graphic)

Please read with care.

PROLOGUE

May 11, 1370—Biertan, Romania

The blood moon hung low in the night sky, an ominous orb glowing crimson—a portent of birth and death, of the eternal struggle between light and darkness. Tonight, the veil between the physical and the spiritual world was perilously thin.

In the small cottage at the edge of the village, the air was thick with heat and the tang of iron. The gray-haired Romani midwife, Zora, worked with fevered hands as the young woman fought to bring new life into the world. But this was no ordinary villager to her—this was her only daughter, Anca. The labor had started normally enough, but as the hours dragged on, her unease grew. Something was wrong. Anca's brow glistened with sweat, her face twisted in anguish. It had been nearly a full day since her waters broke, and the child refused to come.

"The babe's breech," the old woman muttered under her breath. Her gnarled hands pressed and prodded the swollen belly, whispering prayers—some in Latin, others in the old Romani tongue—until, at last, she felt the baby turn.

"On your hands and knees now, girl," she ordered sharply. "With the next pain, you push—hard. Childbirth is no work for the weak. Do it now, or the babe won't last much longer."

Her daughter clung to the bedpost, knuckles white, a strangled grunt escaping as the contraction tore through her. Her face flushed deep red, the veins on her forehead standing out like dark rivers beneath the skin.

"There yes! The babe is crowning," the old woman cried, sliding her hands into position. "Don't falter now—one more push!"

Anca's scream split the air as she bore down with the strength of the desperate, and the child slipped free into her grandmother's waiting hands.

"I have a granddaughter," the old woman whispered, tears springing to her eyes. "A beautiful, healthy girl...she looks so much like you did, the day you came into this world. A head full of hair she has, as black as a raven's wing."

She wiped the child clean and placed her gently to the young mother's breast.

"Magdalena," Anca whispered, her voice raw and fragile from hours of torment. "I want to call her...Magdalena."

At last, her body began to relax, the tension melting from her bones in a long, blissful exhale. She gazed down at the tiny face nestled against her breast, wonder softening the exhaustion in her eyes.

But the joy was fleeting. The bleeding didn't stop. Zora

worked frantically, packing herbs into a poultice, murmuring incantations, but the color drained from her daughter's face.

As dawn threatened the horizon, Anca pressed a trembling kiss to the baby's forehead. "Take care of her, Mama," she whispered, her eyelids fluttering shut.

By the time the first light spilled over the hills, the young mother was gone.

MAGDALENA WAS NOT the only child born in the village that night, nor the only one to lose a mother to the cruelty of childbirth. Under the same blood moon that cast its crimson glow over the poorest cottage, death crept silently into the highest chamber of the walled castle at the village's heart.

There, within stone walls warmed by roaring fires and draped in silks, the boyar's wife labored through the night. Drago Burián, the district's military leader and master of the castle, paced like a caged beast as his wife's screams echoed down the corridors. But all the wealth and privilege of his house could not shield her from the same grim fate. By dawn, she too lay pale and still, her life bled out upon fine linen sheets.

Her son—who would be named Caius—was strong and healthy. A perfect heir. He was as different from Magdalena as two babes could be. His hair shone like burnished gold in the torchlight, and his eyes—an impossibly vivid blue—would not dim nor change with age as most infants' did.

Though born less than a mile apart, they had come into two

entirely different worlds. She, the granddaughter of a Romani midwife in a drafty, dirt-floored cottage; he, the son of a nobleman destined to command armies and inherit vast lands.

Yet the blood moon—a cruel, watchful sentinel in the sky— had bound their fates together in ways no one in the village, neither peasant nor boyar, could yet imagine.

1

THE RUBY

Mira—January 2026

When I finally opened my eyes, Baird was kneeling beside me, his face a mask of worry as I slumped against the cabinets under the kitchen sink. I could only imagine what he had seen—how the ruby, still clutched in my trembling hand, had dragged me under, pulling me into its relentless vortex of darkness and light. I wasn't even sure I could explain it to him. It wasn't like the other objects I'd touched before—simple conduits that revealed emotional imprints of the people who once held them. No, this was different. This was alive, humming with a malevolence that felt ancient and knowing.

"I didn't go looking for this," I said hoarsely. "I swear to you."

Baird's thumb brushed my wrist, near but not touching the stone. "No," he said grimly. "But it looks like it found ye anyway."

My abilities—this uneasy "gift" I'd only recently begun to accept—had overwhelmed me from time to time, but this was different. The power contained by the ruby had consumed me the moment I'd touched it. It had come to me through a picker named Honey, a colorful character who found vintage pieces and gemstones for me from time to time. The color was what gem dealers referred to as pigeon's blood—a deep, rich red with a tinge of blue, glowing from within. When I'd opened the package he had shipped me, I hadn't noticed anything unusual; that was, until I lifted the top on the plastic case the stone had been shipped in. Its surface seemed to pulse faintly, as though a heartbeat within it, and when I touched it, it thrummed with an electrical current that stung the tip of my finger and spread like ink through my veins.

At first, the sensation was intoxicating. Unlike anything I had felt before. With other objects, what I saw made me an invisible bystander at best—or at worst, hurled violently into someone else's reality. I had fought those visions, resisted the emotions they forced upon me. But with the ruby, it was different. Its power coiled through me, heady and electric, and for a moment I felt unbound—no longer flesh and bone but something else entirely. Something vast. I was earth. I was sky. I was no longer human. I wondered if this was how Baird felt when the thing inside him—the part he called the beast—was given free rein.

The air around me thickened, vibrating with energy, every shadow in the room stretching and quivering as if alive. A low whisper rose in my ears, soft yet insistent, threading through my mind in a language I did not know but somehow understood.

We see you...we know you.

And I felt it too—the ruby seeing me. Not my face or form, but the marrow of my soul. It gazed into my very being, and in return, it offered me a glimpse of something limitless. But then everything changed, and what came next was terrifying.

My chest constricted. My breath came shallow and the air around me froze, as though the ruby was drawing not just my warmth, but my very life. And then came the visions. Jagged flashes of other lives and other deaths. An old man with brilliant blue eyes on his deathbed. A young woman with dark hair screaming, dragged away from a child with the same dark hair. A cottage in flames, the smell of burning wood and flesh assaulted my senses. A handsome young man beaten and slumped on the floor in a smoky room. Frantic screams echoed in my ears. The metallic taste of fear, sharp and bitter, flooded my mouth. But amid the chaos and violence the ruby dragged me through, another, more crushing *knowing* bled into my mind.

The young woman I saw was connected to all of them. The old man who was dying, the younger man. And the little girl— no more than a toddler—was her daughter. I just knew it. I felt the love that coursed through her veins for all of them, but it was not gentle, not soft or nurturing. No, this was a desperate, all-consuming love, shot through with violence I couldn't begin to understand. It wrapped around me like barbed wire, sharp and piercing all at once.

Then the visions shifted—jerking me into a room choked with the scent of blood. The woman stood amid a circle of men, her dark hair matted, her clothing soaked crimson. Their eyes bulged with terror as they cowered from her, weapons trembling uselessly in their hands. She moved between them with terrifying speed, a predator unleashed. The blade in her fist flashed like lightning, flesh parting as she cut her way from man to man. Blood spilled in hot, steaming arcs, and she did not pause—her mouth found their throats, and she drank, greedily, relentlessly, until all life left them. Vengeance and hunger fused within her, vast enough to consume the room, the night, the young woman she had been. She was human, and then she was not. This was her beginning—an origin story the ruby remembered.

My vision slowly bled back into the kitchen—the worn oak table, the kettle cooling on the stove, the faint scent of peat smoke—I felt my chest rising and falling in shallow, ragged breaths. But the ruby the ruby was still in my hand. I tried to drop it, to shake it free, but my fingers wouldn't obey. They remained curled tight around the stone, as if it had fused itself to my palm. Its sinister, electric thrum still vibrated against my skin, pulsing in perfect synchrony with my own heartbeat.

"Take it...please," I gasped, holding out my trembling hand to Baird, my eyes wide, desperate. "Take it away from me."

Baird pried the ruby from my fingers, but even as it left my grasp, a cold thread seemed to tether it to me, like part of me was still caught in its pull. I wasn't sure the connection had truly severed.

"Shh, dinnae fash. I've got it," he said closing his fingers around the stone. "You're safe." His voice was low and steady, a balm against the chaos that still churned in my mind. He pulled me into his arms, holding me close until I could feel the solid weight of him anchoring me, his strength defending me against the icy chill that lingered in my veins."Tell me what ye saw, love," he murmured into my ear, his lips brushing the sensitive edge of it.

"Magic," I whispered, pressing a trembling hand to my

chest as if to ground myself. "The stone holds some kind of dark magic. It spoke to me, Baird—the ruby spoke to me." My voice cracked, but I kept going. "It said, 'We see you...we know you,' in a language I've never heard. But somehow...I understood it. It spoke to me before it let me see."

"Mira, lass..." Baird's voice was low, thick with worry. His strong hands cradled my face, thumbs brushing my damp cheeks. "Ye look like a ghost." His gaze searched mine, like he was trying to pull sense from the madness I was spilling.

I clutched his wrists, needing the contact to stay anchored.

"I feel like one." I said faintly.

"Well," Baird replied, "I'd have noticed if ye'd died."

"Don't joke," I said weakly. "A fire, smoke filling a cottage, a group of men destroying everything in their path. They took her—the young woman—ripped her away from her little girl. But then I saw her later...killing those same men. She was a *vampire*, Baird," I said, my fingers digging into flesh, struggling to make sense of it all. "At some point, she was turned—and she used her power to get revenge."

He went very still. "Did she choose it?" he asked.

"I don't think so, but I didn't see that part." I told him. A chill rippled through me at remembering the sequence of events. "When I first touched the ruby, my senses...*shifted*," I said, trying to explain all that I'd seen and felt. "I could see beyond the shadows; the darkness itself was alive. Is that what it's like for you, when you lose yourself to it?" I asked, the last part almost an afterthought.

His jaw tightened, and he took a slow breath. "Aye. Only it never feels quite so poetic as ye make it sound."

"The ruby feels older than she is." I said, the words uneasy as they left me. "Older than the vision itself. What I felt wasn't a moment—it was a cycle. Death, rebirth, over and over, like the turning of a wheel that never stops. What I saw was only the latest turn." I looked up at him then, shaking my head slowly. "And when it spoke to me, it wasn't about her. Not really. I can feel that." I faltered, breath catching as the words to explain slipped just out of reach—close enough to ache for. "Whatever that voice was…I don't understand it yet. But—it *knows* me."

"Knows you…" Baird questioned. "So it spoke?"

"Yes." My throat felt tight. "It knows me."

Baird's eyes narrowed. "Then it's not just a stone." The silence stretched between us. "Not just a vision of someone's memory."

I swallowed, apprehensive at speaking the truth gnawing at my gut. "No."

2

___

MAGDA

Magda—March 1387

The only constant in the history of my village was conflict. Nestled at the convergence of two rivers, in a deep valley hemmed by jagged mountain peaks, its location was both a blessing and a curse. It was the sole north-south passage for a hundred miles in either direction—a prize too valuable to be left unclaimed.

Warlords of the Ottoman Empire swept through, seizing control and forging uneasy alliances with the boyar noblemen of the region. For a time, their power brought a brittle, fragile peace. But peace never lasted here. Others, hungrier for power, soon rose in violence to wrest control, and the valley ran red with blood once more. My father was one of the many who died defending our people, our way of life, before I was even born.

In this place, every healthy boy—whether pauper or prince

—was taught to fight. It was not a question of if they would be called upon to defend their families, their village, their lands, their way of life...but when. The boyar's son Caius was no exception. From the time he was a young boy, I would see him in the village, always shadowed by squire or fight master barking orders as he learned the arts of war. I knew we shared a birthday. I knew we'd both lost our mothers under the same blood moon. Some force seemed to bind us, and whenever he came to the village, he would find me. Sometimes he stopped to play knucklebones with me in the dust of the village square; in his easy laughter and mischievous smile I found a friend. But our playtime never lasted long. Someone from his father's household would appear, scowling, and drag him away by the ear, scolding him for wasting time with "low-born Romani trash." But Caius never looked at me like that. Not once. To me, he showed only respect...and a kindness that felt rare in a world like ours.

"Magda! Stop daydreaming about who'll gift you the Mărțișor and come help me in the garden," my grandmother called, her voice sharp but not unkind.

I kicked at the dirt in front of our cottage, reluctant to leave my spot. She was the only mother I'd ever known, and while the villagers called her Zora, to me she was simply *Buna*.

"Stop moping, girl," she scolded lightly, hands on her hips. "Always so strange. You'd rather run wild in the woods with the boys, playing at wooden swords, than sew or tend a garden. I swear, you'd have been happier if you'd been born a boy—free to ride and fight, not bound to hearth and cradle. Now grab me that basket of straw and help me lay it atop the soil here to protect these seedlings."

She shook her head, a chuckle rumbling in her chest as I came through the garden gate. "Still, you're lucky you're so pretty. If not for that, I doubt many boys would look your way. You're too quick to anger—Magda, the little hellcat."

I smirked at that. She liked to chastise me, but I knew better. Her words were threaded with fondness. Buna loved me fiercely, in her own way.

But Buna was right. I had been thinking about who might give me a trinket tied with red and white twine during the spring festival. At Mărțișor, male family members and friends gifted the women of the village these tokens—a symbol of winter's end and the fertile, sun-warmed days to come. But for unmarried girls, the trinkets sometimes carried a different meaning. A simple cord and charm could speak louder than words, hinting at a young man's affection...or even his intentions.

There was only one young man I wanted to see with such a token in hand—only one whose glance had ever set my heart tumbling—but even I knew it was foolish to hope. The distance between his world and mine was too wide.

And yet...

Buna had been right about something else too. In the past year, the boys of the village had started to notice me. My body, once all sharp angles and restless limbs, had softened around the edges, ripened. The girl I'd been was gone, replaced by a young woman with strong shoulders and lush curves. Tonight, the whole village would gather to eat, drink, and dance—to celebrate the end of winter and welcome the arrival of spring.

Buna had made me a new tunic for the occasion, embroidered with bright threads of red, black, and yellow. Around my hips she fastened a belt of coins, the silver disks catching the light as they clinked softly with every movement. I couldn't help running my fingers over them, imagining whose eyes I hoped might follow their sway.

As night fell, music drifted through the crisp air, carried from the village center on the wind. The sound of drums and fiddles quickened my pulse.

"Will you come and dance, Buna?" I asked, tilting my head toward her where she sat by the hearth, grinding dried herbs in her mortar. I wanted her to come, to step out of the shadows of our cottage and let the firelight touch her face for once.

But I already knew her answer.

The villagers sought her out when they needed her—the only midwife for miles, with her herbs and potions that eased pain and coaxed life into stubborn lungs. Yet when their need passed, they called her witch. They feared her. And by extension, they feared me.

I had learned to bear the word with pride. Let them whisper. Let them believe I possessed some unseen power. They thought their fear was a weapon against me, but I wore it like armor. Buna said my pride would be my downfall. Perhaps she was right. But tonight, I didn't care.

"Wait, Magda...here," Buna murmured, her voice soft as she got up to fasten a small brass bell to my coin belt. The tiny chime rang out, delicate yet clear. "To ward off evil spirits," she said, her lined fingers lingering for a moment on my hip. Then she leaned forward and pressed a gentle kiss to my forehead. "It will protect you tonight."

We were a superstitious people—none more so than my Buna. I couldn't help but roll my eyes at her efforts, though a faint smile tugged at my lips. And then I slipped from the cottage, the door creaking softly behind me as I stepped into the chilly night air. The lane beckoned, thick with the scent of roasting meat and the sound of raucous laughter. Music floated toward me, wild and inviting, drawing me closer to the heart of the village—and to whatever the night held in store.

3

MĂRȚIȘOR

Magda—March 1387

The air thrummed with music, and villagers swirled about in brightly embroidered clothing—so different from the drab browns and grays of our everyday wear. Near the village square, a group of young men lounged, their eyes following the dancing girls. But it wasn't they who held my gaze. It was the two boys standing slightly apart from the rest.

Caius—tall, lean, and powerful—reminded me of a mountain cat. He was striking, with wavy hair the color of honey, golden streaks lightened by the sun. His high cheekbones always seemed flushed, more so when he laughed or was angry. And those eyes—ringed in stormy grey, their centers the clear, cloudless blue of a summer sky.

He was born the same night I was—under a blood moon the old women still whispered about. We shared that beginning, and something else besides. His mother had died bringing him into the world, just as mine had. But where my grandmother gathered me up and loved me fiercely enough for two, Caius had grown under the shadow of a father who never forgave him for surviving.

The boyar remarried, of course. Duty demanded it. His second wife bore him two daughters—healthy, golden-haired half-sisters who carried none of the blame Caius did. The boyar adored them. He tolerated his son. Caius wore that knowledge like armor: bright smiles, bold laughter, recklessness that dared the world to ignore him the way his father did.

At his side was Dani, his ever-present shadow. Broader and taller still than Caius, Dani reminded me of a brown bear— solid and steady. His thick chestnut hair framed a face with soft, sleepy brown eyes that disguised the strength beneath. The son of the boyar's armorer, he was no nobleman, yet far above a simple peasant, raised among tools and iron, craft and discipline.

From the time I was a small girl, the three of us were inseparable. I loved them both—because they treated me as one of their own. Never as the granddaughter of the village witch, but as an equal. Together we raced our ponies across the hills at breakneck speed, stalked deer through the forest, and practiced swordplay—though my "sword" was whatever sturdy branch I could find beneath the trees we climbed, skirts tied up in a knot between my legs.

My grandmother had taught me to read and write, a rare gift in our village, and now and then they'd smuggle me books from Caius's father's library—tales of distant lands and daring adventures, my favorite kind.

But the last few years had changed us. We'd all grown—and I wasn't the only one who noticed. It wasn't just the leering old men of the village whose gazes lingered on me now. Caius and Dani looked at me differently, too. Beneath the laughter and easy familiarity we'd always shared, I sensed something new stirring, a hunger they tried—and failed—to disguise.

At first, I wondered what my approaching womanhood would do to the bond between us. But I could already feel the shift: the way their eyes followed me a moment too long, how a single smile could catch and hold them. There was power in that. A rich, heady awareness that unsettled me even as it thrilled. A peasant girl had little to bargain with in this world—and discovering this, discovering *myself*, tasted unexpectedly sweet.

The other village girls whispered and fluttered their lashes at Caius and Dani—after all, they were the most handsome young men for miles. But if my friends noticed, they said nothing. Their attention never seemed to stray far from me.

I thought of this as I joined a circle of girls dancing, the music of flutes and violins weaving through the air. One of them caught my hand and laughed, "Come—don't stand there!" as they pulled me into the ring and we linked hands and spun. The coin belts at our hips and the bracelets we wore chimed with every rhythmic stomp of our feet and clap of our hands, adding a bright, metallic harmony to the lively tune.

As we whirled, I made a point to catch Caius and Dani's eyes. Caius grinned broadly, lifting a hand in an exuberant wave. Dani's smile was softer, almost shy. He glanced at his friend, then back at me, his expression hesitant.

Where Caius was bold and easy with his emotions, Dani held his close, his quiet reserve shielding an inner world I could never quite reach. The music shifted, a new dance began, this one a dance that included the men. The next time I passed I reached for their hands to drag them into the circle, my long hair flying this way and that. Caius joined in immediately but Dani held back, tugging his hand out of my grip.

"I don't know how to dance, Magda," he said with a soft laugh.

No, he knew how to dance. He simply preferred work that required precision and strength—steel beneath his hands, something useful taking shape because of him. Attention never tempted him the way it did Caius and me. Where we burned bright and restless, Dani was steady—deliberate in all things, even in joy. Reserve was not weakness in him; it was choice.

Between dances, we spent hours feasting on smoked meats, sweet bread studded with walnuts and dried apples, and washing it all down with honey mead and ale. After a few drinks, Dani finally joined us, though he lingered more at the edges than in the center of the revelry. As the night waned and the villagers began drifting back to their homes, I reluctantly stood to say my goodbyes.

"No, Magda—wait! I almost forgot." Caius grinned as he hurried after me. When he caught up, he pinned a Mărțișor charm to my sleeve—a tiny carved flower threaded with the traditional red-and-white string. His fingers lingered at my arm, warm and deliberate, and my heart faltered when I realized I was the only girl he had given one to that night.

I barely managed a breath of thanks before he was gone again. I glanced back to where Dani had been standing, but he was no longer there, and I found myself wondering when he had slipped away.

I watched Caius go, the mark of his touch still burning

through my sleeve, and found myself wondering what it would be like to kiss him—to taste those soft-looking red lips, to learn whether his boldness carried through to that, too. Other village girls had already crossed that threshold. Some were married. Some whispered behind their hands and smiled like they were keeping secrets. I had none of that yet. Only the question, sudden and aching, blooming in my chest.

With the flush of excitement still burning my cheeks, I lifted my hand in a farewell wave and turned toward the road home. The half-mile walk to my grandmother's cottage was quiet, the night air cool against my skin. But then I heard heavy footsteps behind me, boots crunching against gravel.

Startled, I turned—and when I saw Dani alone in the lane, I let out a quiet sigh of relief. He stopped a few feet away, his large frame silhouetted against the moonlight, something small held loosely in one hand.

"What is it?" I asked, glancing around for Caius. But even in the darkness, I could see he was alone.

"I have one for you too," he said softly.

He didn't step forward to pin it to my blouse as Caius had. Instead, he placed it gently into my palm. Another charm, tied with red and white string—this one a wooden heart, painted deep red.

"Thank you, Dani," I said, surprised by his gift.

"It doesn't mean anything," he said too quickly, already turning away. He didn't wait for me to ask what he meant, just strode back toward the village as if distance might undo the words.

But my friend's voice held an ache he couldn't quite hide, and I knew then that it meant more than he was willing to admit. The knowing settled heavy in my chest. Something fragile was shifting between the three of us, something I'd been pretending not to see. I tried to tell myself I owed Dani nothing, but that was a lie. Friendship carried its own vows, spoken or not, and I felt them tightening around my ribs.

4

HELP

Mira—January 2026

We loaded Bunny, Baird's gigantic deerhound, into the SUV and headed for Robbie's pub in Blackwaterfoot. The moment the word *'magic'* left my lips, Baird had said we should ask Robbie what he knew. And frankly, after the year I'd had, I didn't bother arguing. In a little over twelve months, I'd learned two life-altering truths: first, that my ability to touch objects and see fragments of the past wasn't just some psychological quirk—it was real. And second, vampires were real too.

Robbie—the mysterious island fisherman-turned-pub owner, the one the locals whispered about, the one who never seemed to age, and the man Baird had sought out after being turned—had become both mentor and father figure. Robbie had made it clear there were other things in the world that were real too: magic, for one, and those who practiced it. Yet every time he spoke of it, he'd casually make the sign of the cross. A vampire, crossing himself. The irony wasn't lost on me.

And yet, there was something about the way Robbie did it —quick, almost furtive—that suggested his wariness wasn't theatrical. Despite all he was, all he'd seen, speaking about magic seemed to make even *him* uneasy. And if what I'd felt when holding the ruby was any indication, maybe I needed to start making the sign of the cross too.

We sat in our usual spot by the fire, the warmth seeping into our bones as Bunny lay sprawled on the stone floor, blissfully unaware. The three of us leaned close around the small table, voices low, careful not to let the madness of our conversation carry to curious ears.

"Tell me again what ye saw," Robbie said, his voice a low rumble. His iridescent eyes flickered in the firelight, catching and refracting it like polished opals.

To an untrained eye, it might have seemed a trick of the light, nothing more. But I knew better. That shimmer wasn't natural—it was the subtle, otherworldly glow all vampires carried when they weren't actively suppressing it to pass for human. Robbie, though, rarely bothered to hide it here in his own bar.

And if some unfortunate patron caught sight of his eyes—if their gaze lingered too long, lips parting in startled recognition —Robbie would simply glamour them, erasing the memory before it had time to settle. Here, in this place, he could afford to be himself.

"It pulsed with power...and it spoke to me," I said, my voice quieter than I intended. A part of me still felt caught in the ruby's thrall, like it had left some faint, electric residue inside my skin. "There was this endless, spiraling figure eight all around me—darkness and light, birth and death—not separate states but part of the same whole. And what it showed me…" I trailed off, searching for words that felt too small to contain the enormity of it. "It was like a single thread pulled from its history. Just…a glimpse."

"And ye think the woman ye saw was a vampire." Robbie's voice cut through my thoughts, low but edged with skepticism.

The incredulity in his tone set my teeth on edge. I shot him a look, sharp enough to draw blood. "Yes, Robbie. That's exactly what I think." Somewhere deep down, I suspected he didn't entirely trust me—not yet. Maybe he still thought I was one bad day away from packing up, leaving the island, and fleeing back to Massachusetts. Leaving Baird. But I wasn't going anywhere. I leaned back in my chair, folding my arms across my chest.

Baird caught the look on my face and blanched, his jaw tightening. "Mira's sight has never been wrong, Robbie—and ye bloody well kens it. So stop being a crabbit auld git," he said tersely, the edge in his voice cutting through the low murmur of the pub.

I'd never mentioned it, but the way Baird always leapt to my defense made something in my chest ache—in the best way. My love for him deepened each time, impossibly so.

Robbie's mouth twitched, not quite a smile, not quite an apology, his iridescent eyes catching the firelight. "Well…I suppose I ken someone ye could talk tae," he said at last, the words heavy with reluctance. "But she's no the sort to appreciate uninvited guests. Lives alone on a wee island close by. I can go speak to her, see what she thinks." His forehead was creased, and he drummed his fingers on the tabletop, staring into the flames as if weighing his options. "I'll go the morn.

Maybe she'll agree to see ye, maybe she won't. I cannae make any promises."

"Who is she?" I asked, leaning forward, my curiosity sharpening. Whoever this woman was, Robbie seemed both reluctant and wary—and that only made me want to know more.

Baird chuckled low in his chest, ignoring the daggered look Robbie shot him across the table. "She's a witch..." he said, dragging out the words with a smirk. Then he added with a wink, "and Robbie's *old flame.*"

Robbie's kaleidoscope eyes flared in the firelight as he bristled, his voice sharp enough to cut glass. "That's ancient history, and ye ken it, Baird Campbell. Best shut yer geggie afore I put ye through that wall."

But Baird only laughed harder, clearly enjoying himself.

5

A WITCH COMES TO CALL

Mira—January 2026

A soft knock came at the cottage door late in the afternoon, the day after we'd gone to speak with Robbie. When I opened it, a small, middle-aged woman stood on the threshold. A few paces behind her, Robbie hovered with his hat in hand, darting nervous glances between me and the woman like he wasn't sure which of us was more likely to bite.

The stranger wore a kind expression, but there was something disconcerting about her eyes. They were an unnaturally even shade of brown—flat and uniform, lacking the usual flecks and striations you see in an iris. Her salt-and-pepper hair was pulled back in a tight bun, and she wore a faded polyester pantsuit that looked like it had been plucked straight from the 1980s, paired with practical, no-nonsense shoes. Her slender wrist was threaded through the handle of a very prim handbag.

She looked more like a schoolteacher than a witch. Not that I knew exactly what I *expected* a witch to look like.

"Ye are the seer," she said, her voice calm and even—not a question but a statement of fact.

The way she said it—like a diagnosis instead of someone with a name—made my shoulders tighten, uncomfortable with my clairvoyant abilities being acknowledged by a stranger. "Yes," I replied, offering my hand but not sure I wanted to. "My name is Mira. It's nice to meet you." I said, manners taking over. "Please, come inside."

She took my hand in a firm shake, her palm warm and surprisingly soft. "I am Sorcha," she said simply.

I stepped back, holding the door open as they crossed the threshold. Robbie hesitated for just a beat before following her inside, his shoulders stiff, his mouth pressed into a tight line.

"Ye must be Baird," Sorcha said as he stepped forward to greet her, her tone carrying the faintest lilt of familiarity—as though she'd heard stories about him for years from Robbie.

Baird shot a quick, curious glance at Robbie, one brow lifting ever so slightly.

Robbie stood off to the side, wringing his hands in a rare display of unease, as though two carefully separated corners of his life had just collided in a way he hadn't anticipated.

"Robbie says ye have an enchanted stone in your possession, Mira. May I see it?" Sorcha asked, her voice calm but edged with curiosity.

"Yes," I said, my throat tightening. A flicker of unease rippled through me at the thought of touching it again. After Baird had pried it from my fingers, he'd locked it away—sealed again in the hard plastic case and hidden it in the safe. "Let me go get it."

"It cannae hurt you, Mira." Sorcha's voice followed me as I walked down the hall, wrapping me in something calm and reassuring, as though she could sense the dark thoughts clawing at the edges of my mind. In the bedroom, I knelt before the safe and punched in the code. With a muted *click,* the door swung open.

For a heartbeat, I hesitated, staring down at the box resting in the dim interior. The air felt heavier here, as if the ruby's presence bled out even through the case. Then, with a sharp inhale, I forced myself to scoop it up and carry it back to the living room.

I placed the small box gently into Sorcha's waiting hands. Her fingers curled around it with surprising delicacy, as though she already understood the weight it carried. Closing her eyes, she drew in a slow breath, and for a moment the room felt... stiller. Denser somehow, as though even the air was holding its breath. When her eyes fluttered open again, she laid one hand lightly on the lid.

"May I?" she asked softly, her tone respectful but edged with quiet purpose.

I nodded dumbly, my throat too tight for words.

With a slow, deliberate movement, Sorcha lifted the lid and reached inside. Her fingers curled around the stone, and for a moment she simply held it, as if weighing its presence in her palm. She drew in a sudden breath and her eyes widened— whether in awe, alarm, or admiration, I couldn't tell—but the flicker of raw emotion there made my pulse quicken.

She felt it too. Sorcha's eyes flicked to me. She tilted her head slowly to the left, then narrowed her gaze and tilted it to the right, as if trying to glimpse something invisible lingering just beneath my skin. "Ye didnae tell me she was a maker,

Robbie," she said at last, her tone caught between amusement and rueful surprise.

I was used to the word *maker*, but the way she said it held weight, like it was older than language I was accustomed to. It felt less description and more category, and I wasn't sure I liked being lumped into it.

"A...*what*?" Robbie muttered, his brow furrowing in confusion.

"Men." Sorcha muttered, her voice prickly as she tossed her head in irritation. Then her gaze settled on me—steady, unflinching, and impossibly intense. "A maker of things— amulets, sigils, talismans."

The words she used, ancient and heavy with implication, seemed to hang in the air between us like motes of dust caught in a shaft of sunlight. They drifted and twisted in my mind, their edges shimmering faintly, as though I could almost *see* them taking shape. Her phrasing felt odd and archaic, but I guessed it wasn't entirely wrong, especially when the emerald necklace I'd made became something just like that. "I'm...a jeweler. A metalsmith," I said carefully, the words tasting almost foreign on my tongue in the presence of her unblinking stare.

"Oh, nae *just* that. No..." Sorcha's gaze flicked to Baird, keen and knowing, then back to me. "He can see it, eh?"

Baird froze. For a fleeting moment, I saw guilt flicker across his face before he dropped his eyes to the cottage floor, feigning sudden interest in something invisible at his feet.

"See *what*?" I demanded. "I'm standing right here."

Somehow, it felt like Robbie and I had been unceremoniously shut out of an inside joke, one shared only between Baird and Sorcha—a private knowledge that left me prickling with irritation.

"The magic ye wield, Mira." Sorcha stated, as if that explained everything. "Magic seeks magic. The stone found its way to ye because it needs ye. Hold it again," she said gently as she held it out to me. "Let it explain, then ye can decide."

Everything in me wanted to refuse, but I was tired of pretending something that knew my name could be avoided just by not looking at it. "Let it explain *what*, exactly?" I snapped, thrown by the way she seemed to be speaking *about* me and *to* me all at once.

Sorcha didn't answer. She only held the stone out to me, her expression unreadable. I took a deep breath, forcing air into my tight lungs, and swallowed down the knot of fear coiling in my throat. Slowly, I reached out and wrapped my fingers around the ruby. The instant my skin met its surface, a searing pulse shot through my palm, sizzling like fire sinking into my bloodstream. I felt Baird move to my side in a blur, his protective arms encircling me, steadying me as my knees nearly buckled. Then the world dropped away.

The cottage, the firelight, Baird's solid presence—all of it vanished in an instant. I was swallowed by inky darkness, so complete it felt alive. And then the whispers began. Soft at first, curling around me like smoke, their voices neither male nor female—just raw, ancient sound.

We are not whole. We are two. One in your hand...one yet to be found.
Your task is not to keep, but to shape. To forge what binds us. Help us seek the ones to whom we belong. Only then can they be reunited.

We are not yours, yet you are chosen to bring us to life. A maker's hands...a seer's sight. The power lies with you.

The darkness receded, peeling away like smoke until the living room swam back into focus. Whatever the ruby had shown me, it hadn't felt like a threat, not exactly. Something about it made me feel seen, special. And that might have frightened me the most. Three faces stared at me—Baird, his arms still steadying me; Robbie, concern etched plainly across his features; and Sorcha, curious, expectant. The weight of their gazes pressed on me, but it was the power of the ruby in my hand that anchored me most of all. I looked down at it, its surface cool now, innocuous even. Drawing in a slow, deep breath, I held it in my lungs until the tightness in my chest eased. Then I let it out in a long, trembling exhale.

"It said there were two rubies—I only have one. And my task is to shape it into a piece of jewelry. Somehow that would help it find the other, but...that makes no sense." I let out a ragged breath, shaking my head at the riddle tangled in my mind. "Something about a maker's hands...and a seer's sight..." My voice trailed off, and for a moment the weight of it lay heavy in my gut. Then I turned to Sorcha, my eyes narrowing. "And what did you mean by 'I can decide'? Decide *what*, exactly? I need you to be clear," I said. "Because from where I am standing, it doesn't feel like much of a choice at all."

"Ye are not obligated to comply," Sorcha said, her face unreadable. "But I would—*were I a maker*—and been chosen."

"What exactly is it asking me to do?" I shot back, pacing. "Make a ring? A necklace? And then what? Just sit here until someone happens to knock on the door?"

"Is that how ye make a living?" Sorcha asked evenly.

"What? No—I make something, photograph it, then advertise it on social media and my website."

"Then that is what the ruby is asking ye to do. Nothing more. The person who buys it will be part of the chain to bring the person back."

"Bring *who* back?" I demanded, my voice rising.

Sorcha's gaze didn't waver. "The one the woman wants to live again. The rubies hold the power to bring them back. The ruby's spell is one of reincarnation."

Robbie backed away from the three of us, his face as white as a pale-skinned vampire *could* be, his lips moving in a frantic mutter as he made the sign of the cross over and over.

"God preserve us, an' keep the wicked things at bay... Christ's cross be ma shield and ma sword...The Lord's light blind ye and the cold earth bind ye..." His voice cracked on the last words, raw and trembling, and for a moment I thought he might bolt for the door. But then I saw the way his eyes darted toward Sorcha, and I knew—he was too afraid of her to actually do it.

Clearly, Robbie was *not* okay with whatever was happening here. Truthfully, I wasn't either. The ruby had chosen *me* for this...not him. But something had happened to Robbie—something deep enough to leave scars invisible to the eye—to provoke this kind of terror. I made a mental note to ask Baird about it later, when we were alone.

"Think on it, Mira," Sorcha said, her voice level but edged with quiet finality. "I'll come back in a few days to talk with ye." She didn't wait for a reply. "Let's away, Robbie."

She walked out the door first, with Robbie close behind. The ruby was still warm in my hand. Whatever I'd agreed to—

spoken or otherwise—I knew one thing with unsettling clarity. My life had already begun to bend around it.

FOR A LONG MOMENT, neither of us spoke. Baird didn't rush to fill the silence—didn't ask if I was alright, didn't try to interpret what any of it meant. He stayed just close enough for me to feel him there, ready if I needed him.

"So," I said finally. "That went well."

He huffed with a small laugh. "Aye. Very neighborly visit from the local witch."

"When she called me a maker, she said it like it wasn't just a skill." I said. "More like it was a function."

He mused to himself before responding. "I picked up on that. It was odd."

"I'm not sure I like being chosen for things I don't understand," I said quietly.

"Did ye understand your clairvoyance at first?" he countered.

I shot him a pout at being right "No. And I still don't like it."

He pulled me into his arms—the feel of him solid, real, tangible—and kissed my forehead.

I lingered for a moment before pulling away to reheat leftovers for my dinner, and poured both of us a glass of wine. "What do you know about Sorcha?"

"She's old," Baird said after a pause. "Older than Robbie. Older than most things, I think."

I let that sink in. "So she's not just some barefoot hippy with a bundle of sage and a dollar-store spell book?" In truth, I *wanted* her to be that simple and innocuous—to be someone I could laugh off instead of someone who scared a vampire like Robbie. Growing up in Massachusetts, I felt like witch culture was everywhere. Salem merch, *Hocus Pocus* reruns, haunted tours in October. But a *real* witch? Never met one.

"No. She's very powerful I think." He leaned closer to me, his voice low, almost reluctant—as if speaking about her in a voice too loud might summon her. "Robbie told me he met her before he was turned. He was a young lad then, out fishing on the open sea when a storm came from nowhere—black skies, screaming wind. His boat capsized, and he barely survived. Washed up half-dead on an island he didnae recognize." Baird shifted uncomfortably in his seat before he went on. "He said a beautiful redheaded woman found him there. Nursed him back to health. She told him she was lonely...and asked him to stay. And for a time, he did. Happily." He went quiet for a moment, and I saw the tension ripple through him before he continued. "But one day, Robbie went out to collect firewood. As he came back, he saw her through the cottage window...and she wasna the woman who'd found him. She was ancient—a withered crone with skin like parchment and eyes as sharp as glass. She can change her appearance at will, Mira. She'll change how she looks so ye can accept her. That's the kind of power she has."

"What did *you* see her as?" I asked, still processing that she might appear as one thing to me, and someone else entirely to him.

"She looked about fifty, I suppose," Baird said after a moment. "A wee bun on top of her head, a bit of gray in her hair. Eyes the color of a fawn..." He trailed off with a small shrug.

"That's how I saw her," I murmured, the chill of recognition sliding down my spine.

Baird's gaze flicked to mine, and for a heartbeat, the air seemed heavier between us. "She let him go, gave him a boat to come back. Then many years later, after Robbie was turned," he went on, his voice lower now, "he went back to the island. Thought maybe, with her magic, she could make him human again. He said he was never sure if she *couldnae* or if she just *wouldnae.*" Baird's mouth tightened. "Because now she has him. Forever."

"What do you mean?" I asked, my voice barely above a whisper.

"Well...she disnae *have* him. He lives here, goes about his business. But every so often, she calls to him."

"Calls to him?" I echoed, unsure what that even meant. A phone call? Somehow, I doubted it.

"Aye." Baird nodded grimly. "He'll get in his boat and go out to her. Stay with her a few days. Then come home like nothing happened. Says she still looks like the beautiful maiden who found him when he's there. And from the look on his face today..." Baird exhaled heavily. "I'd say to him, she *was* the young woman again."

Every so often, Sorcha made what sounded like a witch's booty call to Robbie, and whatever hold she had on him, he couldn't—or wouldn't—refuse her. Powerful indeed. Then I remembered her cryptic comment—and the guilty look on Baird's face as I sat down at the table next to him.

"What did she mean...when she said you can see my magic?" The words felt strange and heavy on my tongue, like saying them aloud might make them real. I wasn't sure I wanted that. I'd only just made a shaky peace with my clairvoyance, and now this—this suggestion of something deeper, something more—felt like it could undo all of that.

"I told ye before, Mira—sometimes ye glow with it. Literally." Baird's voice was low, reverent. "It's like...an electrical field rippling over yer skin. Shimmering, like the heat waves that rise off a fire. Invisible, but not invisible—if ye ken what I mean."

I swallowed hard, caught between disbelief and a heavier dread pooling low in my chest. The only thing keeping me from going under was the look on Baird's face—one of wonder, and maybe even pride—as he spoke.

"Most times, I see it when you're in the studio," he went on. "Dancing wi the torch in your hand, completely lost in your work. But I've seen it other times too—when ye're in my arms, when ye come for me," he said with a wicked gleam in his eyes, "and I can feel and see the power in ye then, Mira. Strong and wild, like nothing I've ever known."

His hand slid over mine, fingers curling gently. "You're a rare and magical thing, Mira Garvie. And all this time, ye thought I was just bein' romantic."

6

THE MISSION

Mira—January 2026

I was in my studio when she came to call again. This time, she was the young redhead Robbie must see—the one who still haunted him after all these years. Her copper hair tumbled in loose waves over her shoulders, and she wore a pale sundress and leather sandals, as if she'd stepped straight out of a summer daydream.

"Hello Mira." If it weren't for those strange, light brown eyes —too flat, too uniform in their color—I might not have recognized her as Sorcha. But the voice was unmistakable: low, calm, and laced with that same quiet authority I'd heard on her first visit. I couldn't help but wonder why she'd changed her appearance this time. Was it meant as a subtle display of her power? A test to see if I doubted her? Or simply a reminder that she could be whatever—and whoever—she chose.

"Have ye made a decision?" Sorcha asked as I swung open the bottom half of the yellow Dutch door to my studio to let her in. I gestured for her to sit in one of the two chairs in the studio—though this was hardly a space I used for entertaining. I had to move a box of supplies off the other so I could sit down.

"I don't know." The words slipped out before I could stop them. Before I could find a better way to explain what I was feeling. Not that it mattered—maybe she already knew I was afraid. My fingers curled tighter around the arm of the chair. "I worry...about the power it holds. It feels dark somehow. Wrong. Evil." Even saying it made my chest tighten, a heavy pressure settling over me. The thought of shaping the ruby into a piece of jewelry sent a cold shiver down my spine.

Sorcha's eyes seemed to peer through me—beyond me. "What ye feel is the power," she said, her voice slower now, resonant, as if she were reciting something written in an old text. "But power itself carries no will," she said. "It is neither good nor evil—it simply *is*." She lifted her hand, fingers curling in a slow, deliberate arc, as though she might pluck an unseen thread from the air—an ancient truth drifting down to her palm like an invisible feather spun from shadow and light. "Goodness and wickedness are born in the soul of the one who wields the magic. The ruby is but a vessel, holding what was placed within it long ago. That is why I told ye—it cannae harm ye. Nor anyone else. Not unless *ye* give it leave to do so."

"You said I *know* magic, but I don't. I don't know anything about it."

"No, Mira," Sorcha said evenly. "I did not say ye *knew* magic," using my American English in gentle mocking. "I said ye *possess* it." She folded her hands neatly in her lap, her voice slipping into the steady cadence of a teacher correcting a student who hadn't bothered to listen closely. She continued, "There are two kinds of magic. One is learned—anyone with discipline may grasp it, though some are more adept than others. The other is inherent. It is born in the marrow of your bones, the blood in your veins. That kind of magic is rare...and it cannae be taught." She tilted her head, studying me as though she could see it flickering beneath my skin like Baird had claimed to see. "The magic inside ye is inherent, Mira. It has always been there. I, too, was born with magic, different than yours, but still born with it...and I learned the other kind. Ye could learn it as well, if ye choose."

I wasn't sure I liked this detour. She'd come to talk to me about the ruby—*that* was the task at hand. Deciding whether I would, or even *should*, heed its request to create something that could fulfill some magical purpose seemed pressing enough without wading into the murky waters of my supposed natural-born magical talent. That could wait.

I shook my head, hoping for some clarity, "Back to the ruby—what specifically does it want me to make? What metal do I use?" I asked, trying to steer the conversation back to something tangible, something that might actually guide me.

"Have ye asked it?" Sorcha inquired gently.

"*Asked it?*" I echoed, tilting my head like she'd just suggested I strike up a chat with a piece of flagstone.

Her lips tightened into a slight scowl, irritation flickering across her face. When she spoke again, her tone was slow and deliberate, as though addressing a small child. "How do ye know what to make for any stone ye set? How do ye come up with the design?"

I gave a little shrug. "I just...picture it in my head, I guess."

"Exactly," Sorcha said, her voice softening but still edged with that patient insistence. "The stone speaks to the maker, sending an image of what it wants to be. And the maker—*ye*—

receives it. Then ye shape it into being. It's no different with the ruby."

"But those stones...they aren't enchanted. Or magic. Or... whatever this is."

"Correct." Sorcha inclined her head slightly. "In those cases, all the magic lies with *ye*. But the ruby? The ruby may be... more opinionated."

I let out a shaky breath, thinking back. "I don't know. I *did* see it—just for a moment—set in a gold ring when I held it the first time. I assumed maybe it was set as a ring at some point long ago."

"The ruby would only show ye what it needed ye to see. So there ye are," she said brightly. "That," she said, nodding once, "is what it wants to be. A ring." Sorcha said, like it was just that easy. "Remember—it chose *ye* for this task. It knows ye are the right one, or it never would have found its way to ye."

I didn't know if I wanted this—if I was ready for what it might mean. But I supposed the choice had already been made for me. "Okay," I murmured, my stomach tightening just knowing the words that were about to come out of my mouth. "I'll do it."

"Now, that wasnae so hard, was it? I'll return when it's finished," Sorcha murmured, her gaze turning distant, as though seeing something beyond this moment. "It's not often a witch bears witness to work like this—work that will be recorded in our tomes and whispered of for generations." And she stood, preparing to walk out the door.

This wasn't just a magical jewelry repair job. This had somehow escalated into the sort of thing that would be etched into witchy history and talked about for centuries. I was tempted to ask how she'd know when it was finished, but I didn't.

Of course she'd know. She was a thousand-year-old witch who could shapeshift at will and was, apparently, still sexually active. "Thank you, Sorcha," I said with a small nod of goodbye, my stomach in knots. The moment she left and I closed the bottom of the Dutch door, the studio felt smaller.

7

———

A QUESTION FOR THE SMOKE

Magda—April 1387

Buna had been adamant when she taught me her magic: it was to be used only for certain things. Protection—for myself, for those I loved, and for our people. And healing, though I'd always suspected that true healing lived in the plants we used as much, if not more, than in the spells we whispered over them.

She had warned me never to use magic as a means of power for its own sake—or for personal gain. That, she said, was how people lost their souls: by twisting magic until it served ambition instead of need.

Buna was always clear on this point. Magic was neither good nor evil—*people were*. And more often than not, those born with the greatest talent were the first to abuse it.

Luckily for me—or perhaps unluckily—I possessed no great gift. Nothing grand or dazzling. Only a steady hand for mixing healing herbs, and a burgeoning ability to read the smoke.

But Buna was superstitious. And I...I was prepared to wield whatever magic at my disposal to claim what I believed was my true destiny—to stand at Caius's side. To give love and receive his, despite my low birth. Despite her warnings.

Warnings not to be careless with magic. Warnings to stay away from Caius.

I knew the heat in Caius's eyes when he looked at me—the way his gaze lingered longer than it should when we passed in the village, how he leaned in close when we spoke, holding my eyes like he didn't want to let go. Of course there were rumors. Some teased me kindly, calling me the young boyar's sweetheart. But others were cruel. They whispered that I was so blinded by love, I couldn't see the truth—that his father would never allow it, that I could never be more than his whore.

I knew what Buna said—that though Caius looked at me like a man dying of thirst, and I a cool, clear stream, only ruin and sorrow could come if we reached for one another. But what did my grandmother know of the ache in my chest? Of the way my heart clawed for something more—more than my low birth, more than a life of smallness, more than one spent in a drafty, dirt-floored cottage.

Perhaps she was right. Perhaps all roads did lead to tragedy. In our region, tragedy was as familiar as the sound of our own names. Not only for the Romani people—for all of us. We knew violence. We knew loss. We knew illness, and we knew death. It came for the rich as often as the poor, sweeping through our lives like a bitter wind, leaving nothing untouched.

Caius and I had known this truth from the moment we drew breath—each of us motherless from birth, each born beneath the Blood Moon. I was raised by Buna, wrapped in her fierce love and hard-won wisdom. Caius was handed to a nurse-maid until his father remarried years later, left to stand at the edges of his own household, watching affection poured over his half-sisters while he learned to go without. A boy with every worldly need answered and an aching hole inside him.

And still, I couldn't stop the seed of longing from taking root. I had already begun shaping a plan to claim what my heart insisted was mine. But I needed to know—*truly* know—whether what Caius and I felt could take hold, could grow and bind us in a way no one could sever. I needed to know if what stirred in him was as real, as consuming, as the ache that lived in me.

I told myself it would be harmless. A question, nothing more. A looking, not a taking. But even as the thought formed, I felt the familiar tightening in my chest—the quiet place where warnings lived. Where lines were drawn for a reason. Where magic, once bent toward desire, rarely returned unchanged. I did not name that fear. I did not turn away from it, either.

I chose to step over it.

And I knew exactly how.

I pulled the grimoire from the shelf and set it near the candlelight, running my fingers over the worn leather cover before carefully thumbing through its fragile pages. This was why Buna had taught me to read, to write, to count—not just so I wouldn't be cheated at the market, but so the recipes and spells of my people, passed down from woman to woman, would never be lost.

Scrying was a useful tool—but only as a means of preparation, Buna taught, a way to ready ourselves for whatever might come. Scrying was a form of divination, the art of seeing what was hidden or not yet known. There were countless methods, none more effective than another. It was a matter of personal preference. Some witches used crystal orbs. Others gazed into bowls of still water, searching for symbols or images to ripple across the surface. Some turned to fire, watching the flames dance for meaning. But Buna's method was smoke—and that was what she taught me.

It had been a while since I'd practiced, so I turned to the grimoire to refresh my memory. I closed the windows of the cottage—stillness was important. Any draft could stir the smoke, twist the patterns, and obscure the message. I took a few moments to quiet my thoughts, to hush the noise in my mind until all that remained was breath and intention.

When I was calm—my breath even, my focus sharp—I placed a small stone bowl on the table. I reached for the bundle of dried herbs I'd collected and tied with twine, cradled it in my palm, and set my question firmly in my mind.

"Spirit, guide this smoke to reveal to me the truth." I held the bundle—dry tinder—to the candle flame until it caught, then placed it carefully into the stone bowl. The herbs began to smolder, the edges curling, a thin thread of smoke rising before the flame took hold.

"Does Caius love me and want to take me as his wife?" I whispered. I moved my hands slowly over the bowl, one after the other, cupped like I was cradling something delicate and sacred. I guided the smoke with subtle motions, watching as it curled and twisted through the still air, then pulled my hands back to rest on the table.

Softening my gaze, I stared ahead, letting the smoke rise. Waiting for the truth to take shape. The smoke rose in a slender column, then drifted directly toward me—as if it had seen me, heard my question, and chosen to answer.

In a love reading, the grimoire said this was a positive sign. It felt like confirmation. A warm glow bloomed deep in my chest, fragile but bright, and I held perfectly still as the smoke neared. Just before it reached me, the column split in two—one arm curling to my left, the other to my right—parting around me as though my body had cleaved the message in two.

According to the grimoire, smoke that split into two clear streams represented duality—a fork in the road, two possible outcomes. I didn't want to read too much into that. No one could see the future completely, not even those of us who tried. But it was enough for me that the smoke had risen...and reached for me. That was confirmation enough. Caius's heart was mine.

The slam of the door jolted me from my reverie. Buna stood in the doorway, her eyes sweeping the room with a fury I hadn't seen in years. The smoke still hung in the air, curling in lazy ribbons above the extinguished herbs, and the grimoire lay open on the table like a confession. She didn't need to ask. Her gaze fixed on me, blazing with the kind of rage that comes not just from defiance—but from fear.

She knew. Maybe not the exact words I'd spoken or the question I'd sent into the smoke—but she knew it had been about Caius. And that was enough.

"What have you done, girl?" she spat, her voice sharp as a lash. "You couldn't leave well enough alone, could you? What question did you ask?"

Her face was red with indignation, the creases in her brow deepening as her gnarled hands clenched into fists at her sides. There was no use in lying. And truthfully, I was done with her cryptic warnings and half-whispered fears. She wasn't going to stop me. Not now.

"I asked if Caius loved me," I said, lifting my chin in defiance. "And if he wanted to take me as his wife." I didn't flinch. Didn't look away. I was done letting her superstition and fear hold my life hostage a moment longer.

Her eyes widened, just for a moment, and I thought—*foolishly*—that I'd bested her. But then her expression shifted. The surprise drained from her face, replaced by something far more dangerous: calculation. Her eyes narrowed, and her voice coiled like a snake preparing to strike. "And what, pray tell, did the smoke reveal to you?" she asked, drawing out every word, each one laced with slow, deliberate venom.

I forced myself to stand tall, trying to hide the recoil I felt at her disapproval. "The smoke drifted straight up, and then toward me. He loves me, Buna—and he wants me as his wife." I said, as if that settled everything.

"Stupid, reckless girl!" she snapped. "Of course he loves you. It didn't take the smoke to tell you that. Anyone with eyes could see it. So does the other one, the armorer's son. So what?" She stepped closer, her voice rising, trembling not just with anger—but sorrow. "But it doesn't matter what Caius wants. Or what *you* want. You asked the wrong question." Her eyes bore into mine, fierce and unyielding. "You should have asked not *if* he loves you...but *if you'll ever be his wife*. That's the question, Magda."

I was done living in the shadows. Buna couldn't bully me anymore—not with her rules, her warnings, her worn-out sense of right and wrong.

"You're just angry I used magic for myself, Buna," I spat, my ire rising to meet hers. "Well, I did—and you won't make me feel guilty for it."

She crossed the room in three long strides and came to within an inch of my face. Her cheeks were flushed crimson with rage, and though she was several inches shorter, her presence towered. It made me shrink before I could stop myself.

"You think I've never used magic for the wrong reasons?" she hissed. "I *have*, Magda. Just like you." Her voice dropped, but the weight of her words only grew heavier. "And you know what I asked? I used magic to ask a question about you and Caius. The *right* one. And the smoke gave me an answer."

She paused, her eyes glistening—not with tears, but something still sorrowful. "I've done everything in my power to protect you from that answer. To steer you away from the future the smoke showed me. Because that's what it isn't, Magda. It isn't a future. It's an end—and not just yours."

8

THE STRANGER

Magda—May 1387

The stream ran clear and cold over pale stones, sunlight breaking on its surface like scattered coins. Caius had already kicked off his boots and rolled his trousers to his knees, wading in with a practiced ease, fishing spear balanced loosely in his hand as if it were an extension of his arm.

Caius and I were already half-gone, laughing as I plucked berries from the bramble and lobbed one at him for daring me to throw it farther. He whooped and leapt for the river's edge, showing off as he always did—long limbs, careless grace, daring the current to take him. We were restless, reckless—two sparks struck from the same flame.

Dani lingered behind us, methodical as ever. He set down the basket, checked the line he'd brought, and tested the knot twice before letting it sink into the water. Where Caius and I leapt without thinking, Dani paused. Where we broke things, he mended them. He noticed the details we ignored, planned for consequences we never considered, and followed after to set right whatever chaos we left in our wake.

I didn't understand it then—not fully. I only knew that Caius and I burned fast and bright, and Dani was the weight that kept us from flying apart. He carried what we shed without noticing—worry, foresight, responsibility—and bore it so easily it would take me years to see what he'd been doing for us all along.

I climbed to the brambles farther up the slope, where the wild raspberries grew thick and sweet. My skirts were hitched indecently high for the task, and I made no effort to hide it.

"Mind the thorns, Magda," Caius called without looking back, his voice carrying easily over the water.

"I'm not afraid of a little blood," I replied, plucking a berry and popping it into my mouth. "Besides, I thought you liked danger."

That earned me a grin as he turned, sunlight flashing off his wet skin. "And are you dangerous, Magda?"

I laughed, the sound light and unguarded, and held up a berry between my fingers. "You're very confident for a man who hasn't caught a single fish yet."

"Yes," he said, wading closer to the bank, eyes never leaving me. "But I've caught your attention, haven't I?"

Dani cleared his throat softly, crouching to secure the line in the shallows. "If you two could stop talking long enough for one of us to catch something, that'd help. The fish don't like noise," he said, not unkindly.

I watched the exchange with interest, then turned my attention back to Caius. I let my fingers brush my lips deliberately before dropping another berry into the basket. "If you catch something worthy," I said, "I might reward you."

His eyes darkened, a spark of challenge there. "Is that so?"

"I didn't say how," I added sweetly.

He laughed and stepped back into the stream, renewed purpose in his movements. Within moments, he struck—quick, decisive—and lifted a wriggling fish from the water.

"Well," he said, holding it up triumphantly. "Looks like fortune favors me today."

I applauded him, slow and exaggerated. "Impressive. Very heroic."

Dani finally glanced up, his expression tight. He took the fish from Caius without ceremony and dispatched it cleanly, then laid it in the basket.

"You're good at that," I said to him, softer now.

He shrugged. "Someone has to be."

The moment passed, the easy rhythm returning—water sliding over stone, leaves whispering overhead, Caius talking animatedly about nothing and everything at once. I laughed when he splashed water toward the bank, scolded him halfheartedly, and felt the warmth of his attention like sunlight on my skin.

All the while, Dani stayed close but just beyond the circle— steady, silent, watching us with a flinty stillness. There were currents between us that had nothing to do with the river, and for reasons I didn't yet understand, I felt them tug.

I needed to start back before dusk, but I wanted to stop for apples first. After my farewells, I led my pony along the path toward the ridge, less than a quarter mile away. I dropped the reins and let her graze while I reached into the branches, the apples cool and heavy as I set them into my basket.

A horse snorted behind me.

I turned, expecting Caius—his grin, his careless swagger—but the man on the horse was not Caius.

The orchard had gone unnaturally still. No birdsong, no rustle of leaves, not even the soft chew of my pony's grazing. Just the stranger's gaze, fixed and unblinking. At first, it was the animal that held my gaze—tall and graceful, with a coat unlike anything I'd ever seen. It shimmered like pearl, luminous and uncanny, a shifting interplay of cream, rose, and silver-gray. A soft metallic sheen clung to its flanks, catching the light with every restless step. The horse held its head high, its profile straight and proud regal in every movement. And its eyes... they were blue. Strikingly, impossibly blue.

This was no ordinary animal. This was a horse fit for a king.

The man, dressed in a fine jacket, black wool with colorful embroidery on the collar and cuffs, held the reins tightly in hands adorned with rings—bands of gold and silver set with colorful stones that caught the sunlight and glinted like the horse's coat.

I stood, transfixed.

And then the rider, a stranger to me, spoke. Not aloud, his lips still pressed together in a tight line, but he spoke to me all the same. His voice threaded low, into my mind itself.

"You're fascinated, aren't you, young girl? A little fearful I think, but more fascinated." His voice was low—smooth as silk, yet threaded with condescension, like he was playing a game. There was something intimate in the way he spoke, as though he knew me. But I had never seen him before in my life.

I wasn't sure what he was. The fine clothing, the heavy jewels, the horse alone marked him as impossibly rich—but it was more than that. A sorcerer, a shifter, perhaps even a god from the old world. Whatever he was, he was power—undeniable, unearthly, absolute. His face was striking—sharp planes and cheekbones that caught the sun and threw it back at me like a glare. His skin wasn't the ruddy brown of a life lived in the sun but a burnished walnut, smooth and dark. There was something about him that pulled at me, a force. But it was his eyes that bound me. Impossibly black, bottomless. They drank in the light, drank in me, drank in everything.

I wanted to look away, but I couldn't. Some small voice inside me whispered to run—to turn and flee toward Caius and Dani, toward safety. But I couldn't move. Something held me. I felt it—like a tether from him, invisible and unbreakable, snaking straight into my thoughts.

His words entered my mind again, not a figment of my imagination, but real. "*Do you think those young men will protect you?*" he asked, his voice curling around me, slithering like a snake. "*The golden one—you yearn for him, don't you? But you wonder...worry...about what the villagers say. That you're too far beneath him. That no matter how beautiful you are...and no matter how sweet his words...that you'll never truly matter to him.*"

A gasp slipped from me, shattering the mask of indifference I clung to. How could he know what I'd just been thinking? It was as if he were inside me, prying open every hidden thought, every secret fear I'd tried to bury. And then the dread I'd kept pressed to the edges of my mind broke loose—hot, piercing, and undeniable. Panic. At last, I felt it. And it told me the truth. I was in danger.

I reached deep, clawing through the fear to find the fire beneath—the rage that lived just under my skin, curled in my bones. The hellcat Buna always said I was. And when I found her, I let her rise.

I screamed. Not a cry of terror—but of fury. A raw, defiant sound that tore from my throat like it had teeth. If this man meant to hurt me, I wouldn't go down quietly. I would not be easy prey. And the moment the scream left my lips, something broke. His grip on my mind fractured—shattered—and I was free.

In the distance, two voices answered, carried by the wind.

"Magda! Where are you?" Dani's voice, rough with alarm. Then another, farther off—Caius.

Relief warred with dread. I was unprepared. Whatever this man was, I had no weapons for him. No training. No shield but rage.

He gathered his reins, eyes flicking toward the sound of approaching voices. He wasn't retreating in fear—I could sense that much. It was inconvenience that sent him off, not threat.

He nudged his horse forward a few paces, then turned back to me, his dark eyes glittering."I hope we will meet again, Magda." This time he spoke aloud.

And then he was gone—his mount galloping away, vanishing into the trees, in the opposite direction of Caius and Dani. Moments later they came charging up into the clearing on their horses.

I was breathless at what had just happened. "A man on a horse was here. I've never seen him before. But he read my mind—*I felt it*—I know that sounds crazy. He's some sort of *solomonari*, or...or a *maleficius*," using the words my people had to describe a demon or a malicious entity. "He has dark magic, I know it."

"What did he look like?" Caius asked, his eyes narrowing. I could see the wheels turning in his mind, fitting pieces into place.

"Well-dressed. Salt-and-pepper hair, shorn close." The words tumbled out in a landslide of panicked explanation. "The darkest skin I've ever seen, eyes darker still. He wore many rings. But his horse—I've never seen anything like it. Cream-colored, with a sheen like polished metal...and eyes like yours, Caius."

"Eyes like mine? The horse?" he echoed back like I'd lost my mind.

"Yes, the horse—blue." I nodded emphatically, hoping to displace the skeptical expression on his face.

"Which direction did he go?" Caius asked, his tone suddenly sharp.

I watched him and Dani exchange a glance—brief, but meaningful. Then, without another word, Caius wheeled his horse and kicked it into a gallop, racing off in the direction the man had gone.

Dani dismounted and let the reins fall. He crossed to me in a few quick strides, concern etched into every line of his face. His hands settled on my shoulders before he pulled me against him, arms wrapping tightly around me.

I let myself breathe. Just breathe.

He didn't make my heart flutter the way Caius did, but there was a steadiness in him, a goodness that radiated from my friend. I took it gladly, grounding me while my heartbeat slowed. After a moment, he pulled back to look at me, one hand rising to cup my cheek.

"Are you all right?" he asked. "Did he hurt you?" Concern rang in his voice, and in the stricken way his eyes searched my face, my arms, as though he might find some mark he'd missed.

"Yes—no," I said, hoping I was answering in the right order. My body was unharmed, but my thoughts were still in disarray. "He didn't hurt me. Not really." I drew a breath, struggling to put it into words. "But he got into my thoughts. It was as if he reached inside me and knew things—things I'd only just been thinking. He twisted them, turned them against me." I hesitated, heat creeping into my cheeks. "It frightened me," I said at last, letting that be all. I couldn't confess what the stranger had read in my thoughts, and I prayed Dani wouldn't ask.

He didn't respond right away. I could tell he was weighing something, choosing his words.

"Do you know who he is?" I asked, remembering the flash that passed over Caius's face when I'd described the horse.

"No," Dani said. "But I believe Caius does." His mouth tightened. "His father spoke of seeing a man with a pale horse recently. Thinks he is aligned with our enemies from the south."

Dani let out a slow breath, as if he'd been scared too and could now let down his guard. "You're safe now," he said, and somehow the words made it true. He took the basket from my trembling hands and slung it over his shoulder and mounted his horse. "Come—I'll take you home."

When I returned to the cottage, I told Buna everything—about the man on the shimmering horse, and how he had somehow slipped into my thoughts, as if he'd been listening from inside my own mind. How he'd known things he shouldn't have—things I had only just been thinking.

"How do I protect myself from someone invading my

mind?" I asked, the panic still hot in my chest—the awful realization that even my thoughts could betray me.

"You must first recognize it's happening," Buna said, her voice low and deliberate. "And you did. That's a start. Most people don't feel the intrusion until it's too late...if they ever notice it at all."

She paused, drawing a breath, as if deciding how much of the truth I was ready to carry. "But with practice—when you learn to listen for it—you'll begin to sense it in the air around you. You'll know when someone wields that kind of power. Sometimes the moment you meet them." She tapped a finger to her temple. "And that's when you raise your guard. Because that's what it is, Magda—a wall. A barrier in your mind they can't penetrate. You must build it. Hold it. Defend it. Every time."

Over the next few days we practiced. I wrote words on slips of paper, folded them into small squares, and dropped them into a basket. Buna would draw one out and hand it to me. I'd read it, memorize it, and press my hand over it so she couldn't see.

Then came the real work. I'd conjure the word in my mind —wrap it in color, texture, meaning—and then try to shield it, locking it behind the wall Buna was teaching me to build.

She'd close her eyes, searching for what I was hiding. Then she'd tell me what the word was I'd been holding in my thoughts. Sometimes she was close—too close. When my focus had slipped, or I'd let my guard drop, or when I was tired. But other times...nothing. Just a blank void where my thoughts had once been laid bare.

I was getting better.

"But the place you need to get to," Buna said, her gaze

focused, "is beyond just building a wall." She leaned in slightly. "Because if someone reaches for your mind and all they find is a barricade, they'll grow suspicious. The masters of this power —the truly dangerous ones—as I suspect the man you met was —they'll sense you're hiding something. And they'll dig deeper. Harder. And if they can't get to your secrets, they will resort to torturing your body for them."

Her voice dropped, nearly a whisper. "That's why sometimes, you must let them in. Just a little. Let them see what you want them to see—a decoy thought, something believable. You let them catch it, examine it, and walk away thinking they've uncovered the truth."

Buna tapped her temple again, slower this time. "It's not just about strength, Magda. It's about cunning. Sometimes, the only way to protect your truth...is to feed them a lie."

9

____

WEAPONS

Magda—June 1387

I tried to go about my days after the encounter with the stranger in the woods, but I couldn't shake the sense that he had some unnatural power—power that posed a threat to me. I was not a silly girl, easily rattled by shadows or the rustling of leaves, yet something about the way he had slithered into my thoughts left me unsettled for days.

When the man had vanished into the hills, Caius gave chase, disappearing into the shadows after him, while Dani remained at my side. I had never been so grateful for my gentle bear of a friend—broad-shouldered, steady as an oak, his sheer size enough to make even the boldest foe, mortal or otherwise, hesitate before daring to cross him. When Caius caught up with us on our ride home, his face dark with frustration, he reported nothing more than the faint tracks of the stranger's horse pressed into the soft, damp soil of the forest floor.

It was a few evenings later, after supper, that Buna and I

were startled by a soft, hesitant knock at the door of the cottage. We looked to one another, uncertain if we'd truly heard it— then it came again, slightly firmer this time, a hollow thud against the wood. I rose and crossed the room, heart thudding in rhythm with the sound, and pulled the door open.

There stood Dani, his head bowed, eyes lowered to the flat stone that laid on the ground in front of our stoop. In his hands he cradled a parcel, wrapped carefully in heavy fabric and lashed in leather.

"Dani—come in," I said in surprise, stepping aside to let him pass through the door.

He ducked beneath the lintel as he entered, his great height forcing him into a bow that might have seemed humble had it not been so ungainly. The sight was almost comical, and I caught myself pressing my lips together to stifle a laugh.

Dani's mother was one of our own, a Romani, and when she married the village metalsmith, fortune had lifted her from the lowest rung of our people's hierarchy into something nearer to respectability. Their family had a larger cottage than most, with timber walls and a proper floor and colorful rugs to shield them from the cruel winters, so unlike our hard-packed dirt floor. A barn housed their animals, and her husband's forge burned hot through every season. Dani apprenticed at his father's side, his hands blackened with ash long before most boys were trusted with such work.

It often struck me as cruel, the fickle turns of marriage, how a woman could climb one rung higher with the right union, but never leap from beggar's daughter to noble's wife in a single bound. The rules of our world did not allow such miracles— only slow ascents, step by weary step, if fortune favored her at all.

"Hello, Dani," my grandmother said as she crossed the room to embrace him. She stretched her stooped frame as far as it would allow, while he bent low—a giant folding himself down to meet her.

Buna was always fond of Dani. She liked to recall the night he was born—the biggest baby she'd ever delivered, she would say with a shake of her head—though his mother had brought him into the world without struggle, despite his size.

"Doamnă...Magda," he said with a respectful nod to each of us, giving Buna the most formal address.

"What brings you by?" I asked, curious about the reason for his visit. Despite knowing Dani my entire life, he'd never stepped foot inside our cottage.

He cleared his throat, and only then did I notice how pale he looked, his face drained of color. Without warning, he thrust the parcel into my hands, as if afraid he might lose his nerve if he hesitated another breath. "I made these—*for you*—I can teach you how to use them..." The words tumbled out in a rush, clumsy and earnest.

I carried the bundle to the small table in the center of our cottage, the same worn wood that bore our suppers and served as our workbench. Setting it down, I felt the weight of it drag at my arms—heavier than I had expected. Buna and Dani drew close behind me, their presence crowding the air as I unrolled the rough-woven fabric.

The parcel contained two weapons, sheathed in leather. I pulled each away from their housing and the polished metal gleamed in the dim light: a small knife with a wickedly curved blade, and a slim dagger nearly two-thirds the length of my arm. They were smaller versions of the hunting blades the men carried, but no less deadly for their size.

I reached first for the curved knife. Its grip, fashioned from antler, had been carved and burnished until it seemed alive in my hand—warm and smooth, a stark contrast to the cold gleam of the steel. Reluctantly, I slid it back into its leather sheath, meant to ride snug against my belt.

My gaze shifted to the dagger, and I let one finger trail along its edge. A shiver coursed through me—not fear, but the thrill of a power I had never known. These were, I realized, the costliest gifts I had ever been given.

"You made these?" I asked, still amazed—almost incredulous that weapons so finely wrought, with inlaid antler and decorative flourishes etched into their hilts, had been forged for me alone.

Buna kept quiet, watching me with narrowed eyes and a scowl that let me know a lecture was coming as soon as Dani was gone. I ignored her stare as I lifted the dagger, testing its weight. For a moment I imagined driving the blade into a straw dummy, the way I'd seen the boys practice a hundred times.

"These are beautiful, Dani," I said, my chest warming at the thought of how long he must have spent shaping them, making sure they fit me so perfectly.

His eyes lit at once, the pale cast he'd worn earlier fading as color rushed back into his cheeks—the familiar, sun-warmed glow I'd always known. Then he smiled, a grin so wide it seemed to fill the whole room. "I wanted you to be able to protect yourself if Caius and I aren't around..." His words trailed off, the unspoken *if the stranger comes back* settling uncomfortably between us. "I can come by tomorrow," he went on. "In the afternoon. I'll show you how to use them. You'll need to practice—until they feel natural in your hands."

"No," I cut in, too quickly to be casual. Tomorrow was

market day—and I had plans. Plans no one but me knew of, and I intended to keep it that way. For now. "But the day after would work," I added, smoothing my tone, coaxing a brightness into it that felt almost convincing. "If that suits you." I held his gaze a heartbeat longer than necessary, willing him not to question the edge he must have heard beneath the lightness.

Dani studied me for a moment, his brow knitting just slightly, as though he'd caught the faintest wrong note. His mouth opened—then closed again. "Of course," he said at last, the words gentle, accepting. But his gaze lingered a beat too long. "Okay, I'll see you then." Dani tipped his head toward Buna in farewell and moved for the door. As his hand touched the latch, I reached out and caught his arm. When he turned back, I rose on my toes and pressed a soft kiss to his cheek.

"Thank you again," I said, keeping it simple, pushing down the tangle of thoughts that wanted to surface. Things I should have said—like how I loved Caius, which he probably already knew. Or that I loved him too, though not in the way he wanted. But I didn't. Instead, I said nothing more and left him with hope, watching the smile spread across his face before he stepped out into the night. As much as I didn't want to, I couldn't ignore the pull of it—the way his affection gave me a sense of power. And yet, the guilt of not feeling the same gnawed at me.

I shut the door behind him, sliding the metal latch into place with a sharp click, then turned to face my grandmother. As I expected, she was already glowering at me from across the room.

"What?" I snapped, her silent judgment cutting through my thoughts as I pictured myself cutting down phantom enemies with my new blades, fierce and sure as any warrior.

"You could do worse—*far worse*," she said, her tone as pointed as the blades sitting on the table. "I don't see the boyar's son leaving gifts at your door. He could afford them a hundred times over...yet it's Dani who spends what little he has on you." Each word was meant to bite, flung like sparks to the fire already kindling in my chest.

I fumed at her words, wishing she'd stop and leave me alone, and I brushed past her, but she wasn't finished.

"Dani is no longer a boy—just as you are no longer a girl," she said, her voice cold with certainty. "He's a man now, and he wants a wife, even if he hasn't said as much. And he loves you..." She waived a hand dismissively, as though it were nothing. "Despite your stubborn fixation on his best friend."

She closed the space between us in two measured steps, raising a finger already bent with age and aiming it at me like a curse. "He could give you more than this—more than these walls and this hard dirt floor. A home. Children. Protection. Things most women like us never dream of having. And you—" Her voice sharpened, almost spitting the words, "You would throw it all away to chase the fantasy that Caius could ever truly be yours."

"Stop it. Just stop it!" I cried, flinging my hands upward as if I could throw her words back at her. "I don't want a small, suffocating life in this village—raising snot-nosed children, hauling water from the river until my back breaks, scrubbing diapers until my fingers bleed. And at night, lying in a bed with a man who only wants to put another child in my belly."

I turned away, heat flooding my cheeks, ashamed of my outburst yet unwilling to face her scowl any longer. "And then what, Buna?" I went on, my voice shaking now. "I wither away, nameless and forgotten, and die?" I shook my head, the answer rising from a place I had denied for too long. "No. That is not my life."

I swept a hand toward the cottage walls hemming us in— the rough timbers, the shadowed corners. "My life must be something more...more than this."

10

GRANNY MARGARET KNOWS ALL

Mira—February 2026

We drove to Kirriemuir, the small village north of Edinburgh where my father's relatives lived—the nexus of the Garvie family's clairvoyant legacy. After lunch with Evie, her fiancé Davey, and Morag's family, Morag and Evie headed off in one car while Baird and I followed in ours to Granny Margaret's house.

We stepped into her terraced home in the village, and there she was—the same gray-haired, bun-wearing, stooped little woman in orthopedic shoes I'd met just over a year ago when I first arrived, the only link I had to the Garvies, courtesy of Ancestry.com. She had a few more wrinkles now and moved a little slower, but otherwise she was unchanged. Morag had put together a care package after lunch and was busy stacking Tupperware containers in the fridge when I introduced Baird.

"Granny Margaret—this is Baird." I couldn't help but laugh

a little. "The green-eyed man you told me about. I met him the day after I saw you last."

"Aye—weel, I heard from Evie about him. I'm glad ye took my coonsel. Nice to meet ye, lad. Oh, and a handsome one 'an aw!" she said, squinting up—and up—to take in Baird's towering frame.

"I was hoping you might help me again." I said. "You were so spot-on last time."

"Whit's the matter wi' ye, lass?" she asked, her voice kind.

"It's a long story...maybe we should sit," I said self-consciously.

She nodded and lowered herself onto the small sofa. I sat beside her. Evie and Morag took the armchairs, leaving Baird standing—every seat claimed by a Garvie woman. I glanced around the room, then back at Baird. He met my eyes and gave a subtle nod, a quiet go-ahead to share whatever I felt she needed to know. Granny Margaret watched the silent exchange with sharp curiosity.

"Spit it oot," Granny Margaret said, clearly tired of my stalling.

"Okay—" I took a breath. "I know we have a strong family history of clairvoyance, but...has anyone in the Garvie line ever had something else? Any kind of—*oh, I don't know*—magic?" I tried to sound casual, but acting, as Baird had reminded me on more than one occasion, wasn't my strong suit.

Granny Margaret's eyebrows shot up at the question. She looked from me to Evie and Morag, then back again, like she wasn't sure she wanted to answer at all. After a moment, her shoulders eased, like she'd made peace with something.

"Girls," she said, turning to Morag and Evie, "away to the kitchen and make us some tea. And make sure tae bring some biscuits too. We might be here a wee while." Her tone was gentle, but there was no mistaking it was a dismissal.

Evie and Morag exchanged a glance—one of those tight-lipped, silent ones that said *we're not fooled but we'll play along*—and disappeared into the kitchen. Granny Margaret reached for my hand and leaned in close, her voice dropping. She gave my fingers a couple of soft pats, then looked between me and Baird, and then held his gaze.

"Just so ye know," she said, voice low but steady, "I ken what ye are. I'm no afraid—but ma daughter and granddaughter—they havnae worked it oot. And they willna."

Baird gave a small nod, and I echoed it, a quiet pact made between the three of us. "Did you know?" I asked. "Back then—when I first came?"

"Aye," she nodded, her voice still lower than her usual speaking tone. "But ye wouldnae have believed me. And I saw he was the one meant to protect ye," nodding toward Baird. "So...it all worked oot in the end." She patted my hand again, but the gesture felt less reassuring now—more a reflex meant to steady herself than to comfort me."Now, about yer question —aye. My great-grandmother had strong magic. My grand-mother, less. My ma said she had none at all." Granny paused, the look in her eye suggesting she didn't quite believe it herself. "With each generation, it faded. Now all that seems to be left is the Sight." Her gaze settled on me, curious and searching. "Why do ye ask?"

"Well..." I glanced at Baird, trying to piece together a version of the truth that wouldn't sound completely mad. "I came into possession of a ruby. It's enchanted."

Her eyes narrowed with interest, but she didn't interrupt.

"And through a...*friend of a friend*, I guess you'd say, I met a witch," I said, hard-pressed to explain Sorcha. "She confirmed what I felt—that the stone had power. But then she told me something else. She said *I* had power. That I possess some kind of inherent magic—and that's why the stone found its way to me." I exhaled. "I know it sounds far-fetched."

She held a finger up to me, and I paused. She got up on stiff knees and lumbered out of the room without a word, and when she returned a few minutes later, she was carrying an old book—ancient, really. Its leather-bound cover was cracked and curled at the corners, the pages loose and yellowed with age.

"This book's been in our clan fo years," she said, settling it carefully in her lap. "Me ma told me she got it 'cause she was the only lass in her family—but it was meant for the one born wi' magic. I dinnae think we've had a Garvie wi' proper magic in 100 years," she said after a bit of mental math, "maybe longer." She ran a hand reverently over the cover before opening it. "Ah flicked through it when I was wee, hopin' to find somethin' tae help me grasp the Sight. But there's nothing in here aboot it."

She glanced up at me, her eyes soft with understanding. "But the big magic—that had tae be jotted down. Taught. Kept safe. An' ah think that's how our might withered, generation after generation. We just assumed it'd be there...an' now, most o' it's lost."

Granny Margaret looked down at the book again, considering something, and then looked back to me. "Why's the— *witch, ye say?*—thinkin' ye got the magic?" she asked, eyeing me keenly.

I tilted my head toward Baird. This part wasn't mine to tell —only he and Sorcha had seen it—so I let him explain.

"She glows sometimes," he said. "Like her skin catches light and throws it back out. But she disnae see it."

Granny Margaret's brows lifted. "When does it happen?"

Just then, Morag and Evie returned, carrying a tea service and a plate of shortbread. They set it down on the table, but Baird was too focused to notice.

He cleared his throat, then smirked—slow and deliberate, and just watching him made my cheeks burn hot. "Mostly when she's in her studio, working. *Mostly*."

Granny Margaret didn't miss a thing. For the briefest moment, I caught a flash of the sly, mischievous young woman she must've been once, right before she cut him a look that said she understood *exactly* what he meant. "Weel, Mira," Granny Margaret said turning back to me, handing me the old worn book, "it would seem ye are the Garvie with the most use for this at the moment. I'll lend it tae ye, for ye tae learn fae. If Evie —or any of my granddaughters—or their bairns—were to develop magic one day, I'd want ye to pass it back. But for now, I think it's best placed in yer hands."

She looked at the book, now sitting on my lap, wistfully. "My mother always called it *the Mother's Book*. It covers aw sorts o' topics. At first glance, it looks like a domestic guide—how tae mak' tallow candles, pit yer medicinal herbs tae work, that sort o' thing. But tucked awfy tight between the pages are some proper protection spells...spells tae sniff out somethin'—*or someone*—lost...an even how tae keep a vampire oot yer home."

The room went still. I let out a nervous laugh, because Morag and Evie *definitely* didn't know Granny believed in vampires, and I wasn't about to be the one to break that news.

"Ma," Morag said, her voice incredulous. "Does it really say that?"

"The Druid and Celts called it *Abhartach, or Marbh Bheo,* or when a female, *Dearg-Due or Baobhan Sith.* But they a' mean the same thing—a vampire." Granny said. She'd devoured this book as a girl, I could tell, and now she had a reason to share it.

"Mira will be sure to put that last one to good use, won't ye, love?" Baird said, smirking.

I smiled, but my grip tightened on the book. Some jokes hit closer to home than others. "Oh yes," I deadpanned, rolling my eyes. "I've been *desperate* for an effective vampire protection protocol."

Morag and Evie laughed, and I let out a quiet breath of relief. For now, our little act had held. The book was heavier than it looked, as if it carried more than just paper and ink. As I cradled it in my hands, a familiar scent rose from its pages: dry leather, plus stone dust, moss, and something faintly metallic. It hit me like a wave of déjà vu. The box that had held Agnes's portrait had smelled similar. Apparently, ancient Garvie artifacts all carried the same signature odor—dust, mystery, and the weight of secrets.

I was eager to get back to Edinburgh and pore over the unexpected treasure, but there was one more thing I needed before we left.

"Granny Margaret," I said carefully, "would you lay hands on me? I...I don't know if I can trust the witch. *Sorcha.*" I didn't offer any background—no mention of shapeshifting or what the ruby showed me. I'd leave Granny to explain away the strange snippets of my story that Evie and Morag had overheard—including the jokes about vampires—after I left. I just hoped her Sight was as clear as it had been last time.

She nodded without hesitation and raised her arthritic hands to my face. Just like before, her eyes went cloudy, rolling back slightly as she slipped into that trance-like state that would've looked theatrical in anyone else—but in her, it was unsettlingly real.

I leaned in. The room fell still. I could feel every gaze resting on us. I tried to calm my breath, willing myself to be open, to give her every chance to see what I could not.

Minutes passed.

Then she blinked, slow and deliberate, her eyes once again clear and bright. "She's very powerful, Mira." Her voice was calm, but her gaze drilled into mine. I could tell she saw *something*. Maybe how old Sorcha really was. Maybe the way she moved between forms. "I dinnae sense any ill will fae her. She's...pleased wi' whit ye are. Aye, I reckon she thinks hersel' as a bit o' guidin' hand. Keen tae mould yer magic."

I nodded slowly, relieved by her assessment—but just as I relaxed, Granny kept speaking.

"Mira," she said gently, "Ah mind ye spoke aboot the dark man, the last time ye were here." Her expression was guarded, concern knitting her brow. Was she asking if he still lingered? If he still posed a threat? She knew what Baird was, even back then, so I suspected she might also know what Bastien was. Maybe she was seeking closure.

"Ah, yes..." I fumbled. "He was...someone Baird knew." Baird gave me a sidelong look that said *Really?* and *Thanks a lot* all at once. "That's all resolved now," I added quickly, hoping to close the door.

But Granny narrowed her eyes. And when she spoke, her voice carried the quiet gravity of someone who *knew*. "Aye, that might well be. But the woman ye spied when ye touched the ruby...she's got some link to him. I dinnae ken the how of it— but I *ken* it to be true."

As soon as the words left her lips, the swirling infinite—birth and death, darkness and light—coiled through my mind again, wrapping around itself in a never-ending figure eight of color and sound. It was as if her voice had awakened it, stirred the ruby's power that still lingered in me.

Granny Margaret might not have called herself a witch, but her Sight wasn't something to be trifled with. She always down-played her abilities—maybe it made life simpler—but she'd tapped into the ruby's current, and I felt it responding. A silent acknowledgment passed between us. If I'd ever forgotten that the ruby was alive—sentient, watching—this moment made sure I never would again.

I swallowed hard and let out a slow breath. "I guess that chapter isn't closed after all," I said to Baird.

He gave a single nod, lips pressed into a tight line, his whole posture edged with tension. This was the Baird I'd first woken up to on his couch—quiet, guarded, a tempest of thoughts behind troubled eyes. And suddenly, I felt guilty. For dragging him into this mess—me, my magic, the Garvies, now Sorcha. But then again...he was a vampire. An immortal with secrets of his own.

We said our goodbyes outside Granny Margaret's cottage, hugging in the soft afternoon light. I held the book tightly to my chest as I pressed a kiss to her wrinkled cheek.

"Thank you—for everything." I said, and I meant it. Finding them all, but especially Granny Margaret, had been the second-best thing to come out of my decision to come to Scotland last year.

She smiled, and when Baird offered his hand, she batted it away and pulled him into a hug instead, as if to say he was part of the Garvie clan now—*again*. I didn't miss the look in her eye.

Yes, I suspected she'd seen it all. She was clever that way—always giving just enough, holding the rest of her knowledge close to the vest until the moment it mattered enough to reveal it.

We'd nearly reached the car when she called out, stopping me in my tracks. "Mira—perhaps ye'll be the one to have a bairn wi' magic someday. Carry on the line, eh?"

I turned slowly and looked at Baird. His expression mirrored my own—quiet, stricken. He'd told me we'd never have children of our own, that it couldn't happen between a vampire and a human. We didn't talk about it anymore. Not a sore spot really, just one of the things I'd voluntarily given up when I made the decision to come back to Baird.

"Who knows? But you might be getting ahead of yourself—we aren't even married!" I said, half-laughing, throwing the words over my shoulder like a joke to cover the knot forming in my throat. A quick deflection. A way to buy time so I could avoid saying it out loud—that it was impossible.

I turned back to Baird and met his eyes. A quiet sorrow hung in the moment between us—until something changed. A flicker, a shift behind his gaze, like a new question had just taken hold. And just as I saw it, the thought rose in me—unwelcome and undeniable. Granny Margaret always knows more than she lets on.

We were both quiet on the drive to Baird's home in Edinburgh, where we stayed when we weren't on the Isle of Arran, each lost in our own thoughts. For a while, I assumed he was worried about me—but when I stole a few glances his way, I realized the far-off look in his eyes wasn't his normal worry about how I was dealing with things. He was somewhere else entirely, caught presumably in whatever Granny Margaret's words had stirred. His grip tightened on the steering wheel, then eased again like he'd caught himself.

I couldn't help but wonder too—had she seen me having a child someday...*with someone else*? And was that what he was thinking? Or maybe...nope. I wasn't even going to entertain that thought. A part of me wanted to turn the car around and ask her outright. Demand answers. But I knew how that would go. Granny Margaret didn't withhold truths to be cruel—she held them back because she understood that knowing the shape of your future, every twist and turn, could be more of a burden than a gift.

Some paths are meant to be walked, not foreseen.

Maybe I was reading too much into it. Maybe she was just a sweet old lady who thought everyone should be having babies —and didn't know that wasn't exactly an option for us. And maybe—hopefully—that was all she meant. Just a wistful, well-meaning comment.

Desperate to get back to something normal, I asked if we could stop at the stone seller's shop on the way back instead of waiting until morning. Nathan Billings—a fellow jewelry designer I'd met and become friendly with—had a great connection for colored diamonds. I'd placed an order for a dozen quarter-carat yellow diamonds, along with a couple of white ones speckled with salt-and-pepper inclusions, the kind that had become all the rage with Gen Z clients lately.

Nathan's shop was a small storefront just around the block from The Goldsmith's Guild, so Baird parked in their lot and followed me down the sidewalk. The bell over the door gave a cheerful tinkle as we crossed the threshold. Nathan was chatting with a client, so we lingered near the display cases until he finished.

As soon as the client turned to leave, Nathan waved me over, and I pulled up a stool to the counter.

"Mira—how have ye been? This must be Baird," he said, reaching across the counter to shake his hand.

"I've been good—*busy*. Working on some new designs," I said, eager to see the parcel I hoped he had behind the counter. He pulled out a small box and tipped the contents onto a velvet-lined tray—twelve yellow diamonds and a couple of larger salt-and-pepper whites. I leaned in as he handed me a loupe and flicked on the counter lamp. Using tweezers, I turned a few over, watching how they caught the light. There wasn't a single bad one in the lot. Exactly why I preferred to do this in person. You couldn't trust color and fire through a computer screen.

"These are great—I'll take them all," I said, sitting back with a satisfied smile.

Nathan's eyes lit up. "Mira, I know ye love canary diamonds —have I got one to show ye!"

That was how we gemstone nerds operated. Nothing lit us up like the chance to share a perfect stone with someone who'd truly appreciate it. I clapped my hands like a kid in a candy store. He pulled out another box, this one containing a yellow diamond, nearly five carats, oval cut. It took my breath away, and I clutched a hand to my chest, not to be dramatic, but because I'd probably never seen a finer stone.

"Four point nine seven carats, virtually flawless. Fancy vivid yellow, according to the GIA," Nathan said proudly.

He handed me the grading report, and I scanned the diagram, looking for any feathers or inclusions—especially since stones this clean were so rare. The most reputable grader in the world was the Gemological Institute of America, and even here in the UK, it was still the gold standard. If you had an important stone—one that would fetch top dollar—you sent it to the GIA.

I popped the loupe back up to my eye, holding the stone steady in the tweezers I'd just been using. The report said the cut was excellent—and I couldn't disagree. The cutter had known exactly how to shape it to maximize the color play. No dark zones. No dead patches. With oval cuts like this, you often saw what we called a "bow tie"—a mirrored pair of dark triangles in the center that looked like someone had laid a shadowy ribbon right across the middle. But this one? No bow tie, no flaw. Just fire. Just brilliant, uninterrupted golden light. Like a piece of the sun had fallen from the sky and crystalized.

I smiled, searching for a term to describe it: a bucket of yellow crushed ice. Absolutely perfect. I set the stone in my palm and turned to glance at Baird, half-expecting to feel something deeper—some ripple of energy like I had with the ruby. But nothing. No spark, no pull. This one wasn't enchanted. Its magic was purely in its beauty—and it asked nothing of me in return.

"Ye wouldn't be interested, would ye?" Nathan asked. "I had someone looking to design a custom engagement ring, but they ended up going with a slightly smaller stone. I took this one on consignment so they could have a look, but if I can't find a home for it soon, I'll have to send it back."

"No," I shook my head and looked back at Baird, hoping for a little willpower reinforcement.

Baird smirked. "That's no what your face is sayin'."

I rolled my eyes and sighed. The gemstone goblin that lived inside me was practically vibrating with excitement. But I knew the truth: if I bought it, I'd never get my money back—even if I got it wholesale. "The top end of my line sells for nine thousand pounds, and even that's rare. Most of my sales fall under three." I glanced at the diamond again, wincing. "I don't even want to *ask* what your cost was on this."

Then, to save myself, I stuck my fingers in my ears. "And if I bought it speculatively, I'd just find a way to keep it for myself. La-la-la-la..." I sang, shaking my head, fingers still planted firmly. "I'm not listening."

I could hear Baird laughing behind me as I finally pulled my fingers from my ears. I turned and gave him a helpless shrug. I knew myself well enough to recognize the pattern. I had a case full of stones I'd gotten "a deal" on and still hadn't used—none of them anywhere near this quality. No, this would be a terrible business decision. A stunning, sparkling, heartbreakingly beautiful—expensive—business disaster.

I paid Nathan for the small stones I'd actually come for, and we wrapped things up. As we stepped out of the shop, the bell overhead tinkled again, a cheerful chime that felt like it was mocking my self-restraint.

Baird took my hand as we walked, lifting it to his lips and pressing a kiss to my knuckles. I caught the faintest smile tugging at the corner of his mouth—smug and satisfied, like the cat that ate the canary. At least we weren't still brooding over Granny Margaret's cryptic comments. That glittering stone had unexpectedly done the impossible: distracted us, at least for the moment, from our thoughts about witches, ongoing vampiric connections to Bastien, and the grieving of babies we'd never have.

Shiny object for the win. No wonder I love rocks so much.

11

THE MOTHER'S BOOK

Mira—February 2026

It wasn't until we left Edinburgh for the cottage before I really had a chance to explore the book. The leather cover featured a strange embossed design; a circle, and inside the circle a triangle, and then inside that, a flame. A sigil of some sort? I opened the book, the spine creaking and groaning after being closed for so long, but somehow it sounded almost musical to me.

On the inside cover was a faded but still colorful drawing: a young woman, hair full of fire, and a flame held in her hand, the entire image rendered in oranges, reds and yellows. I felt some strange pull to this drawing, staring at it for several minutes, unable to look away, as if she and her flames could erupt from the page at any moment. There were dark rust-colored smudges along the edges, one clearly an ancient finger-print, and a few darker spots, spilled and soaked into the surface. My fingers traced the edge of the drawing, and I felt an almost imperceptible energy, soothing and warm, grounding me. Something that felt so right, holding this in my hands. It was like the first time I held a torch to solder metal, like this was a part of me.

Flames and fire were a recurring theme throughout the book, as was the name Brigid, linked often in relation to the drawings of fire, or different renditions of the embossed image on the front. Interspersed, just like Granny had said, were drawings of different plants, with detailed information on their uses and how to prepare them, how to combine them, *and when not to*, for teas, tinctures, and uses in poultices. Some of the pages seemed like recipes, or medical advice, but other entries seemed to use fire or some of these plants almost ritualistically, for different outcomes. Perhaps these were spells.

Scattered through the pages—in the spaces between lines, the beginnings of new sections, and the quiet corners of margins—were more drawings.

Different hands had left their mark over time. Some were richly detailed, others little more than rough sketches. Many of the drawings showed wheels, and at their centers, a cross-like shape—seemingly depicting something woven from grass or rushes. Each of the four arms was equal in length, and where they met, a small square formed.

The shape tugged at something in me. I'd seen it before—I was sure of it—but I couldn't quite place where. Maybe it was only the resemblance to a traditional cross that made it feel familiar.

The margins were crowded with notes, some illegible, others barely so. Symbols, half-formed words, frantic scratches of ink. My eyes kept drifting back to one entry in particular, written in a hurried, uneven hand that made my skin prickle. The words made my blood run cold.

We are not chosen. Some are spared. Some are not. Our hands record the names and yet the debt remains unpaid.

Several blank pages followed the entry, marked only by deep brown splotches and the occasional smudged fingerprint. As I thumbed through them, searching for something that wasn't there, an ache sparked in my palm—sharp enough to make me pause. The sensation felt focused, deliberate, as though the book had taken note of me and found me wanting.

I flexed my fingers and kept turning pages, but the ache lingered, a quiet insistence that refused to fade. After several minutes, I gave up. I shook my head and rolled my shoulders, forcing myself to relax—to ignore the uneasy sense that I had missed something meant for me alone. Whatever those words meant, I couldn't afford to fixate on them. I needed to learn the book's secrets, not get lost in out-of-context warnings and half-mad scribbles when there was still so much left to decipher.

Some of what Granny Margaret had pointed out was written in a language I couldn't read, but I caught enough words to get a rough sense of meaning. I'd ask Baird to help me translate—maybe Sorcha, if I had to. I tore up a few pieces of junk mail and slid the scraps into place, marking anything I didn't want to lose track of. Either way, I needed to begin transcribing what I could into my own journal. Granny Margaret had kindly lent me the book, but eventually, I'd have to return it to Evie or Morag.

One entry piqued my curiosity, first because it seemed easy to execute, and secondly because it seemed useful. At the top of the page, written in a graceful but faded script, was something called The Call of the Hearthfire:

> *To summon one who is far, when yer need burns*
> *bright and true*
> *Best worked at dusk, or by the hearth flame, on a*
> *waxing moon*
> *Brigid's fire will carry the message, and her well*
> *will stir the heart*

Supposedly, the spell caster was to gather a stone or twig from the place you wanted to call the distant person back to—*easy enough*—a length of red wool or ribbon, a candle or hearth flame—*would my torch work?*—a sprig of hawthorn or rowan—*there was a rowan tree growing next to Agnes's grave*—and a square of linen cloth.

The ritual required you to set the stone or twig on an altar, which I didn't have, or *beside your fire to ground the spell in your land.* I was thinking maybe the top of my jeweler's bench, which was covered in fireproof tiles and was where I soldered and cast molten metal, might suffice. Maybe it was, in some sense, an altar already.

I was supposed to wrap the sprig in the linen and tie it with the ribbon and place it on the altar, and then light it, speaking my need into the flame, and recite the words:

Brigid of the flame and forge, Brigid of the sacred well,

Carry this call on wind and ash, Let my longing rise and swell.

By red thread wound and waters deep, Let their soul be stirred from sleep.

Across the moor, o'er hill and glen, Bring them home to me again.

Let no road turn them aside, Let no doubt within them hide.

By stone and fire, word and will—Let them come. And let them feel it still.

I needed Sorcha's help to unravel this book. But I didn't have her number—or even an address. So I decided to try my hand at what the Garvies had apparently done for centuries: send a witchy sort of telegram and hope it reached her.

The night we returned to the island, I gathered what I needed—everything except the waxing moon, which based on the date couldn't be helped but sounded optional—and set the wheels in motion.

EVER SINCE I'D spoken the incantation the night before—inviting Brigid's magic into me—I'd been buzzing with electricity. Like seltzer in my veins. Even in sleep, I'd felt it: a low, constant vibration that somehow both lulled and stirred me. I moved through the day like I was dreaming, suspended between worlds.

I was in the studio the next afternoon, trying to distract myself from the beehive humming beneath my skin, when she arrived. Despite willing the hearth-spell to work, I still couldn't quite believe it when I saw her—Sorcha—standing at the door. That slightly incongruous *ladies-who-lunch* purse slung over her arm, her eyes fixed on me, expectant.

She cleared her throat. "You rang?"

I opened the bottom of the Dutch door to let her in, my mouth hanging open in shocked disbelief. "It actually worked? Even without the optimal moon phase..." I said, more to myself than her, trying to let it sink in.

"How did ye call me?" she asked with a small smile. "I kent ye weren't in danger. But I felt it as clear as day—ye needed help."

I swallowed hard, my throat suddenly dry. Emotion welled up in me out of nowhere, and I reached with shaking hands for the dusty book I had left on the low table. "This," I said softly. "I need your help to understand it." I didn't know if I was asking for an afternoon of her time, or the rest of my life.

She cocked her head curiously, and then a small, knowing smile formed on her lips. "This is your family grimoire. Oh... what a precious thing..." She took it from me and sat down to leaf through the fragile pages with reverent fingers, and I could see it—a witch's awe in the face of something old and sacred. "Ye just picked it up, found a spell tae call me?"

I nodded dumbly, not sure how else to describe what I did, and explained how Granny Margaret had loaned me the book, and that I wanted to make a new copy—to preserve it.

Sorcha nodded, her voice low. "Aye. These were recopied

again and again. When the old ones fell apart or the family scattered, someone would choose what mattered most and write it down anew. And every woman left her mark."

I looked down at the book she held, suddenly aware I was just the next in a long line—scribing, preserving, adding. Not starting something. Continuing it. "I noticed several references to someone named *Brigid*, and her name was part of the—*spell?*" I shrugged, not even sure if that was the right name for it. "...Whatever that was that I used to call you." I pointed to the page I'd bookmarked for The Call of the Hearthfire. "Who is she?"

Sorcha's entire face lit up. Her usual serenity gave way to wide-eyed excitement as she turned toward me. "Brigid is the goddess of fertility—and fire—and *smithing*," she said, practically beaming.

"Smithing? As in *metalsmithing*?" I asked, stunned.

"Exactly that. It would seem the Garvie clan had a special bond with her," Sorcha said, nodding slowly as she flipped through the pages I'd marked. "I suspect she's the source of the matrilineal magic in yer family. That's why the invocation that called me came so easily to ye."

From the look on her face, this all seemed to add up—one plus one equals magical two. But for me, the math hadn't quite mathed yet.

"And ye channel it when ye wield the torch, aye?" she added. Then she giggled, a wicked gleam in her eye. "And when Baird lights the fire inside ye."

I flushed. "That's what he says," I told her, still unsure I believed it.

My life had been full of strange coincidences lately, but this one landed like a thunderclap. I reached across her and flipped the page back to the colorful image inside the front cover—the young woman, the embodiment of fire. She stood before what I assumed was a cauldron, her right arm outstretched, flames rising from the palm of her hand. Her left arm was lifted high and arced behind her, like a dancer, as if her body was a single lick of flame pulled by the wind. Even the ends of her long hair were rendered as flickering fire. She wasn't just working with flame—she *was* flame.

"Is this Brigid?" I asked, wondering if this was the connection that kept me coming back to the drawing.

"Aye—it is. Brigid is the most high of the Celtic goddesses," Sorcha added. "Did ye know the word 'bride' is derived from her name?"

"No, I didn't." I was about as familiar with Paleo-Christian deities as I was with magic and witches. "Granny Margaret didn't tell me much," I admitted. "Only that the book was supposed to be passed down to the Garvie daughter born with magic, but there hadn't been one in almost a hundred years. She called it the Mother's Book. She said her grandmother was the last to have any magic."

"Dinnae let her discount the Sight ye have—that's magic too—plain and simple. Dinnae ever think otherwise," she scolded.

I hesitated, then added, "She told Baird she knew what he was—even back when she read for me the first time, the day before I met him. She also said she knew what Bastien was. But she didn't tell me outright, not then. When I asked why, she said I wouldn't have believed her. She said she told me what I needed to know, that Baird would never hurt me. I think that was her way of telling me what she could...without telling me everything."

I paused again. "She said something strange when we left, and it's been bothering me ever since." It was a relief to admit it, say it out loud. Despite the look that passed between us, neither Baird nor I had mentioned it. "She called out to me as we were leaving. She said maybe I'd be the one to have a child with magic, to carry on the line. I don't know—maybe she's just baby-crazy. Or maybe she saw me having a child with someone else. But why say that in front of Baird?"

Sorcha tilted her head, frowning slightly, like some part of the story was missing. "Or...maybe she saw ye having a bairn with Baird. Did that no cross yer mind?"

"He told me we could never have children," I added with a small shrug. "That it's just...not possible. A vampire and a human." I repeated it as if it were some universal truth, something everyone in the know would understand. But Sorcha was giving me a look—curious, almost skeptical. Maybe it wasn't such common knowledge after all.

"I mean..." I gave a nervous laugh, trying to lighten the mood, "I *hope* it's not, since I tossed my birth control months ago."

"Do ye no want his child?" Sorcha wasn't laughing.

I froze, caught off guard by the question. "Ah—um—" The words wouldn't come. I looked left, then right, then turned in a slow, ridiculous circle like the answer might reveal itself if I just kept moving. But nothing came—only a thick, charged silence. "Of course I do," I said at last, my voice barely above a whisper. "If that's what *he* wants..." I trailed off, the weight of that *if* settling heavily in my chest. And as the words slipped out, I felt it—a spark of hope, molten and reckless, burrowing into my ribs like it had every right to be there.

"Have ye ever heard of the *dhampir*?" Sorcha asked with an inquisitive tip of the head.

I shook my head. "No. But it sounds a lot like the word *vampire*."

"They sound alike because the words are related. Eastern European folklore, particularly in the Balkan region, has many stories about the *dhampir,*" she said. "In those traditions, it's believed that under the *right* circumstances..." She paused. "...a vampire and a human can conceive. Almost always a male vampire and a human woman. The offspring may carry some vampire traits, like a craving for blood—but no always. They tend to live longer than any normal human."

I stared at her. "Right circumstances? So...like wildly rare, or have I been playing it fast-and-loose with my birth control? Does Baird know?" I blurted out. The question felt absurd the moment I said it—but lately, everyone seemed to know things I didn't.

Sorcha shrugged. "I have no way tae ken what Baird knows. I suggest ye ask him. It is rare—maybe he was only trying to spare ye heartbreak," she added gently, offering him an out.

"Stay here. Don't move." I bolted from the studio, down the stone steps to the house. I found Baird just inside the door, putting on his jacket, readying to head out. "Come to the studio. Now." I grabbed his hand, dragging him along behind me, my heart pounding with every step. Sorcha was still exactly where I'd left her, hunched over the book, leafing through the pages when we walked in.

"Tell him," I said breathlessly. "Tell him what you told me."

She looked up, head tilted, amused. "Which part? That the magic running through your veins was a gift from the goddess of fertility, fire, and smithing herself—or that it's possible for a vampire and a human to conceive a child?"

If I didn't know better, I'd swear Baird was about to faint. He looked pale—green, even, if that were possible. His expression was a mix of disbelief and complete disorientation, and I'd never seen him wear it before this very moment.

We both stared at him in silence until, finally, he blurted out, "Robbie said that wasn't possible."

I blinked. *"Robbie?"* I asked incredulously.

"He seemed sure," Baird replied, like that was a defensible excuse.

Sorcha waved a hand dismissively. "Two men, and one of them Robbie, no less—widnae think to consult a woman when it came to the birds and the bees." She shook her head, clearly unimpressed.

Baird grabbed Sorcha's wrist—fast enough to startle her, and me. For a split second, I worried it might have been a foolish move, even for a vampire. But Sorcha stilled. Her eyes scanned his face, and whatever she saw there softened her stance. The witch in her stepped back. The woman saw a man desperate for answers.

"Like I told Mira, Baird—it is a rare event. But it has happened."

"What are the chances? One in a hundred—or one in a million?" Baird asked, grasping for some understanding.

"That's quite a range, Baird." Sorcha answered with a barely concealed eye roll. "I wish I could give ye a definitive answer, but I'd say closer to one in two, maybe three hundred? But it's not up to ye...it's up to Brigid to bless ye or not."

"Who is Brigid exactly? And what even brought this up?" he

asked, looking between the two of us like tracing the steps of our conversation might change where they led.

"The goddess," I said with an eye roll of my own, figuring I could pick up that explanation later. "We were talking about Granny Margaret—what she said when we left. It's been playing on a loop in my head ever since." I paused, searching his face. "At first I tried to brush it off, chalked it up to her assuming every couple wants kids. But she's smarter than that. She knows what you are. And I can't stop wondering if she saw something...something we can't."

Baird exhaled slowly, as if he'd been holding his breath. "Aye—I wondered too. The twinkle in her eye, like she kens something we dinnae." He turned around and spotted one of the empty chairs and plopped down in it, running a hand through his hair.

Finally, he looked up at me, like we were alone. "Ye're no pregnant...I'd ken." He said softly.

I nodded to agree and then stopped. "Wait...would you know before me?" I asked, incredulous.

"The way ye smell would change. And at some point, I'd hear the bairn's heartbeat—along with yours."

I blinked. I'd forgotten he could hear my heartbeat all the time. But my *smell* would change?

"And your cycles are very regular..."

Ugh. Not even that escaped his attention. Sorcha remained where she was, hands folded neatly in her lap like some ancient priestess, a silent witness to our strange conversation, waiting patiently for us to remember she was still there.

Baird stood and gave a single nod, the look on his face still disoriented, lost in thought. "Uh...I was headed out. Taking Buns."

I waited for him to look at me again—but the look never came. He gave Sorcha a tight nod of goodbye and walked out the door. I knew he hadn't fed in over a week, and he and Bunny usually retreated into the hills alone—either just before dawn or, like tonight, at dusk. Maybe the solitude would help. Give him space to settle his thoughts.

When I turned around, Sorcha was standing, purse in hand, ready to leave.

"Look at the book," she said, "see how your line honored Brigid. Then think on how ye'd shape it yourself—make it personal. Ye must put something of yourself into the invocation if ye want her power to move through your hands." She paused at the door and glanced back, her eyes gleaming."When I return, we'll do a little experimentation."

My eyebrows lifted. "What kind of experimentation?"

"The kind that'll wake her magic in ye—so Baird and I aren't the only ones who see it shimmering just beneath the surface. I'll teach ye to channel Brigid...and to command how her power shows itself."

I WAS IN BED, reading the Mother's Book, when I heard Baird and Bunny return. He'd been gone a long while—and I doubted it was for lack of prey. He paused in the doorway and tugged his sweatshirt up and over his head with one hand. Then he just stood there—shirtless, hair mussed, one hand braced against the frame—and stared at me.

Really stared.

All six foot five of vampire: broad chest dusted with dark

hair, my gaze drawn helplessly down over the hard lines of his stomach. But the real masterpiece was the way his hips narrowed, muscle carving that stark, erotic V that plunged south—an unmistakable invitation for my eyes to follow it straight into his low-slung jeans.

I set the book aside and crossed the room, placing my hand on his chest—solid and cool beneath my palm. I reached up and pulled him down to me, pressing my mouth to his. He hesitated. I didn't. My insistence won.

The kiss deepened, and I tasted it—that lingering trace of blood, gamey, warm and coppery on his tongue. I loved it when he came back from hunting. He was always more alive, charged with a kind of intensity that thrilled me, similar to the strange charge I'd felt for the last twenty-four hours. Tonight was no different. I could feel the electricity crackling between us. And he was already ready.

But there was something else—beneath my hunger, a hesitation. A prickle of guilt. For talking to Sorcha before I talked to him.

Still, he could have told me what he was feeling too—after Granny's comment, when we left. Maybe we still hadn't figured out how to navigate the minefield of hard conversations.

I broke the kiss, the words spilling out like a confession. "I should've talked to you first. I was just afraid to bring it up," I admitted softly. "I thought maybe I was reading too much into what Granny Margaret said—because I wanted to. I wanted there to be a possibility."

The truth of it hung there between us, bare and undeniable.

"And I was scared you'd tell me I was wrong," I went on. "That you didn't see what I did. But I should've asked you... because you *did* see it."

He leaned in, pressing his mouth to mine—a soft, lingering kiss that felt like forgiveness.

"Aye," he whispered, his lips brushing mine with every word. "I am too—"

The slide of his skin against mine made it hard to hold on to anything else.

"I'm guilty of trying to sidestep the hard part," he murmured. "Of not wanting to name the thing I cannae give ye...especially once I knew ye were thinking of it too."

His hands were already moving—unzipping his jeans, tugging down the leggings I'd worn to bed, pulling my T-shirt up and over my head, slipping the clip from my hair so it tumbled free. Every movement was full of urgency and tenderness, like he was trying to lose himself in my body to quiet the ache in his chest. He sat down on the bed, pulling me down to straddle him, my arms wrapped around his neck, losing myself in his embrace.

"Would you—I mean—if we could?" I hesitated, the question snagging in my throat. "Would you even want that?"

Frustration flared, inconvenient and unwelcome. I needed to ask this—*now*—but my body was betraying me, steamrolling straight over my better intentions. His lips were pressed to my neck, to *that* spot, the torturous sizzle of pain and pleasure short-circuiting thought, stealing breath, making focus impossible. The *blood of lovers*—a living connection binding us together, even as I fought my own response, angry at how easily sensation drowned the words I still hadn't finished saying.

His hands were cupping my ass when he pulled back to look in my eyes. "Would I want a bairn with ye? Is that what ye want to ken?" he asked, surprise in his eyes.

I stopped, the realization settling heavy in my chest. This

was what I'd been circling all along—the real fear gnawing at me. I nodded, bracing myself for what I might not want to hear.

"I dream of it, Mira," he said, his voice low and rough. "Of a babe with yer stubbornness and that dimpled chin—God help us both." His eyes gave him away; this wasn't a passing thought, but something that haunted him. "I ache for it. And no bein' able to give ye that tears me in two."

"But it might be possible," I said, my voice barely more than a whisper.

"Aye." His mouth curved without humor. "And I think that makes it harder— to ken there's even the smallest sliver of a chance—than it ever was, this past year, living with the belief it was impossible."

I understood what he meant, but I needed him to hear me. "If there was a way, I'd want to try," I said gently. "Even if it never came to anything. I think I'd need to know we didn't turn away from it—that we held it for a while, together, and let ourselves hope."

"Hope." He echoed and kissed me again—soft at first, then with more urgency. His hands slid down to cup my ass as he lifted me, notching the head of his hard cock against my slick entrance.

When I whimpered, soft and desperate, he smirked. He knew exactly what that sound meant. He thrust his hips upward just as he pulled me down, sheathing himself inside me in one fluid motion. We gasped together at the overwhelming sensation.

I moved on him, rolling my hips, pleasure rising sharp and fast. The buzz beneath my skin amplified everything—each nerve ending sparking with electric intensity. I realized I'd been daydreaming about this all day, flashes of want bleeding into my thoughts when I wasn't paying attention.

His mouth found that spot on my neck—where my pulse beat strongest, just beneath the surface. His favorite. It had become a kind of ritual, this—him feeding from me after a hunt, when the thing he once called a beast still simmered beneath his skin. Not that he needed more blood. It was something else. A hunger of a different kind.

He was demanding when he was like this. Possessive. Consuming. And it made me feel wanton. I didn't want to pretend otherwise. I loved it.

I felt the pinch of his fang at my neck—like the quick sting of a needle when giving blood—followed by the familiar rush, a molten warmth flooding through me. It pulsed with every thrust of his cock, every pull of his mouth as he drank. My orgasm was building already, my body drawn tight, every nerve-ending alive.

And then—something new. A sensation I'd never felt before.

Thirst.

Not his. Mine. Not for water—but for blood.

When he fed from me, I'd always felt the transference—his hunger, his need, even the jagged shimmer of his climax—but this time, something shifted. This thirst bloomed inside *me*. Sudden, insistent, and terrifying in its clarity.

And I wanted it.

I screamed—the sound tearing through the quiet night— not in fear, not even in pleasure, but from a place of raw, unrelenting need.

He pulled back from my neck, startled. His fangs—rarely glimpsed for more than a flicker—gleamed bright white, tipped with crimson. His chest heaved as he gasped for breath, both of us trembling on the cusp of release. His pupils were black, blown by his own hunger.

"Blood," I panted. "Give me your blood." My head lolled back, my body pliant, undone. I didn't know where the thirst came from—only that it consumed me completely. His eyes widened at my demand, but I would accept no refusal. Whatever spell I was under, it had taken hold.

Without breaking eye contact, he slowly brought his wrist to his mouth, pressing a single fang into his skin. When he pulled back, blood welled to the surface—dark, rich, glinting in the low light. Salty tears slid down my cheeks, my entire body suddenly trembling with anticipation as he lifted his arm to my lips. I'd never wanted anything, never craved anything, the way I craved this. I sealed my mouth over the wound, pressing my lips tight, and drew him into me.

The instant his blood hit my tongue—sweet and honeyed, metallic—my orgasm detonated. Shattering. Consuming. The blood ignited something in me, and it reverberated through every nerve, every inch of me, pole to pole. He held me through it, crushing me to him, his mouth at my ear, a hiss escaping his lips as I drank. My thirst quickly eased once I'd taken no more than a mouthful, but the new fire inside me grew, as if the blood had caused a chemical reaction with the buzzing energy just under my skin. I clenched my pelvic floor, my pussy gripping his cock like a fist as I moved up and down. His climax followed, hard and violent, until I pulled my mouth free.

And when we stilled, I stayed there—my head on his shoulder, eyes closed tightly, heart pounding with something far more than just release. "I'm not a vampire, am I?" I whispered

—a small, anxious joke as I tried to make sense of what had just happened.

"Shh, love. That's nohow it's done," he murmured, his lips brushing my forehead in reassurance. "But ye need to open your eyes, Mira."

I did, and I winced. It felt like someone had turned on a spotlight in the room—so bright it burned as my eyes adjusted. And then I understood. Why he'd urged me to open my eyes. The light wasn't coming from above, or any other part of the room. It was coming from *me*.

Radiant flares burst outward from my skin, like solar fire dancing just above the surface arching, flickering, reaching in every direction.

I was blazing from the inside out.

My skin was warm and tingling—but not painful. Like the frenetic energy I'd felt since I'd asked Brigid to send a message to Sorcha, electricity arcing just beneath my skin, had expanded until the confines of my skin could no longer hold it back. Baird still held me close, which meant I wasn't burning him.

"It's not always like this...*is it*?" I asked, astonished—referring to what he'd once told me, how I sometimes glowed when we made love. I raised an arm, rotating it slowly, mesmerized as the flares started to soften—dimming in sync with the slowing rhythm of my heartbeat.

"No, lass," he said slowly, warily, eyes narrowed and fixed on me. "This is new..."

12

ANONYMOUS

Mira—March 2026

Early one morning, I woke to a DM on my Instagram account—someone with the handle @anonymous_a asking if I could design an engagement ring for his girlfriend. He said she'd been following my work for years and loved my designs. His profile was strange: a newly created account, no posts, no personal photos—just a single profile picture of sun setting over a calm sea, no location tagged. If he was trying to hide this from his girlfriend to surprise her maybe it made sense. His only stipulation was that the ring feature a yellow diamond. When I pressed for a budget, he dodged gracefully, saying only that *for the right stone, he'd make it work.* I'd have to test that claim before we got too far into negotiations.

I was uneasy about taking on a long-distance client—especially for something as personal and high-stakes as an engagement ring. Stones, especially rare ones, needed to be seen in person, their color and fire impossible to judge through a screen. I urged him to come to me, but he dismissed the idea outright. Traveling to see the stone, he said, was out of the question.

I told him about the stone I'd seen in Nathan's shop in Edinburgh, the extraordinary canary diamond—nearly five carats, GIA certified, no visible inclusions in the stone, and graded fancy vivid yellow. The kind of stone that, if I were designing a ring for myself, I'd choose without hesitation. My test came when I casually mentioned that a stone like this, set in 18-karat yellow gold, would likely land in the ballpark of fifty to sixty thousand pounds—giving him an easy out if the price was more than he'd bargained for. He didn't so much as flinch. Instead, he replied asking about next steps. I told him I couldn't promise the stone was still available, but I'd make inquiries and let him know.

As soon as we wrapped our initial back-and-forth, I called Nathan. As luck would have it the stone was still available. I asked for the price—yikes. This guy had better be head-over-heels, or wildly irresponsible. Possibly both. At least I'd landed squarely in the ballpark with my initial quote.

I forwarded the buyer the magnified stills, a video of the stone catching the light, and a copy of the GIA certificate. The only way I could justify moving forward was with a non-refundable deposit equal to my wholesale cost from Nathan. That way, if he bailed, at least I wouldn't be left holding a five-carat, fancy vivid yellow heartbreak of a bill.

He didn't hesitate. No haggling, no second thoughts—just a short reply: *Send me wiring instructions.*

I stared at the message for a long moment, waiting for the catch. None came.

The next morning, over coffee, I mentioned to Baird that I might have found a buyer for the diamond we'd seen in Nathan's shop. He gave me one of his patented skeptical brows as he lifted his mug—black coffee, no sugar, no cream. The only concession to breakfast this vampire ever made, and I suspected it had less to do with liking coffee than with the fact that I drank it too.

"What?" I asked, guessing at what he was thinking. "I promise I'm not buying it for myself. Tempting as that would be."

His eyes flicked to me. "It would."

I just rolled my eyes and continued. "Some guy wants me to design an engagement ring for his girlfriend. And he gave me free rein to design it. His only requirement was a yellow diamond."

"Oddly specific," Baird said.

"Right?" I said. "Not 'something classic' or 'she likes ovals.' Just—yellow."

Baird hummed low in his throat. "He *kens* exactly what he wants." He leaned back against the counter, all lazy confidence. "Think ye've time to finish the ruby—and this new ring? Or am I distractin' ye a wee bit too much?"

"You're always a distraction," I admitted. But despite his masterful attempt at seduction, I winced at the mention of the ruby. The wax model sat half-finished on my bench—a design I'd been carving from a solid block, destined to be encased in plaster investment before molten gold filled its every curve. I'd been slow-pedaling the ruby ring on purpose. If I was honest, the idea of creating a ring that might anchor a chain of events revealing the past to some reincarnated soul terrified me. What if the sentient ruby didn't approve of my design? I couldn't shake the feeling that a stone like this might not just disapprove quietly, but rearrange fate entirely. Or what if the person it was meant for rejected it? Ugh—I had to untangle myself from the whirl of thoughts.

"It's coming along. I might even carve the engagement ring next—maybe do part of it now, so I can cast them together," I said brightly, forcing a cheer I didn't quite feel. I tried to equalize the making of an engagement ring to crafting the ruby's setting. But deep down, I knew better. One was important to only two people, and in the end it was simply jewelry. The other...the other might meddle with the cosmos.

No pressure.

THE NEXT MORNING, I woke to a notification from my bank. The incoming wire—in the amount we'd agreed upon—came from Thorndale Ventures Ltd., a nameless, faceless corporate entity registered on the island of Jersey, a notorious tax haven. The funds had originated from a bank in Basel, Switzerland— another refuge where the discreetly wealthy hid assets and identities. My curiosity piqued, I tried to peel back the layers, but every path dead-ended. Whoever he was, he clearly didn't want to be found. The only detail I uncovered was that Thorndale Ventures had been formed in the late 1800s. Old money, then. Very old.

But his days of anonymity had to end, because I needed him to sign something. I DM'd him to confirm I'd received the funds and asked for his full name and email address so I could send over the contract. He replied almost instantly: *Aaron Thorndale* and a company email. Maybe the 'a' in anonymous_a stood for Aaron. I sent my standard agreement—non-refundable deposit clause, binding arbitration in the event of a claim, with me selecting the arbiter, a payment schedule for the balance due. I half-expected him to stall, to pass it to an attorney, maybe even try to redline a few terms. He did none of that. By lunchtime, the signed contract was in my inbox, Aaron Thorndale's electronic signature affixed without a single change.

Now that I had a name, I thought finding a face for my mysterious customer—and his girlfriend—would be easy. I figured I could trace her back to him on social media, maybe get a feel for her style. His glowing *"she loves your designs"* was flattering, but also a little unnerving. I create a lot of designs, and without knowing her, I was shooting in the dark. If I could see what she wore every day, I might be able to narrow in on a direction for the ring—something that would feel like *her*.

Even with his name, I wasn't any closer. I turned up a handful of Aaron Thorndales, but none fit—wrong age, wrong geography. Thorndale Ventures Ltd. might have been formed on Jersey and funneled funds through a Swiss bank, but the listed address was in London. That made the Texas cattle rancher and the California doctor I found along the way unlikely contenders for the Aaron Thorndale buying the ring.

I tried—really tried—to get some style direction from Aaron. After a few rounds of messages, he gave me the least helpful answer imaginable: *"Design exactly what you'd design for yourself."*

"Well," I murmured to no one, "that's either incredibly romantic...or an excellent way to blame the jeweler." Either way, I'd just have to trust my own taste...and hope his girlfriend shared it.

13

A PLANNED ATTACK

Magda—June 1387

On market days, Caius always drifted through the aisles, lingering with the vendors, trading stories and laughter until time slipped its leash. Some had welcomed him first because he was the boyar's son, but now they waved him over, friendships forged with the handsome young man because of the way he listened—how he remembered names, how he made each tale feel singular, important. Caius had a gift for people.

I knew that gift well. I knew what it felt like when his attention settled fully on me, when his warm sunbeam focused until it felt meant for me alone.

I heard that the boyar had ordered new suits of chainmail, delicate work that kept Dani beside his father at the forge for long hours, demanding patience and absolute concentration. No, Dani would not be at the market today.

Knowing all this, I chose my moment carefully—and went

to find Caius. I wore the dress Buna had embroidered for Mărțișor, pinched color into my cheeks, and bit my lips until they were ripe and dark as a plum. None of it was accidental.

I tucked my basket under my arm, two sweet buns cradled inside—traded for a jar of our honey. The pastries were part of my plan—but Caius didn't know that, and I had no intention of telling him. When I reached the main part of the market, two village girls spotted me and bent their heads together, whispering behind cupped hands. We'd once been friendly, but lately their glances had sharpened, their laughter carrying a brittle edge that had little to do with humor.

"Looking for someone, Magda?" one of them called, her smile thin, the implication clear without her needing to say his name.

Only then did I realize how transparent I'd been. Over the past few weeks, I had made a point of crossing paths with Caius at the market—lingering at his side, trading jokes, letting our flirting stretch longer than it should have. What I'd imagined was subtle had been anything but. I forced my expression into something neutral and moved between the stalls, pausing to inspect the vegetables as though their freshness required deep consideration, determined at least not to make my searching so obvious.

I heard his boisterous laughter before I saw him, standing a few stalls ahead, deep in conversation with the cheese monger. I bit my lip once more, then let my attention drift elsewhere as I passed—pretending not to notice him at all, hips swaying as I went, the basket cradled easily against my side. I felt it before I heard it—the moment his laughter faltered, the instant his gaze found me.

"Magda!" he called after me.

My heart skipped, quick and bright, at the sound of my name on his lips. I didn't turn at once. I let him wait a heartbeat longer, then slowly looked around, schooling my face into mild confusion—as though I truly didn't know who had called for me.

"Caius," I said lightly, letting just enough surprise into my voice to make it convincing. His answering smile told me I'd played it well.

"What are you buying?" he asked, peering into my basket, as he fell into step next to me as I walked.

"Sweet buns," I said lightly. "I traded honey for them." I tipped my head, letting a smile soften the edge of my words. "What about you? Don't you have servants who do the shopping for your household?" It was a jest—but not entirely. A reminder of the distance between us that longing looks and years of friendship could not quite erase.

He only grinned. From his pockets he produced two apples and a block of hard cheese and began to juggle them, the rhythm of his hands brushing my words aside as neatly as if he'd never heard them.

A flicker of irritation sparked in my chest—quick, unwelcome—before I smothered it. Caius always did this, turning away from a thorny comment with a smile and a trick, and I hated that some small part of me found it charming. "I was going to sit under the big oak by the river and read," he said. "Care to join me?"

The ease of it startled me. How quickly a glance, a pause, a bit of practiced innocence had shifted the day to my advantage. I accepted his smile, even as a quiet awareness stirred beneath my satisfaction: this had been easier than it should have been.

We settled beneath the sprawling branches, in a patch of

ground warmed by sunlight. He broke off a piece of cheese and handed it to me along with an apple. Conveniently, I had two buns and offered him one in return, and between us it made a fine enough lunch.

I spread my skirts and tucked my legs beneath me as we ate in companionable silence. It felt good, this simple sharing of food—and yet foreign, too. This was a first. My time with Caius almost always included Dani, and while it thrilled me to have Caius to myself, I felt Dani's absence all the same.

When I'd finished eating, I reached for the book Caius had brought with him. "What are you reading?" I asked, turning a few pages.

"A Greek philosopher—Aristotle," he said. "I'm afraid it hasn't been translated."

He knew I could read only basic Slavonic, and not well at that—but the fact that I read at all set me apart from most women in the village. I felt the distance of the language like a closed door and refused to let it stand.

"Then perhaps you could read it to me sometime," I said lightly. Even as I spoke, I could imagine what I was asking—his voice lowered, his attention narrowed to me alone, words meant for no one else. I kept my expression innocent, though I knew well enough that this, too, was a kind of invitation.

"I'd like that," he said, leaning closer, his expression darkening as his voice dropped. "My father hates it when I read anything but military history." He glanced away, then back to me, as though measuring the risk of the words before letting them go. "He says I'm wasting my time."

I saw a vulnerability in Caius I had never glimpsed before —a beautiful, charismatic man, no longer a boy, carrying a wound I had only just begun to see fully.

"Some days I think he truly hates me," he said quietly. "Blames me for my mother's death."

There was a pain in his eyes I didn't fully understand, but I could see it nonetheless. I reached for his hand, aching now myself, desperate to comfort him in some small way. He glanced up at my touch, surprise flickering across his face before something softer took its place. Gratitude. It warmed my heart to know it was something—anything—that might ease what he carried.

"You must understand what I feel," he said, an ache threading his voice.

But I didn't. "What do you mean?"

"Your mother died the same night mine did." He said it as if that explained everything.

In that moment, I understood how different our childhoods had truly been—not merely peasant and nobleman, but something far deeper. My life had been wrapped in love; his had been endured alone. Love had made me resilient in ways Caius had never been allowed to become. My grandmother was firm and demanding, but I never once questioned that I was cherished.

He, for all his servants and tutors, had grown up starved of that certainty, and the wound had been left to fester in silence. I'd seen it from a distance, the whole village had, but I didn't know how deeply that valley had been carved into his heart until that moment.

The thought left me aching—with compassion, and with a shame I couldn't quite name. I didn't want to name the distance between us or admit that I could not fully understand what he carried. And if part of me wanted to comfort him, another part—less noble, more honest—wanted him to feel wanted. So I closed the space between us and kissed him.

It wasn't our first kiss. Before, they had been stolen things—quick, breathless, Caius catching me when Dani's back was turned, all reckless laughter and youthful exuberance. This was different. There was no laughter now, no rush to touch and separate. My lips lingered against his—warm and yielding—and what began as tentative did not stay that way. His hand slid beneath my hair, firm and sure, drawing me closer until there was no space left between us, and I let myself be carried by it, by the heady rush of being wanted so openly.

His mouth deepened against mine, unhurried but certain, his tongue brushing mine in a way that sent heat skittering through me. His kisses traced along my jaw, down the sensitive line of my throat, and for a breathless moment I leaned into it, dizzy with how quickly desire had taken hold.

Then the ground shifted.

The closeness, the certainty of his touch, the unspoken expectation of what might come next—it all rushed in at once, and I realized how far I had stepped without knowing where to put my feet. My body went rigid, breath catching as panic bloomed sharp and sudden.

He felt it immediately. Before I could pull away, before the moment could tip any further, he stilled and withdrew, careful, controlled, as though he'd sensed I was slipping beyond my depth.

"What is wrong?" I asked, relief tangling with the sudden fear that I had done something to make him stop so abruptly.

"You're nervous," he said, a little tentatively.

He wasn't wrong—but I had no desire to admit it. "What makes you say that?" I asked, still mortified, afraid my inexperience had betrayed me, wishing—absurdly—that I'd practiced this with someone else first. My plan to capture him had come together flawlessly. What I hadn't planned for was this—here with him so close, realizing I had no idea what came next.

He took my hand in his and pressed it flat to my chest, his hand covering mine, right over my heart. Beneath my palm it raced—too fast, too loud, a frantic thud that echoed through my whole body.

"Can you feel that?" he asked.

I nodded, suddenly unable to find my voice.

"I can feel it too," he said gently. "I didn't bring you out here for this..." His voice trailed off, the words unfinished between us.

Shame flared hot and sudden. Foolish, I thought—foolish for wanting more. Foolish for thinking a kiss was the answer. Tears stung my eyes as I got to my feet too quickly, smoothing my skirts with trembling hands and turning away to gather my basket.

"Magda—wait." His hand reached for me as he stood. "I'm sorry."

When he saw the tears, his face fell, stricken.

"No," I said, shaking my head. I turned my face away, staring down at the ground because I couldn't bear to meet his eyes. "I'm the one who's sorry. I wanted to kiss you like that—*a real kiss*—I've thought about it so many times over the years." The words spilled out of me, broken and breathless. "And I thought...I thought you wanted it too."

He stepped toward me. I retreated without thinking until my back met the rough, solid trunk of the oak. He lifted a hand and brushed his fingers along my cheek, catching a tear before it could fall. Then he smiled—slow, certain now, the last trace of hesitation gone. "I thought the kiss was because you felt sorry for me."

I shook my head at once, hoping he didn't sense that there was a kernel of truth in it. Compassion was knotted up with everything else—but I had wanted to kiss Caius long before pity had ever entered the equation.

"I want to kiss you too," he said, his voice low now, sure. "Every night, before I fall asleep, I imagine what it would feel like to kiss you."

The words hung between us, heavy and bright all at once. The thought that I occupied his last waking moments each day sent a hot flush to my face that spread down into my chest. Neither of us moved. His hand remained at my cheek, warm and steady, and I felt his breath on my skin—close enough to promise, but not yet to claim.

The world seemed to narrow to that small space beneath the oak—the rustle of leaves overhead, the distant rush of the river, the thud of my heart answering his in a language I was only just learning.

For a long moment, we simply looked at one another, balanced on the edge of something irrevocable, knowing that whatever came next would change us—and choosing, just for that heartbeat, to linger there.

He leaned toward me, taking his time, letting me anticipate what came next. His hand slid from my cheek to the curve of my jaw, steadying me there, as if asking without words. When our lips met this time it was slower, deliberate—his mouth fitting to mine with care, not hunger. There was no urgency, only the quiet certainty of it, the sense that he meant this kiss to be remembered.

"You don't mind that I don't know how to do this?" I asked

when he pulled away, glad to have the truth of my inexperience out between us.

He shook his head slowly, his blue eyes never leaving mine. "I promise I don't mind."

"Will you teach me how to kiss properly?" I asked, brazen now that I'd laid out my desire for him.

"We'll learn together," he said just before he kissed me again.

WEEKS SLIPPED by in stolen afternoons beneath the oak tree, while Dani worked at his father's forge—still oblivious to what was quietly taking root between his two best friends. And several times a week, when his work was done, Dani would come to the cottage to fetch me, patient and earnest, tutoring me in the use of the blades he had made.

One hot afternoon, I looked up from pulling weeds in the garden just as Caius rode past my cottage, his horse's hooves thudding softly against the earth-packed road. When he caught sight of me, he slowed, making a deliberate effort to meet my eyes before pulling his horse to a stop at the gate.

"Where are you off to?" I asked, rising to my feet and brushing the dirt from my apron.

"To the hunting lodge," he said, his bow slung over one shoulder, a sword resting in the scabbard at his saddle. "And what will you do today?" He had a mischievous grin on his face. He often rode alone, or with Dani, to his family's hunting lodge —tucked up in a narrow mountain pass, about a forty-five-minute ride away.

"I was planning to pick berries. Bring them back, make some jam...dry the rest." I moved toward the gate, leaning on it as we spoke.

"I saw some good apples ripening in the trees up by the lake," he said casually. "And the berries near the north shore—some of the best this season." There was an alpine lake about halfway between the village and the lodge—the one he meant. There was a twinkle in his brilliant blue eyes—he was inviting me to meet him there.

Damn him for being so handsome.

"Well," I said, letting a ribbon of sarcasm curl through my smile, "it seems you're the expert, Caius." I might have faltered the first time we truly kissed—my usual boldness momentarily misplaced as I learned the shape of something new—but familiarity had a way of restoring me to myself. The shyness had burned off. In its place was the Magda he knew best: teasing, unafraid, and very much aware now of the effect I had on him.

"I might take my pony up there later," I added casually, brushing a loose tendril of hair from my cheek. "Once I'm done weeding the garden. Or...I might not." I let the coyness hang in the air between us, unwilling to give him the satisfaction of seeing how easily he'd thrilled me.

He smiled broadly, then glanced around to make sure no one was watching before curling one finger to me in a beckoning gesture. I made a show of rolling my eyes, plastering on an indignant look as I slipped through the gate and walked toward him. He stayed perched atop his horse, and I stopped just short of him, lifting my chin in mock defiance. He leaned down, his voice low, barely more than a whisper. "Please come. I'll be heading back from the lodge in the early afternoon. Meet me there—we can be alone."

I nodded in understanding. The great oak had sheltered us well enough—its wide trunk and heavy branches guarding our laughter and stolen kisses—but it had never granted true privacy. We were always listening for footsteps, always breaking apart at the snap of a twig, contenting ourselves with breathless embraces and wandering hands before fear chased us back toward caution.

"I will...if I can get away," I said, letting my practiced indifference soften just a touch. I offered no promise—but neither did I try to hide my smile. The thought of being truly alone with Caius, without the constant dread of discovery, sent my pulse skittering into a restless rhythm. It beat low and insistent beneath my ribs, anticipation and danger twined so tightly I could not tell one from the other.

I knew Buna would be making her rounds with the villagers after lunch, checking in on the sick and the women nearing their time—perfect for slipping away without her asking where I was headed. I would leave her a note, saying I'd gone to gather berries, in case she returned before I did.

THE SUN HAD BEGUN its slow descent into the western sky by the time I reached the lake. Caius was already there, sprawled on his back in the grass near the shore, bathed in golden light. His horse grazed lazily nearby. I slipped down from my pony and looped the reins loosely around its neck to let her do the same. Then I crossed the field to where Caius lay, stepping into the sunlight he'd claimed. My shadow fell over him, and he opened one eye, a slow smile curling on his lips. He patted the patch of grass beside him, wordlessly inviting me to join him.

I was nervous—so nervous I could barely breathe. I'd relived each kiss, each small exploration of our bodies a hundred times over the past few weeks, every stolen moment etched into my mind. And now, here we were. Alone. No one expecting either of us back until dusk. The thought sent a thrill through me, tangled with anticipation that bordered on ache. I was desperate for more—for him. I was tired of holding myself apart, of pretending I didn't want what most girls my age had already discovered. I wanted to be touched. Desired. Claimed.

I knelt beside him on the grass, the sun warm against my skin. I didn't know exactly what would come next, only what I craved. "Kiss me," I whispered, the words heavy with want. I needed the heat of his mouth on mine, on my skin—to wake the fire between my thighs, the way his touches had done before.

He didn't need me to ask twice. He sat up and reached for me, his hand finding my cheek. I leaned in, kissed him, letting his tongue brush softly against mine, his lips warm and salty. I let my mouth wander—his jaw, his chin—tasting him, memorizing him. When I finally pulled back to catch my breath, it wasn't hesitation. I just wanted to feel it all. To be fully present. Not swept away. Not yet.

"I want you, Caius—but..." I faltered, the words catching painfully in my throat.

I was afraid. The girls in the village spoke freely enough of their first times—some laughing it off, others lowering their voices as they spoke of pain that lingered longer than they'd expected. I didn't know which truth awaited me, only that the not knowing terrified me. How could I tell him that I wanted him—that I wanted to give myself to him fully—while still fearing what it might cost me? That desire and dread could live in me at the same time, tangled so tightly I couldn't separate them.

He leaned in as if to kiss me again, then paused, recognition dawning in his eyes. He took my hand gently, placed it over his chest. His heartbeat pounded against my palm—just like mine did the first time under the oak tree. "Do you feel that?" he asked softly. "I'm nervous too, Magda."

"Why are you nervous?" I asked, my voice barely above a whisper.

He gave a soft, breathless laugh, then met my eyes. "Do you think I know anything beyond the obvious, Magda? Because I don't. You are my first."

My lips parted in a silent *oh*, the realization settling over me with an unexpected tenderness. I'd been so caught up in learning the finer points of kissing these past weeks that I hadn't thought of asking if he'd done this before. He had said we would learn together. And only now did I understand that he had meant *everything*.

He tugged gently, coaxing me closer, and guided one of my legs across his hips until I was straddling him. My skirts gathered between us, his hands sliding up my thighs, and I felt the tremble in both our bodies—nerves, want, and the thrill of the unknown.

There was still too much between us—his trousers, my gathered skirts. I ached to feel him fully, the heat of his skin pressed flush to mine. With a needy breath, I hiked my skirts up around my hips, baring myself to him, desperate for his touch. Then I leaned back slightly, fingers fumbling at the leather belt that held his pants in place.

He watched me with darkened eyes, lifting his hips when I tugged, helping me as I worked the fabric down. My hands slid along his thighs, easing the garment past his hips until—

His cock sprang free, thick and flushed and proud between us, and the sudden proof of his desire stole the breath from my chest. I had seen the male body before; babies and ailing old men—but never awakened by me. This was a first.

His hand moved between us, tentative at first, then bolder as his fingers brushed the slick heat between my thighs. He explored gently, his fingertip dragging through the wetness he found there, teasing it back and forth until it glistened between us. I gasped when his thumb found that aching place at the crest of me, moving in slow, languid circles that made my breath catch. I had touched myself in secret, alone at night, muffling my moans in the pillow so as not to wake Buna. But here, beneath the open sky, I was free—free to let Caius hear what his touch did to me.

Then he reached for my hand, lacing our fingers briefly before guiding mine down—between my own thighs, teaching me the motion he'd used. My skin flushed as he helped me slip a finger inside myself, coating it in the same silky arousal that now slicked his own.

When my hand was wet, he moved it to his cock. It twitched beneath my touch, and I gasped again, surprised—the heat, the solid weight of him, alive in my hand. I curled my fingers around his shaft, tentative at first, until he guided me—his hand enveloping mine, showing me the rhythm he craved. The slow, deliberate strokes. The pressure that made his breath catch.

I imagined what it would feel like to take him inside me, to be filled by him completely—and the ache within me deepened, raw and insistent.

I rose up, needing him pressed against me, the friction unbearable in its absence. With my hand, I drew him to me, dragging his length against my wetness, gliding the thick, warm ridge of him across my slick folds. I caught him between my palm and my body, rubbing him there, watching the tension grip his face as he fought for control.

He groaned—a low, desperate sound—and I leaned in, kissing him deeply, hungrily, while his cock remained trapped between us, pulsing and hard, slick with both our desire. His hands clutched my hips, fingers digging in, and I could feel him trembling beneath me.

The knowledge that I could do this to him, that I could unravel the boyar's son with nothing but my body and my want, sent a thrill through me. I felt powerful—more powerful than I had ever been. And as his control frayed and his breath grew ragged, I knew we were both standing at the edge of something irreversible.

He pulled down the top of my dress, baring my breasts to the warm mountain air. Then he rose onto one elbow, his mouth finding my nipple, drawing it in with a soft suck before biting down—just enough to send a jolt of exquisite sensation through me. I cried out, my back arching, not from pain, not entirely, but from the overwhelming rush of feeling.

Something shifted inside me then. Thought gave way to hunger, to instinct. All hesitation burned away beneath the fire in my veins. My body knew what it wanted—what it had always wanted—and it was him.

I rose onto my knees, guided his cock to where I ached for him most, letting my slickness slide along his tip, circling, teasing, until we both trembled. Then I stilled. I took a deep breath, bracing myself for the pain I knew was near, the way I'd heard wetness softened it, turned pain to pleasure. I was ready now. For all of it.

His voice broke just as I was about to take him inside me. "Wait—Magda…" he gasped, his chest rising and falling unsteadily. "I'm scared I'll hurt you, but I can't—I can't hold back much longer." His hands trembled where they gripped my hips. "I want this more than I've ever wanted anything. But once I'm in you…I won't be able to stop."

I pressed my mouth to his, offering him the only answer I had: I was ready—for him, for this, for whatever came next. I reached between us, guiding him to me, and eased back slowly. He slipped inside just a little before my body resisted. I knew what it was—the moment that would hurt. Drawing in a steady breath, I willed myself to soften, to let him in.

Caius hesitated, holding himself still so I could lead. I pressed back, past the place my body resisted, and pain flared —first a sharp sting, then a burn, fire concentrated where we were joined. A cry tore from my lips as tears stung my eyes.

His hands steadied my hips, keeping us both from moving. He leaned up, kissing me in soft, tender brushes—my mouth, the tip of my nose, my eyelids. Each touch soothed, and slowly the burning eased, the tears drying before they could fall.

I rocked against him tentatively. The pain returned with each movement, and still I moved—slowly, carefully, inch by inch, until at last I had taken all of him inside me.

His eyes grew heavy, teeth clenched as I moved against him. The burning gave way to a tingling heat—like the first time he'd slipped his fingers inside me—and my own wetness eased the way, letting me move faster, freer.

His breath soon turned ragged, uneven, and I knew he was losing his grip on control. I couldn't decide what thrilled me more—the deep, consuming fullness of him inside me, or the power of knowing I made it impossible for him to hold back. I pressed my palms to his chest for leverage, my dark hair spilling like a curtain between us. Caius caught it in his hand, winding the strands around his fingers, and yanked me down just as he thrust up into me—no longer content to let me lead.

His grip in my hair, his breath hot against my throat, unraveled me. Every groan that rumbled from him as he struck the deepest part of me sent a shiver spiraling through my body. And each small, helpless sound I gave in return only drove him closer to breaking. His release hovered just at the edge, and I could feel it in the tremor of his body beneath mine.

"I love you Magda," he said as he held me. The words came out rough, the rhythm out of time with the movement of our bodies.

Those were the words I had longed to hear—the proof that what we felt was real, that this was right. The sound that left me was as much from the force of his body as from the impact of his vow; I moaned aloud in triumph. He was mine. And I was his.

The sound I made pushed him over the edge. He cried out as he pulsed inside me, his arms locking around my body until at last he stilled.

I hadn't reached the same release I'd known alone, but I understood—sometimes it didn't come the first time. There would be more chances, more time to learn each other, to discover how to please and be pleased.

When our breaths finally steadied, I eased from atop him. Caius slipped free, though he didn't loosen his hold, and I curled beside him in the grass. In the fragile afterglow I felt suddenly shy, exposed in a way I hadn't expected, while Caius seemed utterly untroubled—his gaze fixed on me as though I were the only thing anchoring him to the world.

The illusion shattered with the thunder of hoofbeats. A rider burst from the trees. We scrambled upright. I turned away at once, dragging my skirts down, folding my arms over my chest as Caius's hand flew to his blade—then stilled. When I turned back, I saw recognition on his face.

His father's man, Ivar. And behind him—Dani.

Ivar reined in sharply, his horse snorting as his mouth twisted into a knowing, lewd grin. "Caius your father calls for you. Our men clashed with a raiding party from the south. He sent your friend with me to find you. Leave the girl—"

But I wasn't looking at Ivar. Dani sat atop his horse several yards away, as though an invisible boundary held him there. He didn't speak. He didn't move. The shock on his face hollowed quickly into something worse—hurt so raw it looked like pain made visible. Not anger. Not accusation. Just the quiet devastation of understanding all at once.

Then he turned his horse. He kicked it into a gallop and fled back the way he had come, leaving behind a silence so complete it rang in my ears. Neither Caius nor I spoke. There were no words that could have followed him—none that could have undone what he had seen, or softened the betrayal he must have felt.

With Dani gone, I turned to face Ivar. Though I had straightened my blouse and tugged my skirt back into place, I felt stripped bare beneath his lingering stare. His gaze traveled over me slowly, assessing, as if what he saw were goods left out in the open market.

"Well," he said just after he spit on the ground, a crooked smile tugging at his mouth, "I suppose some girls are eager to earn their place." The words landed like a punch.

Caius stiffened. His gaze snapped from Ivar to me, then back again. "Mind your tongue," he said, irritated. "She's with me."

With me. Not *she is not what you think*. Not *speak of her with respect*. Just a territorial claim. Heat crawled up my throat—not from shame at what we had done, but from the way they stood there measuring one another over me. Caius bristled, stepping slightly in front of me, shoulders squared, ready for a challenge. But it felt like he was defending ownership, not honor. And somehow, that hurt more than Ivar's words.

Ivar only laughed. "So I see."

Our villagers feared enemies at the gates, men who came with banners and blades. My dread was of a different kind altogether. Ivar and his men were less soldiers than hired brutes— the sort Caius's father kept close for tasks too ugly to soil his own hands. Violence made official. Cruelty given leave. He and his men made my skin crawl.

"We'll follow you down the mountain," Caius told him as I gathered the reins and swung onto my pony. I was grateful Ivar's only reply was a derisive huff before he spurred his horse into a hard gallop down the trail.

As we neared the village, I turned west, urging my pony into a run. I needed to reach the cottage, to help Buna tend the wounded. She asked no questions when I burst through the door after stabling my pony. She had returned to gather supplies, and together we hurried back to the square, where a makeshift shelter held the injured.

We worked deep into the night, scrubbing and binding

wounds. Some men would live to see another dawn. Others would not.

By early morning, Drago Burián moved among the pallets of the injured, dispensing measured words of praise and consolation. He paused beside the families of the dead, commending their sons' bravery, assuring them their sacrifice had preserved our safety. To those whose loved ones still clung to life, he spoke of vigilance—of readiness, of the need for more men, more provisions, more coin should our enemies rise again.

And then his gaze found me.

It was not long, nor obvious. But it lingered a fraction too long to be accidental—cool, assessing, as though weighing something newly discovered. I felt it like a hand at my chin, tilting my face for inspection—forcing a chill down my spine.

Had Ivar spoken? Had he told the boyar what he had seen when he found Caius? The thought hollowed my stomach. His expression gave nothing away, yet something in it had shifted. I was no longer invisible to him.

When I finally stumbled home in the gray light of dawn— two days since I had last slept—I peeled off my bloodstained skirts. The soldiers' blood had dried in dark streaks across the fabric.

And there, smeared between my thighs, was more dried blood.

My own.

14

TROUBLE

Magda—Late July 1387

Since I was fourteen, my monthly bleeding had come as regular as the moon. When I realized I was nearly two weeks late, I knew the reason without doubt. With no small measure of trepidation, I walked through the village that day to find Caius.

I approached the guarded gate set into the stone wall surrounding the boyar's castle and asked the sentry—a young man named Peter—to tell Caius I needed to see him. His gruff expression softened as he unlatched the gate, abandoning formality.

"He's in the courtyard," he said, then added, almost casually, "with your friend Dani."

My stomach dropped. I had hoped—foolishly—that Caius would be alone. I still hadn't found the courage to speak to Dani since the day at the lake, since the look on his face had burned itself into my memory.

I thanked Peter with what I hoped passed for a steady smile and slipped through the gate. To my left, the courtyard opened wide, bordered by the main house, a small chapel, the servants' quarters, and the stables.

I saw them at once. Caius and Dani sat together on the low stone wall, sweat-slick and dust-streaked after sparring with swords laid at their feet. They were talking. There was tension there—I could feel it even from a distance—but it hadn't yet shattered the years of friendship between them. The sight filled me with a fragile, guilty relief...and a selfish hope that if Caius had been forgiven, perhaps I might be too.

Dani noticed me first. For an instant, pain flickered across his face before he tried to mask it with a smile.

Behind him, Caius's expression changed—pleasant surprise tightening into something more guarded. He knew me too well to believe I'd come without reason. I straightened my shoulders, but with every step toward them, doubt pressed heavier against my ribs.

"Hi, Dani," I said, my voice thinner than I meant it to be.

"Uh—I think I need to talk to Magda. I'll catch up with you later," Caius said, giving an awkward slap to Dani's shoulder.

Dani's face said everything—resentment at being dismissed, hurt at being left out. That he was now the odd man out in our triangle of friendship. He gave a single nod and went to retrieve his weapon from where it lay in the courtyard dirt. As he passed, his hurt gaze didn't linger on Caius—it lingered on me.

When Dani disappeared through the gate, I drew Caius into the shadow of the stable door, glancing around to be sure no one could hear. I swallowed hard, forcing down my nerves, and met his blue eyes.

"I am with child." The words left me on a shallow breath—the message delivered, heavy and irrevocable. I waited for his reaction.

His face was still at first, then slowly, a smile began to form. He took my hands in his, and at his touch, my tears came—sudden, unstoppable.

"Don't cry," he murmured, brushing the wetness from my cheeks. "I'll tell my father—and, and..." He faltered, searching for the courage to say it plainly. "And we will be married."

My smile broke through the tears, relief rushing in so quickly it left me lightheaded. In that moment, every fear that had shadowed me seemed to dissolve. All the darkness Buna had foreseen—her smoke-laced warnings and whispered prophecies—burned away like morning mist. She had been wrong, and I had never been so grateful to see her proven so.

"Go home," he said. "I will talk to my father tonight, and we will speak again in the morning." He pressed a tender kiss to my lips and pulled me close. "I love you, Magda."

I clung to him, and for the first time spoke the words I had carried in my heart for so long, afraid to give them voice until now. "I love you too, Caius." I pulled free, lightness blooming in my chest, a smile still warming my lips as I turned toward the path that led back to my cottage. Soon I would leave this small life behind, and all the whispered doubts along with it.

THE NEXT MORNING, I was working in the garden when a woman approached—the boyar's cook. She lingered by the gate, her eyes darting as though someone might be watching. Beneath her nervousness was something else—pity.

"Caius wants to see you," she said quietly. "I'm to bring you to the castle."

I brushed the dirt from my hands onto my skirt and followed her. She said nothing as we walked, and the guard—an older man whose name I did not know—moved aside without a word when we passed through the gate.

She led me through the servants' entrance into the main house, a place I had never seen from within. The corridor stretched long and dim before us. At its end, she stopped before a heavy wooden door, resting her hand on the handle.

For a moment she didn't move. Then, without looking at me, she whispered just two words. "I'm sorry."

The words struck harder than a slap. My first instinct was to laugh, to tell her there was nothing to be sorry for. Caius had sent for me. But the sound stuck in my throat. I stepped inside, the door closing behind me with a heavy thud that made me jump. The room was a library with high ceilings and shelves crowded with books—the same one from which Dani had smuggled me volumes over the years. Against the window stood Caius, his head bent.

"You sent for me?" I asked, hope lifting my voice.

Papers rustled behind me. I turned, startled to find someone else in the room. Caius's father, Drago Burián, stood at the desk, as though only just noticing my presence—casually surprised.

I looked back to Caius. His face held an expression I had never seen before—not anger or fear, but something emptied out, hollow.

"Magda…" he said, his voice flat with defeat.

"Why have you brought me here?" I asked. "Why did the cook apologize to me just now?" I forced my voice steady, though my heart hammered and sweat gathered at my brow.

Drago smiled—thin and cruel. "I spoke with my son last night." He tipped his head toward Caius, who had lowered his gaze again, like a child sent to the corner for disobeying. "He informed me of your…*little problem.*"

"Problem?" The word caught in my throat, still unsure how much the boyar knew.

"His bastard," Drago said. "The one you carry." He spoke as though Caius were no longer in the room.

"Bastard?" My voice rose before I could stop it. "Caius—" I pleaded. "Tell him we are to be married—" I needed to hear it again. Needed something to hold on to. Needed proof I hadn't imagined it.

Drago's laugh boomed through the room, rich and cruel. "Yes," he said, still smiling. "He told me of his plan." Then the smile faded. The amusement drained from his face, leaving only the hard, cold thing beneath. "No son of mine will marry a Romani whore."

The cruel whispers I had ignored for the past year surged through me, each one rising over the last, mocking me more cruelly than even Drago Burián's brittle laughter.

"You love me…" I said to Caius, the words scarcely more than breath. I couldn't tell if I was making a statement or begging for confirmation. "You love me," I said again, forcing the words out, gathering what little self-respect I had left.

Caius stood with his shoulders bent, unmoving. He did not reach for me, did not speak. His silence was the answer. Something in me shifted—desperation giving way to anger, anger hardening into defiance. Magda the hellcat rose in me. I turned to Drago Burián, to defend myself if Caius would not. "Everyone will know that Caius is the father of my child."

Drago didn't even look up. "Caius won't be here," he said mildly. "He leaves tonight to begin his military training—with the warlord Mircea in Wallachia. He will be gone a year. Perhaps more." He shrugged, his attention already returning to the papers on his desk. "You'll handle your mistake on your own."

"My mistake?" I spat, venom bitter on my tongue.

Drago's mouth curled. "Your grandmother's a midwife, isn't she?" He smiled thinly. "Ask her what she gives to girls who forget themselves."

"I will not kill your grandchild," I said through gritted teeth.

"Suit yourself," he said. "You spread your legs for Caius—who's to say the babe is even his?" He held my gaze as he spoke, as if the words themselves might remake the truth. His eyes were Caius's blue, emptied of warmth—winter stripped to bone.

He reached for a small silver bell at the edge of the desk. The chime rang out, thin and shrill, shattering the silence like glass. Then he turned away, already done with me.

A guard appeared. Silent. His rough hand closed around my arm, fingers digging into the tender flesh. As I was dragged toward the door, I looked back at Caius one last time. He had lifted his head. His eyes were full of apology.

He did nothing.

I was hauled through the corridors and thrown outside the gates, my first tears only falling once the doors slammed shut behind me. A man stood only a few paces away, leaning lazily against the stone wall that ringed the boyar's castle—as if he had been waiting for me.

I gathered myself and started toward the road that would take me back to the cottage, refusing to look at him.

"Where are you running off to in such a hurry, Magda?" Ivar's voice drifted after me, amused. Then he laughed.

15

WHAT WE ALREADY HAVE

Magda—August 1387

A week later, as I hung the laundry, I spotted Dani coming down the road toward the house. I ducked behind the sheet I'd just pinned to the line, praying he would pass without noticing me. The last thing I wanted was conversation—least of all with anyone tied to Caius or his father.

There was no escaping him. He had already seen me, and moments later he was striding up the path, his head rising above the very sheet I had hoped would hide me.

"Magda—we need to talk."

I straightened and looked at him over the clothesline. Something in his voice had changed—steadfast where it had once been uncertain. The shy boy I had always known was gone. In his place stood a man.

I couldn't bring myself to meet his eyes—I was afraid I'd cry if I did. Afraid of the disappointment I might find there, of what he would see in me if he truly looked. Maybe he would call me trash, the way some of the villagers did. Maybe I would believe it.

A stupid, foolish girl—old enough to be a woman—dreaming of things that had never been meant for her. My grandmother's words echoed in my head as guilt closed over me, the knowledge settling at last: I had given myself to Caius, and even his love had not been enough.

Maybe it never had been real at all.

And worse still—I carried his child. The boyar's grandchild, growing inside me. Unless fate chose to claim me as it had my mother—death on the childbed. Perhaps that was all I deserved. Better to be swallowed by the earth, laid beneath the soil in a nameless grave, than to live beneath the weight of such guilt and shame.

That was the future Buna had seen for me in the smoke. To think just a week prior I was foolish enough to believe I could outrun that fate.

"I can't talk now, Dani," I said, blinking hard against the sting in my eyes. I focused on the basket in my hands, on the thin crack in its handle—anywhere but his face. "I have to finish my chores." The words sounded brittle, even to me. I turned before he could answer, afraid that if I lingered a moment longer, the wall I was trying so desperately to build between us would crumble.

He came around the clothesline toward me. I turned quickly, clutching the basket to my side as if it could shield me. His hand shot out, closing firmly around my arm, and the sudden grip jolted me still. I looked up at him, my heart racing, every instinct screaming to flee—uncertain of what he knew... and what he didn't.

"Magda—*wait*," he said, his voice low, almost a plea. He swallowed hard, drawing in a breath before the words came. His grip shifted, sliding from my arm until his hand found mine. His palm was warm against my skin, and though I hadn't expected it, the simple, gentle touch eased the frayed edges of my nerves. The air felt heavy, charged with the silence that stretched between us until he spoke.

"I want you to be my wife," he said simply. And though his eyes still held the soft, almost drowsy gentleness I had always known, there was a new resolve burning there. "I've wanted it since we were children—since the days we chased each other through the woods." He stood there, holding my hand. "I've loved you that long," he added, as if time was proof.

I shook my head—not because I doubted his words, but because I knew I didn't deserve them. I could only stare up at him, my throat tight, the truth lodged somewhere between my heart and my tongue. It felt as though the universe had turned a harsh, unrelenting light on me, and I buckled beneath it. I wanted to tell him I couldn't—that my heart still belonged to Caius—but before I could speak, I saw it in his eyes.

He already knew. "You don't have to love me back," he said softly, his words steadying the storm in my head. "My mother says many marriages are built on less than what we already have." He met my gaze, unflinching. "I know you care for me. And that is enough."

His thumb brushed mine. "You will always be enough for me—just as you are."

There it was, shining through him—a calm, steady sense of purpose, as though he had been waiting for this moment all his life. He reached for the basket tucked beneath my arm and set it aside, then took both my hands in his.

My heart hammered. He was too good for me. He knew where my heart truly lay, and still he wanted me. But the baby—perhaps if we married quickly, the village would believe it was his. The thought struck like a held breath. Could this be my way out? The idea felt almost blasphemous. Fate was not merciful—not to someone like me.

Tears slipped down my cheeks, burning with guilt—though perhaps he mistook them for joy. "Are you sure?" I whispered, when what I longed to say was that he deserved better. Maybe I wanted to give him one last chance to turn away, to find a woman who could love him honestly, instead of binding himself to me.

He smiled down at me, and I could have sworn I saw tears glistening in his eyes too. "Yes. I'm sure, Magda. I've never been more sure."

We did not speak Caius's name. It was as if he had vanished, cleanly erased from our lives. I accepted the silence gladly, even as something in me understood it would not stay silent forever.

I swallowed hard and whispered a prayer for forgiveness before I gave him my answer. "Then yes," I said. "I will marry you, Dani."

He leaned in and kissed me. His lips were warm and gentle against mine—nothing like the fire and urgency I had known with Caius. One hand slid to the back of my neck, careful but firm, holding me there, a velvet cage I did not quite know how to escape. Part of me wanted to flinch, to pull away, to run. But another part—smaller, quieter, driven by fear or need—leaned into him all the same.

The kiss was awkward, unfamiliar. And yet it stirred something I wished it hadn't. My heart remained silent, still tethered elsewhere, but my body answered despite me, and the shame of it burned hotter than his touch. I pulled away, breath unsteady, confusion flushing my cheeks beneath his gaze.

"When?" I asked—meaning the marriage.

"Soon—very soon," Dani said, his excitement spilling over, eager like a child at Christmas. "Should we tell your grandmother?"

I glanced toward the cottage. "She's not here just now. Come back tonight after supper." I tried to laugh as I added, "She'll probably try to talk you out of it." It was meant as a joke. But a small, secret part of me almost wished she would—so Dani might yet be spared a life bound to a woman who could not love him as he deserved, who would never be fully happy, never truly satisfied.

Dani beamed as he lifted my hand and pressed a kiss to it. "Till tonight," he said, already turning away.

I raised a hand in return, though guilt and shame closed over me the moment his back was turned. I watched his tall frame retreat, growing smaller as he disappeared into the village—and felt myself shrinking too, hollowed out by the quiet, unbearable weight of deceiving my friend.

Buna returned from her rounds in the village not long after, just as I was pulling a loaf of bread from the clay oven behind the cottage. I set it in the same basket I'd carried the laundry out in earlier and brought it inside. She sat at the table, slicing cheese for a snack. I placed the steaming loaf on a trivet to cool, then turned to stir the stew bubbling over the hearth.

"Dani is coming after supper," I said flatly, my back to her. "He's asked me to marry him. I said yes."

Behind me came a judgmental *hmph*. Had she not stood in this very spot two months ago, telling me I would be wise to do exactly this? Now she made it sound like folly. I could not win. "Does he know you carry his best friend's babe?"

I spun around, the spoon clattering against the pot. "Who told you?"

"Magda—do you forget I am a midwife?" She shook her head. "And a woman besides. It is early days still, but the signs are there for those who know to look."

I turned back to the stew. "No." I said finally. "He doesn't know. Are you going to tell him?"

"I will not betray your secret." Her tone was grim, unyielding. "But for his sake—*and yours*—you had best bed him soon." Her words were a blunt hammer. In that moment I understood she was part of this now, whether she wished to be or not. She carried our secret, but the look on her face said she didn't like the weight of it.

"He knows I don't love him," I said quickly, needing her to see that this was not some girlish delusion. "I told him plainly. He said he didn't care." Even recalling it bore a hole in my gut —low and secret and faintly shameful. He didn't care—but I felt like he should.

When Dani returned later that night, Buna fetched the bottle of pălincă she kept on the high shelf. She poured the sharp brandy—apples, pears, and plums distilled to fire—into three small glasses. Lifting hers, she intoned, "Dumnezeu să vă binecuvânteze uniunea," blessing our union.

But her piercing gaze never left me. I felt it burn through

flesh and bone, straight into the rot at my core—into a restless soul already damned.

16

BLOOD MAGIC

Mira—March 2026

"I was with Baird the other night...*you know*." I gave Sorcha a pointed look, hoping she'd catch my drift. She didn't. She'd wandered into my studio and made herself comfortable while I worked, so I figured I might as well take advantage of the moment.

"No, Mira, I dinnae ken. What do ye mean?" she asked, her voice slow and deliberate.

"I mean," I said dryly, "there was nudity. And feelings. And blood." If I was going to talk about my sex life, we clearly needed to get on more familiar terms. "We were *intimate*. And I had this overwhelming—desire isn't even the right word—need. I needed to drink his blood. It was so all-consuming I screamed for it. I lost all sense of where I was, what I was doing, who I was...until I got it."

Her eyes narrowed the faintest degree. "He let ye drink fae

him?" she asked, her tone clinical, detached—like she was ticking boxes on my medical history.

I nodded. "He didn't hesitate."

"Where did ye drink fae? His neck? His heart vein, perhaps?"

"No," I shook my head. "His wrist."

A low, dismissive sound slipped from her. Disappointment?

"And then—light started flaring off my skin. So bright I had to shield my eyes. It looked like flames, but it wasn't. It was yellow-gold light, blazing out of me like a human signal flare. I'd been buzzing all day—for several days really—something just beneath the surface, just waiting to erupt. And when I drank, it did."

Still no real reaction—just that steady, indecipherable gaze. As if she'd been expecting every word. As if my story wasn't shocking, but confirmation. The silence stretched too long, and in it, I realized: it wasn't that Sorcha felt nothing. She already knew something I didn't.

"No *light show* at the moment, I see. How do ye feel?" she asked.

"The buzzing's still there—like I could tap into that current anytime." It was true. Holding it back now took effort.

"Blood magic," Sorcha said, as if the words alone explained the weight of history. "Witches have used it since the dawn of time. Blood is life itself—the very essence of vitality. We smear it on talismans, on doorways, to charge them with our power, ward off evil. In a spell, even a drop makes it uniquely yours. A magical fingerprint—as personal as your signature."

The smudges inside the Mother's Book flashed in my mind —especially the one that still held a perfect swirl pattern left by an ancestor's finger. Could those dark stains be blood? Garvie blood?

"Blood amplifies magic," Sorcha said evenly. "A few drops when ye cast a spell can help ensure the right outcome. It can consecrate what's sacred. A drop of blood in your grimoire feeds. Binds it to ye."

Sometimes it felt like Sorcha was reading my mind. "There are bloody fingerprints inside the Mother's Book," I whispered, nodding slowly, the realization settling over me.

Sorcha's gaze softened just a fraction. "Aye. You're starting to see it now. The blood of the Abhartach—well, that's the most powerful blood of all," Sorcha added almost casually. "Did ye notice how often it's mentioned in the book?"

I nodded. I had seen the word—*Abhartach*, one of the names Granny Margaret told me our Celtic ancestors once used for what we now call a vampire—scattered through the pages. But I'd only truly tried to read one of those entries: the spell Granny claimed was meant for protection against them.

"So let me get this straight," I said. "The Garvies sometimes used vampire blood in their spells—where exactly do you think they got it? Because I'm guessing you couldn't pick this up at the local drug store."

She only stared, silent, as if daring me to work it out. I hated it when she adopted that elementary school teacher air with me—too measured, too patient. "Where did *ye* get it the other night?" she said at last, her words dropping like a stone, simultaneously a clue and a challenge.

My mouth opened, then closed. "No. No...that's impossible." Was she implying what I think she was implying? "There's a vampire protection spell in the book—Granny Margaret told me. It's supposed to keep a vampire from crossing your threshold. The Garvies were afraid of them."

"I'm afraid that's no an accurate translation of the spell," Sorcha said quietly, her brogue swirling around each word, dropping them as puzzle pieces into place, the picture slowly coming into focus. "I read the spell the other day. It isna meant to bar a vampire from your home, Mira. It's meant to keep one from finding their way into your heart."

"That feels," I said slowly, "like a very specific warning." Maybe I wasn't the first Garvie to fall for a vampire.

17

UNDER HER SPELL

Baird—March 2026

Baird was hyperaware of Mira—blame it on his nature as a vampire. He was so attuned to her now that sensing her felt no different than sensing himself— her body, her reactions, her rhythms blending seamlessly into his own. Almost.

Mira was all graceful limbs and lush curves, her whisky-colored eyes catching the light, a faint scatter of freckles dusting her nose. Dark waves framed her face, and there was that dimple in her chin—absurdly, perfectly shaped to cradle his thumb.

Desire explained some of it. Love, perhaps, even more. But not all of it.

There was the connection he'd forced on her—the one he'd tricked her into with silence when he drank her blood. He couldn't blame it on hunger or desire alone, but something far more dangerous. Something deliberate. A compulsion. A binding. A way to tap into every emotion that moved through her body and mind. A bond that could only take root if love already existed between them.

He had done that. Or the part of him he still thought of as the monster had. He'd spent centuries believing he knew where that line was. Mira had blurred it beyond recognition. Even now, he wasn't entirely sure which part of him had been in control that night. Deep down, he suspected it was he, not the beast, who had wanted it all along—a way to claim in Mira the part of someone that remained untouchable, no matter how close two people came. The *Sanguis Amantium* bond was only meant to form when a vampire drank the blood of his mate, but he'd never truly believed the stories. He'd dismissed them as folklore. Myth.

Until that night. Until one impulsive, selfish act proved they were real.

Most of the time, he didn't think about it. But lately, as Mira changed, he could feel things he shouldn't have been able to. That dark, fragile place inside her—one even his love hadn't been able to fully reach—was healing. Slowly stitching itself closed, as though something long broken had finally found its missing piece. It was an extraordinary thing to witness—humbling even—and yet the guilt of being able to feel it happening inside her never quite left him.

With every hour she spent poring over the Garvie grimoire—alone or under Sorcha's careful guidance—she grew more certain of herself. More whole. He'd seen it just the other day, watching from a distance as Sorcha helped her learn to control the light and fire that had once erupted from her without warning. Mira had been steady then. Focused. Changed.

As if loving him—and discovering the magic that had

always lived within her— were the final elements she'd been missing all along.

Then, the other night, it had caught him completely off guard—her hunger for his blood, sudden and insistent. Violent in its need. He told himself he hadn't had time to level the playing field for Mira, to complete the bond the proper way by letting her take from his jugular or the vena cava—the great arterial paths that, in humans, returned blood to the heart, but in vampires played some mysterious role in the formation of the *Sanguis Amantium* bond.

Was it surprise that made him bite down on his wrist instead?

Mira's hunger hadn't cared. She'd only wanted her thirst sated, and he'd obliged without hesitation. But later, in the quiet that followed, he wondered if it had been more than instinct that made the decision.

Fear, perhaps. Fear of what it would mean to truly let her in. Of what would happen once the bond was complete—when he would no longer be able to keep parts of himself hidden. Not the darker truths. Not the emotions he told himself he buried for her own good. The ones he believed, maybe foolishly, were acts of protection.

One truth had become impossible to ignore—every day with Mira drew him further under her spell. He'd gambled once before, let her walk away, not knowing if she'd ever return, even as the *Sanguis Amantium* bond burned with the certainty of her love.

Never again would he let her slip from his grasp.

18

AMULETS

Mira—April 2026

I'd put it off long enough.

Hours upon hours were spent carving the band and bezel from hard wax—then many more refining the form with rasps and wax files, coaxing the surface toward uninterrupted smoothness. At every stage, I carefully lowered the ruby into its seat, checking and rechecking the fit, unwilling to risk even the slightest looseness—as if the stone itself were waiting for an excuse to object. Once the ring was cast in eighteen-carat yellow gold, I knew there would be no room for correction—only restraint. Every adjustment now would have to be deliberate, precise, and kept to the bare minimum.

The juxtaposition between creating the ruby ring and working on the yellow diamond was night and day. Every moment spent with the ruby was steeped in trepidation—fear of the design, fear of the outcome. My hands were guided by unseen forces; magic prickled beneath my skin, restless, demanding release. I hovered between surrender and restraint, terrified of what might happen if I let go. I couldn't yet see the endgame—only the unsettling sense that the universe was using my hands and tools to reach backward through time and pull someone from the grave.

This ring I was designing was, somehow, meant to call back someone precious to a vampire whose very existence—and the choices she had made afterward—had set terrible wheels in motion. And, if Granny Margaret was to be believed, those same turning gears were connected to Bastien, the vampire who ended Agnes's life and stole Baird's human one, condemning him to centuries of solitude.

And yet, despite all the violence and grief Bastien had wrought, it wasn't lost on me where Baird and I stood now. Together. Happy. As close as two people could possibly be. A life I never could have imagined for myself—more than I ever dared hope for. While I had doubted the depth of Baird's love in the beginning, I had no such reservations now. Still, the pendulum swing of emotions the ruby demanded of me left me nauseous by the end of every session at my bench—too much meaning, too much consequence, packed into something so small.

But the yellow diamond...that was another story entirely. Every second spent on its design—following the very same process as the ruby—was joyful, energizing. Magic coursed through my veins, my hands guided by the same unseen force, yet everything felt effortless, *right*. There was no fear—only that rare creative flow that blesses makers from time to time. Subject to the usual rhythms of the human condition, yes—but untouched by outside emotion or worry.

The yellow diamond was all sunshine and clarity. If the

ruby was a demanding god, the diamond was a golden retriever —eager, enthusiastic, and certain I knew what I was doing. It was almost as if I were creating beings with distinct personalities: one dark, seductive, and stormy. The other bright, lucid, irrepressibly optimistic. Yin and yang.

The casting of both rings had gone flawlessly. I held the still-screaming-hot casts in long tongs, my hands protected by heavy leather mitts, as I lowered them into the quench. A sharp hiss echoed through the studio when the molten metal met water, steam rising as the plaster form slowly dissolved away. At the center of it all, the rings remained joined—golden twins born from the same womb still connected by a thin vein of metal known to jewelers as the sprue.

Once it had fully cooled and the plaster scrubbed away, I dried the piece with a soft cloth. The surface gleamed a warm gold—matte for now, not yet polished. I reached for my flush cutters to free the rings from the main sprue. At the precise moment the blades touched metal, something made me pause —just for a breath.

A sudden, irrational certainty settled over me: that I wasn't merely severing gold but severing pieces of myself I'd only just realized could coexist. The darker part, still burdened by doubt on some days. And the part others had always seen—the light I'd only recently learned to recognize in myself. Were they meant to exist separately? Or did each require the other, bound together to create something greater than the sum of its parts?

I shook the feeling off and pressed on. A sharp click sounded each time the cutters closed, severing the metal umbilical cord that bound them together, followed by a soft *plunk* as each ring dropped free and settled on the bench. I lifted them one by one, holding each to the light, rotating them slowly as I searched for imperfections left behind by the casting. There were none—save for the narrow gold vein where each ring had joined the main sprue, soon to be filed and sanded smooth.

A casting this clean was rare. Two this perfect was nearly impossible.

But then again, it wasn't just my skill as a jeweler at work. I'd had a little supernatural help along the way. I slipped each ring onto my finger in turn, checking the fit. Both were a size six —the same as my ring finger—chosen because my mysterious buyer for the canary diamond claimed his girlfriend wore that size, and because Sorcha had insisted I could make the ruby ring any size I wished. The universe's magic, she said, would guide my hand.

And it had. Some quiet sixth sense had urged me to make it my size as well. Just as surely as the thought had appeared, so too had the understanding that these rings were, in some ineffable way, part of me—like pieces of a puzzle where I was a central figure—designed by forces I didn't yet comprehend.

I softened a couple of chunks of Thermolock with my heat gun until it molded snugly around each ring, to protect the metal while I set the stones. Once cooled, the hardened plastic would shield the shanks as they were locked securely into my bench vice.

I lowered the ruby into its seat—a narrow ledge cut just over a millimeter below the stone's girdle—to check the fit, then shook my head in disbelief. Absolutely perfect. I reached for my ten-power lighted magnification visor, needing a second opinion.

It wasn't necessary.

Steadying myself for the delicate work ahead—bending the

metal over the edge of the ruby, I did some somatic breathing—inhale to the count of four, exhale to the count of four, repeated until I felt still. I picked up my hammer in one hand, bezel pusher in the other, until something made me stop—not fear, but the sudden awareness that this was the point of no return. I dropped them both and called out the Dutch door for Baird.

A blur of color and speed crossed my vision, coming to rest just outside the doorframe. Worry was etched across his face, but it softened instantly into that familiar smirk—the one that melted me from the inside out—when he caught sight of me waiting for him, ridiculous visor and all.

"What is it, lass?" he asked, one eyebrow arched in quiet curiosity.

"I'm about to set the ruby," I said, "...and I don't want to be alone." I winced. "Physically, emotionally...or magically."

"What do ye think is going to happen?" Baird asked—not alarmed, just ready.

"Best case?" I said. "Nothing. Worst case? I invent a whole new category of supernatural OSHA violations. "

The quizzical look on Baird's face told me OSHA hadn't made it into his vocabulary—nor, apparently, into vampire culture at large. "I dinnae ken what that is, love," he said mildly, "but I'll take your word that it's a concern. Either way—ye're safe with me."

God, how I loved that protective streak—the part of him he'd kept hidden from me during that first week we'd met. Only later did I learn he'd spent sleepless nights watching from afar, guarding me without my knowledge, afraid of what Bastien might have planned for either of us. I opened the bottom of the door and he wiped his boots as I pointed to the chair in the small seating area across from my bench. "I have no idea what is going to happen, but whatever it is...I feel better with you here."

He leaned in and placed a kiss on the top of my head as he passed and then squeezed his large frame into one of the upholstered seats. He sat on the edge expectantly, resting his arms on his knees, eyes intently focused on me. I picked up the hammer and pulled my visor down again, pulling the stool up behind me to sit on, and then running my hand along the bench until my fingers found the bezel pusher I'd dropped minutes earlier. "Here goes nothing."

I positioned the tool just off one corner, the face of the pusher angled at forty-five degrees, and delivered a single, confident tap to begin moving the gold over the stone. I rotated the piece in the vise and repeated the motion on the opposite edge. Secure an edge, turn, repeat—methodical, deliberate. Once all four corners were locked in place, I worked my way down the sides between them, always rotating the ring, always pushing metal from opposing directions. After what felt like a thousand tiny taps, the stone was finally held fast—perfectly seated.

The design included four one-millimeter white diamond accents set at the cardinal points—north, south, east, and west —along the outer edge of the bezel, a traditional compass rose. I'd added the element in the hope that its symbolism might help the piece find its intended. Once the ruby focal point was fully set, I turned my attention to the tiny accents.

I let out a long breath and reached for the graver, the small tool with its slightly ominous name. Held at just the right angle and pushed with steady pressure, it carved a clean, bright-cut edge along the inside of the bezel wall that held the ruby, right where metal met stone—the finishing touch that made the piece come alive. After a few careful passes, I nodded, satisfied. All that remained was to heat the Thermolock and free the ring before the final polish. Its surface would stay matte, more reminiscent of an Etruscan relic than the high mirror shine favored by modern jewelry.

No zombies clawed their way from the floor. No mysterious babies appeared in baskets. Just a gentle warmth spreading outward from my chest, like an embrace from the universe itself —*well done.*

"That's it," I said. "Stone's set. No undead surprises." I pulled off the visor and looked up at Baird, still sitting here, watching me.

Baird's mouth curved slowly. "Pity." He said lightly. "I was enjoying standing guard."

"Oh?" I arched a brow. "You look disappointed." I walked over to where he sat and pushed his shoulders back to straddle his legs. His big hands skimmed my thighs suggestively and ended up on either side of my waist. "Sorry it was so anti-climactic."

The sound he made was a low, pleased rumble, a promise of where this was headed. "Watching ye work like that," he murmured, his voice a rough-edged caress. "Steady hands. Total focus. It does things to a man." His hand slid beneath my sweatshirt, unhurried, certain, his touch a brand against my skin.

"Oh yeah?" I purred, arching into his touch. "I think—with a little help from you—we can make this *climactic*." I offered him an innocent look, a transparent challenge I knew he'd never resist.

His gaze, brilliant green and hungry, devoured my face. "Oh, lass," he breathed, tracing my lip with his thumb. "I love it when ye tease me like this. An angel..." I caught the digit between my teeth, biting down gently. A wicked grin split his lips. "...who likes to be very, very bad."

His other hand found the lace edge of my bralette, tugging it down just enough to grant him access. I gasped at the sensation, still humming with the residual warmth of magic from setting the ruby, and realized—suddenly, keenly—how badly my body was aching for his attention. Like a child praised once and greedy for more, every nerve seemed to lean toward him, wanting—expecting—that same approval again. Whether I was tapping into some universal source of magic or losing myself with Baird, the effect on my body was the same: warmth, certainty, and the sense that I was exactly where I was meant to be.

I tugged my sweatshirt higher and slid the other side of my bralette down, craving more—more skin on skin, more contact, less empty space between us. Baird understood the assignment without a word, leaving my breasts only long enough to hook his fingers into the waistband of my leggings and draw them lower, unhurried and sure, as if he'd been waiting for permission all along. I stood impatiently and kicked off my sneakers to help him tug them down the rest of the way. He stood and spun me around, pushing me down into the chair he'd just been occupying, big hands pulling my hips across rough fabric on the chair, until I was perilously hanging off the front of the seat, bare feet flat on the floor. He kneeled in front of me, pushing my thighs wide apart with his, and grinned when he took in the view: me, spread eagle.

"What do you have in mind, Baird Campbell?" I asked, a playful smirk touching my lips even as my body began to hum with anticipation.

"Just realized I haven't given this proper attention lately."

"This?" I asked, tilting my head, coy enough to dare him.

"This," he replied, his tone darkening, every ounce of teasing burned away by want.

A finger pushed between my legs, not teasing, but seeking, delving into the soaking wetness and dragging the slick arousal up to my aching clit. His eyes bored into mine, dark with hunger, as he slipped one long finger deep inside my tight channel, curling it just right before pulling out to force a second in alongside it. I cried out, my spine bowing off the chair as my pussy clenched greedily around the intrusion. Thoughts of the ruby ring disappeared instantly. "Yes," I panted, grinding my hips down to take him deeper, completely unable to hold still as his fingers fucked me with a relentless, expert rhythm. Baird licked his lips, still holding my gaze as he lowered his mouth to my clit, his tongue darting in and out, letting me know this was about me.

Then he slowed his rhythm, his attention narrowing entirely to that sensitive, textured spot on the upper wall of my vagina. He pressed his index finger firmly against it, knowing exactly what he was doing, curling it in a beckoning motion, demanding my body follow. With just the right, deliberate pressure on that spot, that square inch of my body he'd taken full and complete ownership over, he coaxed me toward the inevitable—a messy, uncontrollable flood he treated like manna from heaven.

I cried out, bucking my hips upward to grind against his face—my little tell—the unmistakable signal he'd mastered over the last year. He didn't hesitate, sealing his lips around my swollen, throbbing clit and sucking greedily, all while relentlessly stroking that spot inside me. It was too much, and I shattered, the pleasure cresting until I couldn't hold back another second. Wetness gushed from me in a sudden, relentless surge, and he was right there to catch every drop, his mouth lapping and swallowing until his chin and cheeks were drenched in my essence. A deep, guttural moan vibrated against my core, the taste and feel of me driving him wild. Even now, after all this time, the way he reveled in burying his face in my messy, squirting pussy never ceased to shock me, his sheer ecstasy evident as he drowned in my release.

I dragged myself upright, leaning forward to crush my mouth against his. The rasp of his stubble grazed my skin as I devoured him, tasting my own sweetness on his lips and tongue, sharing the intimacy of every drop he'd just claimed.

He pulled back with a wicked grin, his eyes glinting with that brilliant green fire. "Are ye planning on working late tonight?" he asked, breathless as his gaze swept over my studio, though hope and unspoken desire to carry this right into our cottage was written plainly on his face.

"Um," I breathed, my body still liquid and boneless from the aftershocks. "I'd planned to set the yellow diamond next, but..." My pussy was still fluttering, echoing with spasms that teased a promise of more to come once we were behind closed doors. I met his hungry look and shook my head. "Fuck it." I giggled. "I'll do that one tomorrow."

MORNING DAWNED CRISP AND BRIGHT, a canopy of cloudless blue waiting beyond the windows. Baird was already gone, off with Bunny to check the herd. Cup of coffee in hand, I headed out to the studio to finish the yellow diamond engagement ring.

As I passed the cane chair near the back door, I noticed the leggings and panties I'd discarded on the studio floor the evening before, now washed and folded neatly on the seat, sneakers side by side underneath. I smiled despite myself.

Baird's quiet acts of service still had a way of tugging at my heartstrings. I'd seen my fair share of vampire movies in my thirty years, but none of them featured immortals who were quite so relentlessly neat. He was a baffling contradiction—homebody, trad-wife energy, fiercely feminist to his core—all encased in a body made of sin and certainty. Tender with me. Merciless to anyone who threatened what was his.

I opened the under-counter safe, and pulled the yellow diamond and the cast ring out, the ring still secured in yesterday's thermoplastic cocoon, the very top left open so I could drop in the stone and maneuver it into place. As far as order of operations went, this one was lather, rinse, repeat—familiar, comforting. Just like the ruby—only without the same, bone-deep dread. Like the bright, impossible day outside, the yellow diamond—more shard of sunlight than stone—felt as though it were begging to be finished. Even imagining it in its final state made me nearly giddy.

The design was simple: more eighteen-carat yellow gold, bezel-set like the ruby rather than the more common prongs. The underside of the bezel was pierced to invite light in, to let an expert cut do what it was meant to do—catch, scatter, and return brilliance. My heart felt light as I laid out my tools, and if I focused, I could still feel the lingering effects of the night before—spent breathless and undone in Baird's arms. I should have been exhausted; Baird needed far less sleep than I did.

Instead, I was walking on sunshine. Hammer in one hand, bezel pusher in the other, I turned the swivel vise and made my first strike. My skin flushed, my heart kicking faster—not from fear, but recognition—stepping into a rhythm I already knew. Unlock the vise. Rotate the ring. Lock it again. Strike. Each step familiar, each one newly weighted.

With every measured tap, the metal yielded—subtly, stubbornly—reshaping itself under pressure and intent. I felt it echo inside me. I had spent a lifetime learning when to give, when to resist, when to soften without breaking. This was no different at all.

My magic pressed against my ribs, insistent now, the way heat builds in gold just before it becomes workable. Holding it back took effort, disrupted my rhythm. So I stopped fighting it. I chose to become malleable.

Tap, unlock, spin, lock, tap again. Light spilled from my skin. Flow took me—hands and mind moving as one, thought dissolving into instinct, instinct into motion. Limbs sheathed now in shimmering flares, filling the studio's shadows and claiming every darkened corner.

And just before the final strike, the ring—*this* ring, not the ruby, but this one, the one that felt like part of me—asked for a name. Important diamonds always carried a name—Koh-i-Noor, Hope, Cullinan. "Brigid's Sun," I said to no one. And a thought, fleeting, yet I couldn't force it away, dwelled inside me...something was missing.

Blood.

Instinct took over—calm, certain. I grabbed the box cutter from my bench and willed flame into my palm, passing the blade briefly through the fire to sterilize it. I waved it once to cool, then pressed the tip into the pad of my finger. A single drop of blood welled up. I pressed it to the stone. The diamond answered—igniting into a supernatural supernova. And in that brilliance, a shape emerged in the middle of the studio. Human in form, but wrought entirely of light. And a voice—*her voice*—echoing in my head.

"*You are not merely a smith—you are a poet. Metal and fire your prose and verse. In your hands, a token—an amulet.*"

I looked down at the ring clamped in my vise, the yellow diamond fully set, lit from within by an unearthly glow. My pulse thudded in my ears, questions colliding faster than I could catch them. She was talking about this ring.

"*My name, my blessings and abundance bestowed upon the one who bears it.*"

She meant for me to imbue this ring with magic—somehow—but I couldn't ignore the widening circle of it all. The ruby finding me. The power everyone else seemed to recognize before I did. The Mother's Book appearing when it did. The spellwork that came too easily, too cleanly.

"Why?" I demanded. "Why this magic—the light—the fire?" I flung my hands upward, hammer and bezel pusher still locked in my grip. The questions tumbled out of me, tangled and raw—every doubt I'd swallowed, every question Sorcha dodged with a shrug and a smile. "The ruby—the—why *me*?" It came out in a tumble, the real question. Maybe the only question I needed an answer to. I wasn't afraid of the light or the fire—I was astonished by them. What nagged at me was the reason I'd been singled out. *Why me?* The thought had followed me since the first night light spilled from my limbs, Baird's arms still wrapped around me.

The voice that followed was gentle, steadying, soothing the panic that was knotted tight with exhilaration.

"You believe this is happening to you. But it is happening through you, Mira."

The goddess wasn't going to spill her secrets. She wasn't about to hand me neat, tidy answers and tie them up with a pretty bow.

"You want reasons," the goddess said gently. *"Names. Beginnings. Endings."*

Her presence warmed the air, not with heat, but with certainty. *"Power is not a story told in order,"* she went on. *"It does not arrive with explanations or ask for your comfort before it takes root."*

I huffed out a quiet breath despite myself. Of course she wasn't going to make this easy.

"You ask why you," she continued, unbothered by my irritation. *"You stopped turning from the Sight. A door opened. You began to trust what others saw in you, and then let yourself see. Another door."*

The light around me softened, settling instead of flaring.

"There are bloodlines that remember—" she continued, *"—not in names or faces—but in instinct. In the way the hands know what to do before the mind catches up."*

My fingers curled unconsciously around the tools I still held, wood and steel extensions of my own hands, reacting to the words.

"You are a maker. And some of your people before you," Brigid said. *"Shapers. Those who bind what is seen to what is felt. You do not command fire, Mira—you listen to it, more equal partner than master."*

The diamond pulsed once, warm and steady. A silent nod of agreement.

"That is why the ruby answered you," she said. *"Why the book*

opened to your hands. Why the spells came not as study, but as recall."

I swallowed. "So I was...born for this?"

A pause, careful and measured. "*You were born capable,*" Brigid said at last.

Her voice gentled further. "*Some legacies do not seek power,*" she added. "*They seek return.*"

I turned that over in my head, knowing the choice of words wasn't an accident, yet still unable to understand her meaning.

She offered no clarification, only a final command that lingered long after her voice faded:

"*The blood you gave the yellow gem, you must give to the ruby as well. It requires a piece of you to complete what it was made to do.*"

And then the light—and the goddess—were gone.

I pulled the ruby ring from the safe and laid it on the bench. Then I lifted my finger—the one I'd pierced with the box cutter—and squeezed. Blood welled at the tip, bright and familiar, and the sight of it pulled me backward in time. To the class at the Goldsmith's Guild when I'd cut my finger while making the pendant. The night I'd tested Baird's control by offering him my blood. The night he'd taken what I gave without knowing the chain of events it would set in motion—the bond forming between us before he, or I, truly understood what it meant.

I wondered if that impulse had been mine at all...or if the goddess had been guiding my hand even then. Like the yellow diamond before it, I pressed the drop of blood into the surface of the ruby.

"May Brigid bless the wearer of this ring," I whispered, "and guide them back to the one who seeks them."

The ruby flared to life beneath my touch. Magic stirred

within it—deep and quiet, not brilliant like Brigid's Sun, but just as potent. Its purpose settled into the stone, deliberate and sure. And for the first time, I didn't doubt how this chapter of the ruby's story would end.

Tomorrow, I'd put the final polish on the ruby ring, photograph it from a dozen angles, post it to Instagram and my website, and wait for the right buyer to find it. Then afterward, I'd email Aaron Thorndale to let him know his fiancée's ring was complete, send the invoice for the balance due, and prepare it for shipping.

That part was easy. What wouldn't be easy was boxing up the glittering yellow diamond—the one that had started to feel like a piece of me—and letting it go. That part was going to hurt.

19

WEDDING

Magda—August 1387

Dani's parents had spoken with an uncle who owned a small cottage for rent. It wasn't as large as their own but compared to the place I had shared with Buna, it felt almost luxurious. A clay oven stood outside, shared with the neighbors, and a little outhouse crouched behind the garden patch.

My dowry was meager—only a set of beautifully embroidered blankets and linens that had been my mother's, carefully kept in Buna's trunk for the day I would wed. Before the ceremony, Buna and Dani's mother went door to door through the village, asking after unwanted pots and pans, plates and utensils. The villagers offered their hand-me-downs readily, and soon our kitchen was full.

The gift from Dani's parents was the finest of all—a new bed, wide enough for the two of us, waiting in that small cottage that would be our home.

Buna had worked for days, and long into the nights, to sew me a new dress of pale linen, her needle pulling bright threads of red, pink, and deep blue into patterns that circled the neckline, sleeves, and hem. My only other fine dress had already begun to grow tight as my breasts swelled, betraying the secret I carried. For the veil, I wore my mother's lace—the same she had worn at her own wedding—carefully folded away with the bed linens in Buna's old trunk, waiting all these years for this day.

The ceremony was held on the steps of the church by the village square. When it ended, the guests—Dani's sprawling family, Buna, and the neighbors from beside our little cottage—crowded into his parents' home. We feasted on pit-roasted pig, cornmeal porridge, warm bread still steaming from the oven, bowls of fresh fruit, and sweet cheese pastries layered with sour cream and preserves. After the meal came the toasts, the laughter, the dancing that spilled out into the yard as twilight settled over the rooftops.

It was a good wedding. And yet, as I moved among the well-wishers, smiling when I was expected to smile, lifting my face for kisses and blessings, I could not quiet the strange sensation that I was inhabiting a life slightly out of alignment with my own—as though I had stepped into the place of another bride while the future I had once imagined quietly closed its doors behind me.

At some point, Dani drew me aside. He slipped his arms around me from behind—still unfamiliar, his size overwhelming, his body dwarfing mine. But the warmth of his embrace wrapped around me, and with several cups of honey mead in me, I was not immune to its comfort. I hated myself for wanting it, that comfort.

"It's time for us to slip away...to our home," he whispered against my ear, his voice meant for me alone.

My heart hammered, dread curling tight in my chest—not just for what tonight would bring, but for what it meant that I'd chosen the only path left to me. I knew, with a quiet certainty that hurt more than fear ever could, that I didn't love Dani. Not in the way he wanted. Not in the way he deserved.

But the guests noticed, mistaking my anxiety for typical wedding night jitters, and they began to cheer, shouting their encouragement, their laughter turning bawdy with jokes about the wedding night and crude remarks about Dani's size. He blushed scarlet, while I stood caught between excitement and dread, my heart racing with both.

We said our goodbyes and slipped out, hand in hand, Dani carrying a candle to light the short walk to our new home. The revelers' laughter and music faded behind us, swallowed by the night. At the door, Dani swung it open and stepped inside. This threshold, at least, required only the smallest bow of his tall frame. He turned back, his hand extended to me, waiting.

I lingered there, my breath caught. To step inside was to accept the life I had fought against so fiercely, the life I had sworn I would never surrender to—yet here it was, waiting, claiming me all the same. For a heartbeat, I wanted to run. Then I thought of Dani—his kindness, his goodness that I had never truly earned. I forced the smile to my lips, pressed down the rebellion deep inside me, and placed my hand in his and crossed the threshold—into the cottage, into the marriage bed, into the life that had chosen me.

He passed the candle to me and I carried it into the bedroom, the small space separated from the main room by nothing more than a curtain, and set it on the bedside table. Its flame wavered and snapped, casting erratic shafts of light that made the shadows seem alive. For once, I was grateful for the near darkness. My waist had begun to thicken—it wasn't yet obvious, but I knew—and I whispered a silent prayer of thanks that Dani had never seen me bare before tonight.

When I turned back, he was still in the main room, standing motionless, watching me through the framed opening. I couldn't read his expression. Maybe nerves. I was nervous too, but for a different reason—dreading the question that would inevitably come when he noticed I didn't bleed on the sheets.

Still, I forced myself forward, taking the lead. I kicked off my shoes, unbuckled the wide belt at my waist, and let it fall to the floor with a soft thud. I laughed, quick and nervous, and Dani seemed to take the cue, crossing the room and sitting on the edge of the bed to tug off his boots.

Turning my back to him, I pulled my dress over my head and laid it neatly across a chair, then slid free of my shift, suddenly shy in my own skin. Naked, I drew in a steadying breath before turning to face him. And like me, he wore not a single stitch of clothing. At least I could give him this first—the first time to see a man completely naked, and be seen in the same way.

The sight of him stole my breath. Dani was nothing like Caius—nothing lean or sharp about him. He was built of mass and weight, a wall of solid muscle from the thick curve of his calves and thighs to his broad chest, wide shoulders, and arms like great wooden beams. The reality of what was about to happen hit me all at once, rooting me in place as a cold rush of fear slid through my veins.

I did not know how much experience he had. I had never

seen him with other girls, though he often traveled with his father to markets in larger towns—places where a man might disappear into the crowd and return with secrets no one at home would question. Perhaps he had been with someone there. Perhaps he had learned things I could not even name.

As for me, though Caius and I had spent long weeks stealing kisses and wandering hands beneath the oak tree, I had only given myself fully once—only once crossed that quiet, trembling threshold I now stood before again. I could not decide whether that single surrender made me worldly...or merely aware of how little I truly understood.

The worry must have shown on my face, because Dani reached for my hand. With the other, he gently tipped my chin upward until my eyes met his. There was no impatience there, no expectation—only tenderness. His shy smile was so boyish that a laugh slipped out of me before I could stop it. In that instant, the tension eased, and I was grateful for it.

"We can start with kissing," he said, and the simple earnestness of it made me laugh again.

"Yes, that would be good," I whispered, winding my arms around his neck and drawing him down to me. His lips met mine—warm and soft—far gentler than I'd expected, achingly so. The kiss wrapped around me; a warm cocoon I hadn't realized I'd been longing for. When his tongue brushed mine, tentative at first, then surer when I welcomed him, a shiver ran through me. He drew me closer, one of his large hands sliding over my body until it cupped my breast, and I gasped—caught between surprise and the slow, unsteady thrill unfurling beneath it.

I felt him hard against me, the difference in our height so stark that his cock pressed just beneath the curve of my breast.

The awkwardness of it made me think it might be easier if we were lying down. I pulled back slightly, lowering myself to sit on the edge of the bed, and patted the blankets beside me in invitation.

But instead of sitting, he surprised me. Dani sank to his knees in front of me and gently parted my legs. I gasped, heat rushing to my face, feeling suddenly exposed beneath his gaze, unsure of what he wanted from me in that position. For a heartbeat, fear cut through me—was he trying to test me, to see if I was still untouched? The thought made me freeze. Yet the look in his eyes was not suspicion, but something else entirely, and he mistook the fear on my face for another kind of hesitation.

"I just want to see you—touch you—taste you," he said shyly, one hand rubbing my thigh, as much I think to steady himself as reassure me.

Words escaped me. I hadn't expected this, Caius had touched me between my legs, rubbed the sensitive spot that I touched when I was alone in my bed. But our joining had been frantic, clothes pushed up, pulled down, no negative space between us echoing with yearning and vibrating with possibility. No, this was different.

I didn't want to deny Dani, and if this was what he needed from me, I couldn't turn away. I eased back onto one elbow, still propped up enough to watch him. There was a kind of wonder in the way his hand touched me—tentative at first, as if testing the reality of me. His fingertips traced delicate paths, brushing warmth into places already trembling with anticipation, and when he lingered, my breath caught on a gasp I couldn't disguise.

His eyes widened, awestruck, as though he'd stumbled into a mystery he'd never expected to solve. The weight of his palm, the slow exploration of his fingers, sent shivers scattering across my skin. My head fell back, hair spilling over my shoulders, and a sharp inhale escaped me as sensation bloomed deeper, fuller.

And then he bent closer, his breath fanning over me—soft, warm, intimate. My chest rose in a broken sob I hadn't meant to release, guilt and longing tangled in the sound. I arched toward him, not knowing whether it was Caius or Dani I betrayed in that moment, only that my body was already answering him.

The brush of his lips was a shock, tender and reverent, the sensation a lightning bolt to my core. I shuddered, every nerve awake, every thought drowned in the urgency of wanting more —wanting *him*—while the weight of my divided heart pressed heavy and unrelenting.

"What are you doing?" I panted, disoriented. My voice, heavy with arousal, sounded like a stranger's.

He ducked his head shyly. "I'd heard the men talking...they said women like that." The tips of his ears tinged red. "And I wanted to please you, Magda. Did it not? Do you not like it?" His words hung between us, so sincere they made my chest ache. I reached to touch his face, fingers brushing over the heat of his cheek, still damp with the closeness of me. His eyes lifted, uncertain, searching for any hint of rejection. The innocence in his question nearly undid me. I should have pulled away, should have reminded myself of my loyalty to Caius. But my body betrayed me, humming with the aftershocks of what Dani had stirred. His touch lingered like fire beneath my skin.

"I liked it," I whispered, though guilt pressed heavily against the words. "Very much."

His lips curved into the smallest, hopeful smile, though his gaze never stopped searching mine—wanting only to know if he had done right by me, if he had given me something I wanted.

"I didn't know this was part of...how it is..." I murmured, surprise threading through my breath. "But it feels good...don't stop."

Then a thought struck me and I pushed up on my elbows, searching his face. "Wait—do you like it?" The question tumbled out almost as an afterthought, but underneath it was a true fear—that this was only for me, that he took no joy in it.

For a moment his expression was unreadable. Then his mouth broke into a wide grin, boyish and utterly disarming, the kind that lit his whole face. His eyes—heavy-lidded and drowsy only moments ago—were suddenly bright, alive.

"Yes," he said without hesitation, voice warm with certainty. "I could spend hours here if you let me."

A small laugh escaped my lips at that thought. Satisfied, I let my body soften, sinking back into the bed. There was so much I didn't know—so much yet to learn about all the ways it could be between a man and a woman.

Dani bent to me again, his breath warm as he lowered his mouth, and I closed my eyes to surrender to the rush of sensation. But the instant I did, it wasn't Dani I saw. It was Caius— his face, his voice, the claim he had on my heart. The intrusion jolted me, and I forced my eyes open, desperate to anchor myself in Dani's presence.

I fixed my gaze on him, on the earnest devotion shining in his expression. My heart might have belonged elsewhere, but my body answered Dani without hesitation. That much was real, even if it was confusing. It was something I could give him —something that mattered to him—and perhaps that was enough.

What it revealed about me, I wasn't certain. But for now, I chose not to ask the question.

He moved with an enthusiasm that left me dizzy, each touch more insistent, more consuming. His eagerness carried a kind of intoxication all its own, and I found myself giving over to it—my hand sliding into his hair, urging him closer, while the other fisted into the blankets.

The world blurred into sensation—breathless, urgent, impossible to contain. My body arched against the air, every nerve stretched taut as though I might unravel with the next heartbeat. And then it came, sudden and overwhelming, crashing through me with a force that left me crying out into the stillness of the cottage, praying the neighbors hadn't returned from the wedding celebration.

I caught his face above me, the faintest smile tugging at his lips—quiet, triumphant, as though he'd won some private battle. With an easy movement he slid beside me, pulling me close until my body curved against his. His knee nudged between mine, a silent reminder of the heat still pulsing through him, of the hunger he hadn't yet sated.

He kissed me then, softly, tenderly, the warmth of his lips lingering like the sweetness of the mead we'd shared earlier. There was a new taste to him too—something sweet and salty, and intimate—that made my chest ache with the strangeness of it all. And then the moment came—the one I had been dreading since the day I'd whispered yes to his proposal. He shifted, guiding me gently onto my back, his body moving over mine until his shadow and warmth covered me. One hand braced against the mattress beside my head, the other hovering with careful intent.

The boyish smile that had lit his face only moments ago

was gone, replaced by a furrow of uncertainty. Worry softened his features, though I couldn't tell if it was for him...or for me. My breath caught, fear and anticipation twisting together as his weight pressed over me—a promise I wasn't sure I was ready to meet. But this was the bed I had made, and now I had no choice but to lie in it.

"If I hurt you, just tell me and I'll stop," he whispered, breath uneven. I could see the battle in him—the raw urgency that begged him to claim me, and the fragile restraint that held him back. His eyes searched mine, dark with want yet softened by worry, as though my answer alone could decide which part of him would win.

I nodded, a small gesture that told him I was ready, even if my heart still raced. When he pushed inside me, a sharp gasp tore from my throat. It wasn't pain—more the shock of being opened. The sudden fullness was overwhelming, leaving me breathless, clutching at him for steadiness.

He stilled, searching my face for an answer. I couldn't find the words, so I pulled him down and kissed him hard, letting him feel my answer in the press of my mouth. My hands moved over him, tracing the strong lines of his back, gripping him closer. My body, hesitant at first, began to find its own rhythm —guided by instinct, by the quiet urgency in him, by the simple need to meet him where he was.

He responded with a fervor that left no room for hesitation. Each movement grew rougher, more desperate, until he was lost in it—lost in me—his voice breaking on a cry that tore from his chest. And though my heart twisted with guilt, my body reveled in the abandon of it, in the way he wanted nothing in that moment but me.

And that was what unsettled me most of all: that I liked it.

That part of me thrilled in his desire, even as another part of me recoiled, ashamed. Dani curled his large frame around me, pulling the blankets over us with a protective finality. His arm draped heavy across my hip, and within moments his breath slowed into an easy rhythm, soft snores brushing against the back of my neck. I lay awake long after, slipping into only brief, restless dozes. For years I had dreamed of sharing a bed with a man of my own, of knowing the comfort of that closeness. But it wasn't *this* man I had imagined. That truth pressed against me more heavily than his arm ever could.

At dawn, when the light crept through the shutters, I turned to find him already stirring. Whether he noticed the lack of blood on the sheets—or chose not to see—I couldn't tell. The question I had dreaded never came. And I wondered if it was love that spared me, or simply his choice to guard a secret he did not wish to confront. But I was grateful either way.

20

BLUE EYES

Magda—March 1388

A month after our wedding, I told Dani I was with child. If he suspected anything, he never let on. His face broke into a wide, guileless smile, and soon his joy spread like fire through the village. He told anyone who would listen that we had been blessed so quickly. Maybe it was only my guilt, but I thought I caught the women's glances as I passed in the street—judgmental, knowing looks that made my stomach twist. Every day I feared someone might say something to Dani. But if they did, he never spoke of it.

I still worked alongside Buna for several hours each day, taking over her rounds when her bones ached or illness slowed her—something that happened more often as the years pressed heavier on her. Several times a week, I carried lunch to Dani at the forge.

Even before I reached the barn, heat spilled into the air.

Sometimes I lingered in the doorway, watching him stand before the fire, metal glowing in the flames, his broad hands steady on the long tongs as he drew it free. With a single, practiced motion, he laid the iron on the anvil and lifted his mallet, shaping the molten metal into a sword, a knife—like the one that hung from my belt—or a piece of armor meant for a soldier, sparks flying with each strike.

The tools were heavy, but in his hands they seemed almost weightless. There was always a small smile tugging at his lips as he worked, the expression of a man doing exactly what he had been made to do. His life was simple. And he was utterly content—fulfilled by his work, our home, our child on the way. I wished I could feel the same ease, the same satisfaction. But I was restless. Always restless.

I had settled into the same routine every married woman in the village endured—cooking, cleaning, then cooking and cleaning again. At night, when the house lay wrapped in darkness, I gave my body to my husband. If the days left me hollowed out, the nights with Dani were my only reprieve—the only time I felt truly alive.

As my belly swelled with child, my hunger for release only grew sharper, more insistent, and Dani was more than willing to meet it. My heart still clung stubbornly to Caius, but my body—my traitorous body—had become an instrument Dani knew how to play with practiced ease.

At least I could give him that.

MY PAINS BEGAN one evening as I was clearing the table after supper. Dani's face blanched when I doubled over, but I told him it would be a while yet, and he must fetch Buna when the time came. I forced myself to finish the dishes, pacing the floor to ease the ache, Dani shadowing me, his worry etched so plainly across his face it might as well have been written there: *too soon—the baby isn't due for another month.* Yet he never spoke the words aloud.

Then, hours later as I paced, I heard the faint splash at my feet. I froze, the sudden wetness soaking my skirts and spreading across the floor. Another pain gripped me, sharp and undeniable. I met Dani's wide eyes and nodded. "It's time. Go —bring Buna."

When Dani returned with Buna, none of the fear I had braced myself to see clung to her. My mother had died giving birth, and I thought surely the memory would haunt her now. But if it did, she hid it well. She carried herself like a general, issuing quiet commands with no room for hesitation or doubt.

When the moment drew close, she ushered Dani out the door, pressing a mug of plum wine into his hand. "Bad luck for the father to watch a baby come into the world," she said firmly. And not long after, his absence perfectly timed, I gave one furious cry as the child slipped from me into Buna's waiting arms.

"A girl! A beautiful, healthy girl!" Buna's voice trembled with joy, tears glimmering in eyes that rarely softened. She swaddled the babe, laid her at my breast, then leaned to the doorway to call Dani back inside. "Come, meet your daughter."

The giant of a man entered, stricken at first—but when his gaze fell on her, wonder overtook him. He sat on the edge of the bed with impossible gentleness, bent, and pressed a kiss to her tiny brow. At his touch, her eyelids fluttered open.

Cornflower-blue eyes. The same brilliant blue as Caius.

Not my dark-as-night eyes. Not Dani's brown, warmed with flecks of gold. My gut twisted with certainty. Many babes were born with blue eyes, only for them to darken with time—but if hers did not, if they remained the blue of a cloudless summer sky, they would betray her the moment anyone truly looked.

I wanted him to say it. To admit that he knew. I wanted his anger—his rage—anything that might free me from the crushing weight of this guilt. Buna stood in the doorway, her perceptive gaze taking in everything; she knew exactly what was racing through my mind.

But Dani said nothing. Only that quiet, steady goodness of his—so gentle, so unyielding, it threatened to drown me. Fine. If silence was the game he meant to play, then I would play it too. I wiped my eyes and drew a steadying breath.

Dani looked up at me and lifted a hand, brushing my sweat-damp hair back from my face. "How do you feel?" he asked, his voice unsteady, thick with emotions too large for even his great frame to hold.

I nodded my head to assure him I felt strong, but it was Buna's words that seemed to relieve his worry.

"She came through without trouble. An easy birth...Magda and the babe are both healthy, Dani. No need to worry," Buna said, resting a reassuring hand on his shoulder.

Relief softened his brow. He bent and pressed a kiss to my damp forehead—just as he had to the child moments earlier—then turned back to her, wonder still etched across his face. "What shall we call you, little one?" he whispered.

"Anca. After my mother," I said quickly, the words tumbling

out before doubt could catch them. We had never spoken of names before this moment, and I prayed he would not question it.

"Anca Veró," he repeated, shaping the syllables with care, letting them linger on his tongue. Veró—his family's name, born of the word *to strike*, a legacy of metalsmiths carried down through generations.

21

DREAM OF THE GODDESS

Mira—April 2026

I am in darkness, voices swirling around me—calling, whispering—yet I am not afraid. Their tones are soft, crooning, and they carry light with them, a vortex of gold and white spinning as I stand at its heart, the still point of the hurricane.

I look down and realize I am no longer standing at all. I'm weightless, lifted by the voices themselves. Euphoria hums through me as invisible hands bear me higher and higher, until I am soaring through the night on the wings of sound—protected, guided, urged forward.

Below, the world falls away. I see Glen Chalmadale, the upland valley where my mother's favorite song played when I first arrived on the island, and as I pass, mountains rise from shadow, and I descend toward one—slowly, deliberately—alighting on a narrow ledge just below its summit.

A brilliance bursts before me—sunlight made solid, a crystal flare that blinds. From its heart a figure forms: a woman with flowing *auburn hair, eyes the color of new leaves, robes of deep green that shimmer like moss in rain. Her skin is pale as moonlight, her presence radiates power. Brigid in her human form.*

And as she steps toward me, something in her face—and in the cadence of her voice—feels achingly familiar, looking into the mirror of my own soul.

"Mirren Garvie," the goddess intones, using my full name, her voice a low thrum rising from under the mountain itself. "You have denied your magic long enough. No more. The others who came before you were not enough—they could not wield the flame—but you—you are more than enough. More than I ever required."

I try to answer her, to question what she means, but no sound comes. My voice—the one that doubted, the one that reasoned—is gone. When I open my mouth again, the sound that emerges isn't mine alone. It is hers—our voices joined, echoing through the darkness, layered like a chord. We speak together until I can no longer tell where her words end and mine begin—until belief replaces doubt, and I am her voice.

"You are the chosen one I have waited for—my spark reborn in mortal flesh. The one another spoke of, whose words were ignored, dismissed as mad ramblings. Make no mistake, maker of flame: you may flee from your calling, but you cannot escape it."

I move toward her, drawn by a magnetic pull I can't resist—an invisible current urging me closer. I want to touch her, to feel the heat of her radiance, to brush my fingers against the pulse of the universe itself. Her power is infinite, mesmerizing in its brilliance—yet beneath it runs something soft, almost maternal, a tenderness that reaches for me as surely as I reach for her.

"You are mine now, as you have always been. Let the fire I placed within you burn freely; let it move through your veins as I willed it in the beginning. The world has need of your light again."

Her hand caresses my face and joy floods my body, and then she is gone and I am alone.

I SAT bolt upright in bed, heart pounding, breath coming in short bursts as if I'd just sprinted down the mountain to reach the cottage. Baird, ever attuned—aware of everything and everyone around him—was already alert. A one-man telemetry monitor, more accurate than any machine in the finest hospital, he'd registered every spike in my pulse, every shift in my breathing. A silent alarm had gone off, one only he could hear.

It wasn't a warning alarm, not exactly. I wasn't afraid. But my body's response didn't lie. The dream had been so vivid, so powerful, that for one dizzy moment I wasn't sure I'd woken at all. If I hadn't been naked in our bed—with a slightly worried vampire watching me, wide-eyed and tense—I might've believed I was still there, standing before the goddess herself.

"Love—what was that?" he asked quietly, his voice edged with caution. He reached out, slow and deliberate, as though afraid I might vanish if he moved too fast. "Can ye tell me? Your heart is racing," he murmured. "But it's no fear I'm feelin. It's… something else."

I leaned into his palm like a cat, letting his touch anchor me. "Give me a sec," I whispered. "I just need to get my feet back under me." The moment his skin met mine, the light stirred—flaring where he touched me, spilling through the cracks between his fingers. It shimmered against his skin, my light refusing to be contained, refusing to dim.

"I was flying through the night," I said slowly, still catching my breath, "and I ended up on the summit of Goat Fell. The goddess Brigid was there—she met me on the mountain and told me I was chosen. But I don't know," I shook my head. "...chosen for what?" My head snapped up as the scrawling handwriting from the margins of the Mother's Book popped into my mind's eye. *We were not chosen. Some were spared. Some were not.*

Baird frowned. "Ye were mumbling," he said quietly. "But it didnae sound like just you. It was more...two voices speaking at once."

"Yes!" I gasped, the image from the book slipping from my mind as the dream surged forward. I could hear it again—the way my voice had merged with hers, our words threading together in perfect, chilling unison. I was smiling before I realized it, beaming, the elation still coursing through my veins. "I felt—" I stopped, searching for the word. "Right. Like something finally clicked into place." I was sure of something—something vast and profound—only now uncertain what, exactly, I was so certain of.

I turned to Baird, expecting to see relief, maybe even shared wonder in his eyes. But instead, I found only confusion—the faint crease between his brows deepening, that familiar look he wore when something unsettled him. It was a look I hadn't seen often since I'd come back to him, and its return sent a ripple of unease through my joy.

"Don't look like that..." I said softly, trying to lace the words with humor, to pull us back from whatever edge we'd stumbled onto. I hated seeing him worry—hated the tension he wore in his jaw when he looked at me like I might break. I wanted the other look instead, the one he so often gave me—like I was something wondrous, something not quite of this world. And now that I'd finally started to believe it too, I hoped it wouldn't change things between us.

His stubborn scowl held fast. With a small sigh, I slipped back beneath the blankets, pressing close until I was folded against him. His arms came around me automatically, strong and sure, wrapping me in the familiar cocoon of his protection, a soft kiss pressed to the top of my head. And after a moment, the goddess, the dream, the light—all of it—fell away, and there was only us.

22

———

MAD RAMBLINGS

Baird—April 2026

Baird shrugged into his heavy coat and whistled for Bunny before heading out the cottage door. As he passed Mira's studio, he leaned over the half-door to call out that they were off to check the herd—but stopped short. Mira stood beside her bench, palm upturned, a steady flame blooming from the center of her hand—as natural now as breath. With calm precision, she brought the torch toward it, the hiss of the gas signaling it was ready to catch, and then the flare of the dragon before she adjusted the balance of oxygen and acetylene, the striker that always sat at the ready on her bench now obsolete.

He stayed silent, watching her the way he often did—entranced, half-afraid to break whatever spell she'd woven around herself. Her focus was complete, her face illuminated by the small miracle she'd just performed. He wanted to share her wonder, to let it fill him with the same awe it once had. But lately, something darker had begun to stir beneath that admiration—a whisper of unease he couldn't quite name.

When she finally turned and saw him—lit torch in one hand, eyes bright with triumph—color rose to her cheeks. She blushed, realizing he'd witnessed her summon the flame from within her own palm. Her smile was harnessed sunlight—brilliant, effortless—and the sight of it cracked something tender and painful inside him, because it looked so certain. He only lifted a hand in farewell, a simple gesture to say they were off to the hills. Mira blew him a kiss, her expression bright, before turning back to her bench and to her work.

When Mira had woken from the dream two nights ago—not frightened, not shattered from nightmare—but restless all the same, he had known it instantly. There had been a current in her, a bright, humming energy that did not belong to fear. Excitement, perhaps. He had felt her pulse racing beneath his palm, the swift percussion of adrenaline alive in her veins. It had startled him at first—the intensity of it—but when he searched her face, there had been no terror there. No lingering shadow in her eyes. And for that alone, he had breathed a quiet prayer of thanks into the dark.

She'd mumbled words in a voice that didn't sound exactly like her, too high and too low, the wrong cadence, yet dynamic and omnipotent just the same. But as soon as she was fully awake, relaying what she'd seen, Baird began to feel uneasy. *"I was chosen,"* she'd whispered. *"Many were not enough, but I am. It's Brigid, the goddess—she's chosen me—but for what I'm not sure."* She was confused by the dream, looking for the message that was lingering just past the point of comprehension, and grasping for it all the same.

It struck him then—how her tone mirrored Agnes's fevered prophecies, a photograph negative made flesh. Every trembling, fearful utterance Agnes had once spoken now echoed back through Mira's calm conviction, eerily similar in language, stripped only of the terror and paranoia. Most of what Agnes had said in the height of her episodes sounded wild, unhinged—ramblings that rarely made sense. And now, those words were playing over and over again in his head.

"She's coming for me because I'm not the one. I'm not enough—I'll never be enough. One of us must die each generation for our sins, until the chosen appears—and the ones we love will not be safe."

Those things that hadn't made sense—the tangled mutterings, the half-phrased warnings—had always seemed to circle back to Bastien. At the time, Baird had dismissed the shifting *he* and *she* in her ramblings as confusion, the fraying of her mind. But now, he wasn't so sure. It struck him, with the weight of inevitability, that Agnes had known exactly who she spoke of—and what she meant. The guilt he'd thought long buried rose again, pressing in until it was hard to breathe.

"And one day, after I am gone, she'll come for the one chosen and take her from ye as well. Remember this, Baird. Remember."

She'd repeated it like a warning carved into stone, meant to outlast her. Over and over, urging him not to forget. The meaning had always eluded him. He'd never known whether the loss she spoke of would be a child, or a woman he had yet to meet—but the certainty in her voice had left no doubt that she believed the loss would be real.

When Sorcha first claimed she could see the magic in Mira, Baird had felt a quiet pride. He'd seen it too, simmering just beneath her skin, aching to be known. Mira couldn't see it herself then. Maybe it was that uneasy feeling of being different, strange, that made her deny what she was.

Then Granny Margaret gave her the family grimoire, and everything shifted. Curiosity came first, then confidence, until she began to glow with it—her skill sharpening, expanding, beyond anything he'd expected. Every spare moment found her bent over its pages, chasing meaning, pulled deeper and deeper as the book seemed to unlock something within her, a hidden current of energy that pulsed brighter with each passing day. Everyone could see it now, even Mira. But the dreams, the conviction that someone was testing her, that she was being drawn toward something inevitable...those echoes were beginning to sound hauntingly like Agnes's prophecies. Only this time, Mira *was* chosen. But chosen for what—and by whom?

Baird suspected Granny Margaret knew more than she let on, and perhaps Sorcha did too. The thought unsettled him, a cold weight pressing into his gut. With each new power Mira unlocked, each page of the Mother's Book she turned, the more certain he became: whatever force had chosen her was also taking her farther away from him—into something he couldn't yet see.

The entire walk into the high valley, he'd asked himself a dozen times—more, maybe—how he could learn the truth before it was too late. Granny Margaret, he knew, would speak in riddles if she spoke at all; truth with her always came tangled in threads of misdirection.

But Sorcha—perhaps Sorcha would tell him. The truth about the book. About Mira's awakening powers. About what it meant to be *chosen*. Robbie always said Sorcha had ways of knowing things, that her reach brushed against the gods themselves. She'd become a guide to Mira, helping her draw out the power she'd once denied. And yet, more and more, Baird couldn't shake the feeling that Sorcha wasn't just mentoring Mira—she was watching Mira herself, waiting for more pieces of a puzzle to fall into place.

23
———

THE TELL

Baird—April 2026

Robbie's pub was packed when Baird stepped through the door, the air thick with laughter and the comforting scent of peat smoke and spilled ale. Bunny trotted straight toward her spot by the hearth as if she owned the place, nails clicking smartly against the worn flagstone floor. The locals barely looked up—just a few knowing nods—but the tourists *ooed* and *ahhed*, hands outstretched as she passed. Ever the polite lass, Bunny paused to accept a few pats as she went, her tail sweeping slow arcs of approval, before circling exactly twice and flopping down with a satisfied grunt in front of the fire.

Robbie was hunched behind the bar, mopping up a spill beside a tray stacked with frothing pints waiting to be whisked off to a table. The tang of malt and bleach mingled in the air as he worked, sleeves rolled past his elbows. "What brings ye in,

Baird?" he asked, not looking up, his cloth sweeping one last clean pass over the bar top.

Baird sat with the question for a moment, rolling it around in his mind like a stone he couldn't quite push uphill—not because he was afraid of the answer, but because of where it might lead. The last thing he wanted was to set Robbie off again with talk of witches and magic. The man always turned his most curmudgeonly when those topics surfaced—his lingering disapproval of Mira still grated on Baird, truth be told —and Baird didn't want to hand him more ammunition. He'd learned, the hard way, what happened when he let other people's fears shape the truths he chose to share. He drew a slow breath, steadying himself, and tried to make his voice sound casual, as if this were nothing more than the easy banter shared between old friends.

"Ach, ye know," Baird began, aiming for nonchalance. "I was hoping ye could tell Sorcha I'd like a word with her—at her convenience, of course. But..." He hesitated, rubbing the back of his neck. "...maybe best Mira doesnae hear of it just yet." He added, the words tasting like betrayal even as he told himself they were protection.

That earned him Robbie's full attention. The man straightened, scowl carving lines across his face as he tossed the rag onto the bar with a wet slap. He planted his boots wide, all five foot eight of him radiating the kind of stubborn defiance that usually ended in a row.

"And what am I now, Baird Campbell?" Robbie shot back. "Your messenger between the witches?"

Baird gave a guilty shrug before glancing around. "Lower your voice," Baird muttered. "And Mira's no a witch." Even as he said it, he wasn't sure if it was true, not knowing which side of the line Mira's powers drew from.

Robbie ignored him completely, his tone climbing an octave the way it always did when he was riled. "Oh, is she no?" he shot back. "And that thing ye do—rubbin' the back o' your neck —that's your tell, ye ken. Ye think I cannae see when somethin's troublin' ye?"

Baird stilled his hand at once, irritation flaring—not at Robbie but at himself for slipping. He straddled the nearest barstool, and settled in, knowing Robbie wouldn't be satisfied until he'd heard it all. "Mira's been engrossed in that Garvie grimoire since Granny Margaret gave it to her, and she's never been happier. And I've been fully supportive of it," he said— and mostly that was true. "It's unlocked something in her, something big—powerful."

Robbie cut in when Baird paused. "...*And?*"

Baird shot Robbie an angry glower that cut through the chatter around them.

"She had a dream the other night," he said. "Flew to the top of the mountain and met Brigid herself. And before she woke, she mumbled somethin' about being *the chosen one.*" He paused, catching Robbie's gaze—really catching it this time. "But the voice that came from her, Robbie—it wasnae hers. It was someone else's, and that message about Mira being *chosen* was meant for me, I ken it—a warning." He drew a shaky breath, the old habit taking over as his hand went to the back of his neck. When he caught himself, he slammed his palm flat on the bar in frustration, the sound cracking through the room, loud enough to turn heads. Two days' worth of helpless dread spilled out with the motion, raw and unguarded.

Robbie's eyes widened, the scowl slipping from his face. For a long beat he just watched Baird, the bluster gone. When he finally spoke, his voice had lost its bark. "Aye," he said quietly.

"And if it was *just* that, I wouldnae be in this state," Baird admitted with an exhale. "When Agnes was ill," he said, remembering a time he wanted desperately to forget. "She used to say things about *not* being the chosen one—that *someone* was coming for her—sometimes it was 'her,' other times 'him'— pronouns shifted but the certainty didnae. And she kept warning me—insisting—that the one who came after she was gone would be taken from me as well." He let out a weary breath. "I told her she was confused, that she didnae ken what she was saying. But she kept insisting she did—and that it was *me* who didnae ken."

He stopped then, searching Robbie's face for some flicker of recognition. "But now Mira's saying the same things, only she believes *she* is the chosen one. And she's no afraid, Robbie." Baird shook his head. "No one bit." That, more than anything, was what frightened him.

Robbie leaned onto the bar, elbows braced, eyes locked on Baird's. The pub's din—the laughter, the clink of glasses, the music—seemed to fade to nothing. For a moment it was just the two of them, voices low, the air between them taut.

"And what is it ye think Sorcha can tell ye, exactly?" Robbie asked at last, his voice rough but steady.

"If that voice that came out of Mira in her sleep truly was the voice of the goddess Brigid, then what does it mean to be chosen?"

"I'll talk to Sorcha—and tell her to keep it between us for now." Robbie said, placing an awkward hand on Baird's shoulder.

Baird nodded, relief and guilt arriving hand in hand.

24

HAAR

Baird–April 2026

Baird had never shared Robbie's wariness of Sorcha, but as the boat neared the island—small, windswept and desolate, a place with few trees to break the lash of the sea wind—he began to wonder if perhaps Robbie's fear was justified.

"This is where she stays?" Baird asked, scanning the bleak shore. "Where's the cottage ye spoke of?"

Robbie gave a dramatic harrumph, as though Baird had never listened to a word he'd said about her—about the months he'd spent here as a young man, and the strange things he'd seen. "She'll let us land when she's ready. Same with the cottage. Ye'll see it when she wants ye to."

A wind rose from the north. They were still two nautical miles from the sheltered harbor where Baird planned to anchor when Robbie caught his eye—a look that said this wasn't a weather front. This was Sorcha's doing.

Baird adjusted the sails to meet the sudden shift, but with the wind came fog—dense, white as cotton, rolling over the sea so swiftly it swallowed the world. Within moments, there was no horizon, no sky, only the heave of water beneath them and the groan of the mast above. Both men were seasoned sailors, willing to take their chances with any storm. But a sea commanded by Sorcha—well, that was another matter entirely.

"Just stay the course, when we get into the harbor ye'll want to drop anchor. She'll row out to bring us ashore." Robbie said.

Sure enough, just after Baird dropped anchor, the fog began to lift. Sunlight spilled across a glassy sea, and there—at the heart of the cove—stood a small stone cottage with a thatched roof, perched squarely atop the hill. Baird was certain it hadn't been there twenty minutes ago.

Out on the water, a young woman was rowing toward them —Sorcha, in her youthful guise, long strawberry-blonde hair streaming behind her, a simple sundress billowing in the breeze as though she were any island girl come to greet them.

"Well, hello, gentlemen," Sorcha greeted, her voice lilting across the water like sunlight cutting through mist.

Baird tossed her a rope, though some instinct told him the gesture was unnecessary. The moment before the line hit, it coiled of its own accord around the post at her bow—as if the laws of physics and gravity obeyed only her. He and Robbie descended the ladder and stepped into her skiff, the boat barely rocking, unnaturally steady beneath their weight.

Something in the air shimmered, thick and humming, and Baird sensed that the natural order here bent to her whims. Wind, tide, gravity—none of it entirely right.

He thought absently, but not without a touch of dread, how strange his life had become. How this widening circle around him—Sorcha, Robbie, Mira, Granny Margaret—all bound by forces unseen—had tangled him in a world that no longer felt entirely his own.

At the cottage, Baird stooped to pass beneath the low lintel, and at once sensed the strangeness of the place—the interior was far larger than the modest structure could possibly contain. Magic, of course. He and Robbie stood awkwardly in the doorway until Sorcha gestured for them to sit. Baird chose a sagging couch, its fabric worn smooth by age, while Robbie lowered himself into an armchair near the hearth, eyeing the room with open suspicion.

A matted gray cat slipped from beneath the table, circling their legs in turn. Robbie grimaced when it brushed against him, and the creature turned away with a small hiss as if insulted. It padded back to Baird instead, pressing its head into his hand. He scratched behind its ears, and a low, rumbling purr filled the silence—so deep it seemed to come from the walls themselves.

Sorcha returned with a tray bearing a bottle of whisky and three glasses, the amber liquid catching the firelight as she poured each a careful measure—three fingers, no more, no less. As Baird reached to take his glass, the cat leapt onto the couch and slipped beneath his outstretched arm, settling into his lap as though it had done it a hundred times.

"Haar is a good judge of character," Sorcha said, referring to the cat, her tone sweet but her gaze sharp as cut glass. She leveled it at Robbie, who shifted uncomfortably; he'd never cared for cats, and Baird suspected this was one of many small grudges between them.

Haar—the old word for the sea fog that had rolled in not half an hour earlier. The symbolism wasn't lost on Baird.

Sorcha seemed to trust the cat's instincts, and for that, he was quietly grateful. Sorcha and Robbie always seemed to be at odds, the barbs between them worn smooth from use, but Baird sensed something deeper beneath the friction. Not quite affection, but something perilously close to it—an unspoken tether, as much a part of them as their tempers or their pride.

Baird took a sip of the whisky—fine, smooth, the kind that burned just enough to remind a man he was alive—well, sort of. He held the glass up to the light, admiring the deep copper hue. The decanter bore no label, and he nearly asked the name of the distiller before thinking better of it. Knowing Sorcha, it might have been salvaged from a shipwreck she'd conjured herself a century ago. And Baird, for all his curiosity, had no wish to stay long enough to hear that story told. Another time, perhaps.

The cat's purr was the only sound filling the sitting room until Baird broke the silence.

"Sorcha—what can ye tell me about the Garvie grimoire, and the family's connection to Brigid?"

Sorcha arched a brow. "Oh, straight to the point, Baird Campbell. I do hope Mira gets a bit more foreplay."

Her smirk widened as Robbie cleared his throat, shifting in his chair. Baird only laughed—he should have expected as much from Sorcha. Her joke broke the tension, lifting the edge of the dread that had hung over him since Mira's dream. For the first time in days, Baird felt the tightness in his chest ease.

"Out with it, then. What troubles ye? You don't strike me as the type to fear a powerful woman—*unlike Robbie*," she said, taking a slow sip from her glass.

Her eyes cut toward him again, all wicked amusement and

warning. Robbie shifted in his chair, trying—and failing—to disguise his discomfort.

"I wasnae concerned until the other night, when she had a dream," Baird said. "She began mumbling in her sleep—not afraid, exactly, but her voice wasn't entirely her own. She spoke of being *chosen*, said others had come before her but hadn't been enough...and it felt less like dreaming than a message meant for me." He took another sip of whisky and lowered his gaze to the floor. Haar had stopped purring and now lay fast asleep, mouth slack, a small patch of drool darkening the leg of Baird's trousers—an absurdly ordinary intrusion into an otherwise unearthly conversation. "And it reminded me of things Agnes said—my wife when I was still human, killed by the vampire that turned me—back in the depths of her darkest episodes," Baird went on, explaining about Agnes, not sure how much Robbie had told her. "She spoke of a woman coming for her—because she *wasnae enough, wasnae the chosen one*— and that those closest to her would pay the price. I thought it was her illness speaking." He paused, turning the glass slowly in his hands. "I dismissed it then, like all the rest. But now— hearing Mira say nearly the same words—it chills me. She told me she dreamt she flew to a mountaintop and met Brigid herself—that their voices joined until they spoke as one. She was euphoric when she woke, radiant even. No trace of the fear Agnes had."

Robbie swore under his breath. "That's worse," he muttered.

Baird looked up. "How d'ye figure?"

"Fear makes people hesitate," Robbie said grimly. "Belief makes 'em walk straight into the fire."

Baird turned back to Sorcha and drew a slow breath. "I can't help but feel there's a connection I missed—something that binds them both, though I can't yet see how. Agnes said several times, and was adamant that I remember it, that someday, long after she was gone, the goddess would take another from me."

Sorcha's eyes narrowed as she leaned forward in her chair. "What is it ye're asking me, exactly? Whether the voice ye heard was truly the goddess herself, warning ye—or if Agnes was right? Or perhaps what is the Garvies' connection to Brigid?"

"I wish I kent exactly what I was asking," Baird admitted, realizing coming here may have been a fool's errand.

"Are ye afraid for Mira," she pressed, her tawny gaze fixed on him as though Robbie weren't even in the room, "or guilty for having ignored what Agnes told ye?"

The question struck him like a stone to the gut.

"Cannae it be both?" he said quietly.

Sorcha studied him for a long moment. "And yet ye've told Mira neither." She didn't wait for him to deny it. "There's no use in guilt, Baird Campbell," Sorcha said, her tone softening. "Ye did the best ye could for Agnes."

He appreciated the gesture, but it did little to ease the weight in his chest.

"Let me start by sayin' I dinnae believe the power in Mira is ordinary magic," Sorcha said quietly. "It feels like a door's been opened for her. As though someone's been waiting for her to step through it. And maybe that someone is Brigid herself." Her normally distant composure sharpened, her attention locking onto Baird with sudden intensity that made unease coil in his gut. "As for the Garvies, that book has been copied and recopied over the centuries. The one Mira holds now is at least two hundred years old, likely more—and I'd wager it wasnae the first their family made. It's less a spellbook than a devotional of sorts, every word an offering to Brigid. Families like the Garvies would have worshiped all the old gods and goddesses, but there isnae a single reference to anyone besides Brigid. And the book is laced with fear, not only the feelings I can detect when I lay hands on it, but written in script by the Garvie women themselves."

Sorcha continued to stare at Baird, and he wished silently for a bit of psychic breathing room. "So aye—the connection is real. And if I had to guess, it stretches back at least five hundred years, perhaps more. It's possible Agnes knew of the family connection, but those things she said still may have been because of her illness. Ye cannae know that, so stop beating yourself up for it."

She paused then, her expression shifting, the flicker of firelight catching gold in her tawny eyes. "But power like that—it doesnae come without cost. The goddess is generous, but she's never been merciful. Every gift she gives is a debt owed, and Brigid's debts are always paid in blood or in love—and sometimes, they're the same thing." Sorcha leaned back in her chair, her gaze distant, as if watching something only she could see. "The Garvies bound themselves to her long ago, and the vow hasnae been broken—only passed from one generation to the next. They've denied their magic for many years now. I cannae say why. But it's woken in Mira."

She drained the last of her whisky and set the glass down, her fingertip tracing the rim in slow, thoughtful circles. "Have ye told Mira yet—about what Agnes said?"

Baird raised his brows, pressed his lips together, and shook his head. "No. I wasnae sure how to bring it up."

"Has she mentioned the spell she misread—the one I corrected for her when I visited?"

"No," Baird said warily. "What was it?"

Sorcha rolled her eyes and gave a small, disapproving shake of her head. "Ye two lovebirds need to stop keepin' secrets from each other. Whatever lies ahead, the goddess holds the cards. And the two of ye would do well to remember—ye'll need to face what's coming as partners, or not at all." Sorcha rose from her chair—a small motion, yet one that carried the unmistakable air of dismissal. The visit was over.

"I'll see what I can learn about the Garvies' bond to Brigid," she said, smoothing her skirt with absent precision. "And Baird—get these things spoken between ye and Mira before I come again. Secrets fester, and the goddess—not to mention marital harmony—has little patience for silence."

Baird nodded and thanked Sorcha, and as the three of them rowed out to the sailboat, Baird wondered if the chosen words —*marital harmony*—was a euphemism, or Sorcha's way of letting him know she'd seen something he hadn't yet been ready to speak aloud.

25

THE RETURN

Magda—February through April 1390

Dani and I walked through the market one afternoon. At nearly two, Anca could walk, but she preferred to see the world from atop Dani's shoulders—and Dani could never deny her. Her smallest wish was his command.

I heard a familiar voice ahead of us, and a chill skated down my spine. Dani heard it too and stopped dead. Just feet away stood Caius, speaking with the cheese monger—the same one he'd been talking to the day I dared to kiss him beneath the oak tree.

My hand flew to my mouth.

He looked older. Not merely aged, but forged. His body had hardened the way a soldier's does—shaped by lean rations and relentless drills, by blades raised when life and death truly hang in the balance. Not by boyhood games in the woods with his closest friend. Shadows hollowed his eyes.

I wanted to turn away—to melt into the shadows and run. I had always known this day would come, and I feared my own reaction as anger rose hot and sudden inside me. For the way he'd left me. For the way he'd allowed his father to treat me. My skin flushed, heat prickling along my neck.

Dani stepped forward and bent to set Anca down. Her small legs wobbled as she reached instinctively for his hand, fingers curling tight until they slipped out when he straightened again. Then Dani, his expression hopeful, extended his other hand to Caius.

For a heartbeat, I wasn't sure what Caius would do. His gaze slid past Dani and found me, his lips pressed into a tight line, emphasizing the gauntness in his cheeks. Then his eyes dropped to Anca, lingering there a breath too long—and then snapped back to mine, flashing with a bitterness I didn't understand.

If Dani noticed any of it, he gave no sign.

Caius took the offered hand at last, his grip stiff and awkward. "Who is this?" he asked when he bent to Anca's level, his voice reaching for lightness—and falling short.

She wrapped her arms around Dani's knee and tucked her head against his leg, suddenly shy with this stranger.

A rush of protectiveness surged through me, and I stepped forward to Dani's side. "This is my daughter, Anca," I said bitterly. I almost said *our* daughter, but decided against it, unsure whether Caius would hear it as his and mine...or exactly what I meant: Dani's and mine.

I reached for Anca, lifted her, and settled her on my hip— willing those blue eyes to tell our story. Of how Caius had left me. Of how Dani had gathered up the wreckage his friend abandoned in the wake of his departure.

Caius stared at Anca for several long moments. Then he moved, walking past us close enough that his shoulder brushed mine—not by accident, but by choice.

He offered no congratulations, no *you have a beautiful daughter*. He simply kept walking, leaving us behind as though neither Dani nor I had ever meant anything to him at all. The eager hopefulness I'd seen in Dani's face vanished, and the shocked looks from onlookers twisted the knife already lodged in my gut.

WEEKS PASSED, and the village no longer whispered about Caius—it watched him. The charismatic golden son of a noble house, once all easy smiles and effortless charm, had soured into something harder. He lingered in the tavern long past propriety, drank beyond reason, and bristled at imagined slights. A dice game gone wrong ended with a table overturned. A careless remark earned a bloodied nose. More than once, he struck stone walls until his knuckles split, as though punishing them for refusing to break.

Children were called inside when he rode through the square. Men who had once bowed easily now did so with guarded expressions. His father's steward began appearing more often in the village, smoothing tensions, settling disputes with coin and apology before they reached neighboring estates.

Word traveled. It always did. A noble heir who could not govern himself would not inspire confidence in those he was meant one day to govern. Prospective alliances cooled. Invitations grew scarce. His behavior upon his return was a disappointment to his father, but he was quickly becoming a liability.

One evening Dani walked through the door, later than normal. His face was red, his lip split, blood dried at the corner.

"Dani...what happened? Were you in a fight?" I set Anca down on the rug and rushed to him, my hand skimming his face.

"It was Caius." His voice was flat, his eyes locked on mine, heavy with pain.

A rock twisted in my gut. "Why?" I whispered, though I already knew.

His shoulders sagged. He crossed to the hearth and sank into a chair. I poured a glass of strong plum brandy, set it before him, then dragged the opposite chair close and sat between his legs. My hands began to shake, my face hot with shame. Tears streamed down my face and I hung my head, unable to say the words I should, the truth I owed him. His hand touched my cheek, his thumb rubbing at the wetness from one eye as it fell, and after a moment he pressed under my chin to lift my gaze to his.

"He'd been drinking again. Belligerent. His father's steward and Ivar were trying to drag him from the tavern when we heard the shouting. My father thought I might calm him." Dani let out a brittle breath. "That I still could."

He swallowed. "But seeing me only fed it. I tried to get him home. Told him he'd said enough. That it was finished." His jaw flexed. "He started shouting that I'd stolen you from him." His voice broke. "And then—" He stopped, blinking hard. Tears welled in eyes that so rarely betrayed him. "Then he said Anca was his child. Not mine." The words seemed to scrape his throat raw. "He said it in front of half the village."

This was it—the moment I'd dreaded since the day I accepted his proposal. The rocks of lies and silence that had weighed me down had finally pulled me under.

"I was so angry, Magda. I hit him." Dani looked stricken, as if he couldn't imagine how it had come to this. "He went down, and I thought it was finished. I turned to leave, but he came at me again. Landed a lucky blow before I put him down for good. The whole tavern cheered when he fell. His father walked in and saw it happen—heard the reaction. Ivar and some of the men dragged Caius home."

Caius's accusation that Dani had stolen me could not have been further from the truth. Caius had been the one to leave. The one who tried to win his father's love and approval by casting me aside. But truth had never mattered much in a village hungry for scandal. And no matter how I turned it over in my mind, no matter how I tried to bury it, I could not keep lying to the man who had given me everything.

"I'm so sorry, Dani. I should have told you—should have given you the choice when you asked me to marry you." My voice fractured, a confession between words spoken and not, falling between us like stones into still water, quiet ripples widening the distance between us. "I will understand if you cannot forgive me."

For a heartbeat, silence stretched taut. Then a small, sorrowful smile touched Dani's lips—an expression that cut deeper than anger ever could have.

"Magda—you must think me a fool." Dani gave a tight, brittle laugh, though pain etched hard lines into his face. Not the pain of fists or bruises, but the deeper wound of holding something on my behalf.

"I knew you carried Caius's child when I asked you to marry

me." His voice did not waver, but something in him had already fallen. "I waited for you to tell me—I prayed you would." He drew in a long breath. "But I understood you had your reasons."

He looked away then, toward where Anca sat playing with her toy. "So I kept your secret." His jaw tightened. "And when she was born...those blue eyes." His voice frayed as he watched her. "They told her story the moment she opened them. How could she be anyone else's?" He said it plainly. No anger. No accusation. Just a fact.

I had hurt Dani more deeply than any blow Caius could have struck. And yet, with the truth finally laid bare between us, something inside me loosened—thin, fragile, shameful as it was. "Do you hate me?" The question slipped free before I could stop it, raw and trembling.

"Hate you?" He gave a weary shake of his head, the sad smile touching his mouth again, the lines of his face etched deep by all he had carried in silence. "No, Magda. I could never hate you." His big hand, calloused by hours at the forge, stroked my cheek. "Perhaps I am a fool—but I loved you then, and I love you still. And Anca—*our* Anca," he added, holding my gaze with an earnestness so fierce it stole my breath, "I love her as if she were my own flesh and blood."

I had never doubted that part. I had never seen anyone love a child the way he loved her. In his eyes she was the moon and the stars. I rose from my chair and sank to my knees between his. The guilt hollowed my voice, stripped it bare. Liar. Thief of his trust. Begging for a mercy I did not deserve. "I'm sorry, Dani."

My hand lifted to hide my tears, but he caught it gently and drew it down, brushing the wetness from my cheeks himself.

"No more secrets, Magda," he whispered. His eyes held raw emotion, a wordless plea, asking me to finally let him in. Telling me that I wasn't alone—that I had never been alone.

Anca smiled at us both as she toddled across the floor toward where we sat, blissfully unaware of all that had been laid bare between us. I reached for her and Dani folded both of us into his arms, pressing gentle kisses to the center of her forehead until she giggled. A soft warmth unfurled in me then—for a man whose pure heart held more love than I ever believed was possible.

That night I watched him as we made love, eyes open. No thought of anything—or anyone—else could take root in my mind. I gave myself—no holding back—for the first time.

26

FATE FORETOLD

Magda—April 1390

The door was kicked in with a crash, and our bedroom filled with the sour stink of unwashed men and ale. Anca screamed from her small bed—a bright, urgent sound that cut through the night—and I lunged off the bed for her, but a rough hand caught my hair and wrenched me back; one man held a torch, and raw light illuminated the face of the man that had grabbed me: Ivar, the boyar's enforcer, leering with the contempt of a devil that delighted in breaking things.

Dani's fist landed on one man's nose with a sickening crack, then blows rained in from everywhere—four of them besides Ivar, armed and merciless. I watched, helpless as I screamed for Dani, for Anca. Then, as if in slow motion, a wooden club came down on my skull, sharp and brutal, as my world tore itself into blackness.

Anca's cry thinned and the distance opened between us

until it was only a brittle thread in the dark. As I slipped in and out of consciousness, the hot, acrid smell of smoke threaded in, and with it the hollowing knowledge that something had been stripped from me I could not yet name.

I WOKE LATER to a new smell—the rot of wet leaves and turned earth—my cheek pressed into the forest floor. For a moment I did not remember where I was. Only the cold seeping through my gown, the weight of my own body, the taste of mud thick on my tongue. I groaned and spat, trying to clear my mouth. When I shifted, pain flared through my body, stitching memory back into place. I forced myself to breathe, to listen. The forest was not quiet.

At first it was only a murmur threaded through the trees— low voices, indistinct. Then a burst of drunken laughter, too close to be imagined. It echoed wrong in the open air, careless and ugly. My pulse stumbled. There—another sound. The deliberate crush of leaves. The slow, uneven rhythm of boots pressing into damp earth. Not moving away. Coming nearer.

I kept my eyes half-closed, my body slack against the ground, as the footsteps drew closer and closer—until the sound of them seemed to fall in time with my own terrified heartbeat. With a swift kick to the soft skin at my side, all my breath spilled out in a crumpled grunt. I curled into a ball, batting away hands that groped for me, but another grabbed my tangled hair and yanked me upright, the world lurching as my head throbbed and my gut clenched.

"Why are you doing this?" I screamed. The hand that had

hauled me upright struck my face with a ringing crack. Light burst behind my eyes. I tasted copper and salt almost at once. I turned back toward him anyway and spat blood into the dirt between us. "Why?" I begged again, though the word came out broken now, more breath than voice.

No one answered. I forced my feet apart, willing my legs to hold. The ground tilted treacherously beneath me, the trees bending and swaying as though the forest itself had grown unsteady. My knees buckled. For one suspended second I thought I would be allowed to fall.

I was not. A fist caught in my hair and yanked me upright again. The pain sharpened everything—the cold air, the smoke from the fire, the sound of boots grinding into soil as another man stepped closer. Then another. My vision pulsed—darkness closing in, then receding in ragged flashes. In those fractured glimpses, I saw four of the men had formed a loose ring around me.

One man rose from the fire as if roused by nuisance, each slow step heavy with contempt. The world narrowed; I felt, with a hollow chill, that whatever they intended would not begin until he chose to start it. My vision steadied just long enough for recognition to strike. It was Ivar. His steely eyes were locked on me, cold and incurious. He didn't see a woman standing there—he assessed me the way a farmer might look over a heifer at market, a thing to be used, bartered, consumed.

"The gypsy whore spread her legs for the boyar's son and then wed his best friend." A man with a wine-colored birthmark on his cheek said with a laugh. "Surely she'll let us have a go." He stepped past Ivar and backed me to the tree, his breath foul and close. I tried to flee; their laughter rose and a blow to my jaw split the night into brief, bright pieces.

They held me up against the tree while one of them tore at my nightgown. I floated between fits of black and the feel of hands—each return to sense a small, humiliating shock: the weight of a man, the sting at my lip, the stinking breath across my face. Each time I tried to move, another blow sent me further away.

One by one they came and the night swallowed them. I remember only fragments: the animal shuffle of bodies, the bark of cruel laughter, and the silhouette of Ivar by the fire, a loathsome, indifferent shape, tugging and pulling at his cock as he watched his men have their way with me, waiting his turn. I felt myself slip loose from my own body, as though I could rise above it and watch from some merciful distance—this broken woman covered in mud someone else entirely.

Then a small, obscene sound from Ivar cut through the haze and snapped the fragile thread of oblivion. I was dragged back into myself all at once. Nausea surged hot in my throat. Shame followed close behind, thick and suffocating. The forest rang with the coarse laughter of men who found sport in cruelty, their voices cracking through the trees like splitting wood. And beneath it—clearer than any of them—my child's cries. Cries like a bell only I could hear, sharp and insistent, tolling through the darkness, calling me back to the body I could not abandon.

Another blow to the side of my head split the world again. Hands seized me—two of them this time—hauling, dragging. My heels tore furrows through damp earth as they pulled me through the trees. What remained of my gown caught on briars and splintered branches, fabric ripping in small, helpless protests I felt but could not stop. Each jolt sent a crushing throb behind my eyes, pain radiating outward until thought itself became difficult.

Through the roar in my ears, another sound began to rise—thin at first, almost imagined. Then louder, steady and relentless. Water. Not a stream, but something bigger—the river.

They released my arms without warning. I crumpled forward, then forced myself up onto unsteady feet, swaying. Behind me, from somewhere in the dark, Ivar's voice drifted out—low, controlled, faintly bored.

"Turn her around."

A jerk on my shoulder turned me to face him. Then pain—searing, absolute. I looked down at the knife buried in my belly, Ivar's hand steady on the hilt. When I looked up, he was smiling—slow, cruel, his eyes colder than the steel he held. The blade withdrew with a wet, sucking sound.

His push sent me reeling, my footing vanished, the earth fell away, and darkness rushed up to claim me.

27

SERBAN & OSSIVIAN

Serban—April 1390

Serban had dreamed the night before, a thing almost unheard of for his kind. Sleep came seldom to him, let alone deep enough for dreams to touch him. Perhaps, he supposed, it was closer to a trance than a dream. Still, it was the best explanation he had. Not that he had need to explain it to anyone.

At dawn, he saddled one of his prized Turkoman horses. Their coats gleamed like desert sand turned to metal, iridescent, as though shaped from another world. He could leave behind homes, identities, even whole lifetimes every thirty years or so, when questions grew too heavy. But the horses he never left. They were his constant.

The thing that called to him—the one his father had called *Ossivian*—beckoned from the dark forest. Its pull tugged him forward, and he rode on. With each stride, the connection deepened, glowing within him like a beacon in the night. He'd ridden for nearly two hours when Serban found himself near the mouth of a cave, knowing this was where he would meet the creature. Serban dismounted and tied his reins around the neck of his horse and then made his way into the mouth of the cave.

Serban's father, a man of great magic, and gifted with ability to speak with the gods, first taught him about the cave dweller. Neither wicked nor benevolent, but a conduit, a vessel through which divine will pressed into mortal flesh. This was not Serban's first summons. Two centuries ago, perhaps more, Ossivian's voice had reached him on the continent of his birth. When he called, you went. Always. But Ossivian never asked without offering payment, and he knew Serban's currency: gemstones—some blessed by the gods, some only breathtaking to behold—but all bound with value, all heavy with meaning.

"Why have you called me?" he asked into the black abyss, his voice heavy.

In total darkness the cave dweller scuttered closer, just a faint rattle and clatter echoing off the walls, his voice no more than a faint hiss. "Blood drinker—I have need of you."

"I assumed as much." Serban replied tersely. "Speak plainly —what is it?"

The creature pulled in a breath, the rough sound of wind hissing against stone, before speaking. "A young mother has been taken from a nearby village; her husband and infant slaughtered. Tonight they will finish her—near the bend where the river meets the forest's darkest reach—with a violence only humans can muster."

"And why bring this to me?" Serban asked, impatience thin as a blade. "Do you wish me to stop it?"

"No. You are not to interfere. Simply find her. Take her from human death and fold her into your line," the creature whispered. "When she is ready—when she has learned the rites and rules of your kind—release her. She will answer the cruelty wrought against her with vengeance. Yet her path is hers alone to bear; you are not chained to it."

In the dark, Serban's shoulders sank. To struggle against the will of the gods was futile. "How will I know her?" he asked, resignation heavy in his voice.

Ossivian, wrapped in shadow so dark even Serban's eyes couldn't discern, clicked his tongue, toying with the vampire." You know her. A glade—three turns of the sun past. Picking sweet fruit."

Serban froze, breath torn from him as though by an unseen blow. The young Romani peasant—*Magda*—whose name and face was still etched in his memory. The reckless girl who had trembled before him, yet longed to taste what he carried in his veins. She had wanted power—freedom beyond the limits of her birth. He'd felt the pull even then, the thread tying them. That day had not been chance but design. Now he understood whose.

Sadness cut through him. Blessed or cursed, the gods had marked her. And now, for a time, they had marked him with her. "What do you have for me?" Serban didn't want Ossivian to think he was willing without payment.

The creature edged forward a few inches and set a small box and a velvet pouch upon the ground before retreating once more into the dark. Serban kept his gaze lowered. His father had warned him long ago: it was forbidden to look upon the creature's true form. Some bargains required blindness.

Only when the faint scrape of movement ceased did he step forward and retrieve the offerings. He loosened the pouch's drawstring and poured its contents into his palm—cut stones that caught even the dim light: several diamonds, a sapphire the color of midnight seas, and a scatter of opals that shimmered like trapped rainbows. Satisfied, he returned them to the pouch.

"Those are your payment," Ossivian said. "The box belongs to the girl."

Serban pocketed the pouch and opened the box. Inside lay two large rubies, their glow alive, their magic unfurling like smoke. Power pulsed through his veins—their story threading through him as clearly as any language of men. The rubies spoke of return, of magic that could bring back something the young woman had lost. When the vision faded, Serban exhaled and braced one hand against the cave wall.

"Why do the gods favor this girl?" he asked, the question edged with bewilderment. He had never understood why immortal beings would trouble themselves with the fragile, fleeting dramas of mortals.

"Tsk, tsk," Ossivian tutted, the sound dry as bone against stone. "It is not for me—or for you—to second-guess the will of the divine, blood drinker."

Serban shook his head. He preferred his ties thin and easily severed. He stood there, absorbing the burden until it pressed him inward, bowing his shoulders with its insistence. Without another word, Ossivian turned and vanished into the cave's depths, leaving Serban alone with the echo of his thoughts—and the weight of the task ahead.

28

THE TURNING

Magda—April 1390

I knew I'd fallen far, that my body had come to rest twisted on the rocks near the river's edge. I could hear the roar of rushing water close but I couldn't move. Blood trickled from a fresh wound on my head, a maddening sound—*drip, drip*—onto the stones below. The pain was there, but somehow distant, as though it belonged to someone else.

The night pressed in, black and endless. Somewhere nearby, something stirred. A bear, perhaps. Or a wolf, drawn by the scent of my blood. I could not cry out, could not lift a hand to defend myself—my body was too broken. Was this what Buna had seen in the smoke, the death and destruction she warned of—that I had caused by being foolish enough to love Caius? I surrendered to the thought of teeth in my flesh, of my end, and prayed it would be swift. Closing my eyes, I let go.

A cold presence loomed, leeching the last warmth from my dying body. Even with my eyes closed, I felt it edge closer—the air itself alive with charge, every nerve ending across the surface of my skin prickling with dread.

And then—new pain. Sudden and excruciating. Fangs piercing the hollow of my neck. A wolf. Yet no scent of animal filled the air, only cool breath against my skin.

The last bit of warmth that existed in my body, the last bit of my life force rushed through my veins, then was pulled away, drained until the fire inside me turned to ice.

I remember being lifted, pulled from the rocks, my body cradled as if weightless. My name, a voice low and insistent, and a hand brushing the blood-matted hair from my face.

An angel of death, come at last to claim me.

Then—blood on my tongue. The tang of iron and copper. But not my own; I knew it instantly. A whisper pressed against my ear, faint at first, muffled as though through heavy wool. Then it grew, louder, clearer, tearing through the silence until it filled me whole. A command. Irresistible. Inescapable.

"Drink."

Warm blood pooled in my mouth and snaked down my throat—I thought I'd choke, but my weakened body had no fight left; my muscles lay slack and unresponsive. Then, with a sudden cough, I dragged up a scrap of strength and tried to pull away, but the source pressed harder to my lips and the command came again:

"Drink." And I obeyed.

For an instant I soared; then the musky smell of wet horse yanked me back, and the voice—gentle, vaguely familiar, and inside my head now—decreed, *"Sleep."*

I woke with a start in a bed draped with fine linens. The room was dark, save for a shaft of sunlight streaming through a crack in the window casement—so bright it stung my eyes. I tried to sit up but my body hurt too much. It wasn't the pain of broken bones—it was worse. It was the agony of them knitting back together. Severed ends groping for their mates, reaching through torn muscle and sinew, fusing, binding, forcing themselves whole again. Tendons, once shredded, coiled back around their rightful joints, twisting tight until my body was made anew. The wound in my belly—the one carved by a blade driven so deep the hilt had pressed against my flesh—stitching itself closed again, inch by agonizing inch.

I screamed—raw and unending—unable to make sense of what had been done to me or what was happening now. Then a voice, a whisper close as breath: "Hush, child. That will only make it worse."

I turned my head as slowly as I could. Draped in shadows, a man sat. He rose from his chair and came closer to the bed. I did not know his name, but I knew his face. The man from the glen.

A fine woolen mantle trimmed in fur—a garment made for outside wear—was draped across his shoulders as he lowered himself gently to sit on the bed. His skin gleamed, dark and smooth, and his eyes—black at first glance—were veined with silver, shifting like stars in a night sky as he moved.

He lifted a hand toward me, slow and deliberate, each finger glittering with rings of gold and silver. The gesture was measured, coaxing—like one might soothe a frightened animal. His mouth curved in the faintest smile, a kindness I hadn't glimpsed when we first met, and wasn't sure I could trust.

"My child," he murmured, his voice heavy with an accent I couldn't place, stroking my hair as though I were some pet.

Revulsion surged. I jerked away, pain rippling through me, and I gritted my teeth."I am not your child!" I spat, the words sharp with indignation.

"Aren't you?" he replied, eyes glinting with amusement, but his lips did not move. He was back inside my head again now, I could feel him burrowing in, turning over my thoughts to find the truths buried beneath. "I'm the reason you have a second chance, Magda. To rise out of your life of poverty, to be something greater."

I tried to remember what Buna had taught me, to shield my thoughts from him, plant a thought as a distraction, but I was so tired, and the pain was so great.

"I hear the old woman...she holds sway over your thoughts."

"Stop!" I screamed.

His smile vanished, turning cold, and I felt his grip on my mind slide away—a hood slipping from my head.

Somewhere in the house servants moved: the soft scrape of chair on stone, the rustle of a broom, and outside the window a bird trilled from a branch. What ought to have been muffled and far-off instead pried at my nerves, ordinary sounds made savage. Each note burst in my skull, bright and dagger-like. Despite the pain that came from moving, I clutched my ears, desperate to shut it out. I looked to the man, desperate for explanation, but his expression was stern.

Minutes or hours passed—I couldn't tell—then he stood again and spoke, this time aloud, his voice low and flat. "You need rest, and to finish healing." And then, almost an afterthought, "...You'll need to feed soon."

Feed.

The word landed odd and cold in my ears. Sleep sounded appealing; exhaustion tugging at me like a child seeking attention. He slid into my thoughts again, gentler now—a careful pressure that soothed like a lullaby. Desperate thoughts of Dani and Anca fought for a foothold in my mind, but it clashed and lost against the force he possessed. For the time being, sleep became my master.

29

A BOND COMPLETED

Mira—May 2026

Baird had been acting strange for days. Gone was the attentive, playful man I had spent more than a year with, replaced—almost overnight—by the man I'd first met on Arran. The one I'd woken beside on his couch in the cottage: sullen, gruff, answering my questions with single words, my attempts at playful banter landing with a dull, lifeless thud. Hollow eyes, tight jaw.

At first, I brushed it off. I even tried telling him about the misunderstood spell from the Mother's Book—the one Sorcha said suggested the Garvies had been using the blood of the Abhartach for centuries...and using the spell to keep themselves from falling in love with one. When I told him that, his eyes locked on mine, searching. For a moment, I thought I finally had his full attention. But I didn't get a laugh. Not even the smirk I'd been expecting. I was hoping for questions that turned into a conversation, but it just seemed to drag him down deeper.

Then I wondered if it was me—if I'd been neglecting him. Too much time spent squinting over spells and half-decoded Garvie incantations in the Mother's Book. Too many long hours in the studio, sculpting wax and casting the two rings I'd made between other commissions and replacing stock in my retail line. But something inside me said that wasn't it.

He'd started doing that thing again—rubbing the back of his neck, fingers digging in as if he could work the tension loose from bone and muscle. He avoided my eyes when I caught him at it, turning away under the pretense of checking the fire, the laundry, the dishes, scratching Bunny's ears— anything that gave his hands somewhere else to be. There was grief shadowing him. Not the old grief I'd seen in him when we'd first met—the familiar knot of loss and guilt bound up in losing Agnes. This was different. This was fresh. Raw. New.

Baird was keeping something from me.

He'd been out to hunt—he and Bunny gone for hours— when I heard the cottage door open. Boots shucked and set side by side, careful not to make noise. Quiet hands.

I leaned against the bedroom doorframe, wearing one of Baird's T-shirts, a pair of panties and nothing else, my arms crossed loosely over my chest. Waiting. When he came around the corner, he stopped short. His eyes widened, not a trace of the hunger I'd come to expect after a hunt, but instead I saw only surprise—like he hadn't expected me to be up waiting for him. Like he hadn't expected to be seen.

For a heartbeat, neither of us moved.

Then his gaze dropped, just briefly, before he rubbed the

back of his neck, fingers pressing in hard. I was right, this wasn't just my imagination. He was bracing himself for something.

"You were out a long time," I said softly, all the things I wanted to say but didn't hanging in the air between us.

Baird looked at me, something aching and unresolved in his eyes—so sharp I could almost feel it. But he didn't answer.

I pursed my lips and gave a small shrug, forcing casual into my voice to soften the weight of his silence. As if this were nothing. As if it didn't matter. But it did. I missed him—I missed *us*. The crooked smirk that never failed to undo me from the inside out. The way his eyes used to light up when they found me, like I was something he'd been looking for.

Now he just stood there, shoulders slumped under some invisible weight. I crossed the cold stone floor until I was inches from him and set my hands on his shoulders, steady and sure, forcing him to meet my gaze. "I'm fine," he said at last.

His lie was so thin I could read the subtext right through it. "I need you to tell me what's bothering you." One hand slid to his jaw, my thumb pressing lightly there, holding him in place when he tried to look away.

"Mira," he murmured, the words warning or plea, I couldn't tell which.

"You haven't kept a single thing from me since you told me the truth—about Agnes, about Bastien. About *you*." I leaned in and brushed a soft kiss across his lips, tender but deliberate. Then I turned and walked into the bedroom without looking back. "But this withholding from me stops now."

His voice was low, worn at the edges. "I didnae want to worry ye."

"That's not your choice to make." I said quietly. There it was. Not the why. Not the what. But an admission all the same.

It wasn't much—but it was a start "What is it?" I asked, grasping at straws. "*Money?*"

We'd talked, loosely, about his businesses—plural, and mine—single, but our bank accounts were still separate. Independence by mutual, unspoken agreement. My dad had gone quiet a few times when I was younger—withdrawn, distant—during the recession when estate jewelry buyers dried up and every dollar mattered. I'd learned early to recognize the signs. The careful silences, forced smiles to protect my mom from the truth. Maybe that's what this was.

His look of incredulity—followed by the first small smile I'd seen in weeks told me I'd been way off base. He shook his head, then dragged a hand down his face. "No, lass." He let out a sigh. "Not money. Ye'll never need to worry about money."

"Then what is it?" I asked. It came out rougher than I meant, my patience thinning after days of tiptoeing around him.

He crossed the room and sat down on the bed. He looked defeated, but somehow relieved at the same time. "Sorcha said I should just tell ye, but I didnae ken how."

"Sorcha?" I echoed. "You talked to her?" I said slowly. "But not to me?" A spark of frustration rose, small but it burned bright. "What does *she* have to do with this?" The edge in my voice surprised even me. I was more than a little irritated that he'd gone to her. I still felt like she was withholding things from me, and now it felt like a team sport.

"She kens...*things*, Mira. Ye've got to admit that." He glanced up at me, where I stood. "Robbie agreed I should ask her."

"Robbie?" I spat. "*Robbie* knows what's wrong?" Heat flared in my chest. "Robbie knows what you've been keeping from me?" I crossed the room and stopped directly in front of him, close enough that he couldn't look anywhere but at me.

"I didnae go lookin for opinions, Mira." He said quickly. "I went lookin for answers."

"What is it?" I demanded, the last of my patience gone. Everyone seemed to know the truth. Everyone but me.

His face shifted as he tried to find the words—jaw tightening, then easing, bracing for what I didn't know. His eyes flicked away from mine, not in guilt exactly, but in calculation, as if he was replaying this moment and searching for the version where he could make a different choice. A muscle jumped once along his cheek. He drew in a breath he didn't seem to need, let it out slowly, and when he looked back at me, there was something raw there now. Regret, yes—but layered with resolve.

His mouth opened, closed again. So much for the resolve.

"Spit it out, Baird Campbell. What was so damn important that you went to Robbie and Sorcha—but couldn't be bothered to tell me?" I bit down hard on the last word, daring him to answer.

"Ye were just so happy, Mira." He said it quietly, like that alone should explain everything. "Once ye got your hands on the book and buried yourself in your connection to the goddess...it was like something clicked into place." His gaze dropped, then lifted again, searching my face. "That little dark space inside ye—the one I can feel—that hollow place that's been there since the first day I met ye, even before the bond formed." His jaw tightened. "Self-doubt? Fear? Always gnawing' at ye, even when ye tried to pretend it wasnae." He drew in a slow breath. "But since ye let your magic loose—since ye committed to the ruby ring—that little black hole's been shrinking. Every day. Replaced by confidence. By strength. By joy." His voice roughened. "It was a hole I could never fill for ye. And seeing ye like this...seeing ye *complete*—" He shook his head faintly. "There's nothing that's brought me more happiness than that."

"Then why do you look like you're losing me?" I asked. I couldn't reconcile how this had become a problem—especially when he was right. The ache of not belonging, of being somehow flawed, had begun to fade. Purpose had taken its place. Destiny. And now, quietly, even that was changing, growing, reshaping itself into something bigger I didn't yet have words for.

He saw it on my face. The confusion. The waiting question. Slowly, he lifted his hand between us—not to touch me, but in a silent plea. There was more. "The night ye had the dream of being on the mountain with the Goddess. It started then." It all came spilling out at once—the way I'd said I felt the Goddess had chosen me for some purpose, beyond the ruby. The words I'd spoken without knowing where they came from. The way Baird had heard it too, in the mutterings I'd made in my sleep. *Someone else's voice*, he'd said. The same thing I'd heard in my dream.

And then there was Agnes. The things she'd claimed. The way Baird had once dismissed them as madness, as fear talking. But now...now he wasn't so sure she'd been wrong. And how afraid he'd been to bring her up again—to reopen the wound between us, the one that had driven me to leave him once before.

He believed she'd been trying to warn him. *To warn us*. The Garvie clairvoyance I'd just recently made peace with had perhaps driven her to madness. That being chosen—whatever that meant—wasn't a blessing. It was something dangerous.

"You think this ends with me dead," I said.

It was there in his eyes, the desperation he could no longer hide. He believed this with a certainty that left no room for doubt. And that was what frightened me most. Because Baird was not a man who believed in nonsense.

Still, I couldn't make myself believe it. "I think you're making something out of nothing," I snapped, the words coming faster now, edged with a conviction I wasn't entirely sure I believed. "And I think this has more to do with *you* feeling everything I feel than anything actually happening." I took a step toward him, hands slicing through the air. "Because I don't feel what you feel, Baird. I can't. And there is nothing— nothing—I can hide from you."

"Ye cannae understand what it does to me—" he started, his voice rough.

"No," I cut in sharply. "I *can't* understand it. And that's exactly the point." Frustration flared, hot and unfiltered. "I don't know what you feel unless you tell me. I don't get warnings or instincts or whatever it is you do." I thrust my arms out, the motion a human exclamation point. "You feel *everything* I feel. Every doubt. Every fear. Every joy. Every stupid, transitory emotion that flits its way through my head. You *took* that from me when this—*Sanguis Amantium* bond, or whatever it is— formed." My voice rose despite myself. "Now I couldn't hide something like this from you if I tried. You'd always know. Maybe not the reason—maybe not the details—but the after- math." I shook my head. "You'd feel it. Every time. It's not fair. You don't get to protect me by shutting me out," I said. "Not from this. Not from you."

His eyes flared—not with anger or rage, but with a hard, contained frustration, the kind that comes from hitting a wall you don't know how to break through. Then his expression shifted, tension draining as something settled into place, a decision he'd clearly been fighting finally claiming him. He nodded to himself. "I can make it fair, Mira. I should have done it that night..."

My stomach dropped. Fair meant something very different to him than it did to me. Those familiar eyes, brilliant green and tinted with pain I didn't understand, slowly transitioned to the deepest black, any hint of resignation drained from him, leaving something raw in its wake. It moved through him, reshaping his presence until my instincts screamed predator even as my pulse betrayed me. It should have terrified me. Instead, it felt like leaning forward to meet what he was becoming.

"Baird..." I said quietly when my mind caught up to what my body had already acknowledged.

He let the thing he said caused the blood bond to form rise in him—the part of himself he still hated, still tried to push away. He couldn't see it clearly, couldn't separate it from what he feared it made him. But it was still a part of him that loved me.

Deeply. Possessively.

I clenched my hands at my sides, grounding myself, forcing my breath to stay even—not because I meant to stop him, but because part of me still knew I could. I wasn't ready to let desire cloud my thoughts. I couldn't—not with so much left unsaid.

He leaned closer—so slowly, as if giving me a chance to move away, and yet I didn't step back. The monster he tried so hard to deny knew me too well. Memory stirred against my will: the way he came to me after his hunts, all heat and barely leashed hunger, the way my body had answered his, even when my mind protested.

This was time for talking, not sex. Never—not once—had Baird used sex to avoid a conversation. Me? Yes. I'd done it more times than I cared to admit. Flip the switch. Let pleasure drown out the noise. Obliterate everything I couldn't—or wouldn't—face in the moment. I remembered doing exactly that after Baird had confessed the truth, of how Bastien had killed Agnes and turned him in a rage, overriding every rational thought I had screaming for caution, choosing skin and heat and connection to mute my doubts, if only temporarily.

Now desire crept in again, unwelcome, insistent—curling low and tight—a traitorous ache I fought to suppress. But beneath it, deeper and far harder to fight, the magic in my veins surged in answer to his, restless and hungry, wanting this... wanting him...wanting to *make* something together.

I fought to hold onto the fact that Baird, once again, had held something back from me. And yet my body betrayed me, trembling on the edge of a surrender I was not—*would not be*— ready to give.

"I can make this fair," Baird said again, his voice dropping into that dangerous register that surfaced only when he was at the edge of himself—when he was fighting something that wanted *him*, and wanted *me*, to yield. It threaded through me, rough— stripped of softness, more instinct than language. Less human, more animal. And the way he held it back—made the struggle far more intoxicating than if he'd let it loose.

"What do you mean *you can make this fair*?" I asked, breathless with a need that was confusing—and deeply inconvenient.

Baird opened his mouth just enough. Relaxed his lips.

Fangs gleamed—snow-white against the shadow. Not a warning. An admission.

He closed his eyes and drew a slow, deliberate breath. When he caught my scent, that smirk curved his mouth, darker now—knowing. He already knew the battle raging inside me. And in the most dangerous, morally gray way possible, he believed that letting me lose was how he made this fair.

I braced myself, a silent challenge. Baird answered. The air stirred, and then he was simply *there*, a sweeping force of motion that slammed my hips against the cool, unyielding edge of the kitchen counter. My *why here?* died in my throat, met by a deep, rumbling growl that vibrated through his chest and into mine. He slotted himself between my thighs, his grip proprietary. He pulled my shirt over my head, but it was the sharp snap of delicate silk that made me gasp. I stared at the ruined wisp of a pair of Eres panties on the stone floor and swore. His smirk was a wicked, sharp-edged thing, savoring every flicker of my irritation. This was him unchained, the past and all its ghosts banished from the room. He existed only in this moment, and I was desperate to live in it with him. The second my skin was bared, his mouth descended—a brand against my lips, a trail of fire down my throat, until he found that sensitive hollow. The touch was electric, a current that shot straight down, pooling in my core as a tight, throbbing knot of need.

When I pressed myself against him, chasing the impossible urge to merge, to erase the space between us entirely, the sound he made was less laugh, more resonant rumble—dark with approval, vibrating as if my body alone had drawn it out of him. His hand went to my pussy, tracing an index finger through my wetness before plunging two into my depths. I gasped at the sudden intrusion, the sound torn from me before I could stop it, then dissolved into a helpless moan when he found that place—the one he knew too well. His touch was precise, devastating, playing my body like an instrument tuned only to him, drawing sensation higher and higher until thought itself slipped out of reach.

I reached for his waistband, wanting him as bare as I was —but he caught my wrist and brushed my hand aside. He watched me with eyes gone ink-black, coiled darkness, before lifting his fingers to his mouth. Slow. Deliberate. He lingered there, as if savoring more than just my taste, the faintest curl of a smile playing at his lips as he licked them clean—an unspoken reminder that he was choosing when, and how, this would go. He pushed me back, and lowered his face between my legs, tongue claiming me, every so often letting me feel the sharp tip of a fang, dragged ever so lightly against my labia, just so I didn't forget what I was dealing with. As if I could.

The sound of his zipper cutting the silence was a promise. I rose onto my elbow as he shucked his jeans, my eyes tracing the lines of his body. He stood before me, half-dressed and fully exposed. Every muscle was pulled taut, and the smattering of hair on his chest narrowed, drawing my gaze down the ridges of his abdomen to the deep V to his groin. He was a live wire of power, trembling with it yet perfectly controlled, and the sight made me throb with a desperate want. A smirk touched his lips; he knew. His pupils were vast, swallowing the room's light, but just as suddenly, a terrifying brilliance burned in their black depths as he reached past me.

His fingers found the wood of the knife block. With a sharp tug, he freed the carving knife. A primal fear, cold and sharp, forced movement to my limbs. I scrambled backward, my spine hitting the counter, my brain screaming two conflicting commands: get away or intervene.

"Stop!" The command tore from my throat. He ignored me. He held the tip of the knife to a point just inches above his heart, his gaze pinning me in place as he pushed into flesh. A sharp hiss of pain escaped him as he jerked the blade free, letting it fall with a deafening clatter against the stone. For a moment, there was only the sound of our breathing. Then, a bead of blood welled, swelling into a line that trickled down his sternum. "What are you doing?" The question was a whisper, lost in the horror of it. He stood before me, breath ragged, pain flickering across his features. Bloody—still stroking himself.

The magic in me didn't question. It erupted. Light and heat blazed under my skin, blinding. My mouth went dry, and instinct took over. Then came the thirst—not a gradual wave, but a tsunami, a drowning force that obliterated reason. The scent of his blood—hot, sweet, coppery—filled my head, and a desperate cry tore from my throat. He yanked me against him, sheathing himself in one brutal thrust. His fingers pulled at my hair, a painful grip anchoring me to him.

"Drink," he growled, dragging my mouth to the bleeding gash on his chest. The word was a command. His voice was no longer human, but a low, dark thing threaded with the same ravenous hunger that had made him bleed for me.

I pressed my lips to his chest and drank. His blood filled my mouth, and with every swallow, the fire under my skin burned brighter. I was barely aware of him moving, his thrusts growing from hesitant to demanding. My focus was singular: the exquisite relief of the thirst as it began to wane. It wasn't a deci-sion to pull away, but reluctant release as the craving finally quieted. I leaned back, unsteady, the taste of him still on my lips. When I met his eyes, I saw it: a self-satisfied smirk.

The look of victory.

A cold dread coiled in my stomach as understanding seeped into my veins—slow, poisonous. This was what he'd been trying to do. Not to hurt me. Not to take anything from me. But to fix something. He couldn't give back what he'd taken, so he meant to even the stakes—give me the same terrible advantage he had. He hadn't asked. Hadn't explained. He'd simply acted, driven by the same fear he'd been trying to bury. And I felt it then, bitter and disorienting: the violation of it. The choice taken from me. Again. The echo settling deep in my chest.

And yet—

The magic inside me sang.

It surged with a joy I couldn't deny, answering some ancient call, as if I'd stepped onto a path laid long before I knew it existed. Another hidden threshold crossed. Another step taken in a journey whose end I couldn't yet see.

The beast in Baird hadn't slipped its leash; it had snapped it. Not in fury, but in instinct—a brutal certainty that this was the only way to mend what our fragile human selves had broken. And my magic didn't just answer; it surrendered. His power crashed into mine, not threading but *seizing*, amplifying, binding us together in a way that felt terrifyingly, irrevocably right. It became something new, a force larger and more permanent than either of us alone. Braced against him, dizzy and reeling, I couldn't tell which was more horrifying: that he'd done it...or that he believed this was the only path back to me. He leaned in and kissed me, a messy clash of his blood and my saliva. Both hands clamped onto my hips, yanking me flush against him. My legs spread, ass grinding into the cold countertop as the pressure built to an unbearable peak. His breath was ragged against my cheek, his words a desperate murmur.

"Let me—feel ye—come on my cock, Mira." His words came out broken, barely intelligible—a tangle of command and plea that made one thing unmistakably clear: he wasn't finished with me yet.

He knew exactly how to move his hips, that rhythm coaxing me toward a pleasure so intense it was pain. He was pushing me to the edge, to the only place where I could shatter and be remade. I cried out as the orgasm hit, a blinding wave of release. Golden light exploded from my core, leaching through my skin, the pleasure of both the physical and magical release almost too much to bear. Seconds later, his rhythm began to falter. I knew the sign. I moaned his name, and the sound sent him over. He cried out, his body shuddering against mine. But as his movements slowed, his lips found my skin, his voice a low, muffled whisper. "I'm sorry. I never should have taken this from ye, Mira." The apology wasn't for tonight. It was for the first time. For the choice that made tonight necessary.

The thin trail of blood down his chest had nearly stopped. I traced it with my finger, slow and reverent, then brought it to my lips, tasting the last drop—warm, metallic, faintly salted. "How does this work?" I asked, still breathless. My gaze flicked to the abandoned knife on the floor. "Did you need that?"

"Aye." His voice had steadied, though something fragile still threaded through it. "It had to be from my heart vein—or my jugular. And I preferred to keep it where I could see it."

Understanding clicked into place. Sorcha's odd question the day after I'd first succumbed to the blood thirst—whether

I'd drunk from his jugular or heart vein—suddenly made sense. She'd scoffed when I'd said the wrist. Now I knew why.

He hesitated, then went on, softer now. "I thought about it, ye know. That night the thirst took you. But I realized too late I'd missed the moment." His eyes searched mine, uncertain. "I vowed then, if you ever asked again—*and I realize this wasnae exactly ye asking*—I'd fix this. I wanted to give ye the chance to have what I have."

I hated that I was here again—standing in the wake of something Baird had decided on his own, convinced it was better withheld until it couldn't be. And yet, if completing the bond was the price of keeping us together—of holding onto what we'd built—I knew I'd pay it.

I blinked hard, trying to shake off the frustration and focus on what came next for us. I still wasn't on the same page as Baird—not about this idea that being chosen by the goddess was dangerous. So far, it had meant crafting a reincarnation piece and occasionally burning bright enough to resemble a one-woman fireworks display. Hardly apocalyptic.

"When will I feel it?" I asked, my voice uncertain, searching myself for any hint that something fundamental had already shifted—and finding nothing.

"I dinnae ken—not precisely," he said quietly. "When I drank from ye the first time, I told myself I didn't feel anything until the next morning. Until the moment I told ye I loved ye... and felt that small, impossible glimmer of your love for me inside ye."

His mouth curved faintly, the expression more wonder than certainty. "But if I'm honest, I think I felt ye sooner than that— that night, when I stayed outside." He exhaled slowly. "Frustration, mostly. Ye were frustrated. I was too. It was hard to tell where your feelings ended and mine began." His gaze held mine, steady but vulnerable. "But once it started—it grew quick."

"Don't leave me," I said, reaching for his hand—not because I was afraid of what came next, but because the words felt necessary. We washed the blood from our skin in silence, then curled together on the bed. Baird drew me into his arms, settling me against him, my head tucked into the hollow of his neck. He pressed soft, absent kisses to my hair, my temple, my forehead—small, grounding gestures meant to anchor us both.

We waited.

Somewhere between his steady breathing and the solid reassurance of his body, I drifted off. I woke in the night to darkness pressing down on me—thick, total, and inescapable. Fear flooded my senses, sharp enough to make me nauseous. The strangeness of it struck me—I was completely enveloped, but this emotional signature was foreign.

This was not *my* fear. It was Baird's. I couldn't believe he'd been carrying this— alone.

30

THE WITCH AND THE GODDESS

Baird—May 2026

Baird's phone chimed with a text from a number he didn't know. Just six words. No name. Still, he knew it was Sorcha.

Meet at Robbie's pub this afternoon.

Baird arrived with Bunny at his heels, fresh from supervising the harvest of a winter barley field. The moment he stepped inside, he spotted Robbie behind the bar. Robbie gave a sharp, single tilt of his head, directing Baird toward a small table tucked into a dark corner, where Sorcha sat nursing a pint of ale.

Baird sat and immediately caught the nervous tap of Sorcha's nails against the wood. The woman who was usually so at ease in any room looked unsettled now, her calm stripped away. He'd been about to signal for a pint, but the tension in her face stopped him short. "What is it, Sorcha? Is everything alright?"

The witch sat across from him, middle-aged today, dressed in her usual no-nonsense trousers and blouse, her strawberry-blonde hair pulled into a bun streaked with gray. "I'll tell ye what I can," she said quietly, and the way she said it made dread coil in his chest. "The goddess wants ye to live yer life, Baird Campbell. To love Mira fully. To give her yer heart and soul—no' to ruin today by mournin' something that's no yet come to pass. That's the human part of ye, Baird. The part that grieves the future before it's ever had the decency to arrive." Her words were hushed, careful. But beneath them was fear.

"Ye make it sound like something's coming for her," Baird said. It came out harsher than he meant, fear bleeding into the edges of the words. "Is that what this is? This *chosen* business—Brigid picking Mira for some purpose? What is it?"

"There's a debt the Garvies owe the goddess," Sorcha said. "I don't know how it was forged, or why—only that it exists. And the goddess has been watching, waiting. Waiting for centuries, for the right Garvie." Her voice softened. "It appears that one is Mira." Only then did she exhale, the tension finally slipping from her frame, as though saying the words aloud had been a burden she'd carried too long.

"What do I do—just wait?" Baird asked, the question stripped bare by the need to do something—anything—that might tip the scales.

"Ye've completed the bond with her," Sorcha said softly. "So ye'd best learn to stop poisoning her with your fear. The goddess wants ye walking forward together." She leaned in slightly. "But if ye do anything—anything at all—to turn Mira from her path, the goddess won't hesitate to remove ye from the equation."

The realization left Baird unsteady—that somehow Sorcha, or Brigid, or both, knew he'd completed the *Sanguis Amantium* bond with Mira. *Poison* was the only word for what followed. The first thing Mira had felt through the bond hadn't been love —but his fear.

Fear of losing her. Fear of a world without the one thing that made him want to keep going. He'd meant for her to feel his love first—fierce, consuming, unshakable—but the fear had been louder, stronger for having grown alongside it.

"How did ye learn this?" Baird asked, trying to force down the fear the goddess said would only serve to destroy what they'd built.

"I talked to a being who speaks for the gods. He told me what he could—and no more. But he sent me off with a warning; that he'd never speak to me of this again, and to take the message straight to ye. And that the day would come when Mira needed more answers, he would speak to her when that time came, but that time was not now." Sorcha stood, her purse hanging from her wrist, her expression gentler now but no less serious. "Love her, Baird," she said. "She needs it more than ye ken. The kind of love that brings her joy. That feeds her magic. The kind of love that comes from the part ye're ashamed to name." She stepped closer. "That part of ye gives her power. Dinnae let it fight the rest of you. Find a way to make them one —because when it comes to Mira, that part of ye is never wrong."

Baird woke in the darkest part of the night to light. Blinding, pulsing light, filling the dark stone room as Mira stood at the end of the bed, glowing with an energy that throbbed in time with her heartbeat. Her eyes had turned to molten gold, whirling and alive, waves of her long, dark hair lifting as if caught in an unseen current, the tips flickering with flame.

Power rolled off her in waves.

He knew—instinctively—the being in front of him wasn't entirely Mira. The Goddess was using Mira, her shape wavering like heat rising off stone. When she spoke, it was not loud—but it settled deep, burrowing beneath bone, Mira's voice and yet not   not quite.

"*You are too close,*" she said plainly.

"Too close?" Baird stiffened when he found he couldn't move, some unseen force holding him fast. "To Mira? Never— I'd die for her." That was it really. He wanted the goddess to know.

A flicker passed through the goddess's gaze. Not anger. Something older. Sadder. She nodded in affirmation. "*That is precisely the danger.*"

The air thickened, heavy with meaning he couldn't grasp. "*You see threats where there are none,*" she continued. "*And miss the ones that matter most.*"

His jaw clenched as he strained against the unseen force binding him in place. "Then tell me what I've missed." He'd never considered himself weak—not in life, not even after being turned. The only moments that had ever come close were the ones where he'd failed to protect those he loved. But this was different: helplessness made physical, a goddess's will pressing him into stillness. And with a twist of bitter clarity, he understood it. His greatest weakness had never been his strength or his fear. It was his love for Mira.

She stepped closer. The light dimmed around them, as though the world itself leaned in to listen. "*The woman who watched from the edges. Who warned you. Your instincts failed you then, but no longer.*"

Agnes? Did she mean Agnes?

A pause. "*She merely saw what was to come. That was her curse—knowledge—and it broke her.*"

"What do ye want with Mira?" he demanded. "Because this" —he struggled against the force restraining him—"this is more than just a bloody ruby ring, eh?"

Brigid's gaze lingered on Baird, ancient and unblinking, peering out from behind Mira's eyes. "*The ring is nothing more than a lesson,*" she said. "*A means by which Mira learns to surrender to my will —and, in doing so, becomes the vessel through which my gifts are given.*"

"Promise me ye willnae hurt her," he pleaded.

"*I cannot promise that. No one can.*" Brigid shook her head sadly. "*This is her destiny. You would try to shield her from what's coming,*" Brigid went on, the voice that had been stern gentle now. "*You would pull her back from the fire and call it love.*"

"I do love her," he said, the words bare and desperate. "I'd do anything for her. Anything." The pain that bloomed in his chest at the thought of existing—of *enduring*—without her was excruciating. Only now did he truly understand what Bastien had meant when he'd begged Baird to end his life, when he'd said he could not go on without Clémence at his side. The agony Baird had once seen in another vampire's eyes—one he'd believed long stripped of all humanity—now lived in him with startling clarity. That was what love did. It upended everything

—turned the world inside out, made survival itself feel impossible.

Her gaze softened, her tone gentle as a mother soothing a frightened child—yet weighted with something deeper. "*That is plain for the world to see.*"

He thought of what he'd told Mira once—that he could never bring himself to turn her. And yet, with the weight of loss that hadn't happened already hollowing him out, despite Sorcha's warnings, he realized that perhaps Bastien's bargain had been the only mercy left to him after all.

The invisible restraints eased, as though Brigid had decided he was safe enough to listen rather than fight. He pushed himself upright, the sheet falling away unnoticed.

His jaw tightened. "I willnae let her be used."

A strange expression crossed her face—something like pity. "*You already are,*" she said softly. "*Just not in the way you fear.*"

He let out a breath, full of frustration. "Then tell me! Tell me what she'll become."

Brigid's answer came slowly. "*She is not yours to guard. Not yours to save. Not yours to lose.*"

The words struck him like blows. And then, almost kindly: "*Step back, Baird. Let what is meant to unfold do so.*"

The light began to fade. "*If you interfere,*" she added, her voice thinning like smoke, "*you will not stop what is coming. You will only ensure it comes broken. Face this at her side, and do not make her choose.*"

Just as Sorcha had said.

And just before she vanished: "*Trust me when I say this— what you fear will take Mira from you...*" A pause, deliberate. "*...is the very thing that will give you more than you ever dreamed to ask.*"

Then she was gone.

Mira stood there, emptied of light, her eyes distant and glassy. When her knees buckled, Baird surged forward, catching her as she crumpled, gathering her against him before she hit the floor. Disoriented, her eyes unfocused, she took in her surroundings—head turning slowly right, then left—confusion flashing as her vision cleared and she realized she was cradled in Baird's arms at the foot of the bed, not in it.

"What's happening, Baird?" she asked, her voice slowly returning to the one he knew.

He hesitated, considering whether to brush it off—to tell her she'd been sleepwalking, to offer one of those half-truths that had always come so easily to him. But he knew he couldn't. Not this time. Even if the future was shrouded in shadow, even if he didn't yet understand it himself, she deserved more than that. And every time he'd tried to protect Mira with silence, it had ended the same way—with her hurt, furious, the truth tearing through them eventually.

He looked at her, lifting a hand to her cheek, his thumb settling into the small dimple in her chin. He stroked the soft skin there—more to steady himself than her—and a quiet sound of relief escaped him before he answered. "The Goddess," he said, carefully stripping the panic from his voice. "She kent I'd been worried since your dream."

Mira sat up sharply, but still confused, questions circling in her eyes. Baird knew he needed to do his best to give Mira what he could from the encounter. Maybe it would make sense to her.

"She spoke through ye—like the night of your dream. Her voice from your lips. Your—her—*the light*"—Baird shook his head, trying to sort ownership of the power and realizing it didn't really matter—"comin' from ye, so bright it woke me."

Mira only rolled her eyes. "Well, it would have been nice to be conscious so that I could ask my own questions. Did she mention more about the ruby? She dodged my ruby questions —except for telling me to bless it with my blood that day she appeared to me in the studio, when I was setting the yellow diamond."

"Aye. Said it is some sort of test for ye—one that'll show ye how you will bestow her blessings on others," he said, trying to make sense of Brigid's cryptic prophecies, connect dots in a picture he wasn't sure the goddess was ready to reveal.

"Well that tracks, kind of what she said that day." Mira looked at Baird and blanched when she saw something in Baird's eyes. "What is it?"

Baird's emotions twisted in on themselves, a tangled mess he couldn't break apart. "I dinnae understand most of what she said," he murmured. "But I think she confirmed what I feared about Agnes. She saw the future—and it broke her."

A tear escaped him, sliding down his cheek before he could stop it.

Mira lifted her hand, brushing it away with gentle fingers before pressing a kiss to his skin, lips warm. "I'm sorry," she breathed. "I'm so sorry, Baird."

He drew back to look at her, searching her eyes. "What are ye sorry for?" he asked quietly, unsettled by how quickly the roles had shifted—the woman he'd been trying to steady suddenly the one holding him together.

"I'm sorry," she said softly. "Sometimes I think if you'd never met me—"

"Dinnae." The word tore out of him—rough, urgent,

stripped of gentleness. He caught her face between his hands, not cruelly but firmly, forcing her to look at him. His forehead pressed against hers, breath unsteady, restraint fraying at the edges. "Dinnae ever say that again." It was not anger that sharpened his voice, but desperation—the raw command of a man who had already endured too much loss and refused to let fear or guilt come between them.

An ache threaded through his voice, stripping it of pride. "I'd relive every moment—*gladly*—just to love ye, Mira Garvie."

Her smile—vulnerable, luminous with relief—spread slowly across her face, and the sight of it struck him with unexpected force. The joy it stirred in him was bright enough to burn, stirring regret for the weeks he had allowed to slip past without giving her reason to wear it.

"Something she said settled inside me—that the thing I fear will take ye away is the very thing that will give me something so great I couldn't even dream it—and we needed to be in this together."

Sorcha's words echoed in his mind. *Love her.* And he knew that was it, the thing he needed to do above all else. Right then, without fear. Without holding back. He let go of the part of himself that had been bracing for loss, knowing it had no place here—no place with her. He pulled her close, fierce and certain —and the moment he did, the light of Mira's magic surged in answer.

31

THE MAKER

Magda—May 1390

I woke again to find the sun gone from the window. In its place, the golden hour draped the room in warm light and deep shadow. Every sound still struck too sharply, reverberating in my skull, but the searing agony from before had ebbed, leaving only a dull throb in its wake.

I tried to rise, but one hand would not obey. An iron cuff bit into my wrist, bolted to a heavy ring; a thick chain threaded from it into another ring set in the wall.

"You devil! Let me go!" I screamed, throwing sound into the empty room in the hope the sorcerer—if he lurked nearby— would hear. Footsteps answered, slow and deliberate, then the hard click of a key in the lock.

Beaten, raped, stabbed, and hurled from a cliff hours before —and this was my reward. The world tilted; bile rose hot in my throat. He had bound me like an animal. My hands trembled against cold iron, and fury flared where fear had been.

He walked into the room and sat on the bed beside me. I jerked back, yanking on the cuff until it clattered against the wall. Frustration welled up, and a desperate cry tore from my throat. "Who are you? Why am I chained here?" My voice cracked as I squirmed against the sheets. "I need to go back to my village—to Dani, to Anca, to Buna—"

He raised a hand to silence me, then laid it gently over the one not bound in iron. His face was grave, and had I not been his prisoner I might have mistaken it for tenderness.

"I am called Serban. The chains hold you for your own safety," he said, as if that explanation alone should make it bearable. "You do not yet understand what change has been wrought upon your body, nor the hunger that comes with it. Until you learn to master that hunger, you are a danger—to yourself and to those around you."

His voice was low and honey-smooth, his accent shaping each word into something both foreign and strangely familiar. He spoke in riddles. *My own safety*? I pushed myself upright, kneeling on the bed. The chain allowed little slack, the iron biting into my wrist—cold, unyielding against the softness of the linen.

"Control my hunger...what do you mean?" I spat at my captor.

He rose from the bed and stepped beyond its edge before turning back to face me. With deliberate precision, he unfastened the cuff of his shirt, letting the sleeve fall loose, then lifted his wrist toward his mouth.

His dark eyes glowed—fierce, possessive—holding mine so completely I could not have looked away even if I'd tried. Slowly, his lips parted, revealing teeth white as sun-bleached bone against the warmth of his skin.

Then came the shift. His upper row aligned and altered, lengthening with unnatural grace until two teeth gleamed—sharp enough to pierce.

The world tilted. Dizziness swept through me. His words echoed back—*my own safety*—*control your hunger*—not because he had forced them into my mind, but because of their sheer absurdity as I watched this monster, this devil, unveil himself.

But I knew now what he was. Buna had told me of the *strigoi* —how they drank blood to live and walked the earth in darkness. Terror swept through me; whatever bravery I had drained away. I shrank back, pressing into the bed. Then he lowered his head, and with one swift motion sank a fang into his own wrist, his eyes never breaking from mine.

The tang of blood—sharp, sweet—hit my nose, and hunger roared through me, thirst rising like fire in my veins. A force not my own seized me, propelling me toward him with the speed of flight before thought could catch me. The chain, forgotten instantly, snapped me back onto the bed. I hissed—at the shackle, at him, at the monstrous thirst that was no longer his alone but mine.

"Now you understand the need for restraints, my child," he said, using that term again.

Child, me.

Maker, him.

Feed.

Yes—this was what he had meant. I needed to feed.

A moan tore from me, half whimper, half plea, as I strained against the chain like an animal. Iron bit into my wrist, but I barely felt it. Some part of me still begged, still reached—

though I knew I could not get closer, could not touch the very thing my body screamed for.

My mind and body split apart. My mind knew I was chained. Knew I could not reach him. My body did not care. It had one purpose. One purpose only.

Blood.

He stepped closer to the bed. The scent hit me—warm, tinged with iron, alive. Saliva spilled from the corner of my aching mouth. When I tried to catch it with my tongue, I felt them—two teeth descending, lengthening. Mine. Like his.

His eyes never left me. Curious. Measuring. Waiting.

The last of my confusion drowned beneath the thirst, and he saw it.

He came nearer and extended his arm. Revulsion flared—but my hand shot out anyway. I seized his wrist and dragged it to my mouth. A sob tore through me. I tried to pull back. I tried to resist.

I could not. My fangs sank into the wound Serban had already opened, piercing deeper. Heat flooded my mouth. I drank. And drank.

When he tried to pull away, I only tightened my grip.

"Stop," he said firmly.

I whimpered at being denied, the blood dripping down my chin. I tried to wipe it away with the back of my free hand.

Sated, at least for the moment, I tried another tactic. "Please let me go...I have to get back to my husband and daughter..."

He lifted his eyes to mine, and I saw sorrow flit across his face like a shadow.

"No—no—what do you know? Tell me." I cried.

He sat again next to me, his lips set in a grim line. "I sent a man to your village, Magda. To ask around. He said your husband and daughter died when they set fire to your home." There was pity in his eyes. "They are gone. Nothing is left for you there."

No. No—he lies. He must. Not Dani. Not Anca—her little lungs, smoke would choke her, but Dani would have saved her. He promised me. He swore he would keep her safe. He swore.

The fire—was it our cottage? Someone else's? He was trying to break me, that's all, to bind me tighter. If I ran now, I would find them in the woods, alive, waiting. Dani's laugh, Anca's small hand curled around mine. They were there. They must be there.

But the smell   smoke clung to memory, charred wood, hair singed. I could hear it—crackling, the walls collapsing. No, no, no. My fault. If I had stayed. If I had fought harder. If I had never let Dani love me, if I had never brought this curse to his door. My daughter—my baby—gods, I wasn't there.

"Did you do this? Did you watch them burn? I will tear the black heart from your chest, I will drink you dry." I screamed at him pulling again against the iron cuffing my wrist.

"No, Magda. I found you after those men left you—"

I cut him off and sound died in my ears. "Get out," I begged the room, the chain biting into my wrist as I writhed. For a breath I expected him to slither back into my mind, to unravel me into that soft obedience he could coax; instead he stood there—distant, composed, sorrow carved across his face. Let me keep the pain, I told myself: let me taste the loss of the man I had failed to love in time, the man whose whole heart I'd given away to another. And my child—small, innocent—who bore the consequence of every wicked choice I'd made.

The click of the door locking when he left me echoed in my head. Alone with the weight of my pain, I thought that erasing my memory might have been the truest mercy. Instead he walked away and left me to the slow burn of torment.

I wept myself empty, the tears dried but the pain still throbbed raw and open inside me. I sat crumpled in the corner of the bed, hollow as a husk, and only then did I notice—I was clean. At some point, while my mind had been veiled in that unnatural sleep Serban forced upon me, my torn and blood-stiffened gown had been taken and replaced.

Was my body not my own? Had it ever been? Last night had shown me the truth—in the eyes of men, I was an empty vessel, existing only for their pleasure. Some took their pleasure and offered something in return—attention, perhaps even love. Others took with violence, and repaid me with death.

Even this man had taken something. Perhaps he believed it kindness—tending my body, dressing it decently—but without my consent, it was only another trespass.

THE CEASELESS CADENCE—THE lock turning, his blood against my lips, the darkness he summoned over me—blurred waking and sleep. Every sound was too sharp, too loud, setting my head to ache. Cruel mornings burned into nights, nights into a week or more, until time unraveled completely.

The sound of the lock turning echoed again—still too sharp for my aching ears—yet it had become a herald, a grim announcement of his presence. He entered with casual grace, long limbs moving with deceptive ease, his frame lean but powerful, his shoulders broad enough to fill the space. From his pocket he drew another key and reached for the iron cuff at my wrist. The lock snapped open with a higher, sharper pitch than the door's, and the distinction sent a shiver through me. My cell may have been outfitted with fine linens and soft rugs, yet I was still a prisoner.

The bed frame groaned under his weight when he sat, the sound striking through my skull like a hammer on iron. His hands folded loosely in his lap, but his face betrayed him—eyes shadowed, mouth drawn with weariness—as he looked at me.

"The sun," I said at last, my voice raw, foreign to my own ears. "It burns my eyes in the mornings, but not yours." I nodded toward the window, though the light had long since fled. Only the cold night pressed through the casement now, a draft that should have prickled my skin, but oddly did not.

"No. Not anymore," he said. "When you are newly born, as you are, the sunlight sears the eyes, and every sound claws its way into your skull like a nail dragged across slate. But you'll adjust soon." He rose then, crossing to the window to pull heavy curtains over the wooden shutters. Why, I could not guess. The cold night pressed in, but my skin gave no shiver, no reaction at all. His gesture felt almost human—an instinct, a habit carried over from another life. Perhaps some remnants we never truly lose.

He turned toward me, his face a mask of pity. "I'm sorry, Magda. I know you don't believe me, but I am not to blame for what happened to you. Perhaps you think death would be kinder now that your husband and child are gone from this earth. But I saw something in you that day in the glen—your defiance, your fierce conviction that you were born for more than this."

I huddled on the bed, arms wrapped around my knees,

gutted. The day he spoke of was three years past, and yet it felt like a lifetime ago.

"You feared me," he continued. "Yet when you felt my power, you moved it around inside you for a moment, testing its weight, to see if it fit. It was only when you realized I was inside your mind that the fear took hold, but even then I felt you grasp for it." He looked in my eyes, but I refused to let him win. "We are alike, you and I. I was never meant for a small life—just as you are not."

"Life? Don't speak to me of life. I have none—I am undead." The ache in my chest burned at the thought of Buna, the iron-willed woman who loved me with a tenderness she rarely showed. "What would my grandmother say, seeing me like this?" I said to no one but myself.

"When you are ready to leave, perhaps you should ask her." He said lightly. "I know it's small consolation, but your grandmother still lives."

"Buna?" I whispered. "Take me to her." I begged.

"You aren't ready yet, Magda," he said, loosening the button at his cuff and lifting his wrist to my mouth. It was the same wrist he'd offered me before, yet the skin bore no mark, as though teeth had never pierced it. I brushed a fingertip across the spot, expecting to find a scar and surprised I did not.

He caught the unspoken question in my eyes. "We heal quickly," was all he said.

He raised his wrist the rest of the way. This time there was no revulsion, no hesitation. The blood beneath his skin called me, and I answered.

At the mere thought of that honeyed scarlet syrup, my fangs slid long and sharp, the ache startling me. The skin gave way so easily—warmth flooded my mouth—life itself streaming down my throat—and I drank greedily until his voice cut through my hunger with a single command to stop.

I pulled away obediently now, a thin trail of blood sliding down my chin. I lifted my hand to wipe it, but the thought of wasting a single drop made me catch it with my tongue, licking the red line from the back of my hand.

"Your lessons begin tonight," he said, his voice calm, measured, as though this were nothing more than instruction in a trade. "You'll come with me, and I will teach you to hunt game. There will be times when it is more convenient to rely on animals to sustain you. Once you've mastered that, we will move on to humans." He gestured toward the wardrobe. "There are clothes that should fit. The boots may be a little large, but I will see you properly outfitted soon."

He rose, moving toward the door. Before leaving, he paused, hand on the iron key. His gaze lingered on me. "Be ready within the hour." The lock turned with a sharp click, leaving me alone with the echo of his words and the lingering taste of blood on my tongue.

I found a pair of men's trousers and a rough-spun tunic. Save for the leather belt drawn tight at my waist, they would have slipped past my hips. A long woolen cloak completed the ensemble. The boots were far too large, but with two pairs of thick socks I managed. Even worn and ill-fitting, they were the finest boots I'd ever had on my feet.

I paced the room, restless, rifling through drawers and the trunk in the corner. At last, I pushed back the curtain and opened the shutters, peering through iron bars into the court-yard below. A stone barn stood north of the main house, torches flickering against its walls. Several horses' heads jutted from the stalls, busily pulling at hay. Two of them had the same pale cream coats as the mount I had seen him astride in the glen.

A knock sounded at the door—an odd, hollow thud that rattled inside my skull. Another followed, and then his voice: "Magda—did you find the clothes in the wardrobe?"

I cleared my throat, unsettled by the gesture of privacy, especially after he had stripped, bathed, and dressed me himself when I'd arrived. "Yes. I am dressed," I answered.

The dull click of the key echoed in the room as the door opened. "Come," he said, stepping aside to let me pass over the threshold. A short hallway opened to a narrow staircase, the beams so low in places that I had to stoop to keep from striking my head. At the bottom, another corridor led into a large chamber. Stone hearths anchored both ends, vast enough that I could have stepped inside their mouths.

A long table stretched between them, its surface crowded with candelabras that lit the scatter of maps and heavy books. To one side, several chairs ringed a fine rug, and behind them a case overflowed with books—stacked haphazardly on shelves, toppled into teetering piles on the floor. These were not for ornament. Serban lived in these pages, used them, wore them thin.

The heart that once belonged to the old Magda—the girl who had dreamed of far horizons and salt winds, who once yearned to see the sea—gave a sudden, foolish skip. Then the memory struck: that girl had died long before her human life was taken, the moment she set aside those silly dreams to marry a good man who gave her daughter a father.

Serban's eyes followed mine to the overflowing bookcase. "Do you read?" he asked.

"Yes. Some," I admitted, careful not to overstate it, afraid he might put me to the test. "Buna taught me. I know it's uncommon—for a peasant, and even more for a woman. But Dani—" My voice faltered, the name catching like a thorn. "He used to sneak me books from Drago Burián's library."

His expression darkened, as though my grief sat heavy in the air between us, something he did not know how—or perhaps did not wish—to touch. "You may choose some to keep in your room when we return," he said. "Later, when you can be trusted—when you're free to roam the keep—you may take whatever you like."

"Why do you keep me locked away?" I asked.

"The newly turned are unpredictable. I can't watch you every moment," he said, voice grim.

"Unpredictable?" I echoed. "What is it you're afraid of?"

"That you might hurt someone. Or be hurt by those who work for me. I'd rather neither happen," he said plainly.

"Who could I possibly hurt?" I asked, not knowing what he meant.

He gave a small shrug. "Any of the humans who serve me."

I stared. "There are humans here? In the house?"

"Petra," he called from the doorway to the main room, down another hallway. I heard shuffling footsteps grow closer and after a moment an old woman appeared.

I heard the pitter-patter of her heartbeat the moment her steps ceased. She saw me and inclined her head. "You are awake."

Serban's gaze stayed fixed on me. My limbs began to tremble as my vision sharpened, every detail etching itself painfully into my mind—the hollows beneath her eyes, the creased skin of her throat, the brown speckles scattered across her cheeks and hands. Her heavy breasts strained against the plain weave of her dress and apron.

But then I saw it: the faint flutter at her temples, the steady rhythm beneath the curve of her jaw, the pulse pushing life through her veins. My fangs slid down, and a hiss—feral and unbidden—escaped my lips.

I took a step toward her. A flicker moved at the edge of my sight. Before the thought had even fully formed, Serban had me pinned against the wall, his hand clamped around my throat, holding me as though I weighed nothing at all, my feet dangling inches above the stone floor.

His dark eyes—the nexus of his power—locked on mine. I couldn't look away, though my body strained to focus on Petra.

"This is why you are locked in your room, Magda," he said. "You will learn control, but the early days are the hardest." His voice was firm, yet threaded with an unexpected sympathy.

Strength flooded me, a heady rush that made my pulse race even though my heart no longer beat. Power surged through my limbs—intoxicating, dangerous.

"Why isn't she afraid?" I demanded. Some part of me wanted to taste her fear; its absence stung like disappointment.

"She knows I wouldn't allow any harm to come to her." His gaze never wavered. "I enthralled you when you first came, so you were powerless when she bathed you and changed your gown."

I had assumed Serban had done it. No man—save Dani— had ever treated my body with respect. But I had misjudged this one. The shock must have flickered across my face.

His expression hardened, almost affronted. "After five men had abused you, I thought your healing should begin with the gentler touch of a woman."

I swallowed; words caught rough in my throat. "How many other humans serve you?"

"There is a groom in the stables. A boy." His hand eased at my throat, the pressure loosening once he was certain I understood, and I slid down until my feet again touched the floor. He turned toward Petra and dismissed her with a nod. "That will be all. Thank you."

She dipped her head, obedient, and disappeared down the hall from which she had come, her footsteps fading into silence.

We stepped into the night, the courtyard glowing with the unsteady light of torches. The barn loomed ahead, its doors wide, two horses—one cream, one dark brown—already saddled and waiting. No groom in sight. Serban mounted with effortless grace, pausing only to glance at me. When I swung into the saddle, he turned without a word, spurred his horse, and vanished into the darkness. I urged mine forward, the sound of hooves striking stone echoing between us.

For nearly an hour we rode through the hills—sometimes flying in a loose gallop across open ground, sometimes reduced to a cautious trot as the path twisted into rocky passes. At last Serban crested a ridge and raised his hand, commanding me to halt. He dismounted in one smooth motion, boots crunching against the gravel, and waited until I joined him on foot.

He moved so quickly I barely saw it—his hand clamped against my face, firm but not cruel, forcing my gaze to his. The shock of it jolted through me, his fingers holding me still, commanding every flicker of my attention. He inhaled, slow and deliberate, as though tasting the night itself. His pupils widened, black swallowing silver, and I felt the shift before I understood it. A scent carried on the cold air brushed my senses—musky, acrid, animal. Beneath it, a faint sweetness, earthy and wild. His gaze went to the direction of the scent. "Fox," he murmured, voice dropping low. His grip eased, but his eyes stayed fixed beyond me. "Her den is near. Listen."

From deep in the ravine came a sharp, dog-like yip. My ears caught it instantly, every vibration reverberating inside me. The sound rolled around the stones and trees, until I could pinpoint its source with uncanny clarity. The hairs along my arms prickled upright.

"Give chase." His voice was low, certain, as he nodded down the slope.

I hesitated. "Can I catch it?"

"You are faster now than any beast in this forest," he said. "Go. Feel the slope beneath you. Smell the air. Listen."

I stood frozen, the command burning in me, half disbelieving it could be so simple—that I might master the night with nothing more than instinct.

"You don't need to think, Magda. Your body knows how to survive." And he nodded again. "Go."

I gave in and let my body carry me, feet skimming over the rocky slope. Gravel scattered and tumbled beneath me, but nothing slowed my momentum. The night itself seemed alive inside my skull—sounds too sharp, reverberating like struck metal, each one urging me on.

The scent was my tether, sharp and musky, pulling me first straight toward the den. But the fox sensed me, bolting into the brush. My power surged, and I veered after her, each turn as effortless as breath.

At last, I cornered her beneath a fallen log. Her body crouched low, trembling, eyes wide and wild as she cowered in the shadows. I bared my fangs at her—another predator, an alpha staking claim—making it plain how this would end.

I seized her, pulling her warm body to my lips. Before thought or revulsion could slow me, an inherent *knowing* roared to the surface. My ears caught the frantic patter of her heart, racing faster and faster as if she already knew her fate. My fangs sank into the soft vein of her neck, and hot blood rushed into me—this small creature giving her life for mine.

It was gamey on my tongue, sweet—tinged with earth and rot. So unlike Serban's blood, which had been golden honey on my lips. I drank until she was dry, until her small body lay limp in my arms, and only then did the enormity strike me: I had killed her. An animal, yes, but one that trembled and resisted like any soul who wished to live. I stood there, holding her lifeless weight, not knowing what to do.

Serban's voice cut through the night behind me, his boot steps crushing dried leaves and pine needles as he came nearer. "Put her down, Magda. Her carcass will feed the scavengers—and then the earth."

Kneeling, I laid her gently on a bed of pine needles, a clumsy echo of reverence. That was when I heard it—the high, frantic yips from deeper in the ravine. Kits. Her kits. Calling for the mother who would never return. I stood and looked toward Serban, the unasked question in my eyes.

"Finish them off," he said with a nod toward the den. "I've caught the scent of a wolf nearby. When you're done, find me."

Then he was gone—no more than a blur in my sharpened vision, a rush of air as he vanished into the trees. A breeze stirred after him, carrying with it the musk of wolf. Similar to the fox, yet heavier, darker—my senses catalogued it hungrily, as though the forest itself was writing a new language in my blood.

The yips drew me back. Thin, frantic cries that tugged me closer to the den. I crouched low, my vision keen, but even with this new clarity I could not pierce the darkness of the burrow. Instead, I listened—three tiny heartbeats, quick and desperate, hammering against the earth.

I slid my hand into the hole. Warm fur brushed my palm. I closed my fingers and pulled. The young fox was no larger than a kitten, trembling in my grip, its body feather-light. Its eyes blinked open, glassy and wide, fixing on me with a silent, instinctive terror. Its small heart battered against my hand, a frantic drum calling to the hunger still uncoiling inside me. I reached in and gathered the other two, cradling all three against my palms. At least they would have the small comfort of each other in their final moments. Tears blurred my vision, because what Serban hadn't said aloud was true—that ending the lives of these motherless kits was an act of mercy. Yet when I was done, the only thought clawing through me was not of kindness to them but to myself. What mercy exists for a mother without her child? Certainly not this life.

With a hollowness inside me, I made my way to where Serban had killed the wolf, letting the new creature inside me carry me forward, step after step, pushing down the emotions that threatened to break me if I held them, examined them too long. He stepped back when I approached and let me drain the last of the wolf's blood.

When our night's hunting was finished, we rode east toward Serban's keep. The first blush of dawn painted the sky, and when the sun's pink rays struck my eyes I winced.

"Pull up your hood. It will blunt the worst of it," he said, matter-of-fact. "Your eyes won't fully adjust yet for weeks."

I tugged the hood forward, angling my head so the heavy folds of fabric shaded my pupils. Even so, I flinched at every stray shaft of light. As we rode, Serban went on.

"I suspect the sensitivity we suffer in those first weeks—along with the lack of impulse control—is what gave rise to the legends and falsehoods humans whisper about our kind. Once our bodies adapt, once we master restraint, we can walk beside them in the market or on the street and never be suspected. The curse of the undead, hiding in plain sight."

"Why are you teaching me?" The question escaped at last, sharp and restless, rattling around in my mind since we left the stables hours before.

"Because it is what we do. I was taught, and now I teach. One day, if you choose to make another as you are now, you will do the same. That is the way of it." He might as well have been reciting scripture, so devoid of feeling was his tone.

"When may I leave? To return to Buna?" The question slipped out before I could bite it back.

"You'll go when you are ready. Not before." His eyes flicked to mine, cold and cutting, a look sharpened to a weapon. The shiver it sent down my spine carried fear—but twined within it was a thread of exhilaration. I could not pretend the hunger of this new self explained it. No, even the girl I was before had found danger intoxicating. And now, that girl and this creature both stirred at once.

"Tomorrow night you learn to take from a human," he said, his eyes straight ahead as if they'd hadn't just cut me to the quick. "Enough to sustain you without taking a life. And then to wipe the memories, so the human wakes in the morning none the wiser."

My fingers dug into the rough wool of my hood, and I wondered what awaited me.

32

NEW PREY

Magda—May 1390

The next day, I spent my time in the library. Serban lingered nearby, watching me from the corner of his eye, hovering like a nervous milkmaid whenever Petra appeared. His nearness grated on me. Never had I been so closely watched, so carefully managed. Still, I wasn't locked in my room while he monitored me, and that was something—a small, pitiful freedom.

Petra went about her duties, lighting candles on the long table, though out of habit, I thought. The main hall had no windows to draw in daylight, but with the sharpness of my vision, I hardly needed it.

I sat in a large chair, thumbing through a stack of books I'd gathered from the shelves—tales of Christian Crusades to the Holy Lands, hand-illuminated and lavishly decorated copies of the Bible, the Quran, the Torah, most in languages I couldn't read. Bestiaries describing mythical animals, their margins crowded with creatures half-lion, half-serpent—I wondered how many had once walked the earth in truth. Star charts mapped the heavens in painstaking detail, constellations inked in gold and lapis.

I tried to imagine the lifetimes Serban must have lived to gather such treasures. I looked up at him. "How did you come to be here?"

"I don't stay in one place for long," he said, not looking up from his ledgers. "I've lived in Rome. Across the sea the Turks call the Akdeniz. In Constantinople. At the foot of the Altai Mountains—that's where I discovered my fondness for the horses in my stable." A small smile touched his mouth before disappearing. "Athens, for a time. Among other places."

I didn't even know most of the places he'd spoken of. To see the world like that—it was a life I'd barely imagined was possible. Certainly not for a peasant. "But why here?" I asked. Of all the places he could have chosen, a war-torn land seemed the least likely.

"I follow war," he said tersely, irritation knitting his brows together. "You will find it is a convenience for our kind. Battlefields are full of men already dying, living conditions breed sickness. To hasten the end a soldier knows is coming is a mercy."

Were we—what I had become—no better than vultures living on carrion?

His voice did not waver. "And if someone goes missing between battles, who is to say what took them? It is easier to blame the enemy at your gates than a thing most men refuse to believe exists."

He looked at me pointedly. "And war is here." He slid from the perch where he'd been watching me—pretending to work —and began to pace. "...skirmishes along your borders. The Ottoman Empire forcing its way north—enslaving your people, buying loyalty from those with means."

Buying loyalty from those with means. Those words settled on me, somehow separate from the rest.

"And in the brief stretches of peace," he continued, "your people turn on one another. They always do. No different than anywhere else I've been."

"That day in the glen. Caius said he thought he'd recognized you." I said.

"The golden-haired one? Or the other?" he asked, referring to Dani.

My heart hurt at remembering—the foolish infatuation I thought was love that lived inside the naive girl, hot and reckless. Now only a gaping void in my soul remained. "Caius was the one with the blue eyes and light hair, the son of the boyar," I said softly.

"I don't recall seeing him before, but I know of his father... and his father's men. The ones who took you," he added grimly. "I've been here for many years now. We are only a few hours' ride from your village."

For the first time, I had some idea of where I was. Knowing I was so close to Buna made my heart ache.

He stopped pacing and folded his arms across his chest. "And I've traveled near to your home before, so perhaps he recognized me." He shrugged. "My horses are..." He searched for the word. "...unique."

They were that. "If your intention is to blend in, the fine horses and the glittering rings may not be the best approach." I didn't soften my observation, nor did I particularly care how he received it.

For a moment, amusement threatened at the corner of his mouth. He mastered it quickly, smoothing his expression back into something more guarded.

"Why were you there—near my village?" I asked, curious about the way it seemed he watched us go about our lives.

"I don't interfere in the squabbles of humans, but you could say I play both sides." He shrugged, as if that explained anything. "I'd heard the boyar's men met with a go-between for a small group of Turkish forces—a few summers ago." He paused, searching his memory. "It was the summer I saw you picking apples." A faint nod. "I tracked the meetings. Once, even the boyar himself met with a Turkish general. I watched from a hill." His mouth tightened slightly. "I think he saw me."

"Why?" I asked. "Why would the boyar meet with our enemies?"

"To broker a battle," he said. "A small one. For coin." There was a hint of dry humor in his tone, as though he were explaining something obvious. "Both sides gain what they want. The boyar reinforces his warnings about foreigners—fear keeps people obedient when they share a common enemy. The Turks receive payment, secure a tentative alliance with someone powerful in case the conflict grows, and can report back to their superiors that an engagement took place. Everyone wins—except for those who fight, of course."

"The summer we met?" I asked quietly. "Was it the fighting later that season?" Memory rose unbidden—the orchard heavy with fruit, the reckless sweetness of the day I gave myself to Caius. And then the aftermath: the wounded carried back on carts, blood soaking through linen, Buna and I tending them for days while the village mourned its "narrow escape."

Serban considered the question, then reached for a small journal tucked beneath a stack of books near his chair. He thumbed through several pages, scanning quickly until he found the entry he wanted.

"June—1387."

My head was still reeling from what I learned when we rode into a nearby village long after dark, and left our horses hobbled in a field. Serban wore the fur mantle again, and I a dark dress that had mysteriously appeared in my room, along with a new pair of boots, these ones a perfect fit.

"Pull up your hood, Magda." Serban cautioned as we walked in the shadows between the buildings.

I shot him a questioning glance. It was dark, the sun was no longer a threat, and even then my eyes were becoming more accustomed to the sun a little more each day.

"We aren't that far from your village. You are supposed to be dead. I don't think you are ready to answer questions about how, and why, you still walk."

Begrudgingly I pulled up my hood and hid my face in the shadows.

Within moments we both heard it, the singsong of a drunken man who had spent too long at the tavern drinking ale, trying to find his way back home in the dark, weaving with steps unsteady down the lane.

Serban reached out a hand to slow me and indicate to watch.

The man was nearly upon us before he realized we were there. He looked up and smiled, at Serban and then me, and then his smile slipped away. Fear for an instant, and when I saw his eyes widen every nerve in my body fired. Even in the dark I could see the way the pulse point in his temples thrummed in time with the beat of his heart, the goosebumps forming on the bit of skin exposed on his neck. The awareness of those changes was intoxicating...and arousing. The way my body flooded with pleasure when I'd touched myself or laid with Dani, I felt it again. I was confused as I watched Serban look in the man's eyes, make no move toward him, but I could see and hear the voice Serban wove into the man's thoughts, gentle, soothing, the same one he'd used on me. The man's heartbeat immediately slowed, and then he took an unsteady step toward Serban, one, then another. It was painful watching his lumbering gait, and it was all I could do not to step forward and offer him an arm to steady him. As if Serban read my thoughts, he cut me a look that made me recoil.

Serban beckoned the drunk, and after a few more wobbly steps he fell into Serban's embrace. The small man was almost completely wrapped in Serban's mantle. I saw him dip to drink from the man, and I heard the small weak sound his skin made as it parted for Serban's fangs, and then the whoosh of the man's pulse as he drank. The smell hit me and I dropped to my knees and trembled, fearing Serban's wrath if I did what I wanted and joined him.

Serban kept one eye on me as he drank, his watchfulness a constant stifling shackle on me. But then he pulled his mouth away and his eyes told me it was my turn. The man lolled in his arms, twin crimson rivers snaking down his neck.

Serban held the man as I fed. My teeth were closer together than Serban's and I made two new punctures just inside the two he had left. I pulled from him until I heard Serban command me to stop. Like the first few times I fed from Serban's wrist, I did not want to release him. The hunger had a will of its own, tightening its grip the longer I drank, until it felt less like sustenance and more like surrender. Back then, when I failed to pull away, Serban had forced the distance himself—rough, unyielding—reminding me who held the line.

Now the sensation shifted. What had begun as hunger deepened into something warmer, more intimate. Sexual pleasure unfurled through me, slow and insistent, threading along my nerves until it pooled low in my body. My breath hitched. Awareness sharpened in ways that had nothing to do with blood. It wasn't attraction for the drunk man, I knew that much, but the confusing feelings overwhelmed me.

"Listen, Magda." Serban said into my head, snapping me back to attention. Not risking speaking aloud for fear of someone overhearing, he continued to communicate with me silently. "Listen to the speed of his heartbeat. It's faint now. If you take more—it wouldn't take much—his heart will stop. Don't risk taking more." Serban leaned down again and licked the man's neck, and I saw the four piercings close, slowly at first, and then faster, until not a single mark remained.

Serban looked into the man's eyes, which had stayed open during the encounter. Through his connection to me, he patiently urged me to try the same, to put thoughts into the drunk man's head, soothing, gentle but firm, and to ask the man to speak if he understood my instructions.

The man nodded dumbly, and repeated in a low whisper what I'd said to him. "I walked home from the inn. I had too much to drink. I saw no one."

'What is your name?" Serban said silently to the man.

"Albert," the man responded.

"Go home to your wife, Albert." Serban whispered.

Albert, with an unsteady gait and a faint smile, meandered his way down the lane.

Serban looked at me, his dark eyes glittering with something like pride. "Well done." He said softly, and then looked away from me and started into the dark night.

We retraced our path to the horses, his silence between us heavy. When we mounted, he turned back toward me, eyes narrowing. "How do you feel?" he asked.

How did I feel? Alive. More alive than I'd felt at any point in my miserable life—save the night Anca was born—and that realization cut deep, a dagger of guilt burning low in my gut. The trembling hesitation that had seized me the night before in the forest was gone.

Perhaps Serban's mercy—Albert still lived—had made tonight's lesson easier. But the power I'd summoned to cloud Albert's mind, that same intoxicating trance I'd felt under Serban's hands the first time three years ago, now flowed through me. It was heady, powerful. Arousal threaded through every moment, the hands of a dozen invisible lovers caressing every inch of my skin, first at the moment I scented Albert's blood in the cold dark, then again when I snaked my thoughts into Albert's mind and controlled him.

Serban still sat astride his horse, waiting for my answer. But I suspected every thought crowding my mind had already found its way to him—and that this was what he truly wanted to know: whether I fully understood what I had become.

I nodded, uncertain at first, then steadier as the pulse of something new took hold in me. I raised my chin to meet his eyes. The movement sent my hood sliding back, my hair cascading down my shoulders.

"I feel strong." It was the simplest truth I had.

Serban said nothing, but I thought I saw a small smile tug at the corner of his mouth before he turned his horse and kicked him forward into the night.

After our return, a young boy waited in the stables. Fifteen at most, all bones and long limbs, his head bent low. He wouldn't look at me. Fear? Deference? I couldn't tell. But the tilt of his lashes, the color of his thick, unruly hair—warm, deep-brown—stirred a sorrowful memory—Dani at that age.

"That will be all tonight, Nicolae," Serban said, passing him the reins of both mounts. The boy nodded silently and dipped his head, his boots crunching on the gravel as he walked the horses back to their stalls.

I must have lingered on tender Nicolae a moment too long, because Serban's hand clamped around my wrist. He dragged me behind him through the servant's entrance of the keep and didn't stop until we reached my chamber. He flung the door open, pushed me inside, and shut it hard behind us.

I could have pulled away—should have—but instead I clung to him. My arms wound around his holding my wrist, drawing it tight between my breasts, seeking the pressure, the friction. The excitement still thrummed through me, my body alive and unrelenting, the ache between my thighs, the place wet and swollen, pulsing with the memory of the ride home and the rhythm of the saddle beneath me.

Serban's expression hardened—anger, discomfort, something like pity flickering behind his eyes.

"I can smell it on you, Magda," he said sharply. "Feeding from a human awakens everything—sight, sound, scent, touch. It floods the body with hunger and pleasure both. It's disorienting, I know." He pushed me back, gently but firmly, disentangling his arm awkwardly from me. "In time, you'll learn to tell the difference between that hunger and what is truly desire."

He was right. I could smell it too—my own arousal, hot, thick, and sweet. But knowing the cause didn't lessen the ache. I whimpered in frustration, arching my back, a cat in heat, every nerve alive beneath my skin. The old Magda would have been appalled at the way I was acting, but who I was now knew no shame. The hunger had nowhere to go, curling tighter inside me until I could hardly breathe. I raised a hand absently and squeezed one of my breasts, my lips parting at the sensation. A wanton moan escaped my lips and Serban's eyes went wide, consumed by blackness.

The flicker of change in his face—hesitation, awareness— made the air thicken. I was still a woman, and this, this allure, was the only power the world had ever granted me. And I would wield it, even if it damned me further. I used my newfound speed to push Serban against the door, catching him off guard. One hand held his neck the way Ivar's men had held mine against the tree, and my other went to his crotch. His cock was thick and hard, and I felt the phantom pleasure imagining it inside me.

His face closed off, any sympathy gone. The shove came quick and hard, sending me stumbling until I hit the floor. My pride, not my body, took the blow. I looked up at him, breathless, waiting for softness that never came. His stare was winter-cold.

"Testing your limits tonight, are you?" His tone was bleak. He turned and left the room. The hollow echo of his key in the lock reverberated through my skull.

The sweet scent of my desire still lingered in the room, but with it, a hint of another scent mingled with mine. Musky, earthy smoke mingled with my honeyed spice. I knew without a doubt what the foreign scent was.

Despite his denial, desire answered in him as fiercely as it did in me.

33

TRUTHS

Magda—May 1390

Petra shuffled down the corridor, broom in hand, her gaze lowered not in fear, but in habit long ingrained. She did not look at me—nor at Serban, who sat bent over his ledgers, though there was less secrecy in the posture now than burden. Matei, another vampire, had vanished again, swallowed by the night on errands I was no longer certain were entirely mysterious, only necessary.

This household—humans and vampires under one roof— still unsettled me. They were not chained. They were not cowering. And yet everything here moved in quiet orbit around Serban.

"Why do you have humans serving you?" I asked, keeping my voice calm, but I was tired of being kept in the dark.

I had noticed how closely he watched me whenever Petra or Nicolae drew near—not suspicion exactly, but vigilance. Habit, perhaps. He had lived too long not to anticipate the worst in his own kind.

He was master of this keep—of that there was no doubt—but I had never seen cruelty in the way he commanded it. No raised hand. No careless threat. Petra moved with the ease of someone long accustomed, not terrified. Nicolae lingered without flinching. Also still, the truth pressed against me. We were predators by nature. And they were not.

Serban looked up slowly this time, not bristling, not snapping. His eyes searched my face as if weighing the question for what it was—not accusation, but need.

"Why does that trouble you?" he asked quietly.

There was no irritation in him now. Only caution. And something else—an understanding that I was no longer asking to provoke him. I was asking because I deserved to know.

"Explain it to me," I said, trying to keep the edge out of my voice. "You've made yourself my teacher for some reason. So go on—explain."

Serban exhaled slowly, the sound controlled but weary. "I did not *make* myself anything," he said firmly. "I turned you. That binds me to you whether I wish it or not." He straightened from the desk, pushing the ledger aside. "You deserve to understand what you are now. Not because I seek obedience. Not because I enjoy authority." His gaze held mine steadily. "Because what awaits you will not spare your ignorance."

The words carried no threat—only gravity.

"When the time comes for us to part," he continued, quieter now, "I will not have you unprepared." He did not look away when he said it. "I want you to be ready."

Serban's careful stillness shifted—just slightly. Not weakness. Not surrender. But the focused composure of a man deciding whether to carry something alone a while longer.

"You've never told me why you turned me," I said quietly. "You could have drained me—finished what Ivar and his men began. Or you could have kept riding, as you claim you always do. You don't interfere in the squabbles of men, remember?" I held his gaze. I did not flinch. "So why was this any different?"

Silence settled between us. For a moment, he did not look like a creature weighing whether to dominate or deflect. He looked like a man tired of holding a secret. And in that pause, I felt it—not a crack in armor, but the weight behind it. The truth he had kept not to control me...but because speaking it would bind us in ways neither of us could undo.

He had broken his rule. But not lightly.

He closed the ledger and rose. Two steps brought him closer, and he stopped—not looming, not crowding, but near enough that the air between us felt charged. Power lived in him always; that would never change. But it was held in check, leashed by will rather than temper.

His hands curled once at his sides, before he drew in a slow breath and let them open again. The movement was subtle, almost weary. For the first time since I had known him, Serban did not look like a creature carved from iron certainty. He looked like a man carrying something heavy—and deciding, at last, to set it down.

Maybe honesty—not defiance—would bring me closer to the truth. "You have to understand my position, Serban," I said, my voice steady but stripped of its earlier edge. "Weeks ago, I was powerless—a peasant, a wife, a mother—living in a quiet village only a few hours from here. My world was small, but it was mine."

I swallowed. "Now I wake with strength I never asked for, in a house that is not my own. I walk among the living as something no longer alive. My husband and child are dead. I was hunted, brutalized, nearly erased...and remade."

The words felt strange spoken aloud—too stark, too real. "I do not even know why it happened," I continued, meeting his eyes. "Not truly. You tell me I am meant for something. That I must be prepared. But prepared for what? For whom?" My voice softened, not accusing—aching. "You ask me to trust you while I stand in the ruins of my life." I held his gaze. "I am not your prisoner, Serban. But I am not yet free either." I was not demanding answers. I was asking for them.

He drew a chair toward him, the legs whispering across the stone, and turned it before sitting—close enough to speak plainly, not to dominate. He rested his forearms along the back. When his eyes lifted to mine, they were no longer shuttered.

"Keeping you in the dark has not protected you," he said at last. "It has only widened the distance between us. You deserve better than that." The admission settled between us—simple, unadorned. "You asked first about the humans."

He leaned back slightly, gaze drifting—not evasive, but reflective. "I was a man once. Flesh and breath. Fear and hunger. It is easy, after enough years, to forget the weight of a heartbeat. To forget how fragile a life is when it ends only once."

His eyes returned to me. "I keep them near because I must remember what I was. What we were." A pause. "You will need that memory as well, Magda. This existence stretches long. If you sever yourself from who you were—wife, mother, daughter —you will not become stronger." His voice lowered. "You will become less." There was no superiority in the warning. No lecture. Only experience.

The life stretching before me—unchosen, unasked for—settled over my shoulders like a cloak I had not agreed to wear. How many times must a woman of twenty be remade by forces beyond her will? Even now, the road ahead felt charted by hands not my own.

Serban's voice drew me back. He did not speak down to me now. Nor around me. He spoke as if the truth belonged to us both.

"Petra worked for the man whose name I carry," he said quietly. "She was younger then. Thirty, perhaps. I never thought to ask." A faint, almost self-reproachful breath left him. "He was not a merciful man." His jaw tightened. "He beat her. Often."

There was no embellishment. No drama. Just fact. "When I killed him and assumed his place, she begged me not to send her away. Said she and her family would not survive it." His gaze lowered briefly, thoughtful. "I offered to turn her—I would not have done so without her consent. She refused."

His eyes lifted to mine again. "She chose mortality. And she chose to remain here."

A quiet pause stretched between us. "I believe she understood that I was not her enemy," he added. "That whatever I am, I would not harm her." The words were not boastful. If anything, they carried the weight of responsibility. "She has been in this house nearly forty years now," he said. "Not as chattel. Not as prey. Because she wishes to be."

He did not ask me to approve. He simply trusted me with the truth. "And the young boy, Nicolae?" I asked, needing to understand everything Serban kept so carefully hidden.

"Petra's grandson," he said quietly. "Matei's son."

The name lingered between us, and something in his expression eased—just slightly. "Matei fell ill years ago, after his wife died. Fever took him slowly." His gaze drifted. "On his last night as a man, he asked me for the gift his mother refused. He did not ask lightly. He asked because he could not bear the thought of leaving his boy alone in the world."

Serban's voice did not carry pride. Only gravity. "I warned him what it meant," he continued. "What it would cost him. He chose it anyway."

I found myself wondering what I would have done, had death stood at my bedside and a choice been placed in my hands. To live like this. Would I have taken it?

He looked away then, the lines around his mouth tightening. "He is a good man," Serban said quietly. For a fleeting moment, something sad crossed his face—something like fear of eventual loss, though vampires did not age as men did. Immortality did not spare one from grief; it only stretched it thinner across centuries.

Serban had not stolen a family. He had preserved one. And the loyalty I had sensed in Petra, in Nicolae—even in Matei— no longer felt like obligation. It felt chosen.

I found myself wondering how many times he had done this—how many fragile human lives he had steadied at the edge of ruin, only to step back and let them remain—or be— what they wished.

"And keeping humans around can be...practical," he said after a moment. "I send Nicolae—and Petra, when she was stronger—to the nearby villages. They blend in, go to the markets, listen. They bring back information." His eyes met mine. "It was Nicolae who brought me the news of your husband and child."

The air between us thickened. He did not look away from the truth of it. "He did not understand what he was carrying when he returned," Serban added quietly. "Only that something terrible had occurred."

The restraint in his voice was no longer iron discipline. It was sorrow kept contained. I had always wondered why Nicolae avoided my eyes. I had assumed it was fear—of me, of what I was becoming.

Now I understood. It was not fear. It was the memory of being the one who bore news that shattered what remained of my world.

"And you are right," he said at last. "I broke my rule." There was no defensiveness in the admission. Only acceptance. "It was not coincidence that I was there that night." He drew in a slow breath. "I was summoned in a dream by something older than men and older than our kind—a being called Ossivian. It moves in darkness, a messenger between us and the old gods."

His eyes did not leave mine. "It spoke your name, Magda." A faint tightening in his jaw—reverence, not fear. "It showed me what would unfold. The path set before you. And the part I was to play within it."

He did not rush the next words. "I was told to wait in the woods. To interfere with nothing. To act only at the moment appointed." His gaze darkened, not with anger at me—but at the memory of restraint. "If I stepped forward too soon, you would have died beyond my reach. That was made clear."

The air felt thinner. "I did not stand idle because I was indifferent," he said quietly. "I waited because it was the only way you would survive." There was no plea in his voice. No demand for absolution. Only truth.

I stammered, words failing me. "What do you mean? What is this thing? Where does it live? I have to speak with it."

"If I took you to the cave where I met it that night, it would no longer be there. It only comes when it wishes to speak to you."

I sat in stunned silence, and when I didn't speak, he continued.

"My charge was precise—turn you, heal you, teach you... and then release you when you are strong enough to stand alone." There was no triumph in the words. No sense of accomplishment. His gaze deepened, solemn. "What was done to you was witnessed," he said. "The old gods are not blind. Justice does not move swiftly—but it moves." A pause. "And you, Magda...you are meant to be its instrument."

Not a weapon. An instrument.

His hand lifted then—but hesitated, as if uncertain of its welcome. When his fingers brushed the loose strand of hair from my face, the touch was light. Careful. Something closer to apology. In his eyes I saw no pity—only sorrow for what I had endured, and maybe a fragile hope for what I might become.

He rose without another word and went to his room, leaving me alone with the terrible understanding that both my death and whatever future awaited me rested in the hands of the gods.

That night, for the first time, my door stood unlocked. And still—I was not free.

34

ANONYMOUS NO MORE

Baird—June 2026

Baird had asked himself a dozen times over the last couple of months whether his absurd plan would hold together. Surely Mira suspected something. A faceless buyer who didn't haggle, who refused guidance, who'd only said, *"Make what you'd want to wear."*

That should have given him away.

But perhaps the pressure of perfecting the ruby ring had absorbed her so completely she hadn't stopped to question who this one was truly for. He'd even considered waiting to ask —or abandoning the thought altogether—his fear and uncertainty clouding what should have been simple. But everything Sorcha had said, everything the goddess had shown him, led to the same truth: only by loving Mira fully could they come through this together.

He didn't know if he had another year with her, or a human lifetime. And in the end, he realized it didn't matter. Whenever doubt seeped into the cracks of the life he was trying to build, the beast inside him stirred. Now he didn't fight it. He let it rise.

Because if that part of him knew anything, it was how to live in the moment—how to love without hesitation. The vampire took hold, flooding him with a certainty so complete there was no space left for fear. He let it flow through the bond between them, and Mira felt it at once.

Each time he did, she answered him with joy—fierce and unwavering. And sometimes, just for a heartbeat, he thought he saw something else behind her eyes. A presence. A knowing. As if the Goddess herself were watching...and nodding in approval.

The day came bright, blue skies and high clouds, the kind of morning that felt like an invitation. Baird knew then he wouldn't wait another second. When he asked her to walk with him up Glen Rosa to check the herd—a daily ritual he shared with Bunny—she eagerly agreed, happy for the excuse to leave the studio behind and be with him. They walked hand in hand along the path beside the stream that ran through the valley. Bunny trotted happily at their side—darting off now and again to chase one of her namesakes, her long legs barely touching the earth when she hit her stride.

They passed the footbridge, that familiar mile marker just beyond where Mira had once found him after returning to the island—after she had fled back to America, unsure then if she could trust the depth of his feelings. Now, with her fingers laced through his, that doubt felt distant, softened by the quiet certainty of her presence beside him. He smiled to himself, remembering her running down that path, bundled in her heavy coat and hat on that cold winter day—how it had taken everything in him to stand there stone-faced while she stumbled through her awkward apology for not believing him.

The moment replayed in his mind like a highlight reel. How he'd managed to stay stoic for a few heartbeats, until he realized what he truly wanted—what he'd been aching for—was to see her smile. The one he'd missed during the long month it had taken her to understand that what they shared was something fated. When it finally came, it was like watching a sunrise for the first time. A thing a vampire never took for granted, even after his eyes had learned to bear the light again.

Around the bend, the Blue Pools came into view. When he found her here the first time, she'd been a goddess come to life —dipping beneath the waterfall, standing tall in the frigid water as if the cold couldn't touch her. Even knowing he'd intruded on her private moment, he couldn't look away. In that moment, she had owned the entire valley. And now he was sure why.

He'd felt it with every fiber of his being—something ancient in her, something she couldn't yet see. Back then, she was at war with herself: the tug between living a so-called normal life and surrendering to the power pulling at her. Now, watching her, he realized how much she'd changed. She almost didn't seem like the same person anymore.

He couldn't explain it, he knew it was time. He was on edge, a strange, restless energy had taken hold of him, the ring box burning a hole in his pocket. He slowed, letting her hand slip from his. Mira continued on, a few steps ahead, eyes wide as she soaked in the valley, as if seeing it anew.

"Ye ken," he said softly, and she turned back toward him, curious, "there are things I've done for ye I never told ye about.

Not because I wanted secrets—but because I wanted the timing right."

"Baird?" Just his name. A question.

He took a deep breath and exhaled, then sank to one knee. Mira's eyes went wide, and for the span of a heartbeat—what remained of that organ in his chest—clenched in fear. But when her hand flew to her mouth and that smile broke free behind it, wide and radiant, he knew he'd never had anything to fear.

He lifted the ring box he'd slipped from his pocket a moment earlier, opening it as she turned back toward him. When she saw what lay inside—*Brigid's Sun*—her eyes went even wider, and then she laughed, that deep, belly laugh that always undid him. He couldn't help but laugh with her. "I wondered how long it would take ye to realize ye'd been working for me," he said softly, voice cracking just enough to betray how hard he was trying to keep it steady. "I couldna risk having anyone else do it," he said. "So I asked ye to make it." He took the ring from the box and held it out to her.

She took a tentative step toward him, and he reached for her hand.

"Mirren Faith Garvie," he said, her full name catching slightly in his throat, his voice not quite his own yet. "Will ye be my wife?"

She nodded quickly, not a second of hesitation in her response, tears crowding her lashes before spilling freely down her cheeks. A shaky, half-laughing gasp tore from her as she tried to speak.

"When—I—oh, ugh," she choked, laughing and crying all at once, words tripping over each other. "When I boxed it up to ship it to the buyer"—she shot him a bright, watery look, almost disbelieving—"...it felt like I was ripping a piece of my soul right out." She broke then, joyful sobs shaking her as she laughed through them, breathless, unable to stop smiling.

"That's because it was never meant to leave ye." He said quietly.

Baird slipped the yellow diamond onto her finger, and in that moment, the sun broke free of the clouds, its light gathering into a single radiant beam that caught the stone and set it ablaze. "The Goddess said this ring would bless the wearer..." Mira let out a soft laugh, shaking her head in disbelief. "Oof."

He knew it was another truth, another answer, falling gently into place at the very moment the Goddess wanted it to, and not a moment sooner. As if in answer, light erupted outward from Mira's skin, refracting through her in a dazzling display, making Mira gasp in awe. Not just the usual golden light, this time iridescent color radiated across her skin, bleeding past the fabric of her clothing: rose, aqua, lavender, peridot—all shimmering together in a kaleidoscope of brilliance, threaded through with golden flares. She stumbled back a step, brow furrowed in astonishment, until Baird caught her hand and drew her close again with a reassuring smile.

"Dinnae retreat from it, Mira," he said softly. "The Goddess —or wherever your light comes from—approves. Sorcha told me once not to fear what feeds your magic," he added softly. "I think I finally understand what she meant."

Mira laughed, trembling with awe as the radiance began to fade. She lifted her arm, still sparkling faintly with flecks of color, and admired the ring Baird knew she'd secretly loved from the moment she began to shape it—her heart, her magic, her soul all poured into its making.

As she watched, a honey bee drifted down and settled lightly on her forearm.

Her eyes widened briefly, and Baird murmured, reassuring Mira. "Dinnae move—she'll be gone soon. I think she's admiring the show too."

"Maybe she thinks I'm some new kind of flower..." Mira whispered.

Then a second bee landed on her hand. And a third. Within moments, her forearm and the back of her hand were covered in honey bees—not swarming, but resting gently, their wings trembling in a slow, rhythmic harmony. Their thrum filled the air—soft, resonant—echoing the electric pulse that seemed to hum beneath Mira's skin.

Baird met her gaze, and they both understood: the bees meant no harm. This, too, was a blessing.

"Or maybe," Baird said very softly, "...the bees ken exactly who ye are."

One by one, the bees lifted into the air and drifted away, a golden stream rising toward Goat Fell until they vanished into the light.

35

APIS ET LEPUS

"So, Mira," the woman said, her attention fully on me. "Tell me about the wedding. Formal or casual? Destination or local? Indoor or outdoor?" The bridal consultant—Sylvia—a tall, elegant woman with silver hair and a serene energy—settled us into plush seating area and placed flutes of chilled champagne into our hands. Anne had made an appointment for dress shopping at a boutique in downtown Boston as soon as I said I was coming, pulling significant strings to make it happen on such short notice. Sylvia gave me her complete, undivided attention, as though I—and my wedding—were the only things on her schedule that day.

"It's going to be small. On the Isle of Arran, in Scotland. A destination wedding for these two," I said, motioning toward Anne and Dillon, who had drifted to a rack of dresses and were murmuring to one another. Clearly, they already had ideas about what I should wear. "I'm originally from Boston, but I live there now—with my fiancé, Baird." Even after weeks to let it sink in, the word still sent a shiver of excitement down my spine.

Thinking of him tugged at something deep inside me—an invisible thread pulled taut by distance. I'd barely been apart from him since returning to Arran, his presence settling into my life like a second pulse, the *me* slowly, willingly subsumed by an *us* that felt destined. Inevitable.

The ache deepened without warning. I turned away before the sting in my eyes could betray me, missing him with an intensity I felt in my body—and mourning, all at once, the absence of my parents, who should have been here for this moment. I pressed my hand to my chest, breathed through the tightness, and forced the emotions back into their proper place.

"Dillon is going to walk me down the aisle, and Anne"—I glanced toward them as Anne gestured animatedly, shaking her head, her distaste for the enormous ballgown Dillon was holding unmistakable—"will be my maid of honor...just her. Like I said...a small wedding." I smiled, trying to find a way to make Sylvia see the picture as clearly as I did. "The ceremony will be in a summer house on the grounds of Brodick Castle, and the reception on the terrace, overlooking the gardens." The place had claimed me the moment I first walked its paths—as if it had been waiting, patient and certain, for me to arrive. I remembered looking back from the gardens to the castle the first time I'd visited, imagining fairy lights at twilight and soft music, and feeling as though the scene I'd dreamed up belonged to someone else. But maybe—just maybe—I hadn't been imagining at all. Maybe I'd been glimpsing the future.

My future.

Warmth spread through me, my breath loosening, my pulse

steadying, as if my body had known the truth long before my mind allowed it: my gift of sight had been at work all along, guiding me. In moments like this, the distance I'd once felt—from the world, from men I'd dated, even from myself—threw the connection I felt now into sharp relief. I hadn't been whole until I learned to trust my true self, accepted my gift. And in return a greater gift took root and blossomed within my body: Brigid's power, steady and patient, just beneath my skin—though I still questioned why *me*.

"That sounds beautiful, Mira," she said, her hand warm and steady against mine—a touch that should have felt too familiar, but didn't. Sylvia seemed to have a way of sensing exactly how much reassurance a bride needed, and at that moment, I needed more than I wanted to admit. "Any must-haves?" she asked softly. "Or silhouettes I should stay away from before I start pulling dresses?"

Anne's voice carried across the boutique. "Absolutely not."

Sylvia and I shared a look and turned in unison toward the source—Dillon frozen, another ballgown in hand, Anne already shaking her head.

I pulled myself away from the unfolding scene and turned my attention back to Sylvia. "I'm drawn to lace—something that feels a little bohemian," I said. "Flowers in my hair instead of a veil. And I'll be wearing an emerald pendant, so I'll need a neckline that lets it be seen." I shrugged, unsure I could give more guidance than that. I'd never been one of those girls that had all the details of her wedding planned years in advance, and I'd started to wonder if my two best friends had been doing the dreaming for me. I leaned closer and added softly, "But bring in a ballgown. If Dillon doesn't get his moment, I'll never hear the end of it."

With a knowing wink Sylvia set to work, directing a second consultant as dresses disappeared toward the fitting rooms—lace, tulle, satin passing in soft waves. When she returned, I was still on the couch, champagne cool in my hand, my pulse ticking just a little faster. "Ready?"

The first dress was the sacrificial ballgown, worn only so it could be ruled out. It was stunning—heavy satin, beaded bodice, sweetheart neckline, an enormous train—but the weight of it pressed down on me. A dress for a princess in a cathedral, not for the rustic wooden structure overlooking Brodick Bay.

Sylvia walked ahead of me, silently announcing my arrival. Both Dillon and Anne fell quiet as I stepped into the viewing area and onto the small platform. I lowered my hands, letting the full skirt fall into place for maximum effect, then looked to my friends for a reaction.

Anne smiled sweetly, but the tight set of her jaw betrayed her. She knew—correctly—that this silhouette was all wrong for me. And Dillon, who had wanted so badly for this to be *the* dress, sagged as the truth reached him.

"Fine," he said at last. "It's wearing you. Not the other way around. Anne is right, as usual." I laughed as Dillon raised the white flag, the look of defeat unmistakable.

Anne's face relaxed, reassured now that I wasn't in love with the dress. "It's overwhelming you," she said. "All I see is the dress."

Satisfied that we were all on the same page—at least where ruling out the ballgown was concerned—I gathered the billowing skirt in my hands and returned to the dressing room. The next thirty minutes blurred into a procession of dresses: sleek sheath gowns that clung too tightly, A-line skirts that felt overly polite, long sleeves that weighed me down, strapless bodices that left me cold. One by one, they were stripped away, wrong for reasons I couldn't always name. But when I stepped into a trumpet silhouette, the lines finally made sense—enough that Sylvia and her companion exchanged a look before heading back to the racks to pull a second round.

When they returned a few minutes later, my gaze went straight to the dress on the top of the stack. Intricately embroidered ivory lace lay over a nude lining, the pattern almost alive beneath the boutique lights. The entire stack was beautiful—Chantilly lace, soft beading, moiré satin—but something about the first dress made everything else fall away.

A tingling warmth flooded my body when I reached out to touch it, my fingers brushing the delicate detail as my hand trembled slightly, my newfound magic stirring beneath my skin as I examined it.

"The lace on this one is truly special," Sylvia said offhand as she unzipped the gown and slipped it from its padded satin hanger. "It just felt like you," she said simply. "We only received it yesterday." She paused, studying it thoughtfully. "You're the first bride to try it on."

My heart began to pound the moment I stepped into the dress, Sylvia held the bodice open as I slid my arms through. When she zipped it up, the gown settled against me like a second skin, light and fluid, moving easily when I breathed. The neckline plunged into a clean V, sleeveless and elegant, while the lace overlay traced my curves—skimming my waist, following the line of my hips—before releasing into soft gussets mid-thigh that let the skirt fall and flow to the floor. A modest train fanned out behind me, just enough to whisper against the ground.

"The style is called *Flora and Fauna*," Sylvia said. "If you look closely at the hand-embroidered accents, you'll see plants —leaves, vines—along with insects and butterflies. Very *Queen of the Fairies* vibe."

I exhaled and took one last look at myself before stepping out of the dressing room, asking myself the question I already knew the answer to. Then something caught my eye. I stopped mid-step and leaned closer to the mirror, the room narrowing until there was nothing but the embroidery near the neckline.

A bee.

My hand flew to my mouth—it wasn't my imagination. It was stitched there, deliberate and unmistakable. Tears welled and spilled over, tracking hot and sudden down my cheeks. A reminder from the universe—blatant, unnecessary, and devastating all the same—of the day Baird proposed. Of the honey bees that had gathered on my hand and arm after he slid the ring onto my finger. I wiped my tears away quickly, careful not to let them fall onto the lace, the fingers of my other hand trembling as I ran them lightly over the fabric—this dress that somehow already knew my story.

When I walked into the viewing area, two sharp inhales greeted me—both Dillon and Anne momentarily speechless. I stepped onto the platform and turned slowly, studying myself from every angle the wraparound mirrors allowed. Sylvia said something quietly and nodded to her assistant, who crossed to a nearby cabinet and returned with a flower crown—silk instead of fresh flowers, but strikingly close to what I'd imagined. She placed it on my head, and I couldn't envision any other adornment with this dress. Simply perfect.

I let my mind wander, envisioning Baird's reaction, seeing me for the first time in this dress, half-listening as Sylvia explained the unique stitching on the lace to Anne and Dillon, until Anne tilted her head and went still.

"Wait," she said softly. "What's this on the train?" She stood and stepped closer for a better look.

I turned, craning to see over my shoulder, and my breath left me when my eyes found it—not decorative, not playful, but deliberate. A rabbit, embroidered in the same shimmering silver-gold thread as the bee, the focal point at the very center of the train.

Something tender gripped hard in my chest.

The universe, it seemed, had remembered Bunny too.

36

CONFESSIONAL

Serban—May 1390

Both Serban and Magda had dreamed of Ossivian the night before, and he told her that was the sign—that the hour had come for her to hear the gods' design with her own ears. That night they stood in the stables while Nicolae saddled the brown mare and his cream-colored gelding, the air thick with the scent of hay and the soft clatter of metal buckles being drawn tight. Magda paced the corridor just beyond the door, restless as a young doe sensing a coming storm.

"You can return, you know," Serban said. It slipped out more gently than he intended. She didn't have to fumble through this new existence alone. She could come and go as she pleased—so long as she was discreet, so long as she did not endanger his household.

She paused, her brows drawing together. "I didn't think you

wanted me here. I felt like I was a burden." Her words trailed off softly.

A burden. He winced at the term. He would never have chosen it himself—not even in those early days when Ossivian had first laid this charge at his feet and resentment had bloomed in his chest. The guilt lodged sharp as a thorn beneath his ribs. He cleared his throat, steadying his voice, hoping the sincerity would carry. "I am sorry I made you feel that way, Magda. It was never my intention."

And it was the truth. Somewhere between her questions, her fiery temper, and her unbroken will, he had come to enjoy her presence—more than he cared to admit aloud. Despite all she had suffered, despite the grief that would likely haunt her for centuries, she still carried curiosity like a flame cupped in her hands. A keen mind, unafraid to probe or challenge. It had been a very long time since he'd met anyone who could do that.

"Any time," he added quietly. "The room will remain yours. Unlocked." He added, small smile at his lips, trying to convince her that he finally trusted her, almost wishing she'd use that sarcastic wit against him.

She shifted uncomfortably. "I don't know what to say, Serban. I appreciate the offer. Truly. But I know you have your rules—and I'm afraid I would break them. Stepping into the petty conflicts of men, the very disputes that put my countrymen at risk...that is exactly where I would find myself." Her voice thinned as she searched for more justification, then abandoned the effort with a small shake of her head. "But before any of that, I need to speak with this cave dweller."

In that moment her face looked unbearably young. He forgot, sometimes, that she was still only a girl—though she had lived through more in a handful of years than many did in a lifetime. "The offer stands," he said simply. "Come. We'll ride to Ossivian. I'll teach you how to find him, should he ever call you again when I am not there." His father had served as conduit for the creature, just as Serban now did—an unwanted bridge between mortal will and something older. He had always assumed that strange ability passed through blood like any other inheritance. But watching Magda now, pale and resolute in the lantern light, he wondered whether the tether binding her to Ossivian had formed by lineage—or by design.

They rode in silence for many miles. Then, without warning, Magda's voice drifted across the space between them—soft at first, fragile. She began to speak of her life and the twisted path that had delivered her to his doorstep. He wasn't sure if she spoke to him, or if she merely spoke the words to hear them aloud.

"I fell in love with Caius when we were children. Dani, Caius, and I were inseparable, even though each of us belonged to a different world. When we were small, no one cared. But Buna warned me to stay away from Caius. We shared the same birthday, and both of our mothers died that night..." She explained how her grandmother saw the signs in the smoke that foretold her tragedy.

He slowed his horse until he rode beside her. She kept her gaze fixed on the road ahead, the night swallowing her expression as she continued her story. She was speaking to give shape to what had broken her, to hear the pieces laid out in order. She spoke of her foolish infatuation, and how she had lain with the boyar's son. There was no shame in her voice—none. Another girl might have whispered such a confession, but Magda carried it like a truth she refused to hide. She was weary, yes, worn thin by grief and violence, but not bowed. If anything, her chin lifted a fraction higher in defiance of all she had endured.

Serban imagined her briefly, scared, discarded on the street, a young woman with no options, and his heart—what was left of it, he supposed—hurt for her. Hurt in a way he hadn't let himself feel in centuries. The only sound between them was the dull thud of hooves on the packed earth, and the steady unraveling of the truth she had kept locked inside her. Tears slid down her cheeks, glinting like dew in the moonlight, but she did not hide them. She spoke as if the night itself had demanded a reckoning.

Only now did she trust him enough to reveal the moment her life shattered—and the horror that followed. And he found himself wishing he could go back and shield that girl she had been from the brutality of the world that had shaped her. If he could have warned her that day he saw her picking apples, he would have. But she would not have listened, just as she hadn't to her grandmother.

She went on, speaking of her husband Dani with a reverence usually reserved for saints, and he found himself wondering at the sort of man capable of loving with such steadiness—without demand, without condition. It was a kind of devotion he had rarely witnessed, and never fully trusted. He kept his horse even with hers, careful not to crowd her, careful not to fall back. Close enough that she would feel his presence if she reached for it. Far enough to let her speak without the pressure of his gaze.

Her eyes remained fixed on the road ahead, as though the narrow ribbon of earth were drawing the truth out of her step by step—each word pulled loose by the rhythm of the ride, each confession laid down behind them like hoofprints in the dust. She fell silent, her pain hanging in the air between them like a living thing.

"I loved my daughter, and I loved Dani in my own way, but I hated my life." She said at last, spilling out with a shuddering breath, the kind one releases only when a secret finally escapes the walls built to contain it.

Her honesty struck him—not for its revelation, but for the steadiness with which she held it. There was no shame in her voice. Only the weight of someone who had seen too much, survived too much, to pretend anymore. He let the silence stretch a moment before he spoke. "You were never meant for a small life, Magda," he said quietly. "No wonder it felt wrong on you." And he meant it.

They rode on in silence, her mind finally still. He could feel her sensing Ossivian now—those faint, instinctive signals that tugged at her just as they did him—drawing them closer with every mile.

After a time, the road split before them. To the right, the path wound down toward the river bend. To the left, the trail climbed sharply, curling up the hillside toward the bluff and, beyond it, the cave where the creature had summoned Serban five weeks ago.

He drew his horse to a stop. Magda, feeling the same pull he did, turned toward the rise. She looked at Serban, a question written plainly across her face. "To the right," he said quietly, "that is where I found you that night." He tried to keep his voice gentle, though the memory cut like a blade. She deserved the truth—all of it. She deserved the right to choose whether to face that darkness again.

Magda drew a slow breath and straightened in the saddle. The young woman he had taken in—frightened, grieving, raw —was gone. In her place sat a young woman who had endured the unendurable, died in agony, and clawed her way back into the world. Strength born from violence, ash and blood. It struck him then—this was the first time he'd seen her not as his charge, or a task given to him by the gods, but as what she had become. Fire once, now tempered with ice.

"Show me," she said, no tremor in her voice. She reined her horse to the right and he kicked his to catch up.

Just a few minutes ride further brought them to the place where he had found her—the scent of her blood pulling him through the trees that night, her body battered and broken in ways no human should survive. He remembered it with bitter clarity: how she had felt no fear when he approached her, only that steely, impossible resolve. He reined in his horse and dismounted, letting the reins fall as he walked toward the spot. Magda followed, silent, steps sure despite what this place meant. "Here," he said quietly, resting his hand on the granite boulders—ancient stones tumbled long ago by the force of the river and time. "This is where your body came to rest."

Her dried blood still marked the stone, dark flecks stubborn against the weeks of soft, unceasing rain. She stepped closer and set her hand beside his, as if the granite might offer her an answer, some meaning to anchor herself to. But there was no sense in any of it, and the proud tilt of her chin faltered.

Serban's reaction was instinctive. He reached for her without thinking, drawing her against him, tucking her into his chest as though he could shield her from the memory itself. That was when she broke—silent, wrenching sobs shaking her slim frame—grief she had carried alone for far too long.

He told himself this was a small offering to her—to give her a place to rest, to be seen for all she had been and all she was becoming, before she gathered the hard armor she wore now and steeled herself for what lay ahead. But something else stirred in him, something he had not invited. A seed, planted without his consent, had taken root. Some part of her had lodged itself inside him, and he knew that when she tore it free, it would leave a hollow behind.

A memory surfaced—the night he had taught her to feed from a human. The first rush of blood had overwhelmed her, heat and strength surging through limbs still untrained in containing it. Hunger had sharpened into something perilously intimate, power tangling with instinct until the two were indistinguishable.

For the briefest instant, he had imagined not stopping her. Not stepping back. He had wondered what it would be like to close that final inch of distance. To let desire override restraint. To answer the pull that had nothing to do with the frenzy of blood. He had been close—close to staying—close to taking comfort where he had no claim. Close to turning a moment of vulnerability into something neither of them could have undone. Instead, he had pushed her away. Not because he felt nothing, but because he felt too much.

This time it was Magda who pulled away, turning her face from his watchful gaze as she wiped her tears with the back of her hand. Then she straightened—shoulders back, chin lifted—and walked to her horse. By the time she swung into the saddle, every trace of vulnerability had vanished. She wheeled toward the fork in the road they'd left behind, toward the path that led to Ossivian, toward whatever destiny had set its claws into her.

Serban followed, keeping a respectful distance. The trees thinned, the shadows shifted, and in what felt like the space of a single breath, the mouth of the cave came into view—gaping like a black maw in the hillside. As Magda urged her horse forward, he found himself wishing she'd slow. Just a little. He wasn't ready to let her go.

37

MAGDA AND THE RUBIES

Magda—May 1390

"*Why have you come?*" In total darkness the cave dweller scuttered closer, just a faint rattle and clatter echoing off the walls, his voice no more than a faint hiss. "*The young girl who believed herself destined for greatness, now one of the undead...did your grandmother not warn you?*" He let out a brittle laugh.

"Shh." I cut him off, weary of riddles. Had I still been human, I might have felt fear. But now? I had nothing left to lose. I could not be more dead than I was—unless he chose to obliterate me. Perhaps that would be mercy. "I came because you called to me. I have the rubies you gave Serban—what I need to know is how their magic works."

"*Who will you bring back, Magda? Dani? The one too good for you, who gave everything to protect you and your daughter—never to have the only thing he ever wanted: your love. The love you squandered on Caius instead. Or will it be your daughter? Stolen from you too soon, denied her life barely after it began. And if you succeed—what then? What if she makes the same mistakes you made? Will you damn her to the same fate?"*

"Stop. This is none of your concern. Give me only what I ask." The command left my mouth, rough and caustic, steadied by a confidence I did not entirely possess.

"As you wish, blood drinker. Under the blood moon's gaze, let your lifeblood fall upon hair, or tooth, or bone of the one you crave. Set it to flame. When the fire leaps bright, cast the two rubies into the heart of the blaze. When the embers die and the stones grow cold, take one for yourself, and spend the other. The ruby given is loosed into the world, beyond your will, beyond your hand.

His words swirled around me, cryptic, strange.

"At the next Crimson Convergence, more than six hundred years hence, the soul you seek shall draw breath again. They will not know you. Their road is their own. Yet the wandering ruby will return in time—first to the hands of a maker and seer, the daughter of flame. She will bring you together with the one you seek, and the ruby shall awaken their memory. Then shall the lost life burn anew, and the chance denied shall be lived once more."

I stared at Ossivian, the words refusing to settle into meaning. Six hundred years. I bowed my head because my neck would no longer hold it upright. The number tolled inside my skull—slow, merciless, an inescapable funeral bell. Six centuries of waiting. Six centuries of watching the world turn and rot and renew itself while I remained unchanged. Six hundred years to carry a love that had already broken me once.

My breath hitched, then shattered entirely. My shoulders shook with it. How could I endure so long? How could any promise survive that span? What if memory faded? What if I did?

And beneath the grief, another thought coiled, colder still. What if this was not mercy? What if the gods, in their vast and distant wisdom, had not granted me another chance—but merely stretched my punishment across the centuries?

Ossivian read every frantic turn of my thoughts and answered them with a dry rattle of bone that might have been laughter. *"You have nothing but time, blood drinker,"* it said. *"Nothing but time. Make yourself useful."*

I KNOCKED TWICE on Buna's door. Footsteps shuffled closer, then stopped—as if she'd frozen just short of the threshold, wondering who would come knocking at this hour.

"Open the door, Buna. It's me." My voice was barely more than a whisper against the draft seeping through the lock.

The bolt clicked. The door creaked open. A single candle trembled in Buna's hand, its light throwing long shadows across her face. She didn't look surprised to see me. Her face was carved into stone; only her eyes moved—cold, filled with a quiet, bitter contempt. She stepped aside to let me in, her eyes never leaving mine as I ducked under the low doorframe. I had to bend farther than I remembered—another reminder of what I'd become. In all the years I'd lived here, I'd never had to stoop. A few inches in height, a few degrees less human. My turning had changed more than I'd realized.

She did not recoil when she saw me. No gasp. No sign of the

cross. No whispered prayer against evil. If anything, her gaze sharpened—as if she had expected this reckoning.

"You should not have come back," she said at last, her voice steady. "What you are now...there is no place for it here. Not among the living."

The lack of fear unsettled me more than hysteria would have. She had always been devout. Superstitious. Quick to warn of *strigoi* and wandering spirits. Yet she looked at me not as a monster—but as something inevitable.

"I came to know if it was true," I said. My voice did not tremble, though something inside me did. "That Dani and Anca died that night."

Her eyes softened then, just slightly.

"You are the only one I have left," I added. "The only one I still trust to speak plainly to me." Whatever I had become, whatever name the village might give it—she was still my grandmother. And I was still her blood.

Her shoulders sagged, the strength draining from them as if she had been holding the weight of it alone.

"Ach...yes," she said at last, and the words came laced with something darker than grief. "Ivar and his men burned the house." Her mouth tightened. "We found Dani near Anca." A breath hitched in her chest, but she did not let it break her voice. "But we never found you."

Her eyes lifted fully to mine then—not in fear, but in searching. As if she were peeling back the pallor, the stillness, the unnatural quiet of me...looking for the girl she had once held as a child.

For a moment, something like pity flickered there. "I knew you had been taken," she said softly. "No body in the ash. I knew." Her gaze sharpened, not accusing—demanding truth.

"But this..." Her hand gestured faintly, encompassing what I had become. "How did this happen to you, Magda?"

Not *what are you*. *How*. And beneath the question, another: *Who* did this to you?

I knew she meant my turning. All the village knew Ivar was a monster, but only the mortal kind—the kind that killed, not one that had the power to create the undead. "Ivar and his men beat me. Raped me. Stabbed me. Then they threw my body over the cliff...into the river like trash."

The candle trembled in her hand.

"The man I saw in the glade that day—the one I said was a *maleficius*—he found me. Only he isn't a *maleficius*. He is *strigoi*."

Buna huffed, her face twisting. "And now you are like him." She spat on the packed dirt floor—her disgust, her grief, her final blessing and curse in one gesture.

"Where are they buried?" I asked, my voice breaking finally as tears stung my eyes. Tears for them, and tears for myself, alone now. Disowned.

"In the cemetery," Buna said. "Caius buried them."

"What?" I demanded, the word catching somewhere between anger and disbelief. "Why?" The thought of him grieving—of him claiming any right to sorrow—ignited anger inside me. "He did not care about them," I snapped. "Not enough."

My hands trembled, though whether from rage or old hurt, I could not tell. "He let his father decide who he could and could not love. He let that man choose his future—choose *for* him." The bitterness in my voice surprised even me, raw as an open wound. "When it mattered, he left. He let them send him away. He let them turn me out."

The memory rose vivid and merciless—the day the door

closed behind me, the day I understood exactly how small my place in his life had been. "He is weak, Buna," I said, the word falling heavy between us. "Weak." It was not a revelation. It was a truth I had swallowed the day his father severed us—when I learned that love meant nothing beside obedience.

"He is weak," Buna agreed softly, though the sharpness had left her tone. "That much is true." Her eyes held mine—not chastising, not dismissing. "You know it now because you have known the love of a man who was strong. Strong not only in body, but in heart. A man who chose you openly." There was meaning in the distinction.

She drew a slow breath. "But weakness does not erase love, Magda. It only corrupts it." The words were worn with age, not accusation. "Caius may have lacked the courage to defy his father. He may have failed you—and Anca." Her voice thinned, tired as old linen. "But it does not follow that he felt nothing. A man can love...and still choose wrongly. Both can be true."

That struck deeper than I expected.

Her hand lifted and settled briefly on my shoulder—light, uncertain, as though she were no longer entirely sure what I was made of. She searched my face one last time, then withdrew her touch.

Without another word, she turned toward the cupboard, leaving me alone with a truth I had no desire to carry.

"Why aren't you afraid of me?" I asked, irritation fraying the edges of my voice. She still addressed me as though I were an impulsive girl who had come home in disgrace—not something the village would whisper about after dark. She knew what I was. I could taste the revulsion in her. But there was no fear.

"I know how I die," Buna replied, her tone brisk as she

rummaged through the cupboard. "And it is not by the hand of a *strigoaică*." She said it plainly, without bravado.

Buna's gift for reading smoke was no secret. Villagers had come to her for years with bundles of dried sage and questions about harvests, marriages, illnesses. I would not have been surprised if she knew the season—perhaps even the hour—her own breath would leave her.

The cupboard door creaked on its hinges. The scent of iron and crushed herbs thickened the air. She withdrew a small bundle wrapped in cloth and placed it on the table beside the candle. The flame flickered, light trembling over the rough wood as though aware of what lingered between us.

With deliberate care, she began to unwrap it. Inside lay two blades. Their leather sheaths were charred and split from the fire, blackened and brittle—but when I drew the longer one free, the steel beneath caught the candlelight and held it. Untarnished. Untouched. As though flame had bent around it. The smaller, curved knife was the same—its edge bright, keen, waiting.

For a heartbeat, I was no longer standing here with Buna. I saw Dani's face instead—how proud he had been the night he placed them in my hands at this very table. The way his eyes had shone when he said they were forged for me, balanced for my grip. It had been just after I met Serban in the glade, when my only fear had been of a stranger.

"Did you clean them?" I asked quietly, turning the blades over, searching for soot, for warping, for any mark of what they had endured.

Buna shook her head. "No. We found them in the ashes when we searched for your body." Her voice thinned, but did not break. "The house was gone. The roof collapsed. Everything burned." Her fingers tightened against the edge of the table. "But these..." She looked at the steel as though it were something sacred. "These lay beneath the wreckage, untouched."

Her gaze lifted to mine. "Whether angels guarded them, or the old gods turned the flame aside, I cannot say." She swallowed. "But Dani's love for you—and for Anca—was a living thing—fierce, protective." She paused. "I believe some part of it lingers in these blades."

The words settled deep.

Pain and certainty lined every crease of her face as she added, "I kept them for you."

"Did you know I'd come back?" I asked.

"I saw this—*all of it*—in the smoke years ago," she murmured, her hands lifting, gesturing toward the blades... toward me.

There was a heaviness in her eyes that only comes from knowing a storm will crest and being powerless to turn it aside. She had warned me about Caius more times than I could count. Warned me of pride. Of weakness. Of men who bend too easily beneath stronger wills. Even if she had told me everything—every flame, every loss—I would not have believed her. Some fates must be walked into blind.

Her hands began to tremble. When she looked at me again, sorrow filled her gaze—but beneath it, stubborn and unextinguished, was love. "There is something you are meant for, Magda," she said, her voice roughening. "Your life...and even your death...are not without purpose." Her words were not comfort. They were her prophecy.

"I cannot see its full shape," she admitted. "Perhaps it lies too far ahead for smoke to reveal. But it is there. I have seen enough to know that." She drew in a steadying breath, mastering herself as she always did.

Then she crossed the room and took her cloak from its peg. The fabric rustled as she settled it around her shoulders. "Come," she said quietly. "Let me take you to their graves."

We walked to the small cemetery where I had so often visited my mother's grave. Just beyond the gate stood two new headstones—marble, gleaming even in the darkness. They were far grander than any others in the village, too fine for simple folk, no matter their standing.

No, these belonged among the resting places of the boyars, not here among paupers and farmers. I wondered what stories would be told, centuries from now, about how two monuments so proud came to stand in a graveyard so humble. Perhaps I would be around to hear them.

On Anca's headstone—smaller than Dani's—an unopened rosebud was carved beside a simple cross, with her name and dates below.

On the larger stone next to hers, the name *Dani Veró* was etched deep into the marble, his own dates beneath it. A cross adorned the top, and below it, the words: *Husband, Father, Friend.*

The sight made my blood burn. *Friend?* How dare Caius call Dani that now, when their last meeting ended with Caius striking him—bloodying the lip of the man who'd been like a brother to him.

I was sure Caius knew about Ivar, his father's right hand, being the one to kill my family. The way he deferred to his father, he may have known about the plan in advance. Maybe these fine graves were a display of guilt.

"He comes each day, Magda. He comes and he weeps," Buna said, a warning in her voice that I didn't miss.

"Why are you protecting him?" I said bitterly.

"I am doing nothing of the sort," she said heavily. "But you'd do well to remember that if all you look for is blame and fault, that is all you will find. Your life, or whatever this thing is you live now, will be filled with bitterness. Don't allow that to become your legacy."

38

VENGEANCE

Magda—May 1390

When I left the cave after talking to Ossivian, Serban had pressed the reins of the brown mare into my hand as though sealing a pact. A small leather pouch followed—heavy with gold and silver, more coin than I had seen in all my years combined. Enough to travel. Enough to survive. He said it wasn't generosity. He called it preparation. But the truest gift he gave me was the last.

"There is a village north of yours," he had said, his tone measured, offering information—not instruction. "A tavern near the square. Ivar and his men drink there most nights when they are not riding."

He did not tell me what to do with that knowledge. He did not ask what I intended. He simply trusted me with it. I remembered the way he turned from me and mounted his horse without looking back, and how alone I felt in that moment.

Now I stood just beyond the doorway of that tavern,

surveying my targets as they drank in the great hall. The room stank of smoke and sweat, the sour musk of unwashed men. I knew all the faces, but only one name among them—Ivar. He lounged on a bench at the back, a woman draped over his knee, her blouse tugged low to bare a breast. He toyed with her lazily, pinching and prodding as if she were no more than a bored distraction. The look on her face told me everything— she didn't dare cross him. Perhaps she already had. Her left eye was swollen, her throat mottled with bruises, purple and angry.

I knew what it was to be a plaything for these beasts. Men who were more monstrous than any creature our people called a monster—like the one I now shared my name and nature with. At least I needed blood. At least my hunger had purpose. These men? They harmed because they could. Because cruelty made them feel bigger, stronger, more powerful.

How wrong they were. And it was time they learned the truth.

I tugged the hood of my cloak lower, shadows clinging to my face as I stepped into the room. The first to notice me was the woman. Her eyes caught mine, and I felt it— her fear stabbing like a knife now, instead of the dull, familiar dread she held for Ivar. This was different. A lamb sensing the lion. But she was not my prey.

I did not break her gaze. My power unfurled around her mind, a silken snare, just like Serban had taught me, irresistible and absolute. She stiffened, her will crumbling in the face of mine.

"You will tell him you're fetching more ale. When you rise, walk slowly. Do not run. Then you will leave through the back door. Tomorrow, when people ask what you saw—tell them I came to put

an end to the evil of these men. Tell them I came to protect you—all of you—the poor, the rich, the weak, and the strong."

And even as I released her, my command lingered—a whisper in her bones, impossible to disobey. She bent low to his ear, but he shoved her aside with a scowl. She stumbled a step and then slipped past me without so much as a glance, as though I were a shadow clinging to the wall.

I pulled down my hood, loosened the cord at my neck, and let the cloak fall to the ground. The flicker of torchlight shifted and rolled in the room, an eerie backdrop for the power that unfurled from me—slowly, like a beast stirring in its sleep.

Heads turned. Eyes lifted. At first, there was only sluggish curiosity—drunken men surprised to see a woman standing in their den. But then...recognition dawned. One pair of eyes, then another, and another.

They knew me.

They had believed I was dead, my life ended when they pushed me from the cliff to the rocks below. But here I stood, alive—and not. As my gaze swept the room, I felt my eyes shift, a molten light flickering to life—embers roused from long slumber. Then the glow receded, leaving only blackness, deep and endless. I was the void, staring back at them. Whatever doubts they had about what I was dissolved in that moment. There was no room left for questions.

A new scent cut through the stale air, sharp and metallic. The tang of fear. Five men, and not one of them could hide it. One brave—or perhaps just reckless—fool stood. The man with the birthmark on his cheek set his hand on his dirk, knuckles white. His eyes were wide with terror, but still...I had to grant him this: he was the only one with enough will to fight.

The others? Cowering. Hands trembling. Even Ivar had

risen, his face pale as he stumbled backward. I hadn't even bent their minds yet, and still their true natures lay bare, exposed for the gods to see.

Cowards. All of them.

No, I wasn't ready to enthrall them—not yet. I wanted their eyes clear. I wanted them to watch as the shape of their ending came to claim them. This was their penance. For hurting me. For hurting every woman like me.

I moved with the newfound speed I'd gained, the kind of power they'd only imagined in their fevered nightmares. I was at the doorway, and then—before the man with the birthmark could even blink—I was behind him, the blade from my belt pressed to his throat.

All eyes fixed on me. I saw the tremors in their hands, smelled the fear bleeding from their pores. It fed me. Propelled me. With one elegant motion, I opened his jugular. The red line blossomed across his neck, widening as a rivulet of crimson slid down to soak his shirt.

"*Watch,*" I commanded. My voice coiled around their minds, holding them in place, forbidding them to look away. And as they obeyed, I bent to the wound, lips brushing the hot skin. His blood filled my mouth—vital, potent, and bitter with the weight of his sins. Just as Buna said it would be.

I drank deeply, his life force spilling into me in a rush of heat and power, his body softening, sagging against mine. When he was emptied, I let him slip from my grasp. His corpse crumpled to the stone floor with a hollow thud, and I stepped over it without hesitation, blood still warm on my lips.

Another man lunged for the door, desperation twisting his face. But he wasn't fast enough. The same blade—still wet with his friend's blood—swept cleanly across his throat. He gasped, a wet sound, and I caught him before his knees hit the ground, drawing him in close. My mouth closed over the wound, and his panic surged hot against my tongue, the taste of it laced with rot and salt.

One by one, they watched their brothers fall—if they'd ever known the meaning of brotherhood. Perhaps not. But now they understood what it was to lose everything, to be rendered powerless as death moved deliberately from man to man.

And Ivar...Ivar knew he was last.

Blood coated the lower half of my face, warm and tacky as it dried, the bite of iron lingering on my tongue. I knew what my eyes must look like pupils blown wide, devouring the color from my irises until only a thin ring of light remained.

A predator's gaze. Just like Serban's when he fed. The first time I saw that look on him, it frightened me—not because it was monstrous, but because it was honest. There was no pretense in it. No civility. Only hunger, laid bare—and a terrible beauty.

I moved toward Ivar, letting him see the same in me now. His eyes darted from my face to the blade in my hand—the one Dani had crafted for me with such care. A man who, despite everything, had clung to scraps of love and fashioned something pure from them. A good man, who wanted nothing more than to protect those he loved. Who died, like my daughter and I did in Ivar's wake.

The blade gleamed, slick and red, heat rising from it in curling tendrils of steam—as if the metal itself had come alive, pulsing with intent. I brought it to my lips, drew my tongue along its length until it was clean, then slid it back into the sheath at my belt.

I stood before Ivar, close enough to hear the ragged pull of his breath, to watch the sharp bob of his Adam's apple as he struggled to swallow. His eyes—wide, unblinking—clung to mine as if I might let him live if he stared long enough.

"Did you think you'd seen the last of me?" I asked, each syllable laced with a cool, deliberate amusement. I let the silence after it linger—slow and tightening, a noose drawn firm around his throat. "Come now. You've always known your life would end in violence."

I tilted my head, studying him as one might examine a specimen pinned beneath glass. Desperation bloomed in his eyes, wide and feral, and I allowed a smile to curve my lips—measured, patient. I wanted him to see that I understood precisely what he feared. "But not like this." I stepped closer, unhurried, letting the air between us thin and tremble with my nearness. "Not at my hand." My voice softened, almost intimate. "Isn't that true, Ivar?" The smell of piss, and the dark stain on his crotch told me everything I needed to know.

I was conflicted—just as Buna warned I would be. Part of me wanted—no, *needed*—to make these men pay for everything. For my daughter's tiny body, stilled before its time. For Dani's goodness snuffed out. That hunger for retribution felt righteous. Pure.

But another part of me was frightened by the shadowed place inside me that *enjoyed* the killing. That felt the rush of power like a drug, curling in my chest. For so long, men like him had stripped me of agency, reduced me to nothing. Now I had it in spades, and this twisted, electric joy felt almost as strong as vengeance itself.

For a fleeting moment, I wondered what that made me. Goddess? Monster? Or some terrible thing in between? The question curled in the dark of my mind, but I didn't let it slow me. I pressed it down at the same time I inhaled the scent of blood and let wrath fill my lungs like fire.

Ivar had slunk off the bench and pressed himself into the corner, one hand fumbling at his dirk, the other splayed against the wall, as if he might push off—make a desperate break for it, or at least slow me down.

But I didn't move. I only watched, as the fragile thread of hope in his eyes frayed, then snapped, leaving only raw, animal fear behind. Let him sit with it. Let him feel it crawl through his bones. I wasn't even going to bother pursuing this coward. That would have been too merciful. No—I could make this far worse for Ivar.

I let my mind seep into his, coiling through his fear-soaked thoughts just as I had with the woman moments ago. But there would be no gentle command to leave this time. No—my will gripped him like a vise, forcing his piss-stained legs to drag his wretched body toward me.

"Come to me," I whispered into the hollow of his mind. *"Crawl if you must. Bow before me. Beg for the mercy you never gave."*

A strangled cry tore from his throat as his shaking limbs betrayed him, pulling him closer and closer. I stood still in the center of the room, a statue drenched in blood, the bodies of his men scattered across the floor, broken toys at my feet.

And then the thought came—dark and venomous. A small, gleeful demon whispering that I should push him onto the nearest table, visit every cruelty upon him that he had inflicted on me. A twisted eye for an eye. Would that not balance the scales?

But then Buna's voice cut through the darkness, stern and steady, and I forced my demon down into the pit where it belonged. It was enough to see him tremble. To feel his terror roll off him in waves. I didn't need more blood tonight; my clothes were already soaked in it, and his death would not cleanse me of my pain. But this—this would be the last thing he saw: me, terrible and unyielding, standing over him like a goddess of ruin.

He half-walked, half-crawled until he was within a foot of me. My will crushed his resistance until he collapsed to his knees, head bowed.

"Tell me your crimes, Ivar," my voice a silky command against the sound of his frantic, shallow breathing. "So that I may decide your punishment."

"I did what I was told...nothing more," he sobbed, the words tumbling out between gasps, snot glistening as it streaked down his face. "I had to...I didn't have a choice, I...I swear." His words came in a tumble from his thin lips.

Did he think I was stupid, that I believed he had not been complicit? I let my gaze travel over him slowly, deliberately, until he squirmed under the weight of it. "Ah, ah," I scolded at his lie. "What else did you do, Ivar?" I asked, my voice low and silken. I already knew the answer. But I wanted to hear him say it.

"I'm sorry...I'm sorry," he whispered, his lips trembling as his voice fell to a rasp. "I couldn't help it."

I took a single step closer, and he flinched as if I'd struck him. "What couldn't you help?" I murmured, my voice curling around him like smoke—heat and malice woven into every syllable. All the while, my mind slipped deeper into his, coiling tight, fingers of thought wrapping around the string knotted to his truth. And then, with a subtle tug, I began to pull.

His confession tore free in a guttural rush, wet and trembling.

"I wanted it, Magda. I wanted to watch them hurt you. The lowborn granddaughter of the village witch...who thought she was too good for the likes of me and my men, who fancied herself better than she was." His voice cracked, and for a fleeting second I thought his fear might rein him in. But no—his last scraps of self-preservation crumbled. "I wanted to fuck that sweet...*cunt*," he spat, the word raw and jagged in the air, "before I finished you." The shock on his face said it all. He understood now—he didn't even control the words spilling from his mouth. Not anymore. Not even the thoughts he buried deep in his mind were safe from me.

"So there it is," I said quietly. "You wanted to take what was never yours. And where are you now? On your knees before me." I had only one question left. "Who told you to do it?" I asked.

Tears streamed down his face—not out of fear for the answer, but because he understood what would come after it. There was no escape now. "Drago Burián," he choked, his voice barely a whisper. "He wanted you...eliminated. Said Caius was never the same after he was sent away. Said you were a poison... that would eventually kill him."

My face may have been imperious, but the truth gutted me. That Caius's father could hate me so deeply, that he would let fear twist love into a threat—believing the affection his son held for me could somehow weaken his grip on power. Anger coiled in my chest, slow and venomous. His arrogance, his prejudice, had set fire to everything: caused the death of his own granddaughter, the slaughter of his son's loyal friend—who had tried so desperately to pick up the shattered pieces the boyar's hatred had left behind.

And me. What I suffered. What I became. Reborn into

something that would never again bow to men like Drago Burián. I would decide how to deal with the boyar—but not tonight. Judgement would come for him another day.

I willed Ivar to rise, and he staggered to his feet, legs quivering like saplings in a storm. I took a single step forward until we stood eye to eye. He trembled violently, as though the air itself had turned to ice, though the room was warm and thick with the coppery scent of blood.

I pulled the long dagger from the fire-crazed leather sheath slung across my back in a fluid motion. My other hand, small but unyielding, slick with the blood of his fallen men, closed around his throat. I lifted him effortlessly until his boots barely scraped the floor. He struggled weakly against my grip, but I held his gaze.

With a single thrust I drove my blade up beneath his ribs, the steel slipping through flesh with elegant precision. Slowly, deliberately, I dragged it downward, carving cleanly through him, past his groin before I pulled it free. His body jerked and twitched, but I held him aloft until the wet slosh—the contents of his abdomen—struck the floor.

His face drained white, his mouth sagging open in a soundless scream. The muscles needed to summon a cry were useless now, severed and lifeless. A faint, pathetic gurgle bubbled from his lips as I released my grip and let him crumple in a heap at my feet.

I turned from him without a word, unhurried, and reached for a pitcher of strong mead. Pouring it across the table nearest Ivar, I let the liquid seep into the wood. Then I plucked a torch from the wall, the flames flickering hungrily in my reflection, and lowered it to the mead-soaked surface.

Fire bloomed instantly, crackling to life as the table ignited and the flames began to spread.

"Watch, Ivar," I said softly, almost tenderly, as the fire's glow painted me and the room in shades of gold and crimson. "As the flames cleanse this place of your filth."

And when the fire reached him at last, I did not look away. I stood still as the flames took hold, watching until the entire structure was engulfed—until the place where Ivar and his men once schemed and brutalized would stand no more.

I picked up my cloak before I walked out into the night.

The townspeople had gathered, drawn by the flames and the rising smoke. They lined the lane, eyes wide, lips parted in shock as I passed. I knew what they saw.

A woman, drenched in blood.

I walked slowly down the center of the narrow road, head high, shoulders steady. Terror incarnate. And justice. I sent my thoughts outward, to each man, woman, and child. The same message I had planted in the mind of the woman I'd spared in the great hall:

"I came to end their reign of terror. To protect our people—all of you—the poor and the rich, the weak and the strong. And I will not stop...until all our people know peace."

39

REVENANT

Magda—May 1390

I lowered my hood so the guard could see my face. It was Peter. Recognition flickered first—he had known me since I was a child—then shock, and finally, fear.

I reached into his mind—not roughly, but with deliberate precision—brushing the edges of his thoughts until I found the tight coil of duty and eased it loose. His resistance did not shatter; it softened. Curled inward. Then it gave way. Of all the abilities awakening inside me, this was the one that felt the most dangerous—and the most intoxicating. Not strength. Not speed. Control.

I did not speak. The main street lay too near, too exposed for careless risks. Instead, I pressed a single, silent command into the center of him.

"Open the gate."

He obeyed without question, his hands moving as if the

thought had always been his own. The latch lifted. The hinges sighed. And I slipped inside.

I crossed the walkway and entered the courtyard, my steps unhurried, as though I had every right to be there. The servants' door—the same one I had slipped through beside the cook the day Drago Burián first summoned me—gave beneath my touch without protest.

A young servant girl stood just inside. She couldn't have been more than fifteen. The color drained from her face the moment she saw me. Her fear was uncomplicated, innocent: I was a stranger where no stranger should be, and she would be the one blamed for it.

"I won't tell," I murmured softly, as if we shared some small conspiracy. Before her panic could sharpen into a cry, I reached for her thoughts. Not to break them. Not to take anything she would miss. I only smoothed the rising edges, gentled the spike of alarm, let her believe—just for a moment—that everything was as it should be.

Her shoulders loosened. Her mouth closed. The fear dissolved before it could take shape. And I walked past her as though I belonged.

She nodded, relief softening her features. A small, grateful smile flickered across her mouth. Before she could turn the moment over in her mind, before it could settle into memory, I reached back in and stirred the surface of her thoughts. Just a blur. Edges dissolving. Details smudging into the ordinary haze of a forgettable afternoon.

By the time she turned away, I was already fading from her recollection. I moved down the corridor, unhurried, listening. The great wooden doors of the library loomed ahead. I did not know which room would hold the boyar—but I did not need to.

There it was—a heartbeat—steady, measured, strong. I paused just long enough to savor it—the calm cadence that always preceded the moment of recognition. The fragile illusion of control. I had learned how quickly it shattered once my face came into view. I pressed my palm against the heavy door and pushed. It opened with a low groan. He sat behind his vast desk, head bowed over a scatter of papers, ink staining his fingers. Unaware.

He did not look up. Did not so much as shift in his chair. In his sanctuary, a servant was no more than a draft beneath the door—felt, perhaps, but never acknowledged. I closed the door softly behind me and walked farther into the room, stopping directly before his desk. I did not speak. I simply stood there. And waited.

An irritated sigh broke the silence. He rolled his eyes before he even lifted his head, already prepared to reprimand whatever fool had dared disturb him.

The shock struck him the instant his gaze found me— before the thought could fully form, before my name could surface. It flashed through his pulse, a violent stutter in the steady rhythm I had heard outside the door. But to his credit, he mastered it quickly. By the time his eyes narrowed, the surprise had been buried beneath something caustic, assessing.

His lips twisted, turning his face into something ruinous— something that might once have been a grandfather, but was now only bile and bone. How a man could despise me so completely—despise me enough to wish death on his own granddaughter for my crime of loving poorly—was beyond reason. Beyond mercy.

I had come to the castle for truth. That was the story I told myself as the iron gates shut behind me and the old stones of

Castle Burián watched my approach. Truth. Answers. Closure. But beneath that tidy lie, something uglier uncurled. A question—thin as smoke, black and treacherous—slipped into my mind before I could crush it.

Did I carry hatred the same way? It would be easy. So easy. To let it root. To let it bloom. My desire to make him suffer pulsed through me, fierce and intoxicating. I wanted him to feel the terror he had sown in others. Wanted to see his composure fracture, his pride split open. I imagined stepping closer, speaking softly, letting him glimpse precisely how powerful I had become. Letting him understand—too late—that he had not destroyed me.

The hunger sharpened at the thought. Not just for blood. For dominance. For fear. For the exquisite moment when the light would gutter in his eyes and he would finally understand what he had made.

My grandmother's voice rose in my memory, steady as prayer. Do not let the darkness choose for you, child. And Serban's warning threaded through it—quieter, heavier, to remember what it was to be human.

The two voices stood between me and the abyss, fragile as glass. I could feel the new thing inside me testing its wings. It whispered that cruelty would taste sweet. That vengeance would be cleansing. That I had earned it.

I straightened, forcing my hands to still at my sides. Let him see the war in me. Let him wonder which side would win.

"How did you escape?" he asked, insolent. "My men said they'd taken care of you."

How fitting that he assumed only incompetence. "Your men did take care of me," I said, my voice steady—almost conversational. "They killed my husband and daughter. They dragged me into the forest. They beat me. They violated me. They stabbed me and threw me from a cliff."

I watched his face as I spoke, searching for it—remorse, shame, even discomfort. There was none.

"I died, Drago Burián." I let the words settle between us like ash. "Died as surely as if it had been your own hand around my throat. No...they did not fail in the task you gave them."

Silence thickened the air. For a heartbeat, I considered describing it in greater detail. The cold of the river at the bottom of the ravine. The way the sky had dimmed. The terrible, helpless awareness of my own blood leaving me. I could have forced him to see it. Forced him to sit inside the horror he had ordered.

The darker part of me urged it. Make him choke on it. Make him taste it. My grandmother's warning brushed the inside of my skull like a rosary bead passing through fingers. *Do not become what you hate.*

I took a step closer instead. "You see," I continued, my gaze never leaving his, "I did not escape." A faint smile curved my lips—not warm, not kind. "I was remade."

My hunger stirred at the word, stretching languidly inside me. I could end him here. I could make his death slow. But I wanted something else first. I wanted the truth. And I wanted him afraid long enough to give it.

I summoned every ounce of power I possessed and let it rise. Rage answered first—hot, tidal, intoxicating. It surged through my veins and into the air between us, thickening it, bending it. The candles along the wall guttered. The shadows lengthened toward me as if in allegiance.

His smug expression faltered. It did not vanish all at once. Realization dawned slowly—his mouth closing mid-breath, color draining from his cheeks. A chill rippled visibly across his skin; the fine hairs on his forearms lifted beneath the sleeves he had so arrogantly rolled to his elbows.

Now you understand, I thought. "I killed Ivar and his men last night," I said, and the calm in my voice was more terrible than any snarl. "I made it slow." The memory flickered behind my eyes—moonlight on steel, pleading voices, the copper scent of terror saturating the air. "I drank their fear first," I continued. "Let it steep. Let it ripen. I wanted them to know exactly why they were dying."

The darker thing inside me purred at the recollection. "I opened their throats and drained them dry I thought it might ease the ache in me..." My lips curved faintly. "But it didn't." Not even close. I leaned forward, planting my palms flat against his desk. He had always used that slab of wood as a barrier, a stage from which to dispense judgment. To me, it was nothing more than a suggestion. A line scratched in dirt I could erase with a breath. "But Ivar..." I tilted my head, as though savoring a fond memory. "Ivar was my favorite."

I watched the pulse in Drago Burián's throat quicken. "He begged." I leaned closer still, until he could see the inhuman stillness in my eyes. "He pissed himself before I opened him from belly to spine." Silence roared between us. The devil within urged me to reach across that desk, to demonstrate. To let him feel the first slice, the first bloom of helplessness. My grandmother's voice trembled at the edge of my thoughts. This was the precipice.

The color drained from the boyar's face when he realized who was in control now.

"Why?" I asked, needing to know. 'Was it worth it?" The boyar's lip twitched, the stink of his fear making saliva pool beneath my tongue. Yet despite that fear, I sensed no lie in what he said.

"You weren't what I wanted for Caius. I wanted a politically ad—advanta—advantageous marriage..." He stumbled over the word, and in that instant something inside him gave way.

The steady whoosh of blood I had grown accustomed to in every human body—a soft, constant tide beneath skin—hitched, then broke rhythm entirely. The current within him turned chaotic, misfiring in frantic, uneven bursts. His heart fluttered wildly against the cage of his ribs, no longer driven by fear of me alone but by a dawning, animal awareness that something vital was betraying him from within.

His eyes widened—not in defiance now, but in confusion. Still, stubbornness carried him forward. "I thought he'd f-forget you when I sent him away." The words assembled themselves in his mind, but his mouth lagged behind, clumsy and uncooperative. One corner of his lips dragged lower than the other. "I d-didn't c-care that he'd s-sired a brat in the village."

The scent of him shifted—acrid, threaded now with rot of failing flesh. His hand lifted as if to steady himself, but it rose too slowly, fingers curling inward against his will. The predator in me recognized the moment before the man did. Something in his brain had torn.

The boyar's blood pressure dipped—slowed—and then surged violently, his body scrambling for a rhythm it could no longer hold. A thin rope of spittle gathered at the corner of his mouth. I felt it then: his mind cleaving, one half struggling to reason with an enemy, the other half slipping, confused, trying desperately to understand what was happening inside him. "I've—I—tried to arrange his marriage twi—twice," he forced out, each word a battle. "And he...he refused both women. Sss—sssaid he'd never forgive me."

A chill crept over the left side of his body, the blood there faltering, failing to reach the far half of his mind. The muscles on that side of his face—so tight with scorn a breath ago—went slack, sagging in a slow, inevitable melt.

Had fear done this to him? If it had, I felt no guilt. Drago took a few steps around the desk before his knees buckled, one hand reaching out as if I might steady him. The irony of it almost made me laugh—this man who had destroyed my life now seeking my help. His eyes widened in the instant he understood, whether surprise that his legs no longer held him or that I wasn't going to catch him, I couldn't say. The great and powerful Drago Burián fell to the cold stone floor like a tottering child, and I watched.

"I was so naïve...thinking our dear boyar would protect the people he governed," I mused as I walked slowly around the desk. "How wrong I was. You protect only those who can serve you—never the low-born, never the poor, even when we pay your taxes and your rent for the land beneath our feet. All this time, you let us believe the danger to our way of life came from the Ottoman Empire." I circled his slumped form, the only arm his failing body still answered to braced against the floor, holding him up by sheer stubborn will.

I saw his gaze flick toward the small bell resting at the edge of his desk—the one he'd used to have me dragged out of this room in what seemed like a lifetime ago. "Oh...would you like me to ring it?" I teased, my voice a pleasant singsong. "Shall I summon one of your servants? Or Caius? Yes—Caius I think." I nodded as I reached for the bell. "What a good idea." The delicate chime that followed was so light, so dainty, it felt almost absurd—an oddly feminine sound for the monstrosity who wielded it.

I turned as the door creaked open and caught the eye of the servant—the same young girl I'd encountered upon entering. I slipped into her mind before her second step crossed the threshold, stilling her like an insect caught in tree sap.

"Fetch Caius," I murmured. "The boyar is unwell. Tell no one. Go straight to him."

Her expression slackened, obedient, and she turned on her heel without another sound. The girl did a small curtsy to me before heading out of the room, closing the door behind her, just as if I'd asked her to bring me mulled wine.

I looked down at the boyar, his body crumpled on the floor.

"Ppp—please. Don't let him sss—see me like this," he begged, words slurring, his pride leaking out of him as surely as the strength from his limbs.

"He will see you like this," I said. "And so will every soul in this house." I crouched beside him, letting him see the truth in my eyes. "After what you stole from me, did you really think I'd spare you a moment of dignity?"

He whimpered. The sound might once have startled me—might have fractured something inside me to hear fear in the voice of Drago Burián. I moved closer to him. He flinched as I neared, shrinking into himself, as if proximity alone might draw blood. I did not touch him. Not yet.

Behind the desk, the world looked different. A map lay spread across its surface, thick parchment pinned at the corners with brass weights to keep the edges from curling. Inked roads branched like veins. Forests were rendered in dark crosshatch. My gaze snagged on a mark pressed hard enough to score the paper—a village an hour's ride to the east. Marked?

Or targeted? I leaned forward with interest. Was this what Serban had spoken of? A few moments later, the library door creaked open.

Caius stepped inside. His eyes were wide with worry—real worry, desperate and raw, when they landed on his father prone on the floor. It transformed his face, the one I'd glanced these past months in the village, from afar. Drawn, hollowed, usually drunk or feeling the effects of the night before. Now, just for the briefest moment, I saw the man I had once believed him to be.

Then he saw me. Standing behind his father's desk. Concern twisted into confusion. Confusion sharpened into disbelief. And then— like a crack splitting stone— something surfaced beneath it. "Magda…" My name left his mouth like a desperate prayer.

I studied him in silence. How many nights had I imagined this moment? Confrontation. Answers. Regret. He looked between me and his father, taking in the pallor, the tremor in Drago's hand. Understanding dawned in him far faster than it had in the old man. "You're alive," he breathed.

Alive. The word scraped at my mind. "I was," I said softly. "I am no longer."

Caius took a tentative step forward. "Magda, whatever you think—"

I lifted one finger. He stopped. "You will not lie to me," I said, my voice calm and terrible in its restraint. "Not in this room. Not after what your father ordered while you stood by with your head bowed."

His gaze flicked to the map on the desk. He saw the mark. Confusion crossed his face. Good. Let him question the kind of legacy he'd turned a blind eye to.

He looked again to his father, slumped there between us,

drool spilling from the slack corner of his mouth, his body half-collapsed—a puppet with its strings cut.

"I was just speaking with your father when he was suddenly struck by some kind of...palsy," I said, all innocence, lifting one shoulder in a small shrug.

Caius reeked of alcohol, his hair as disheveled as it had been every time I'd seen him since his return. But despite the drink clinging to him, his eyes were clear. Whatever else he'd drowned, he had not drowned his mind.

"I told him I'd dealt with Ivar and his men," I said evenly, nodding again toward his father. "After that, he confessed. Why he had your daughter killed. Why he murdered your closest friend." I held Caius's gaze. "He was afraid he was losing his hold on you. And once he was rid of me, he believed he could pull you back into line. That you would simply forget us."

Caius went pale—truly pale—and then slowly turned to look at his father. The expression on his face was not confusion. It was betrayal.

"Your father hasn't protected the people of our area," I said quietly. "He's used us to protect his interests."

Caius's jaw tightened, but he didn't interrupt.

"The attack the day we were at the lake—" I let the memory hang between us: sunlight on water, laughter, the last uncomplicated afternoon we'd known. The beginning of the end, though we hadn't understood it then. "He orchestrated it," I finished. "Manufactured the threat. Used fear to tighten his hold, let the innocent pay the price with their lives."

I watched him absorb it, saw the shift behind his eyes—the slow churn of reckoning. Belief warred with denial, each refusing to yield ground. For a moment, I considered pressing harder. Forcing the truth past whatever defenses he still clung to.

But I didn't. Conviction born of coercion would never hold. If he was going to face what his father had done—what he had failed to see—he would have to arrive there on his own.

"Control," I said. "That's all it's ever been about." I let him sit with that truth for a moment before I continued.

"It's time to become the man you were meant to be, Caius—the man our daughter could have loved, the man Dani believed you were. It isn't too late. Not yet."

The words left me softly, weighted with everything we had lost—and everything he might still salvage.

I shook my head once, slow and deliberate. "I don't know if he will recover," I said, glancing at his father's slumped form. "But he is your responsibility now." My gaze returned to Caius. "You can keep drowning in guilt, drinking yourself toward an early grave...or you can rise and become the leader your father never was."

He looked stricken, but his eyes never left me.

"But hear me—you must lead all our people. Not just the wealthy, not just those who can serve your family's ambitions. All of them. The poor. The sick. The ones your father ignored." I took a step closer, letting him see the truth of what I'd become, and what I expected of him. "Be better, Caius. Be the man he was not. Because if you won't...if you choose cowardice again...then so help me, I will be the one to put you in your grave." I let my eyes flare with that unholy fire—silent, inhuman, unmistakable—the living embodiment of my threat.

Caius stared at me, eerily still, and then looked down at his father. Disgust carved hard lines into his features, but beneath it was something else—something that had been festering for years. At last, he tore his gaze from his father and looked at me.

The man who met my eyes was not the boy I had once loved, nor the broken creature who had drowned himself in wine and grief. He looked like someone standing at the edge of his own reckoning. The blue of his eyes, once bright with mischief, now clouded, haunted...yet in their depths, a spark caught.

He swallowed hard, his throat working, and for a fleeting instant I saw the boy he had been—golden, untested, full of promise. A boy who once dreamed—until he chose obedience over love, chasing a father's approval that was never worth winning.

"I don't know if I can live up to what you're asking," he said, his voice roughened by more than drink. "And if I fail them again—Dani and Anca—" His gaze shifted to his father, collapsed on the floor. "—then I deserve the grave."

40

BLOOD AND FIRE

Mira—October 2026

The string quartet spun a dreamy, lilting spell as I stepped onto the flagstone path leading from the gardens. Dillon looked especially dapper in his suit, and I clung to the steadying comfort of his presence as we moved forward together—but the ache in my chest was relentless. It should have been my dad at my side, and that absence throbbed with every step.

We walked as though time itself had slowed, sunlight filtering through the downward-draping fir branches overhead, dappling the path and the ferns that climbed the hillsides. Ahead, the Bavarian Summer House revealed itself, nestled into the wooded slope overlooking Brodick Bay, appearing less like something constructed, and more like something that had quietly grown there—roots and timber rising from the earth.

The small octagonal structure was just large enough to hold the officiant, a few attendants, and—of course—a bride and groom. Guests gathered around it in a gentle ring, standing shoulder to shoulder, the double doors thrown open wide as an invitation to witness something sacred and intimate.

Inside, the walls were wrapped in dark, branch-like timber-work, arranged vertically and diagonally like entwined vines and roots. Tall, arched windows welcomed the last wash of golden sunlight from the early fall evening, bathing the interior in warmth. As I approached, a soft murmur rippled through the guests as they turned to look—camera flashes punctuating the hush, mingling with the chorus of crickets and the quiet calls of birds perched above us.

Just ahead on the path, Anne walked beside Robbie, finally arriving and stepping into the structure. And there—waiting inside—stood Baird, impossibly handsome next to the vicar. A full head taller than Robbie as he settled at his side. Beyond him, a floral arch framed by glowing candles marked my destination, and for a moment, my breath caught—as though the world had narrowed to that single point of light, waiting for me to cross into it.

I'd given up hope of this—though I couldn't say exactly when that surrender had taken place. Somewhere along the way, the imagining had quietly stopped. And yet here I stood, on the cusp of an entirely new life, the man who would share it waiting just beyond the threshold. Not fully human, perhaps—but still a man who loved me with every fiber of his being. The certainty of it washed over me so completely that, for a fleeting moment, I felt foolish for ever having doubted it at all.

The look on his face told me everything I needed to know. Quiet wonder softened his features, his eyes wide, missing nothing as Anne bent to straighten my train. When our eyes met, the air tightened, then steadied, as though the moment had found its balance. I placed my bouquet into Anne's hands, and when his fingers closed around mine, warmth spread—deep and deliberate, a slowing down of time and space that flooded me with a sense of peace. The vows were spoken aloud—human words—but they carried a weight that went beyond sound, a spellwork to bind us. Each promise sank into place with quiet precision, syllables settling like something being fitted exactly as it should be. I felt them move through me, through him, binding without strain, without doubt.

When the rings were exchanged, the moment my band slid into place beside the ring that bound the Goddess's magic to me, and to him, the pulse came once, strong and sure—then settled into a steady hum. The heat softened, cooling as it sealed the bond, the way forged metal tempers as it rests. What remained was not fire, but strength—solid, unyielding, and permanent.

When the vicar pronounced us husband and wife, Baird hauled me hard against him—possession and promise bound together in the strength of his hold. I felt the vampire in him rise, powerful and undeniable, his eyes flaring green, alive with iridescent fire. It was a show meant only for me, a heartbeat before his mouth found mine.

Cheers swelled around us, a rush of sound from the gathered crowd, but it reached me only distantly. In the still, quiet center of that moment, I offered a silent thanks to the Goddess Brigid. Whatever time she chose to grant me—a mortal—with my immortal husband, it would be enough.

THE RECEPTION WAS in full swing less than an hour later. Guests wandered the garden paths once more, drifting up to the upper terrace where strands of fairy lights glowed overhead, casting a warm, golden shimmer across two long tables dressed in crisp white linen. In the gentle night air, most of the men had shed their suit coats, sleeves rolled, ties loosened. Laughter rose and fell throughout the grounds, light and unrestrained.

There were many toasts, including one from a handsome white-haired gentleman, one Aaron Thorndale, who spoke with fond humor about his part in Baird's plan—and who, Baird whispered in my ear, was distantly related to the business partner Baird had once shared a shipping company with before marrying Agnes. When the last toast ended and the terrace glowed with warmth and affection, Baird pulled me into his arms. We swayed together in our first dance as husband and wife, the world falling away until there was only us and the quiet certainty that we belonged here.

When the music shifted and others joined us on the floor, a memory flooded me—of Agnes's vision—the day I touched her caramel silk dress. The whirl of dancers. The wild, unguarded joy she'd felt for a few precious moments that night in Baird's arms. And I found myself smiling, grateful that I'd been given the same chance to feel it.

The song ended, a low murmur rippled through the crowd. At first, I thought it was about us and didn't pay it much mind —until the movement on the dance floor shifted. The people nearest us began to step back, one by one, until the crowd peeled away like a red sea under fairy lights and a starry sky.

Only when the bodies cleared did I understand why.

A woman—no older than her early twenties, yet with eyes that carried the weight of time—glided through the space toward us. My arms stayed looped around Baird's neck, his hand pressed into the small of my back, as though we were still dancing. But the moment he saw her, I felt the tension ripple through him.

She was tall and spare, all long, elegant lines balanced by the sinuous curve of a hip. The blood-red bias-cut silk dress clung to her like a second skin, the high slit flashing a length of thigh as she moved toward me. Her hair—black as a raven's wing and cut into a sharp, shoulder-grazing bob—swayed like a pendulum with each step.

She was breathtaking—but it wasn't her beauty that rooted me where I stood. It was her presence. I had never seen anyone with such command; she radiated an intoxicating mix of power and danger, holding every gaze as though the air itself bent toward her. I was as transfixed as everyone else.

She looked achingly familiar. Had I seen her on TV? No. Not on TV. In a vision—the ruby's history: the young woman, brutally beaten and left for dead, who took her revenge the only way a vampire can—through blood and oblivion.

A hush swept across the terrace as she came to a stop before us. I let my hands fall from Baird's neck and turned to face her. He instinctively stepped in front of me, an arm outstretched to shield, but I laid my hand on his forearm, halting him.

She was dangerous—I was certain of that much. I'd seen her mete out vengeance in the vision the ruby had allowed me, and I suspected she'd claimed many more lives in the time that had elapsed since. Yet I didn't feel threatened. Not exactly.

"Mira," she began, her voice low and smooth, each word carrying the faintest trace of an accent—eastern European, though I couldn't place it. "I am Magdalena Veró," she said by way of introduction. "But those who know me call me Magda."

She glanced around, a self-satisfied smile on her lips as she took in the scene. "I hope you'll forgive me for interrupting the celebration of your union."

I made no move to ease her concern—if she really had any at all—and I hoped my silence told her she hadn't earned any forgiveness.

"I've come for two reasons," she said, her gaze shifting to Baird. "First—" She hesitated, as though testing the word. "—to congratulate my..." Another pause. Then, with the faintest curl of amusement in her eyes, "...*grandson*, I suppose."

I turned and watched Baird's expression shift in quick succession—wary, confused, then blooming to anger when he understood what she'd meant. She was Bastien's maker. Granny Margaret had seen it when she warned us they were connected in some way.

"And secondly," she said, turning her eyes to me again, "to find out what you are." Her voice was ripe with curiosity, not hostility.

I didn't understand what she meant. Did she mean who I was? She already knew my name somehow. Or did she mean what I was to Baird? In my white dress and flower wreath, cake on a table just waiting for us to cut it and shove it into each other's faces, it shouldn't have been so hard to guess.

Out of the corner of my eye, I saw my engagement ring flicker to life. Brigid's Sun began to cast golden rainbows across my hand, spinning like something alive. With all the terrace lights twinkling around us, I couldn't tell how obvious it was to the others—but I knew. It was reacting to her question, ready to answer for me.

The confusion on my face must have been all the permission she needed to continue. "More than six centuries ago," she said, "when the two people most precious to me were brutally murdered—and I with them—the rubies told me to seek *the daughter of flame.*" Her gaze never left mine. "I know you are a metalsmith. Descended from a long line of clairvoyants. I know your name." She hesitated then, her voice lowering, a flicker of vulnerability breaking through her resolve. "But what I need to know is whether you are the one who can help me."

At her words, the buzzing under my skin swelled, warm pins and needles racing over every inch of me. I knew that sensation—Brigid's power, waking and stretching inside me. And though this was the *last* place I should give in to it, something powerful deep in my bones wanted to claim it here and now, in the open, before everyone. After months of questions, I had no such doubts now. I was the one she sought.

I scanned the crowd, still unsure if it was wise to let the fire take me, knowing only two had seen it before—Baird and Sorcha. Sorcha's face was as serene as ever, as if this were no more remarkable than pouring tea. Then again, maybe it wasn't remarkable at all—an uninvited guest challenging the bride to reveal her supernatural power—just another day at a witch's wedding. I wouldn't know. This was my first.

Robbie, on the other hand, had turned away, muttering the same half-rhymed limericks he used to ward off evil, his fingers tracing the sign of the cross over the suit jacket I'd never seen him wear before tonight. He looked distinctly uncomfortable with the saga unfolding around him, his eyes flicking from me to Magda, to Baird, to Sorcha—only to land back on me.

I knew there were two vampires here I could trust to glamour the humans afterward—make them forget the woman in the red dress, her words, and everything that was about to happen.

I made my choice.

I stepped past Baird toward Magda. My arms lowered, palms open, angled outward as if to offer myself to the night. Power surged from beneath my skin—crackling, electric—until the air itself seemed to vibrate. And then it broke free.

Flame—yellow and blinding—erupted across my body in a single, searing bloom. It licked along my arms, arced from my shoulders, and flared upward like solar storms escaping the sun. Gasps rippled through the crowd. Magda's gaze locked on mine, her dark eyes swallowing the light until her pupils were nothing but a void. And in the blackness of her eyes, I saw reflected back exactly what she saw—my gown haloed in fire, my hair crowned in living gold.

The heat kissed my skin but did not burn. The ends of my hair fluttered in the updraft, edges glowing as if each lock had been forged in a smith's fire. Even the yellow roses in my hair had caught the fire—open blooms glowing like embers, unopened buds unfurling into delicate tongues of flame—until the whole crown blazed into a halo of golden fire and light. Around us, the guests drew back, their faces lit by my light, looks of awe and fear caught in stark relief.

I was Brigid in that moment—still myself, yet also her. The triple goddess of poetry, fire, and fertility. Keeper of sacred knowledge. Patron of smithcraft and artisans, whose gifts are bound to the forge itself and the forging of fates. She, the one prayed to for blessed harvests and the blessings of motherhood. She from whose name the word *bride* is born. In that moment, I was both bride and daughter of flame, blessed by Brigid herself to wield her power.

The ring on my hand, as if refusing to be outshone, demanded its place in the moment. It flared brighter—its rainbow refractions sharpening into the very thing they evoked: a crystallized shard of the sun itself. Iridescent and golden light blended and spilled from it in wild, prismatic flares, as if it could reach the heavens themselves, illuminating the stone terrace of Brodick Castle.

And then, with the grace of a dancer, Magda—regal as an imperious queen, and as deadly as an assassin—sank to her knees at my feet.

She was bowing to *me*. Absurd. Impossible—and undeniable.

If I were standing in front of the being I saw reflected in her eyes, I would have bowed too.

I glanced around, wanting to etch this into memory before my mate and his kind erased it from human history. Even Baird —who'd seen me illuminated like this more times than I could count—was transfixed. And in Robbie's eyes, I caught something unexpected: the quiet confession as he stared not at me, but at Sorcha, that said Baird wasn't the only vampire to have fallen hopelessly for a woman with magic.

Anne and Dillon looked terrified, and my heart ached for them, though I knew the fear would be gone soon enough. The same with our friends from the island—their stricken faces would be smoothed clean by glamour. Knowing Robbie, it wouldn't be the first time he'd done it to them, and perhaps not the last. Then my gaze found the Garvie clan. Morag's boys and husband stared, awestruck and confused; Evie's fiancé wore the same expression. Evie and Morag themselves looked stunned but not afraid.

And finally, I found Granny Margaret. She stood near the group, tears shimmering in the corners of her eyes as she looked at me. She said nothing, she didn't need to, the emotion she felt written clearly across her face.

Pride. Familial pride.

"It would seem I have found the one I seek," Magda said as she rose to her feet.

I willed the fire on my skin and in my hair to roll back like a receding tide, forcing it deeper and deeper until it was nothing more than a faint fizz beneath my skin—champagne bubbles under the surface. Silently, I thanked Brigid that I'd finally begun to learn to control how and when her power coursed through my veins.

Turning to Baird, I placed a hand on his shoulder and rose onto my tiptoes—still dwarfed by his height, even in my four-inch heels—to whisper in his ear. "Can you and Robbie..." I let the rest hang, tilting my head toward the stricken crowd still gathered around us on the dance floor, my eyes pleading: *Please fix this.*

He nodded and began to turn away, but something in him shifted—he pivoted back, pressing a soft, lingering kiss to my forehead. When he lifted his head, his gaze found Magda. Wary. Measuring. A silent warning in the steel of his eyes. If looks could kill, she would have crumpled to the terrace stone. Then he stepped into the sea of stricken faces, leaving her in his wake.

"He doesn't trust me," she said without preamble.

My answer was just as plain. "No. He doesn't."

She didn't hesitate to press on, but my attention drifted past her to where Baird and Robbie were at work. I watched them move through the crowd, speaking a few calm words, their eyes glowing faintly with that particular brand of vampire magic—

gently pulling at the threads of memory, unwinding the last five minutes from each human mind.

"I don't hold him—*or you*—accountable for Bastien's death," she said.

My head snapped back to her, startled—by both her words and the notion that *this* was the time or place to air the dirty laundry that belonged to our strange vampire family. She tilted her chin toward a small table for two at the far edge of the terrace, choosing a more private corner before continuing. We walked together, her voice calm—almost casual—but the weight of her words cut through the night air like a blade.

"Baird gave Bastien what I refused him *absolution.* I know it was never mine to give..." She shrugged as I looked at her in confusion. "I went to Paris to see Bastien after Clémence died..." Magda said, letting the words trail off, and I thought I saw a flicker of sadness in her smile. "But enough of this story —it can wait for another time," Magda's gaze swept over the guests again, scanning the terrace, before turning back to me. "Tonight is for celebrating."

I followed her line of sight. Most faces looked happy, if faintly puzzled. A few wore sheepish expressions, as though the hazy gap in their short-term memory was nothing more than the effect of the generous pours of wine, champagne and whiskey that had flowed freely all evening.

"I am anxious to speak with you—about the ruby," acknowledging the comment she'd made minutes ago. "And about Bastien. But..." I hesitated, choosing my words as if each one might tip the balance. Magda was not someone to be trifled with. "Not tonight. My place is with our guests."

"Yes, of course. I will go," she said, starting to rise.

I caught her hand. "Please—stay. I didn't mean you should

leave...unless there's somewhere else you need to be. I only meant...tonight wasn't meant for magic, or enchanted rubies, or vampires." My voice softened, a reluctant smile tugging at my lips. "I want it to be...as close to normal as it can be for us."

Her eyes glittered with amusement. "If it weren't for magic —and vampires—you wouldn't be here at all."

She wasn't wrong, but before I could answer—a sharp, commanding "'No" rang out from across the terrace—cutting through the fragile laughter that had begun to replace the stunned silence. Only moments ago, Robbie and Baird had begun smoothing away the terror—moving from guest to guest, glamouring their memories, replacing the vision of a bride engulfed in golden flame with something softer, benign: music, wine, laughter. Robbie was making his way toward Granny Margaret, who stood squarely in front of Evie and Morag, shielding them. The rest of the Garvie clan had already succumbed—chatting animatedly with other guests, laughter spilling easily, one of them waving down a waiter for another drink—blissfully adrift in the false memories the vampires had spun for them.

Granny stood her ground, chin lifted, her voice low but iron-clad. "Stay back, *Abhartach*," she snapped, using the ancient Celtic term for a vampire-like creature. "Ah dinnae need yer bleedin' help. Let me keep ma memories—I'll explain to ma daughter and granddaughter in ma own way." She was indignant. "They've just seen the first Garvie tae wield Brigid's might in a century! I'll no let ye tak' this gift fae us." Baird had started toward Robbie as soon as he'd heard Granny's initial protest. He reached Robbie in three long strides, his presence a quiet command. He gave him a single, deliberate nod, then turned to Granny. With a wink and a finger pressed to his lips, he sealed between them a wordless pact. Not the first.

Granny's stern gaze lingered on him for a heartbeat, then her features transformed. She smiled—a fierce, radiant thing, crooked teeth and all—and in that moment she was every inch what she had always been: the living heart of the Garvie line, the keeper of the flame's legacy.

THE REST of the evening unfolded quietly. One by one, then in pairs, guests took their leave. Magda vanished without a word, though I knew in my bones our paths would cross again. Our closest friends lingered to see us off, helping me into the Range Rover, my skirts gathered carefully in their hands. The car gleamed beneath the lights, freshly washed and waxed, *Just Married* written across the back window in shaving cream.

41

BELLE ÉPOQUE

Mira—October 2026

We pulled in just after half past midnight, not exhausted but giddy—worn thin in that breathless way that follows too much joy, too much feeling pressed into a single day. Baird opened my door and lifted me easily into his arms, carrying me over the threshold and nudging the door closed behind us. Bunny raised her head in sleepy acknowledgment—but something immediately felt different. The fire was lit, casting a warm glow across the room, and yellow rose petals traced a path down the hall.

I stared, speechless, and Baird only grinned at me—wicked, satisfied—having once again pulled off a small miracle right under my nose.

He loosened his tie, his golden-brown hair tousled from a night of dancing, our heady kisses stolen between hugs from friends and family. He tugged open the top buttons of his shirt, and reached for my hand, pulling me toward the bedroom with that grin that promised trouble. "Let's get ye out of that dress," he murmured as we passed a silver ice bucket—a bottle of Perrier-Jouët Belle Époque Rose chilled and waiting, two flutes standing ready on a low table near the bed.

"Wait," I said, my voice catching with laughter as I pulled the hairpins free securing the flower crown and laid it aside. I took his hand and guided it to the neckline of my dress, tracing the detail that had drawn me in from the start.

"A bee?" he asked, blinking—clearly as stunned as I'd been—his gaze fixed on the golden threads stitched into the patterned lace.

I turned, fanning out the train as I craned my neck over my shoulder. "Look."

He sank to his knees, eyes widening as his fingers brushed the rabbit stitched in the same shimmering thread at the center of the train.

"Buns," he whispered, awed. "I've never seen anything so perfect. So...*you*. Did ye have it made?"

"No," I said softly when he looked up at me. "It was just there. Waiting. Exactly like this." Even now, I couldn't quite believe it.

His hand found the ribbon on the hidden zipper at the back of my dress, drawing it down slowly before he leaned in, his kisses cool against warm skin as the straps slipped from my shoulders. I gathered the fabric and stepped free, laying the gown carefully across the chair before reaching for the hanger. Baird took the dress from me and hung it on the closet door, where it lingered like a piece of art—a sentinel waiting to witness what came next.

Baird's gaze devoured me—the creamy Swiss dot of my strapless bra and thong, the crystal-encrusted heels still strapped to my ankles. He tore at the last of his shirt buttons, but I remained still, a silent challenge, letting the heat of his gaze wash over me. I watched his eyes, glittering green, darken until they swallowed the light. I knew the part of him he'd stopped fighting was rising, ready to claim his bride. I popped the champagne cork, the sound a sharp crack in the charged air, and set the bottle back in its bucket. He answered by stripping off his trousers and flinging them aside, a careless discard that made me laugh and contrasted sharply with the reverence he'd shown my dress. I walked to the bed and, with a single hand on his chest, pushed Baird down. His eyes flared, his muscles coiled tight, and the tip of a single fang showed in the shadow of his smile. A low growl rumbled in his chest—a protest against my control. Tonight, the beast had met its match.

I lifted my leg and straddled Baird, settling myself atop his cock, letting him feel the g-string between my legs slip across his hardness as I slid myself along his length. He made a move to grab it but I caught his hand. "Tsk, tsk...not this time," I chided. "This pair has sentimental value." I tugged at the bow tied at my hip. One end slipped free, then the other, and with a knowing smile I let the ribbons fall, tossing the small wisp of fabric onto the pile of Baird's clothes on the floor.

Even with the vampire so close to the surface, I caught the smirk—that familiar glint of Baird beneath it all, remembering more than one moment when his restraint had failed him entirely. I reached behind me and unhooked my bra, letting it fall to the floor to join the small, careless trail of discarded clothing a few feet away. Then I lifted my hands to my throat and unclasped the emerald necklace. I held it there for a moment before setting it down.

I'd made it the week I met him—worn it the night before I left, before I ran home, away from something too big, too powerful for me to understand. Something I hadn't been ready to believe in.

But he had known. Somehow, in the quiet intimacy of that night, he'd known exactly what to do. He'd asked me to wear it. He touched it. Left something of himself behind. Changed it, blessed it. Turned it into something more, a message of love only I could read. The final proof I'd needed.

The ring on my hand was anointed in the same way I realized, and an exquisite pain bloomed in my chest, the undeniable truth that we were fated to be one. Two people changed by loving each other, greater than the sum of our broken parts.

I sank onto him, slicking my wetness along his length. I let the head of his cock catch, then pulled back, drawing a ragged inhale from him each time. I was enjoying this—teasing him, feeling his control fray. The next time I let the head slip inside, his hands clamped onto my hips like a vice. He bared his fangs, twin points of white that meant only one thing: my blood was his to take. His sustenance. His drug.

He drove into me. The sudden, full intrusion made me gasp, stealing my breath. Even with my own slickness, there was no time to adjust. He held me fast, grinding up into me, a brutal mix of pleasure and pain that left me reeling. I tried to shift, but it was a token effort. I didn't want to escape this; I wanted him to take me.

This wasn't submission. It was a tactic. I let him believe he'd won, let him revel in his power while I studied every inch of him, every darkness he tried to hide. I was awestruck by his raw claiming, and I wanted all of it. This was my move in the game, letting him think he was the one in control.

Baird surged upward, sitting until his chest was flush against mine. He hooked an arm under my ass, hauling me up and forcing my legs to wrap around his waist. With every powerful thrust, he lifted me, impaling me deeper. My head fell back, spineless, my body surrendering to his brutal rhythm.

His hand found my breast, his grip rough as his fingers closed around my nipple, pinching hard. A gasp tore from my throat. I retaliated by sinking my fingers into his hair and fisting them, yanking his head back until I met his eyes—dark and utterly animalistic. I slowly licked my bottom lip, my mouth a breath from his. Then, I tilted my head, baring my neck and shaking my hair free in a clear, deliberate invitation. I tightened my grip in his hair, pulling his mouth toward the offered flesh, leaving no room for misinterpretation. This was what I wanted. This was what I would take.

My blood pulsed hot under my skin, a familiar tingle where his lips touched me, fusing with his dark intent. But tonight, it was different. Something was driving me, something waiting to be born of this union.

When he hesitated, I commanded him to drink. The voice that emerged was not my own. It was lower, deeper—not the harmonious convergence of the goddess within me, but something else entirely. It was a dark, ancient sound, echoing the primal force that came from Baird in his moments of pure instinct, yet this was older. Vaster. It was a voice from the origin of the cosmos, speaking through me.

He didn't need to be told twice. He surged forward, fangs bared, and when they pierced my throat and he latched on, the world dissolved into pure sensation. With every pull of his mouth, pleasure flooded my veins, a bright, overwhelming tide. Iridescent light flared across my skin, emanating not just from my limbs, but from the very points where his mouth held me fast. It was as if he weren't just drinking my blood, but drawing the very fire of my magic into himself, consuming me from the inside out.

We'd only been joined for minutes, but there was nothing slow about this. A frenzied coupling had seized us both, a raw collision of need, neither of us bothering to control the storm. He tore his mouth from my neck, and the imagined tether between us—the trail of fire I'd always felt—ignited into a living, physical connection. Blood and light merged, searing my skin.

I gasped at the pain, my body arching. Out of the corner of my eye I saw the champagne bottle—just an arm's length away. Our bodies still joined, I stretched with one hand to grab it— my pace never faltering. I ground against him, chasing my own release even as I tilted the bottle, pouring the icy liquid down the side of my neck to quell the fire.

Frothy pink rivulets streamed down my chest, my blood mingling with the champagne, parting around and between my breasts. Between thrusts, Baird leaned in to lick the mess from my skin. I arched my back away from him, his large hand planting firmly against my low back to hold me, letting me cantilever my body for his view. I was on display: firm, flushed mounds; tight, rosy nipples; the faint traces of blood; a small well of pink bubbles caught in my navel.

A low growl rumbled from Baird's chest, and my body answered, light flaring brighter as I hurtled toward orgasm. I pulled myself up, wrapping my arms around his neck, my pace demanding he fuck me harder, faster. That strange, ancient voice rose from me again, a command to bind him to me. "Come with me," I said, not a question, but an order.

And I felt it—that same surge of electricity, but now focused where our bodies were joined. Pleasure tore through me, bright and overwhelming, and I cried out as it crested, the force of it dragging Baird with me. His answer was a raw, guttural sound, more animal than man or vampire.

Around us, our bodies still echoing with release, the light flared brighter still, gathering and condensing until it burned between us—an imploding star, white-hot, brilliant, impossibly dense. Then, with a sound like a rushing breath, it collapsed inward, no larger than a coin, and drove itself into me just below my navel.

A deep ache bloomed where it entered me, bringing tears to my eyes. I did the only thing I could: I pushed myself down on Baird's cock, crushing the head of it against my cervix. That sharp, familiar pain was a welcome distraction, temporarily eclipsing the burning thing now lodged deep in my belly.

My pain blurred into a desperate, mounting pleasure as I ground against him. Through our bond, Baird felt my agony and tried to pull back, confused, but I held him fast. The deep ache in my belly was being consumed by a sudden, blazing arousal. With tears of pain in my eyes, I cupped his face. My moans left no room for questions, and he understood without a word: I needed another release, to erase the hurt with ecstasy.

"Take what ye need from me, Mira. Take it," he whispered against my cheek, the words repeated like a vow.

And then it happened.

The sensation surged through me—no longer contained, no longer held back—stealing my breath as it expanded outward, the inverse of what had come before. Where the light had gathered and burrowed into me, now it burst free, radiating through every part of me at once.

The world fell away.

There was only sensation. Only release. Only the echo of something vast and bright moving through us both. Whatever pain had ever existed dissolved in that instant, erased as if it had never been there at all.

I trembled in his arms, exhausted yet electrified, a confusing mix of spent and elated. Baird's breath was still ragged against my cheek. "Are ye alright, Mira?" he murmured, his voice thick with concern, a smear of blood still dark on his mouth.

When I pulled back to answer, a laugh escaped me, shaky and absurd, as I took in the glorious wreckage of us—blood, sweat, sticky champagne, and his release painting my skin. My laughter seemed to quiet his worry. "I didn't know wedding night sex could do that, " I said breathlessly. "Someone should have warned me."

My joking eased his concern, but not completely. His hand stayed firm at my back, anchoring me as though he didn't quite trust the world yet. He brushed his thumb under my chin, wiping away a spot of blood—but his touch lingered, careful. Listening. "That...felt different." His voice tinged with the wonder of what we'd just experienced, two people with almost two years' worth of supernatural lovemaking between them, awestruck at something that defied even their explanation.

"Yeah," I said. "Different." I shook my head slowly, still picking through bits and pieces, flashes of light and brief memories of pain. "I thought for a moment, if this was how I died, it would be incredibly inconvenient," I offered lightly.

"Ye don't have any pain now?" Baird's voice was low, a sheepish guilt that shadowing his eyes. "I could feel it inside ye, and then the pain you were creating for yourself, pushing me as deep inside as ye could." He swallowed, his gaze dropping for a moment before meeting mine again. "Does it always hurt that much when I'm deep like that, when I hold ye and ye can't ease off?" His expression was a fragile thing, torn between a desperate need to know and fear of the answer.

"I'm not going to lie to you," I started, my voice still breathless. "Sometimes it hurts, but sometimes...I want it to hurt. My orgasm is different then, pushing past that point of pain." Just trying to explain it with him still inside me, soft now instead of hard, made me throb again with want. "...those times, the pain makes the release even more intense."

I squirmed off him, stretching out beside him on the bed. He reached a hand between my legs, his palm covering my swollen flesh, and I arched against him, reveling in the masterful way he always seemed to know exactly what I needed. "But I don't have the faintest explanation for what just happened," I admitted, still dazed. "I'm guessing that wasn't on your wedding-night bingo card."

"No, Mira Campbell," he said, and my heart gave a foolish little leap at the sound of my new name on his tongue. "That was not on my bingo card—though I'm still no' entirely certain what one is. But I appreciate the sentiment all the same."

I caught his hand before he could pull it away, holding his gaze as I lifted it to my mouth. I tasted him—me and him, heat and hunger tangled together—bold and unashamed.

"I'm sorry," I whispered, licking his hand clean.

He laughed softly, eyes bright, something tender threading through the humor. "What are ye sorry for, lass?"

"For all the laundry," I said, stretching languidly like a satisfied cat, the wicked smile tugging at my lips entirely unrepentant.

42

BRUNCH

Mira—October 2026

I woke to the scratch of beard against my cheek, soft kisses trailing over my skin. I blinked slowly, letting the pale morning light filter in through lashes still heavy with sleep, expecting to find a naked Baird sprawled beside me. Instead, he hovered over me fully dressed.

"Thirty minutes, Mrs. Campbell," he murmured, his voice a lazy purr, his thumb brushing the curve of my jaw as if he couldn't stop touching me—a touch that made me want to drag his annoyingly alert morning-self back into bed where he belonged.

But the words registered a second too late. I bolted upright and squinted at the clock. Damn it. He was right. We had to be at the inn for the morning-after brunch before Anne, Dillon, and the rest of the Garvie clan caught the early afternoon ferry back to the mainland. I launched myself out of bed and into the shower, his hand skimming my hip as I passed, wincing just slightly at the pleasant soreness the night had left behind—made worse—or better—by the second round, slower and sweeter than the first, but no less effective at leaving its mark on tender skin.

Ten minutes later, I was dressed—soft knit tunic, leggings, and suede boots tugged on without ceremony. My hair was still damp, twisted into a messy knot that would either fall beautifully or betray me at the worst possible moment. My cheeks were flushed, my body humming, and all I needed was a quick swipe of mascara and lip gloss before facing the world.

Baird and I piled into the Range Rover, *Just Married* still scrawled across the back window, and made the short drive up the coast to the inn. I hopped out before he'd even cut the engine, bounding up the steps two at a time, hand already reaching for the door when I heard him say my name.

"Mira."

I turned.

He stood at the bottom step, hands in his pockets, that familiar smile tugging at his mouth. "Do ye remember?" he asked quietly.

And I did.

The first night. The way he'd walked me back here after I'd collapsed at the grave, still disoriented and shaken. How I'd stood on these very steps with my hand on this handle, unsure of everything except an irrational desire to kiss him. How he'd lingered at the bottom then too—but that evening his face had been carved with something heavy. Grief. Loneliness. A sorrow so deep it had made my chest ache for reasons I hadn't yet understood.

But the man standing there now, bathed in morning light,

wore none of that weight. His smile was easy. Unburdened. And it wasn't lost on me that I was the reason.

He took the steps two at a time and caught me in his arms, pulling me into a fierce, breath-stealing kiss the moment my hands slid around his neck. His grip was unashamedly tight, fingers splayed at my lower back like he was anchoring himself to me. The heat of our wedding night still lingered beneath our skin. We were both lost in it—smiling, breathless, entirely unconcerned with the world—until a chorus of catcalls and applause broke through the moment.

"Christ," someone called, "get a room—*oh, wait.*" Our friends had spotted us through the window.

I pulled back just enough to laugh as cheers echoed from inside, the sound full of affection and well-earned teasing. Baird only grinned wider, forehead resting against mine, utterly unbothered by the audience.

It had taken some coaxing—from both Sorcha and the goddess herself—but Baird was finally learning how to loosen his grip on restraint when the human part of him faltered. The vampire didn't hesitate the way the man did. Didn't soften the touch or lower his voice just because there were witnesses. Didn't second-guess or pull back. Baird Campbell might have been mortified by the little scene we were making on the inn steps, but the vampire in him had no such qualms.

I was his. Heart, soul, and every inch in between—and he wanted the world to know it. The certainty of it thrummed through me, heat pooling low and dangerous, the kind of possessive devotion that felt less like a claim and more like a vow. And God help me, it was the most intoxicating aphrodisiac I'd ever known. As if I'd ever needed help where Baird was concerned.

It was Evie who opened the inn door with a giggle and ushered us into a room of our closest friends and family, sprinkled here and there with strangers staying at the inn who'd decided to join in the well-wishing.

"Look wha's finally decided tae join us," Granny Margaret called, as if we were an hour late instead of five minutes.

"Dinnae blame me, Granny Margaret," Baird said with deliberate slowness, the widest grin I'd ever seen still firmly in place. "My bride had a bit o' trouble waking this morning..."

A ripple of laughter moved through the room. I felt it then—how many eyes were on us, how little either of us cared. Before I could protest, he spun me around and lifted me off my feet, pressing another kiss to my lips, before addressing the room. "I kept her up until the wee hours," he added, far too pleased with himself. His gaze dropped again, just briefly, to my mouth. I caught the unmistakable glint in his eye—the one that promised he had every intention of doing it again.

Baird always laughed when I used the term *dick-drunk* to describe the effect he had on me, but ever since we'd walked through the door the night before, that term didn't even begin to cover it. Saying we couldn't keep our hands off each other felt like a wild understatement—more like space between us had ceased to exist entirely, even now, even here.

I spotted Anne and Dillon first, deep in animated conversation with Morag and her boys. But it was Sorcha who made me slow to a stop.

She sat tucked into a corner table with—*of all people*—Magda.

They'd only met the night before at the wedding, and yet they spoke now as if they'd known each other for years, heads inclined close, expressions far too knowing for two women who were technically strangers.

Baird's arm tightened around my shoulders, just a fraction more possessive, the moment he noticed them too. A subtle shift—but I felt it. A warning. Or maybe an instinct neither of us could name. I leaned into him without thinking, my hand sliding to his thigh, mutual touch providing a united front.

A few feet away, Robbie stood with a pint in hand, watching the pair with open suspicion. The disapproving shake of his head told me everything I needed to know—he had absolutely no control over Sorcha, and he trusted Magda about as far as he could throw her.

I gave them a small, self-conscious wave. Sorcha, apparently having decided mimosas were beneath her, had opted instead for a glass of whisky. Magda sat beside her, a highball of cloudy red liquid cradled in her hand.

"Bloody Mary," she said, lifting the glass with a single raised brow, daring me to think otherwise.

Baird snorted softly behind me, and Magda's smile widened at the sound—warm, knowing. The first shared vampire joke between them, landing easier than I would have expected.

I slipped away from the little tableau, not quite ready to witness whatever a Sorcha–Magda–Baird conversation might entail, and made my rounds instead—quick hellos and hugs with the extended Garvie clan—before finally reaching the table where Anne and Dillon were seated.

"I don't know what kind of sex magic you're dabbling in, Mira," Dillon said in a theatrical whisper, leaning back in his chair to give me an exaggerated once-over, "but whatever it is, you're going to have to share. No exaggeration—your skin is actually glowing."

Heat rushed straight to my cheeks. If only he knew how accidentally accurate his joke was.

"Stop it," I muttered, swatting lightly at his arm. "You're going to give me a complex."

He grinned, clearly pleased with himself, while I tried—and failed—to smooth the telltale smile from my face.

"He's not lying, Mira," Anne added softly, her eyes shining just a touch. "You know I was skeptical at first—worried about how you'd adjust to living here, so far from everything familiar." She hesitated, her gaze drifting past me to where Baird sat, animatedly telling the story of how he'd managed to trick me into designing my own engagement ring without realizing it. Laughter rippled around him.

"But..." she continued, her voice gentling in a way that made my throat tighten, "...he's good for you."

There was no teasing in it. No qualification. Just relief.

As if he felt our gazes, he looked up, catching my eye. The expression on his face—open, happy, and so full of love, even with the wildcard Magda sitting across from him—made my chest ache in the best way. I turned and pulled Anne into a tight hug, holding on a second longer than usual, before looping an arm around Dillon and pulling him into the Yankee group hug. "You too. Get in here."

Two hours slipped by, several of the guests mentioning how bits of the reception were hazy—laughing it off, blaming the generous flow of alcohol. I smiled along, even as a prickle of unease traced my spine. Soon those catching the ferry began making their rounds—goodbyes exchanged, bellies full, bags packed and loaded into waiting cars.

Out of the corner of my eye, I spotted Granny Margaret speaking quietly with Robbie. She seemed to be offering an apology of sorts for her behavior last night when he tried to glamour her. He waved it off easily, no harm, no foul, but the look in her eye showed gratitude, and maybe even relief. She must have carried this secret for so long, held it close and carefully guarded, and she could finally share it. Not just with her girls, but with an ever-widening circle of people who now knew the truth about the return of Garvie magic.

When the cars finally pulled away to the east, it was just me, Baird, Robbie, Sorcha...and Magda. I wanted to retreat to the cottage with Baird and pick up exactly where we'd left off—*literally*—the ache between us had grown almost painful. I felt it in my gut and under my skin, and when I looked at him, I saw the same hunger reflected back at me. The *Sanguis Amantium* thrummed between us, a two-way current of want and awareness neither of us could ignore. Baird's mouth brushed my ear. "Soon," he murmured—promise, warning, and plea all wrapped into one word.

I swallowed and nodded, because if either of us said anything more, we weren't making it out of the inn fully clothed.

But it was clear Magda had no intention of waiting any longer—as if patience itself were something she'd spent lifetimes mastering, and was unwilling to spare any more. Something about her presence set my nerves on edge in a way I couldn't quite name—not threat, exactly. I found myself oddly eager to show her the ring, as though some part of me already knew it mattered. Maybe she was supposed to be the buyer. Maybe not. The ruby hadn't exactly been forthcoming with answers, and for all of Sorcha's insight, even she didn't seem to know everything.

Which, somehow, made the moment feel heavier. I had the

distinct sense that whatever came next had been set in motion long before any of us arrived here. The three of them—a strange trio, if there ever was one—followed us back to the cottage. Middle-aged Sorcha and Robbie, eternally dressed in plaid, looked like they belonged together. Magda, on the other hand, was the odd one out. Her uniform today was off-duty model: black denim, biker boots, a fitted T-shirt, and a leather jacket thrown on with confidence. Impossibly chic. Effortless in a way I'd never been, and suddenly was acutely aware of. In the centuries since her turning—since the violence the ruby had shown me—she'd clearly refined more than just her survival skills. She knew exactly what worked on her body, wore it with intention. And suddenly, I felt faintly ridiculous for the image I'd built of her from that single glimpse of the past: a flat, one-dimensional woman fueled by vengeance alone. She was... more than that. And whatever she'd been forged into hadn't dulled her edges.

While I'd been sleeping late this morning—trying to recharge after an exhilarating, if utterly draining, day and night —Baird had quietly put the cottage back to rights. The rose petals and empty champagne flutes were gone, the bed stripped and aired while I showered, leaving the place looking deceptively calm. He moved to build a fire as I settled Magda and Sorcha into the small living room, the sound of him behind me a steady reassurance, while Robbie poured another round of whisky. Watching the amber liquid slosh into the glasses, I had the distinct feeling this afternoon was going to require more than a single bottle. When I handed Magda the glass, her hand lingered on mine and she caught my eye.

"Tell me how it came to you," Magda said softly. "The ruby."

And so I did.

I told her how Honey had found it and sent it on to me. How the stone had shown me visions—of *her*. Of how its arrival had coincided, far too neatly to be chance, with the first stirrings of my magic. I told her about meeting Sorcha, about Granny Margaret and the Mother's Book, a relic I still didn't fully understand, along with the mystery of what the Garvies' connection to Brigid actually meant. I told her how Brigid had begun to speak through me—never plainly, never fully—only enough to guide my hands. Enough to tell me the ring was a test, not so much of skill but of willingness. A measure of readiness for something she still refused to name.

And as I spoke, I realized just how much of my story remained unanswered.

"You had it once, didn't you?" I asked quietly. "The ruby. With another one?"

Magda nodded without a word. Slowly, she slipped a hand into the neck of her T-shirt and drew out a long chain. At its end hung the ruby's mate—set simply in a prong setting, firelight catching the facets with a gentle glow that belied the power that lay within. She brushed her hair aside, lifted the chain over her head, and held the pendant out to me.

A flicker of fear sparked in my chest, the memory of what the stone's twin had already shown me, threatening to steal my nerve. But Sorcha's voice echoed in my mind. *It cannae hurt ye, Mira.*

I swallowed and let the pendant fall into my outstretched palm. My heartbeat thundered in my ears—too loud, too fast—the familiar warning that a vision was coming, that something was already reaching for me from the other side.

A hand steadied my shoulder. Baird's. He wouldn't let me

slip into the ruby's pull without him close, anchoring me. Then the darkness closed in.

I was swallowed by the vortex of the stone's magic, my curiosity burning even as the world fell away. I braced myself, wondering if this ruby would show me something different than the first—if its message might change depending on the hand that held it.

But beyond the spiraling dark that stole my sight and sharpened every other sense, the same vision rose to meet me.

Scenes from Magda's life rose again—at the old man's bedside, his hand clasped in hers, his face already half lost to death, life lingering only in the piercing blue of his eyes. The night of her bloody vengeance, righteous somehow. A child crying in the doorway. Magda reaching for her. Laughter—cruel and sharp—as someone tore the girl away. A young man, kind eyes filled with terror, lunging across the cottage toward the child just before a club cracked his skull. Smoke curling through the room, thick and choking and final.

Time continued to reel back, unspooling with cruel precision—to a new scene: three young teens, Magda and two boys, the tall boy with the kind eyes filled with love so deep it hurt to watch him be ignored, while Magda flirted with the other boy, one with golden hair, an easy smile and piercing blue eyes.

Then the foreign ancient language, more sounds than words that somehow I understood, the ruby's chant filling the head, the room, the heavens. Different than last time, a new message:

Now two found, we will begin.

Your hand forged our purpose, your eyes saw our truth,

Through you the goddess rights one wrong, to return what was taken

And in doing so forges her own vessel to right another...

"Mira," I heard only distantly.

Baird.

My vision swam back into focus, and I found four pairs of eyes fixed on me as I sat on the edge of the couch, Baird still steadying me at my side.

"What did ye see this time?" he asked softly, his voice careful, his thumb brushing small circles into my arm as if to remind me where I was.

And he wasn't wrong to be cautious—but I realized, distantly, that I felt different this time. Less disoriented. Less shaken. Maybe it was because I'd stopped fighting the pull of the visions. Stopped mistaking surrender for weakness. Instead, I let them take me—like drifting with a current, sometimes slow, sometimes rushing toward its destination, just trusting it to carry me where it would.

I rubbed my eyes, buying myself a moment. The vision's meaning pressed at the edges of my thoughts, but I refused to chase it down—not with its subject sitting right beside me. I'd tell her what I saw. The rest...she could supply herself. I looked at Magda when I spoke, meeting her gaze without flinching. "I saw you," I said quietly. "Same as last time. And an older man —dying. Blue eyes. You were holding his hand."

Warmth flickered briefly in Magda's eyes. "Caius—my first love," she said softly. "We shared a birthday. Born under the same blood moon." Her breath caught as she exhaled. "We lost our mothers that night." Her jaw tightened, the memory still sharp despite the centuries."We were alike," she went on. "Reckless. Quick to anger. Impetuous. But I had my grandmother's love." Her gaze dropped. "Caius...I don't think he ever truly had anyone. Not until me. And Dani."

Dani.

The name settled into place. The other young man from the vision—the one whose eyes had never left her, whose body had moved without hesitation when danger came. I didn't need to ask to know. I skipped past the revenge. Everyone in the room had already heard that story, and Magda had lived it. Her reasons were not a mystery to me.

I chose my next words carefully. "I saw the night they came," I said quietly. "I saw what happened—to your daughter. And the man who tried to protect you both." I hesitated, then added, "Dani?"

Her composure finally cracked. If she'd spoken of Caius with restraint, the grief that crossed her face now was something else entirely—raw, brutal. There was no mistaking it. Her daughter and Dani—they had been the love behind her vengeance.

"I fell in love with Caius," Magda said, her voice barely more than breath. "Buna warned me—my grandmother. She read it in the smoke, said destruction would follow if I gave my heart to him. Loss had etched the same scar into us the night we were born; to join our lives would tempt whatever hand had carved it."

Her mouth trembled, just once. "She saw everything. She *begged* me to listen. But I was young. I was certain love could outrun prophecy." A bitter smile flickered and died. "I called her superstitious. Met him in secret. Believed myself clever."

Her gaze dropped to her hands. "And we conceived a child."

The words landed like a funeral bell.

This wasn't the story of a reckless girl chasing romance. It was a tragedy written long before either of them had taken their first breath—a cruel, inevitable spiral of love and loss, of fate tightening its grip no matter how fiercely one fought it. I felt it then, the unbearable weight she'd carried across centuries.

I'd judged her. Branded her with the same cruelty I'd reserved for Bastien. But even monsters, I was learning, were often born of grief so vast it hollowed them out.

People were complicated. Vampires even more so.

I reached for her hand, gently, offering what little comfort a stranger could give across lifetimes of sorrow.

"Caius's father was the boyar," Magda said quietly. "A powerful man. Wealthy. Influential. When he learned of us, he forbade Caius to marry me—sent him away as if distance alone could erase what we'd done." Her fingers curled in her lap.

"And I was cast out. Turned away in the village square, pregnant and terrified." She swallowed, the memory still sharp after centuries.

"Dani—who had loved me all along—married me then. I thought I'd gotten away with it. Thought I'd fooled him into believing Anca was his. That marrying so quickly had sealed the lie." A hollow breath tore out of her. "But I hadn't." Her throat worked. "He'd known. All along. Every moment of it."

Silence closed in around us. "He let me keep the lie," she whispered, "until the guilt ate me alive and I broke." Her voice cracked. Just barely. "He did it for me. And...I think, in his own way, for Caius too." Her eyes shone—grief laid bare, no guard left to raise. "I wasted the love of a good man." Her voice broke finally. "The best man I ever knew. All for a foolish, reckless love I mistook for destiny."

The room was silent. Too much to process. We sat for a bit before I pressed on, hoping Magda could help me make sense of the rest.

"Your ruby told me the two stones reunited would right a wrong," I said carefully. "That they would return what was taken." I hesitated. "Do you know what that means?"

Her gaze drifted past me, unfocused, the regal composure she wore like armor slipping away. In its place was something hollow. Worn thin by time.

"The cave dweller gave me the rubies," she said at last. "Told me what power they carried. What I was meant to do." Her voice faltered, just slightly. "And then he told me to wait." She let out a breath that sounded more like a laugh than a sigh. "Wait," she repeated. "And wait. And wait some more. Six hundred years, Mira." Her eyes finally found mine again, anguish shining brightly in their darkness. "Do you know how many times I thought I was a fool? A stupid, desperate fool clinging to a lie? How many times I wondered if I'd imagined it all—if I'd thrown my second chance at a life away for a promise that was never meant to be kept?"

The air in the room felt heavy, a lead weight pressing down on us all.

She swallowed hard. "I waited anyway."

Sorcha lifted a hand gently, a silent request to speak. Magda turned toward her, granting permission with a nod.

"This cave-dweller you mentioned," Sorcha said carefully. "Does it have a name?"

It. The word landed strangely on me.

She didn't seem unsettled by the lack of gender—if anything, it appeared to make more sense to her and Sorcha than it did to me.

"Serban—*my maker*," Magda continued, "called it Ossivian. He said it was a conduit for the gods. That it led him to me the night I was dragged from the cottage." Her voice remained steady, though the words themselves were anything but. "Beaten. Raped. Stabbed. Thrown from the cliff."

The air felt suddenly thin.

"The being said the gods used him to turn me. That my suffering was...necessary." Her mouth twisted. "That I was to be their instrument of vengeance—for what was done to me, and to Anca, and to Dani."

My stomach tightened.

"Serban told me Ossivian gave him the rubies that night," she went on. "Said that once I had learned what it meant to be a vampire—once I was ready to leave him behind—I was to return. That Ossivian would tell me how to bring her back."

I glanced at Sorcha.

For the first time since I'd met her, she looked shaken—sitting rigid at the edge of her seat, eyes wide. She opened her mouth to ask something else, but I cut in before she could.

"Bring *her* back?" I asked quietly.

The question that had been clawing at me since the ruby's vision finally found its voice. My pulse pounded, echoing in my ears. And I saw it in Magda's dark eyes for the first time since we'd met.

"My daughter. Anca."

43

THE RUBY SEEKS

Mira—October 2026

There it was.

The answer to one of my questions, circling for months, finally landing—and instead of relief, it left me hollow.

"Ossivian told me to keep one ruby, and to spend the other as currency. That one—cast to the wind and beyond my control—would find its way, after more than six hundred years, to the daughter of flame. The one who was both maker and seer."

The realization echoed through me, ricocheting inside my chest like it couldn't find a place to land. This being she called Ossivian had spoken of me six centuries ago—and somehow, impossibly, part of that felt right. But another part of it felt wrong. Not incorrect, but misaligned. Like a truth spoken too soon, or not fully enough. I felt the urge to speak, to correct something I couldn't yet name. Baird felt it too—I saw it in the way he went suddenly still, alert, as if something inside me had shifted and he'd sensed the change. Restlessness surged through me, questions tumbling over one another, my mind scrambling for reason, for proof. As though logic alone might save me from what instinct already knew.

One question clawed its way to the surface, scattering the others. "The gods told you to seek me," I said. "But how did you find me?"

Magda regarded me for a long moment, her head tilting, her gaze confused, searching. "Bastien," she said at last. "I'm sorry, Mira. I thought you already knew."

I shook my head, unease coiling tight in my chest as I began to pace before the hearth. "I don't understand."

"He told me of his visions—a seer who looked like Agnes, set on a collision course with Baird. He was nearing the end then, his will to live already gone after losing Clémence. The coincidence was too precise. The timing too perfect. He knew my story. He knew how long I had waited." Her gaze moved from me to Baird, heavy with something like remorse.

"I told him to watch her. For me. And when he followed her to the Goldsmith's Guild, when he saw her in that classroom, he knew. She was the one."

Baird finally spoke. "Did ye ken?" The calm in his voice was wrong—too measured, too controlled, completely at odds with the fury in his eyes. "Did ye ken he came here to ask me to kill him?"

"Did I know?" Magda said, lifting a shoulder casually, almost flippant. "No. But did I suspect? That's another matter entirely, Baird."

He turned away from her then, and the anger radiating from him was almost physical. The anger of a man who real- ized he'd been maneuvered, used. Even without the *Sanguis*

Amantium bond, Magda could see it clearly. It was etched into his posture, his clenched jaw, the way his hands curled at his sides. Despite his near constant teasing about me not being much of an actor, Baird Campbell wasn't much of one either.

"Stop acting like a child, Baird. Didn't that act change you? It stripped away the guilt you'd carried for centuries and left room for something else—for love. The man you were before that night couldn't have loved Mira the way you do now." Magda's conviction was steadfast.

Baird was unwilling to drop it. "Ye used me and Mira. The same way ye used Bastien."

For the first time I saw Magda's anger flare. Baird's power was a predator's instinct—brutal at times but honest. Magda's anger seemed calculated, someone who could justify any sin if it served her purpose.

"Don't speak of Bastien. You knew nothing of him—you made him into the monster you wanted him to be, and now you speak to me about being used?" she said coldly. "Spare me your outrage." Her voice sharpened as centuries of resentment bled through. "I was used by the gods themselves. Molded into a weapon because I failed to heed my grandmother's warnings. They made me pay for it—made others pay for it so they could feel powerful through my suffering. And if they were truly gods..." Her lips twisted. "Anca and Dani would not have died that night."

The escalating tension in the room was a fraying high wire to my nerves, the rising tide of anxiety flooding me. I scanned the room and noticed Robbie gone.

"He took Bunny for a walk." Sorcha said in answer to my unspoken question. She sat there in the way she sometimes did, a mindful watcher letting things unfold, hands clasped in her lap. But the twinkle in her eye signaled she wanted to cut in. "Magda—so Bastien told ye about Mira, but that was almost two years ago. Why did ye show up now?"

"Yes!" I added quickly, the question that had been circling in the back of my mind suddenly shoving its way to the front. I was grateful to Sorcha for deflecting the anger—at least for the moment—between Baird and Magda before it could ignite into something neither of them could take back.

Magda regained her composure. "Ossivian told me I'd know when the ruby was ready to be found. I've been watching you from afar since Bastien found you, and when you listed the ruby ring on your website, I know it was the one...it was time."

The echo of my heart's contractions pounded in my ears until my stomach roiled in protest, the reverberation increasing in intensity by the minute. An awareness shattered what little calm I had left. I'd been here trying to decipher answers to all the questions I'd asked myself for the past few months, and I couldn't piece it together. But there was someone with answers, and I just realized what I was feeling was anger. Not mine, not Baird's through our bond.

Brigid's anger.

My chest heaved, and I held my arms out away from me awkwardly. Even hanging at my sides they were too close, too constricting. The ache I'd been carrying for Baird all day surged hot and insistent, along with my magic, buzzing to life in my veins. Sensation crowded in from every direction, too much, too fast.

"Baird," I said, my voice pitching high, unsteady—betraying how close I was to losing control.

He was at my side before the thought had even finished taking shape.

The words spilled from me in a rush. All this circling, all these fragments we'd been clawing at—human, vampire, witch—trying to make sense of a story none of us fully understood. And all the while, the one who held the answers had been right there, waiting for me to finally ask.

"Get the ruby ring from the safe," I said quickly, panicked. "It's trying to show me something. Something I can't see yet. A piece of this I'm missing."

I heard the familiar tones of the code being entered on the safe lock, distant as the swell of anxiety took me, pulse thudding, a cold sweat trickling down my neck. Baird swept back into the room and dropped the ring into my hand. I motioned to Magda for her necklace.

When they touched, the two rubies thrummed with power, bleeding red—dense at the source, fading at the edges beyond my cupped hands. The heat built fast, searing my palms, and then, like a spark to dry kindling, Brigid's Sun leapt to life. Glittering light burst outward, scattering the red haze of the rubies. At first—like the time in my studio—her light coalesced into the shape of the goddess, bright but indistinct, standing in my living room. Then Brigid spoke, light and heat cascading off her in waves, transforming before our eyes. No longer the washed-out silhouette I'd seen before, but a woman of flesh and blood: copper waves of hair, green eyes—the same Brigid I'd met on the summit of Goat Fell in my dream. Called here by me, but it was not me she addressed first. It was Magda.

"Make no mistake, blood drinker. When you speak of the will of the gods, it is I you name. The gods may have sat by and watched the crimes against you and your family, but it is my power—and mine alone—flowing through the one you call daughter of flame, for she is my hand upon the earth."

Her hand thrust out in my direction, but her eyes never wavered from Magda. *"The hand that turns the wheel of time and fate. The hand that brings your daughter back—the child too young, too innocent, who paid the price when you turned from your grandmother's warnings. Your grandmother carried the Sight, like Bastien did from his mother—like Mira."*

Brigid's anger was palpable, carried in a voice that made me cower for the first time. Gone was the gentle mothering tone that—despite speaking only in riddles—always filled me with peace. *"I used you—not some nameless, faceless god—to exact my vengeance upon Ivar and his men for what they had done."* Brigid laughed, the sound of archaic judgment—sharp and caustic. *"Humans believe they know the gods, but you are too consumed by yourselves to see the truth. The ones other people may call Persephone, Ostara, Flora, Freyja, Vesna—we are one and the same. Different names pressed upon a single will."* Her final word, almost a snarl, left no doubt.

"Mine."

I glanced at Magda; her black eyes held only shock, Brigid's power pressing down hard enough to smother even a vampire's darkness.

"I saw your fate. It was I who set the wheel in motion—to grant you a second life, and your daughter a second chance at breath." Brigid's next words came softly, deliberately, each one placed where it would hurt the most. *"But know this, Magda: it is not your wish I now fulfill through Mira's magic. I answer the dying plea of another."*

Brigid moved a step closer to Magda, power coiling in every syllable. *"A man pure of heart. A maker—like Mira—another smith who forged metal with fire. One who loved you, and your daughter, beyond what even I believed a mortal heart could bear. A man who loved so fiercely that, at his passing, all the gods wept."*

Magda fell to her knees, trembling at the sheer force of Brigid's will and the power of memories and regret.

"The one you called Dani. It is his wish I grant—Let Anca live."

Brigid turned to me, dismissing Magda as if she were no longer present. *"Mira—the questions that still haunt you, let them go for now. The one who will bear the ruby ring will be revealed soon, but for now you—and Magda—must wait."* Her corporal body began to fade, reverting to the outline of pure light.

"No! Wait!" I cried, unwilling to let her slip away again without answers, despite her admonishment. "Why did you choose me for this?" I pleaded, all the while knowing my hope was foolish.

"Your hands ache for truth, but I haven't hidden it from you, Mira." Her form dimmed, then the flame was snuffed. The silence that followed was wrong. She was gone.

Her words echoed in my head—and then I felt it. An ache bloomed in the center of my palms, the same hands still clutching Magda's necklace and the ring. I held the necklace out to Magda and set the ring on the counter.

I rubbed one palm and then the other, pressing my thumbs into the hollows until the pain sharpened. When that didn't help, I pinched harder, trying to smother it with something new. Erase one pain with another. I'd done the same thing the night before with Baird, when the ache in my belly had swallowed everything else.

I'd taken in too much—too much information, too many other people's feelings boring straight into my heart. Too much for my introverted self. I needed time to process. Alone. With

Baird. To hold him in the quiet of the bedroom, with only the crackle of the fire and the thick stone walls pressing close.

"We need to be alone," I said. No apology. Just fact. My voice stayed level, even as Brigid's cryptic words pressed in—and the ache lingered in my hands.

I glanced around and realized Robbie hadn't made it back. Baird caught my look, gave me a brief nod, and headed for the door to find him—and Bunny.

Magda and Sorcha stood. Magda looked confused, as if dismissal were a sensation she hadn't had to interpret for centuries. Sorcha, for all she normally kept hidden and patiently waited for me to discover on my own, suddenly wore a look that said she had a secret—and wanted to share it with me. Magda slung a leather bag over her shoulder, Sorcha already waiting in that odd way she did with her wrist threaded through the arched handle of her bag.

I ushered the witch and the vampire toward the door. According to Brigid, Magda and I had more waiting to do. And although Magda knew how—and where—to find me, I had no way to reach her when, not if, a potential buyer came calling about the ruby ring. It was another reminder that everyone seemed to know more than I did, even as everything kept circling back to me. I was the common thread. The point of contact. Whether I liked it or not.

Magda opened her bag and withdrew a card holder. She slid out a business card—white linen stock, the ink a deep, blood-dark crimson. Her name was set in a modernist sans-serif font: clean, elegant, and faintly cold. Her email and phone number followed beneath. Entirely on-brand. No flourishes, nothing else—only what you needed to know, and not a bit more.

It felt like there was a version of Magda she allowed the world to see. Tonight, I'd been shown more of the story that made her—and the knowledge settled between us, quiet and shared. I suspected very few were ever let that close.

Outside, Baird stood with Robbie near his car waiting. The look on Robbie's face seemed to indicate Baird had relayed the visit from Brigid, and Robbie was glad to have missed it. Just before Sorcha got into the passenger seat, she pulled me aside and whispered in my ear.

"We should talk about the creature Magda referred to as Ossivian. Ye know how to reach me." She meant for me to use The Call of the Hearthfire again. "When ye are ready." That was the look I saw in her eyes moments ago in the living room. I gave her a quick nod and a squeeze on the shoulder, for the first time feeling something close to trust in the odd witch.

44

BLOOD SPILLED

Mira—October 2026

I woke hard from a deep sleep.

I'd been dreaming of the Mother's Book—of flipping through it with aching hands, my fingers dragging over the pages as if touch alone could pull centuries of Garvie knowledge into me. In the dream, I was ravenous for answers, certain I was meant for something I was finally close to understanding. I kept flipping back to the blank pages. The ones that followed the warning:

We are not chosen. Some are spared. Some are not. Our hands record the names and yet the debt remains unpaid.

When I woke, the ache was still there. Worse. My palms throbbed, hot and insistent, as if the dream hadn't let go of me.

It wasn't just memory—it was a nudge. A pull. Baird sat up beside me, already alert. He reached for me, concern etched into his face, but I waved him off and threw back the covers. I didn't stop until I was in the living room, breath shallow, standing in front of the bookshelves.

The Mother's Book sat where I'd left it, dark and ordinary. No glow. No warning. And yet I knew—whatever waited for me was already awake, and Brigid's words echoed in my head—*Your hands ache for truth, but I haven't hidden it from you, Mira*—as I reached for it on the shelf.

Light exploded out of me, filling the cottage wall to wall—as if to say *yes, this is what she meant.*

Book in hand, I crossed to the kitchen counter and flipped through the pages until I found the blank one. The ache in my palms intensified, pulsing now, unbearable.

I reached for the knife in the butcher block—the same one Baird had used to pierce his heart vein so he could complete our bond—just as he entered the kitchen behind me.

"No, Mira," Baird said.

I turned and threw out a hand on impulse, stopping him before he could take another step.

Baird froze mid-stride, suspended as if the air itself had turned solid. Light spilled from my palm, a barrier between us. The only sound was our breathing.

I didn't have time to wonder how I'd done it—how I was holding a vampire still, countering his speed with something raw and instinctive. His eyes widened, just for a second.

"This is what she meant," I said, my voice shaking despite myself. "My hands ache for truth—but she hasn't hidden it from me. Whatever this is, it's been here since the moment I touched the book."

When I lowered my hand, the light faded. Baird relaxed—but he didn't move closer.

I drew in a breath and dragged the blade across my palm. The sting was sharp, immediate. Blood welled—and with it, the ache vanished.

I cut the other hand without hesitation. New pain bloomed, clean and bright, replacing the deep, relentless throb that had haunted me constantly since Brigid spoke those words. I cupped my hands, letting the blood pool, and then spilled a drop on the page, mine bright red splattering on the parchment, mingling with other drops of Garvie blood given to the Mother's Book over the centuries. A name appeared, as though my blood was siphoned into an invisible quill, marking the page.

Maelina Garvie - died 1391–Abhartach

More blood from my hands, more names.

Seoras Garvie, and child Ailis–died 1415 –Flood
Elspeth Garvie–died 1433–Murdered by husband
Duncan Garvie Wallace–died 1460–Baobhan Sith

Deaths recorded in the Mother's Book. All Garvies. A generation apart, as if measured. Each one untimely. Two taken by vampires.

Dread hollowed me out, carving something deep and dark inside my chest. I feared the answer even as I needed it.

I spilled more blood onto the page. More names surfaced—some single, some paired. Some deaths were tragic and ordinary: sickness, famine, childbirth. Others were violent. Burned at the stake for witchcraft. Murder. Clan wars.

Until I spilled the drop that tore a cry from my throat. The sixteenth generation listed, the one I'd known was coming, but had refused to believe until I saw the names revealed in the ink born of my own blood:

Agnes Garvie Campbell and husband Baird—died 1785—Abhartach

Baird started toward me—then slowed. He closed carefully, as if approaching something newly dangerous. He stopped at my shoulder and leaned in, just enough to read the names. His gaze tracked the page from top to bottom until it reached the entry that bound him to Agnes—and to me.

I turned to face him, bracing for shock—for denial—but what I saw instead was grim recognition.

"This," he said, his voice hollow. "...this is what Agnes meant. She saw it all." His gaze lingered on the page longer than it needed to. "When Brigid referred to the woman who watched from the edges"—he nodded once, jaw flexing, face twisting with the bitter taste of truth—"she meant Agnes. This was the madness that haunted her."

He exhaled slowly, a sound caught somewhere between awe and remorse.

I picked up the knife again. The cuts were already stitching themselves closed, but my palms were aching again. There were more names that demanded to be seen.

Baird caught my hand. I waited for him to stop me—to spare me the knowledge he already knew would break something in me. He didn't.

Instead, he took the knife. His grip slid from my wrist to cradle my hand, careful, devastatingly gentle. He looked ruined, like this was a choice that would stay with him forever.

I had come to the book alone, chasing answers I thought I had to face by myself.

When his eyes met mine, I knew I'd been wrong. There was no hesitation—I saw only a resolve to carry this together, whatever it demanded of us. He pressed the blade into the half-healed cut, just enough. Blood welled. There were still more names waiting—and he knew that he would not be permitted to heal me until they were seen.

Baird didn't let go. He folded my hands into his, our bodies close, aligned, and together we tipped the blood onto the parchment. More names surfaced. More death. More tragedy. Two more taken by vampires.

The seventh name stopped me cold. My paternal great-grandparents—James and Sarah Garvie. Dead in 1948, the night a fire destroyed their home. I reached out and touched their names, a piece of tragic family history I'd only ever heard about, never once considering their deaths might be connected to this.

"Family, love?" Baird murmured when I stalled.

I nodded, distant—the same way he had when he'd been forced to face his own entry in the Mother's Book. I spilled another drop. *Helen Garvie.* Dead in a plane crash in 1984. The cause of death felt wrong beside the ornate, looping script—too modern for ink that curled like a curse. I didn't recognize the name, but I was sure in my gut that Granny Margaret would.

I touched our hands to the parchment one last time.

Baird's grip tightened before I could read it myself. His

breath caught hard in his chest. "Mira," he said, something broken in the way he said my name. I followed his gaze to the final entry.

William Garvie and wife Faith—died 2024—automobile accident

45

ONCE IN TWO LIFETIMES

Baird—October 2026

Mira stood in front of him, broken open by grief. Her eyes were wide—not the frightened woman who had fled when he'd told her the truth about Agnes and Bastien, about himself, less than two years ago. Back then, it had taken her clairvoyance to accept what logic could not.

This was different.

This was the woman who had learned to live with the unexplainable, who had stepped into it—with courage and choice. And still, this—this dawning truth that the magic she'd chased since finding the Mother's Book was not a gift but a family curse, one that had claimed generations of Garvies, including her parents, including him—was going to gut her before she ever made it to the other side.

Baird pulled her into his arms and simply held her, his fingers sliding into her hair to cup the back of her head, cradling it against his chest. He bent into the soft spill of her hair and whispered in Gaelic, a message meant to soothe her.

"Thoir dhomh do phian, Mira," he murmured the translation. "Give me your pain."

She drew back and looked up at him through tear-stained lashes, her eyes filled with soft wonder, shot through with agony. Through their bond, he felt her surprise echo—anchored by something he rarely sensed from her. Guilt.

"What about *your* pain?" she cried. "This thing—this blackness that's haunted my family." Mira shook her head, anguish spinning into anger. "What about your pain?" she cried again. "It took your life, Baird. And Agnes's. It took my great-grand-parents. My parents."

Her voice broke, then hardened again. "This thing that brought us together—it's nothing more than the Garvie curse. And I unknowingly dragged you back into this."

She wrenched herself from his arms, sobbing. "I did this to you, Baird. I'm the reason—"

Baird reached for her, already moving. He would not let her spiral. He caught her by the shoulder and spun her back to him —harder than he meant to, urgency snapping through his restraint. The vampire in him didn't care how he'd been made. He had no anger left to spend on fate or circumstance.

"Where do ye think you're going, Mira Campbell?" he demanded. "I won't have ye walking away—not when I need ye to hear this. Not when I need ye to *ken* it." His gaze dropped, and only then did he notice the blood smeared across her palms—fresh, vivid.

The realization startled him. He had been so consumed by her that he hadn't felt it. The hunger that had ruled him for over two centuries. The pull of sweet, honeyed blood—*her* blood—so close to his lips. Nothing had ever mattered more to him than that need. His teeth ached in response, instinct snapping awake. He forced it down.

"Hear me when I say this," Baird said, his gaze never leaving hers as he lifted her hand and pressed a kiss to her palm, his saliva sealing the wounds he could see—hoping his words might mend the ones he couldn't. "I would live this life—*and the last*— a thousand times over. I would endure every loss, every shadow, just to stand here with you. Right here. Right now." He held her face in his hands, his thumb settling into the dimple on her chin, refusing to let her turn away—done with secrets that festered in the name of protection.

"What if I am the next name on the list, Baird?" Mira asked softly.

Baird thought of the goddess's visit—the night she'd spoken through Mira in their bedroom. He couldn't pinpoint it exactly: her meanings were always veiled, but somewhere deep in his soul he knew that the goddess wasn't going to take Mira like that.

"Brigid said to me that night, '*Trust me—what you fear will take Mira from you*'—meaning her and this damned purpose she won't reveal—'*...is the very thing that will give you more than you ever dreamed to ask for.*"

Mira's brow furrowed. "What does that even mean?" Her voice wavered, caught between confusion and a hope that ached to believe.

"I dinnae ken exactly," Baird admitted. "But in that moment, something settled in me. Something real. It changed me."

His thumb brushed her skin, steady, grounding. "I stopped mourning a future that might never come—and started living in what we have. Here. Now."

Beneath the words, the vampire in him stirred—not in defiance of his will, but alongside it. What had once felt like a fracture eased into a quieter balance, almost companionable. A coexistence that had taken root that night with the goddess, leaving him steadier than he had ever known himself to be.

"What if you are wrong?" she asked, her voice barely above a whisper.

"I may well be," Baird said softly. "But it dinnae matter, Mira. I love ye—and I was *made* to love ye. And if I'm wrong, if the goddess takes ye...she'll take me too."

He sighed, the truth of it resisting language, irrational and absolute all at once. "I cannae live a moment on this earth without ye." He leaned down and pressed a gentle kiss to her lips, savoring the warmth, the desire threaded through with tenderness that met him every time.

"I didnae ken true joy until ye came into my life," he murmured, his mouth hovering over hers. "And if it was the Garvie curse that brought ye to me, then I'll turn it on its head and call it my blessing—because that's what ye are."

At the word *blessing*, Mira's engagement ring flared to life. Brigid's Sun spun in a wash of molten gold and prismatic light, scattering rainbows through the cottage's midnight dark.

Mira let out a skeptical huff as she looked down at the living glow. "Blessings," she said. "That's what she told me the one who wore this ring would receive—her blessing." She lifted her gaze back to him, uncertainty threading her voice. "Whatever that means."

Despite the bite of the night and the painful truths unearthed by the Mother's Book, something warm took root inside him. Not an answer—only a knowing. A certainty he couldn't yet name, couldn't yet give to Mira in any way she might accept.

But it didn't matter.

He would carry it for them both—this faith, this stubborn hope—until she believed, or until fate proved him wrong. And if that was the shape of their destiny, then he would fill her life with a love so steadfast, so undeniable, that she would never question the cost. Never doubt that whatever curse bound them had been worth bearing, if it meant choosing each other.

He swept her up into his arms, earning a startled gasp and a look of pure disbelief.

"Where are you taking me?" Mira asked, her brows knitting as she searched his face for answers.

Baird didn't give her one immediately—not with words, anyway. Instead, he reached for his favorite unfair advantage. The one he wielded with wicked precision. His smirk unfurled slowly, deliberately—just exaggerated enough to be theatrical. One eyebrow arched. One corner of his mouth tugged upward, all promise and trouble, the look that had undone her a thousand times before.

It was the same one that always made her laugh, or blush, or forget whatever weight she'd been carrying. Usually all three.

"To bed, lass. Where we belong."

46

———

THE CAVE DWELLER

Mira—October 2026

We woke the next morning to a tentative knock at the cottage door.

Sorcha stood alone on the threshold, her expression drawn, the sea wind tugging at her hair. She didn't offer pleasantries. I hadn't even had time to contact her, but the look on her face said this was too urgent to wait.

"There's a cave on my island," she said instead. "And something that lives within it."

Baird went still beside me. "Something," he repeated carefully, "or *someone?*"

Sorcha's mouth tightened. "A creature of the dark. One that speaks for the gods." Her gaze slid to me, heavy with meaning. "I've gone to it before. More than once."

Baird's eyes widened in surprise as if a piece of a puzzle I'd never seen fell into place.

"Aye, Baird—" she said, in answer to his wordless question,

before her eyes turned to me. "The day Baird came to me, askin' after Brigid. After *you*." She hesitated, as if weighing the cost of the next words. "It told me when the time came, it would speak to you."

Baird swore softly under his breath. "And ye believe that time is now."

Sorcha nodded. "When Magda spoke of Ossivian, I kent it in my bones. Different name. Same voice." Her eyes moved between Baird and me. "Crepitus has been waitin' for ye, Mira. It said so."

An invisible weight pressed down on me—that familiar feeling of a tight bolt constricting my breathing. This decision had already been made and was only now catching up to me.

"If it speaks for the gods," I said slowly, "then it knows why this is happening."

Baird turned to me at once. "Ye don't have to do this."

I met his gaze—whatever waited in that cave, it wasn't something I could outrun. "I do," I said. "If it's been waiting for me...then so has the truth."

Sorcha exhaled, something like relief flickering across her face. "Then we shouldna delay."

I dressed without another word.

Less than two hours later, the three of us were cutting across the water in Baird's sailboat, Sorcha's desolate island rising dark and jagged against the horizon—silent, watchful, as though it already knew we were coming.

THE CAVE MOUTH yawned black before me, the air spilling out damp and cold. I walked deeper into the cave, the ambient light around me dimming by the minute. The cave was damp so close to the sea, the air thick with the smell of salty brine and decay. My fingers slid against the rough rock wall, and as I struggled to see, touch was the only thing guiding me forward. My breath sounded too loud in my ears, thin and uneven, as if the cave were already deciding how much air it would allow me.

Words slipped into my mind unbidden, coming from somewhere in the bowels of the cave, a barely audible hiss slithering across other thoughts, snaking around them, capturing them and twisting them this way and that. My heart thudded in my chest and echoed in the tight confines. Wet sand underfoot gave way to rocks, a quiet splash here and there as I crossed over puddles, each step deeper into the darkness.

"*Mira...*" The whisper coiled around my name, soft as breath. "*Why do you tremble?*"

The promise of answers tugged me forward, one shivering step after another into the dark. Sound prickled the hairs on the back of my neck. Low at first, it grew louder with every passing second—drawing closer. It was a hollow, uneven clicking, threaded with a papery rustle, like parchment scraped across stone. The stench of decay shifted too, carrying a new top note: dry and fibrous, the scent of something once alive but now only a hollow husk.

My hands clenched at my sides. "Who are you?" My voice came out steadier than I felt.

"*One who remembers,*" it replied.

I heard the grind of stone sliding behind me, heavy and

final, and then the last glimmer of light winked out, leaving me swallowed in darkness.

I was trapped.

The realization landed without panic—only a bone-chilling stillness that froze everything inside me.

I pressed back against the stone wall, listening as the drag and hiss crept closer. In the pitch-black I could see nothing—only feel it. Something closed around me, less physical restraint, more supernatural field pinning my body against a wall of rock. A whisper of breath brushed my skin, cold as ice, fetid with rot and something familiar. My heartbeat thundered, a beat so loud it filled my chest cavity, the sound reverberating against my eardrums from the inside.

"You're the cave dweller," I said. "Ossivian—or is it Crepitus?"

A pause. Then: *"Names, nothing more. I have many."*

Something smooth and polished stroked my cheek. Like a finger, but without softness—no flesh, no give at the tip. I tried to lean away, but the stone wall bit hard into the back of my skull. The contact carried no heat—no life—but it lingered with deliberate curiosity.

"Why are you here, Mira Garvie?" the voice asked.

I flinched at the name, suddenly wishing for the shelter of my married one. "Sorcha said you would speak with me."

"Has the daughter of flame come for answers?"

There was that term again, the same thing Magda—and Brigid—had called me. The title didn't feel metaphorical. It felt like a claim.

The velvet blackness of the cave was absolute. I kept expecting my eyes to adjust, to find shadows or edges, but there was nothing—only the oppressive closeness of the being, the suffocating certainty that I was entirely surrounded.

"I saw the names," I said, unwilling to waste time on riddles.

"*Names?*" the being echoed, feigning curiosity—baiting me into saying more.

Fine. I would play this game. "In the Mother's Book," I said. "Brigid told me my hands ached for truth. They did—*literally*—until I cut them and bled into the pages, like the Garvie women before me."

"*Your blood changed nothing,*" the voice said. "*It only showed you what was already true. The goddess led you there because you required convincing.*"

The voice hovered an inch from my face. Breath washed over me, carrying stone, dust, petrichor—like the Mother's Book and Agnes's portrait—the slow rot of Garvie secrets made scent and memory. The cave dweller did not just know them. It carried them.

I was tired of being kept in the dark. Ossivian—Crepitus—used the blackness like a weapon. Not seeing it might have been a mercy, but the buzzing electricity under my skin swelled with my fear.

I shoved it down with sheer will. The pressure built, unbearable.

Then something ancient inside me took over.

Before doubt could catch hold, I released the damper on my power and let it tear free. Not in desperation—but in decision.

The cave burst into light—brilliant, blinding. I wanted to shield my eyes, but I forced them open, to see what was waiting for me. Light waves danced across every inch of my body, rising and twisting, joining together and splitting apart, alive and pulsing, the now familiar warmth a constant companion.

Before me stood a creature I wasn't supposed to see: a human skeleton, impossibly animated, its brittle frame held together by nothing more than stubborn strands of sinew, dried ligaments clinging to their last scraps of dominion. Darkness pooled in its eye sockets, yet within the void flickered faint pinpricks of light, like stars in a moonless sky.

It was terrifying—and it was strangely beautiful.

It wore a hooded robe of coarse black wool, the heavy fabric hanging in folds. The skull hovered inches from my face. Fleshless, muscleless, incapable of expression—and yet, I could have sworn it smiled.

Flares like flame spilled gold across the cave walls, mapping every bone and desiccated strand of sinew in grotesque relief. For a heartbeat, I thought it might recoil. Instead, it froze— head cocked, the hollow sockets catching the light. The faint glimmers within shone like suspended diamonds.

"Yes..." The voice slid over me like a shiver. "*There it is— power. Not borrowed, not begged—yours. The first with the power to pull back the shroud of my darkness in a thousand years...*"

The bones rattled—not in fury, but in something disturbingly close to approval. Through my fear, the power inside me rose to meet it—answering as if it, too, recognized the truth and took pleasure in finally being seen. At last, the creature withdrew, gliding a step backward. The sudden space it granted felt both like reprieve and invitation, just enough that I could peel myself from the damp cave wall where I'd been pinned.

"*The Garvie line carried many pretenders. I had to be certain you were not one of them. Light born of blood...you are the one destined to serve her. The one foretold.*"

"Born to serve? Brigid?" I demanded, forcing my light to

shrink back to something less blinding—enough to see, but still unsteady. My control had improved, but precision wasn't exactly my strength yet.

"*Brigid,*" it intoned—confirming what I already knew. "*You are the daughter of flame, chosen to walk as her hand upon the earth.*"

There it was again. Daughter of flame. I'd been so eager—following blindly, playing at magic, angry at Baird for worrying.

"Why? I didn't ask for this..." My voice cracked, dismayed at the thought of being torn from the life I'd only just begun with Baird.

The voice coiled and hissed, wrapping itself around the thoughts in my head like a snake. "*Because your family owes her a debt. And debts to a goddess are never left unpaid.*"

"And if I don't want to pay it?" My voice sharpened, fear spitting at the edges. "Then what?"

The creature's shrill laughter echoed and bounced off the cave walls. "*Make no mistake, child. You have no choice in this. Brigid may guard her flock with fire and mercy, but when she is crossed, her wrath consumes not only the guilty—but all they love.*"

"Then tell me why—explain that at least." I demanded. I didn't yet know the crime, only the cost—one life taken from every generation, sometimes more. Interest compounded in blood, demanded because a goddess could.

The creature sighed—an oddly human sound—then turned and settled onto a rock at the cave's center. "*Brigid's daughter, Lasair, laid down her immortality to wed a mortal man and bear his children. When death claimed her, Brigid lost her only daughter.*" The voice that had confronted me moments ago now carried the faint echo of grief.

A chill locked around my ribs. "What does that have to do

with me? With my family?" The question was almost a formality. The answer was already burning its way through me, old as myth and just as cruel. I didn't want it—but my blood did. It recognized the truth before my mind could catch up.

"The man Lasair gave up her immortality for was a Garvie. From his line you carry the Sight—but the light that burns in you, the flame that will not die—that is the blood of the goddess Brigid herself."

Daughter of flame. So that was it. Not chosen. Inherited.

"What happens to me?" I asked, my voice barely a whisper.

"You fear your name on the page," the cave dweller said, statement instead of question. *"That fate belongs to the unchosen."*

Relief loosened my lungs—brief, fragile. "Baird said she wouldn't hurt me."

"The blood drinker has learned to listen," the creature replied. *"That is not the same as knowing."*

I couldn't tell if that meant Baird was right or wrong. Tears threatened as the weight of knowing so much—and still understanding so little—became suddenly unbearable. The creature seemed to sense I was at the end of my rope.

"I know simply that you are her vessel," the creature said softly. *"Not an offering. But even I do not see the end of your path. The conclusion is not yet written."*

Vessel. Brigid, and the rubies, had used that very word.

Stone scraped against stone as the cave entrance began to unseal, the sound filling the chamber—final, unmistakable. Light spilled in from the mouth of the cave. I turned back, the question tearing free of me—"What does it mean to be Brigid's vessel?"

The cave was empty.

Ossivian was gone.

I had come fearing death, but I left fearing purpose.

47

BLUE EYES AGAIN

Mira—December 2026

A few weeks after the cave, the world slipped back into something that passed for ordinary. The days shortened. The light softened. Life settled into familiar rhythms—bench work, quiet meals where I ate and Baird nursed a single glass of wine, the low hum of the sea beyond the windows. I held to those small rituals, telling myself the unease lingering under my skin was only the price of fragile peace—not the weight of what being a vessel would one day demand.

Then my phone chimed.

I almost ignored it. Instagram was usually a trickle of likes and the occasional polite inquiry—custom pieces, timelines, budgets. Nothing urgent. Nothing that made my pulse hitch.

This message did.

> Hi Mira. I hope this isn't too forward. I came across the ruby ring you posted a while back and I can't stop thinking about it. I'd love to talk about purchasing it, if it's still available.

Her username was unmistakable. Verified. Blue check. An author whose vampire novels had dominated bestseller lists for the better part of the last five years had also secured a new movie franchise. I stared at the screen longer than I meant to.

Of course she wrote vampire novels. I told myself that meant nothing as I typed back, keeping my reply light, professional.

> Hi—yes, the ring is still available. I'm happy to answer any questions you have.

Three dots appeared almost immediately.

> Perfect—I'd like to buy it.

Just like that. No haggling. I swallowed, fingers hovering, then added the question I always asked—routine, muscle memory.

> Before we finalize things, I should check. Would you need the ring resized?

The reply came fast.

> No need. I wear a size six.

The room seemed to tilt. Size six. Exactly what I'd made it, just like Sorcha said.

I sat back slowly, the phone warm in my hand, my thoughts

skittering in half-formed directions I didn't like. The ring had never been measured against a client's hand. I hadn't guessed. I'd simply *known*. Trusted the quiet insistence that had guided my hands that day I carved the wax. I closed the message thread without replying and opened my browser instead. Her press photos were everywhere—publisher sites, interviews, red carpets. Mid-thirties. Beautiful. Dark hair worn sleek and loose around her shoulders. Everything about her appearance was polished, deliberate. And yet—there was something faintly off about the way she held herself, as though she were playing dress-up in a life that didn't quite belong to her.

Physically, she looked so much like Magda it made my chest tighten. The same sharp cheekbones. The same mouth. The same effortless grace. But where Magda wore her body with presence—with command—this woman carried hers more carefully, almost apologetically, as if she were inhabiting a form she'd never fully claimed.

The other difference was her eyes.

Where Magda's were dark and unreadable, this woman's were a startling cornflower blue—bright, almost luminous, lit from within. And yet even they held a searching quality, as if they were always looking for something just out of reach. I scrolled through image after image, my unease deepening with every swipe. Different outfits. Different cities. Always the same face. A reflection—shifted just enough to feel wrong.

I clicked through a few interviews next, then excerpts from her books—blurbs, quoted passages pulled for reviews. I hadn't read her work before, but I didn't need much. The themes repeated themselves with quiet insistence. Characters unmoored from their origins. Immortals who survived centuries without ever quite knowing who they were meant to be. Lovers bound together by blood or fate, searching not just for each other, but for the missing piece that would make them whole.

It wasn't subtle.

Her vampires didn't fear death so much as they feared *being unfinished*. Trapped between lives. Between names. Always powerful, always admired—and somehow still lost. Spending lifetimes circling a truth they couldn't quite touch.

The ruby pulsed warm in my thoughts. Not coincidence, my instincts whispered. Not at all. When I finally picked up my phone again, I didn't open Instagram. I opened my messages and scrolled to Magda's name.

> I think we found the buyer for the ruby ring.
> Call me when you can.

I didn't add anything else.

Some things were better said out loud.

AFTERWORD

Turn the page for a sneak peek at the final book in the Sanguis Amantium series, *The Memory Writer,* coming January 2027.

THE RIVER OF DREAMS

Thia—Now

My dreams always fall into one of two categories: before, and after.

The *before* dreams are the happy ones. A little girl—dark hair, wide smile—standing in the doorway of a cottage. Her parents are there with her. It feels like another age entirely. The Middle Ages, perhaps—I can't say when, and I'm not sure where. They speak a language I don't know, yet somehow I understand enough. There is love in that house.

The mother is gentle but distant, as though part of her is already elsewhere. The father's hands are rough and calloused, and when he looks at the little girl, his eyes shine with a devotion so fierce it almost hurts to witness. I can feel it—the weight of his love, steady and certain.

It is a simple life. A warm one. But something terrible happened to that family. I never see it. I only feel the shadow of it creeping closer, inevitable as an approaching winter.

The *after* dreams come more often than the happy ones. They always leave my chest aching for reasons I can't put a finger on. It is the same woman—the mother from the cottage—but she is alone.

She searches for someone. Or something. She is no longer the woman who baked bread and mended clothes by the fire. The little girl is gone. The broad man with the calloused hands and gentle smile is gone. Whatever warmth once filled their lives has been stripped away.

I don't see how she lost them—I only know that she did. In these dreams, I watch her move through life—or something like life—stronger than she once was. More powerful. And utterly broken.

She doesn't age. Centuries turn around her like pages in a book, yet she remains unchanged—young, beautiful, untouched by time. People watch her the way I do—drawn in, captivated, unable to look away. But unlike me, they can reach her. They can touch her. Speak her name. She sees them, studies them, uses them. Bends them gently—or cruelly—to her will.

I am just a shadow that trails behind her, unseen and unheard. I try to reach her. I try to call out, to warn her, to beg her to turn around. But there is something between us—a thin, invisible veil. I press against it and feel nothing but distance. She moves through the world like I don't exist.

Maybe I don't.

Circumstance turned her into something else—something that feeds on the blood of living. Not exactly like the beings in the vampire books I read as a child, or the silly things we see on television. Sunlight does not burn her. She casts a reflection. She doesn't sprout wings or dissolve into mist.

She is fast—terrifyingly so. And strong. And sometimes she kills.

When she does, she knows the evil in her victims. I feel it too, as though her judgment lives somewhere inside me. As though her vengeance belongs to me as much as it does to her.

People see her beauty but miss her intelligence. They never notice how perceptive—*cunning*—she is. She can slip into a mind as easily as a room—draw out secrets, bend will, make her prey kneel without ever raising her voice.

In the *after* dreams, her lives are rich—rich with purpose, with power, with rooms larger than any she had ever dared to enter before. As though death was the doorway to everything she was never meant to have.

But these lives are empty of love. And beneath the power she wields, beneath the elegance and control, her heart still aches for what she lost.

I feel that ache as if it were my own. When I wake, the details of her face begin to dissolve. They melt at the edges first, frost beneath sunlight, until only the barest bones remain— dark hair, a slender build, the memory of graceful movement that can, in an instant, become something terrible.

I try to hold on to her, but sand sifts through my fingers. I am certain her face—the first detail to go every time—contains the answer to something I am missing.

My psychiatrist told me to keep a journal beside my bed. The pen and paper are always there. The moment my eyes open, I reach for them and write frantically—anything I can salvage. Impressions. Fragments. The shape of the story before it scatters. Most mornings I have less than a minute before it all unravels into nothing.

I have had these dreams for as long as I can remember. The

journaling came later—only the last ten years or so. Now I have stacks upon stacks of notebooks filled with these fragments. Their covers are bright and harmless—hummingbirds, butterflies, impressionist landscapes—images that lie about the darkness and loss inked across their pages.

That is all I truly have—fragments. They became fuel for my writing. What began as a way to keep the dreams from swallowing me whole followed me to university and became something else entirely. "You have talent," they told me. "You have a gift for storytelling." So I wrote.

This has been my life for as long as I can remember. Sleep. Dream. Wake. Forget. Until this morning.

This morning, the dream did not fade. I remembered it, clear and whole inside my mind.

All of it. Every last detail…

ABOUT THE AUTHOR

Rebecca Byron lives in Grapevine, Texas. When she's not writing or planning her next travel adventure, she's reading—voraciously, obsessively, and with complete disregard for whatever might be on TV.

As a teen she read hand-me-down paperbacks from romance icons like Janet Dailey, LaVyrle Spencer, and Kathleen Woodiwiss. But after she read Salem's Lot, vampires took up permanent residence in her heart. These days, she fangirls hard for Diana Gabaldon (she once wrote her a gushy fan letter in the early 2000s and has no regrets), Christopher Buehlman (because if horror could write poetry, it'd be him), and Mary Roach (science, but make it weird and funny). In addition to all things vampiric, Rebecca has a deep love for ghost stories, witch-lore, and all forms of clairvoyance—which she may or may not secretly possess.

Rebecca was born in Southern California, where she grew up riding horses, hanging out at the beach, and serving as president of her high school FFA chapter—because honestly, if you've never learned how to castrate a lamb or aren't fluent discussing chimeras in citrus crops, are you truly living? She even spent a year working on a horse ranch in Italy—mainly for the pasta.

Her hobbies include eating, baking (not really cooking, just baking—let's not confuse the two), drinking cocktails, swearing a lot, barely exercising, parking with chaotic energy, and hiding her disaster of a closet from her ultra-organized husband.

For more books and all the latest:
www.rebeccabyron.com